BEWARE THE CHILD

Ruth Foster

A DELL BOOK

Published by
Dell Publishing
a division of
Bantam Doubleday Dell Publishing Group, Inc.
666 Fifth Avenue
New York, New York 10103

ISBN: 0-440-20303-1

Printed in the United States of America

Published simultaneously in Canada

April 1989

10 9 8 7 6 5 4 3 2 1

KRI

THE CHILD WAS SINGING AGAIN

The worms crawl in,
The worms crawl out,
The worms crawl into Tracy's mouth.

Tracy suppressed a scream at the gross image, unaware of what was going on in the classroom.

"Perhaps Tracy can tell us what causes thunder and lightning," Mrs. Hendricks said with her knack for calling on the pupil who wasn't paying attention. The students were as curious about the recent unusual storms as the rest of the city.

Tracy looked up in a daze. It wasn't as if she thought of the song, or even remembered the voice of someone singing it. It was as if the child were in her head. She wondered how a child could sound so sinister.

"Tracy, I asked you what causes thunder and lightning."

"He's angry," Tracy said with a shudder.

"I expected a more sophisticated answer than a preschooler's view of God," Mrs. Hendricks said sarcastically.

Tracy sank in her chair. She hadn't meant God. She meant *the child*.

For Jeff

Special thanks
to
Rosemary Carpenter
and
Rosie Springsteel

1

He was bad. He screamed and screamed. Now the figures in white were coming for him.

He's crazy. He killed the only woman who'd ever loved him.

. . . Coming to take him away. Coming to tie him down and take him to the room with the snakes.

In his nightmare Adam heard the attendants' steps as they neared his six-by-eight-foot cell with bars on the window, bars on the door. The squeak of their rubber-soled shoes on the concrete floor reminded him of gremlins' excited squeals of delight at the prospect of an imminent game.

He tried to stop the screaming so they would go away, not put him in the straitjacket that bound him like a mummy, not put him on the rolling bed with the unoiled wheels that creaked raspily. But he couldn't stop the screams. They grew in his chest and bellowed out his mouth. They bounced off the olive-green walls and ricocheted through the hostile corridors. Where was the nurse with his pills? The screaming would stop if she brought the pills. The demon would accept the sacrifice and rest appeased. They both would stare through his eyes at the four walls and smile obediently at the bars. Adam's screaming continued as the squeaky shoes and creaking table came nearer.

He's crazy all right. He killed that girl with his bare hands. The jury said he was crazy. No sense hanging a crazy man. Send him away. Lock him up. Let them electrocute him at the funny farm. They'll kill him over and over with the electric snakes. He's a bad one. Even his mother didn't want him; left him on the steps of the Catholic church when he was newborn. She knew. She knew even then.

The figures in white were outside the barred door, turning the key. They rolled the bed next to him and stood above him, grinning. In his nightmare they were replaced by the nuns from the orphanage where he grew up.

We told him what would happen if he didn't mend his wicked ways. We tried to warn him.

Now the figures in white were back, holding him down, wrapping him tightly. Adam's robe twisted around his body, cutting off the circulation in his arms and legs, but they kept holding him and tying him to the bed that would take him through the maze of corridors. He struggled, kicked, screamed, as they put him in the straitjacket. He wanted to say he was sorry, but only screams came out of his mouth. He was bound so tightly, he could barely breathe. Still the screams came.

His girlfriend was afraid. He put his hands around her throat and squeezed. She couldn't breathe. She gasped, then silence.

The figures in white rolled him down the halls. The wheels squeaked like the laughter of a hysterical woman who was pleased he was getting his just deserts. The hall was a shrinking tunnel leading him to the pain. The walls grew closer. They breathed deeply, sucking the breath from Adam, sucking away the screams. The fluorescent lights blinded him. He wanted to cover his eyes, but his hands were bound. He had to shut his eyes. With one tiny movement of the protective lids he could block out the terror, but his eyes were locked open watching the nightmare unveil its secrets.

The hideous metamorphosis continued. Sister Mary Xavier's face burst before him on the ceiling, angry, vindictive. Adam flinched. The hall and ceiling were covered with Sister Mary Xavier's face, never leaving his sight though the attendants continued rolling the bed. The nun kept changing. First her expression was accusing and angry. Then she was beautiful and alluring. He was drawn to her beauty, despite his fear. He was hypnotized by her eyes, forgetting momentarily about the straitjacket and the attendants. But the nun changed again. Her face twisted and distorted until he saw that it was not Sister Mary Xavier. She was inhabited by a demon. Its red glowing eyes looked through him to his soul. The lips, which were still the nun's, smiled. Little nubs of horns protruded from its scaly, reptilian head.

"You're mine, Adam Smith," the demon said. "You've been mine since you were sixteen years old. You will ask for what only I can give you, and on that day I will claim you through your heart's desire and feed on your fear and anger to become invincible; then you will serve me through all eternity."

"No," Adam moaned. "It's not true."

The demon laughed and disappeared. The table stopped. The squeaking shoes stopped. He was at the end of the tunnel. Before him was the door. The thick gray door grew as a thunderstorm grows, massive, threatening, shooting electricity from its bowels. The doorknob was the demon's head, snakelike, triangular, its mouth open wide, revealing sharp, curved fangs that dripped electrical current. The drips became horizontal balls of lightning whizzing by Adam's body as the demon hissed its welcome.

Adam Smith's scream pierced two worlds as his nightmare and his sleeping body joined, forming a dimension so terrifying, it snapped in his head and catapulted him into the waking world.

The attic apartment filled his eyes, illuminated by the flashing neon lights from the bar at the corner of the alley: LIVE REVUE, GO GO DANCERS, flashing on and off in hundreds of colored bulbs. Adam sobbed quietly. He was shaking and sweat poured off his face and body like blood gushing from a bludgeoned pig. Finally his limbs and mind were once again able to work as a team. He lay in his usual position with his head at the wrong end of the bed. He reached out his rough hands and turned on the television, which was always close by to bring relief from the nightmares. He blinked at the sudden brightness of John Wayne's blurry image and at his voice, tinny through the old speaker.

"Oh, my God, my God, will it never end?" Adam said aloud to the bare walls. He looked around the apartment to make sure the dream was over. The dusty window was tightly locked. The chipped porcelain stove was coated

with layers of grease. The small refrigerator, covered
with daisy contact paper that was sagging and parting at
the seams, hummed hesitantly. It appeared defeated, like
the residents of the Arms Apartments.

Adam turned his attention back to the television until
he heard a hissing noise behind him. He whirled around,
dreading a rerun of his years in the institution where the
wires injected a demon into his brain.

But Adam's conscious mind knew nothing of the demon. He remembered the creature from the doorknob as
a snake. His mind couldn't handle the truth. He whirled
toward the hissing in an instant that spanned decades of
memories, then breathed a jerky sigh of relief as the
steam heater hissed again and fought to keep the damp
Midwestern winter wind from taking over the drafty
room.

Except for a distant siren the city streets below were
quiet. The silence of the building was broken only by the
sounds of the wind. Although it had been fifteen years
since Adam was released from the mental hospital, he
still was not used to the solitude of his apartment. Only
nineteen of his fifty years had been spent outside the
boundaries of overcrowded institutions. Though he made
few friends at the institutions, the constant barrage of
noise helped fill the void of his loneliness.

He had grown up at the Mothers of Charity Orphanage, where they arbitrarily assigned him a name of conve-
nience. All the children were given Biblical first names.
One-syllable last names were tacked on for identification
and tax purposes. At the orphanage prospective parents
walked right by the shy boy who didn't speak up. They
would come and he would stand back and wish they
would take him away and make him their child.

*Sister Mary Xavier: What are you doing, Adam? Come
here. I'll teach you to mend your wicked ways.*

Adam rubbed his throbbing temples at the intrusion of
the jumbled memory. Sister Mary Xavier wasn't at the
orphanage when he was small. She didn't come until he
was a teenager. When he was young, Sister Teresa was at
the orphanage. She was old and jolly and used to let
Adam sit on her lap when she told the children stories.

She was just what Adam thought a grandma should be, with her wide, soft lap and wrinkled smile. Once he called her Grandma and was afraid he would get in trouble for being disrespectful. Instead, she wrapped her arms around him, pulled him to her voluminous body, and told him anyone would be proud to be his grandmother. Adam adored her.

When he got sick, he vaguely remembered Sister Teresa trying to get him to eat soup and kissing his forehead with her cool, rough lips. Then she didn't come to take care of him anymore. Another nun told him she had caught a virus from him. Adam got well. Sister Teresa died. After that Adam kept to himself.

When he was thirteen, Sister Mary Xavier came to live at the orphanage. She was younger than the other nuns and pretty. Adam followed her around and tried to please her and get her to pay attention to him, then . . .

"I was hiding behind a curtain. She found me and . . ."

He untangled the blanket on the sagging mattress as though the act would also untangle his memories, but he couldn't remember. He knew he had been bad, but after the years of electric shock there were voids in his past like black holes in space. He would start to remember, then his mind would be blank. He knew that sometimes he had nightmares about the things he couldn't remember. He'd wake up and the images would dangle on the edge of his mind, then dissipate. The only nightmare he always remembered was the one about the electric snakes, and it didn't answer his questions. If only he could pull the dreams from the edge of his mind into the sunlight maybe he could get rid of the nightmares forever, and more importantly, find out what really happened to Marie.

"I know I didn't kill you, Marie. I love you."

When he was a child, he dreamed about growing up and marrying a beautiful woman. They would have lots of children who would love him and play with him. He never would be lonely again.

Sister Mary Xavier: Sex is only for having children.

The nun's admonitions from his childhood haunted

him so regularly, he could visualize a miniaturized Sister
Mary Xavier living in the recesses of his brain, rapping
his skull with a tiny pointer and creating his blinding
headaches.

When he was sixteen, Adam was given a suit of clothes
and ten dollars. He couldn't stay at the orphanage.

"They caught me. They found out I was . . . was
what? God, I can't remember."

Adam had hated the orphanage, but it was the only
home he knew. The confines of its strangling walls didn't
prepare him for a world of which he had no knowledge.
He was more alone than ever, until he met Marie.

"Marie, my precious Marie. To me you are beautiful.
They said I killed you, strangled you. All I remember is
your crumpled body at my feet and your blood covering
me. Where did the blood come from, Marie? People don't
bleed like that from being strangled, and I could never
hurt you."

He remembered standing next to Marie's limp body,
screaming. The police came, then the figures in white
locked him up. The screaming lasted fifteen years and
still invaded his sleep.

He turned off the television and, praying the dreams
were over for the night, drifted into a fitful sleep; but
soon he was back where the demon snake doorknob
hissed its welcome. The door opened silently by itself.
The silence swallowed Adam's screams before they could
explode from his throat. The door devoured every sound
in the massive building, then extended outside the walls,
beyond the twelve-foot fence. Adam felt his eardrums
would burst from the overwhelming absence of sound.

The creaking wheels broke through the noiseless void,
mocking him as the figures in white rolled the table into
the demon's room.

*We'll show him what happens to murderers, to crazy
men. How many volts should we give him? Turn it on high.
We'll stop his screaming.*

They rolled the table next to the machine. Its cold
metal was more terrifying than the figures in white, more
horrible than Sister Mary Xavier's accusing face. The
nun played a lute while the demon grew multiple snake

heads that writhed from the holes in the machine, twisting, curving their snakelike necks upward in time with the music. Their hissing and the high pitch of the lute filled the air while the heads slithered toward him. They moved gracefully, content to take their time while their victim waited helplessly. Their evil eye slits looked at him hungrily. Their triangular heads gaped open. Their fangs glowed with electricity and moved toward him in anticipation. . . .

They struck . . . their fangs sinking deep into his temples, filling his rigid, jerking body with electric venom.

Adam bolted upright in bed, his scream blending with the buzz of the windup alarm clock. Another night was over. He covered his face with his weathered hands and rubbed his throbbing temples, then turned on the television and pulled himself shakily out of bed. In the bathroom red sunken eyes stared back at him from the mirror. His wrinkled, ashen face gave him the appearance of a man in his sixties. Short, wiry brown hair sprinkled liberally with gray flopped in disarray around his forehead and ended abruptly above large ears. A receding chin quivered under pencil-thin lips. It was a face that appeared to rush as quickly as possible from birth to death.

Adam climbed into the wobbly stand-up shower and washed away the sweat and the dream. He dried himself and threw on the blue janitor's uniform he wore every day at the Third Precinct. He unconsciously rubbed his temples, where for fifteen years the institution's attendants had attached probes and sent electric charges through his body. His head ached, as it always did after the distorted memories that came during the nights. He longed for the pills that would take the pain away. He didn't miss them as much as when he'd been released fifteen years ago, when the craving was a physical need that left him pacing the floor, but the longing still was there. When they turned him loose, the doctor had given him a prescription and referred him to an outpatient clinic where he could get more pills if he needed them, but Adam was afraid to go, afraid if he asked for help

they would lock him up again. So he rubbed his temples
and wondered about the nightmares.

He sat on the kitchen chair and lit a cigarette.

"If only I could remember, then maybe I could live in
peace," he said, puffing nervously on the cigarette and
rubbing his temples. "But I can't remember, except in the
dreams."

He flipped off the television, put on his coat, and
started down the icy fire escape that served as the only
entrance to his apartment.

Maybe Miss Laura will talk to me again today, Adam
thought. The other people at the precinct station don't
even notice I'm there, but Miss Laura does. Sometimes
she smiles at me when I empty her wastepaper basket.
Sometimes she says, "Hi, Adam. How are you today?"
That Miss Laura is a nice lady. She's a lot like my Marie,
but Marie would never want to be a police detective.

Adam pulled the collar of his coat around his neck and
shivered, then hurried through the city streets to work.

If Sergeant Brady were still around, he'd talk to me,
too. I wonder why he got me my job after they let me go?
None of the old-timers are around the precinct anymore.
At least people aren't looking at me, thinking: There's
the guy from the funny farm. Better they don't notice me
at all.

2

Tuesday, January 15

"Rise and shine, all you early birds. It's going to be another beautiful day in the city," the radio announcer
blurted cheerfully.   .

"That man should be fired," Laura mumbled, turning
over and pushing the snooze button. "It's obscene to be
that cheerful this time of day." She pulled her pillow over
her head and snuggled next to Darryl, relishing the comfortable feeling of his warmth next to her as she promptly
fell back to sleep. The ten-minute grace period soon was

over and the alarm once again was doing its job. She groaned when Darryl pulled the pillow off her head.

"Good morning, sleepyhead," he said, kissing her eyelids.

"It can't be morning. I just went to bed," Laura complained. She opened her eyes tentatively, then closed them again when Darryl began kissing her neck and running his hands along the curves of her body. She turned to return his kisses and soon forgot about being sleepy. They made love tenderly, but with an intensity that spoke more loudly than if Darryl had shouted his concern about the potentially dangerous assignment Laura faced that day.

Later she stretched luxuriously in the king-size water bed and smiled at the intricate pattern of ice crystals reflecting through the skylight, before pulling herself out of bed and rushing through the cool room toward the bathroom for a hot shower.

Laura loved the skylight, and her entire house, for that matter. Since Darryl was a contractor, they originally planned to build their own home, but when they saw the nineteen thirties farmhouse, they both fell in love with it. With Laura's knack for decorating and Darryl's carpentry skills, on a limited budget they had turned it into an attractive home. They enjoyed the neighborhood too. It had been one of the first areas to be swallowed by the city during the post–World War II boom and now had a comfortable, established look.

Laura hopped in the shower while Darryl shaved. "I'm so excited," she said. "I want to leave early. I don't want anything to spoil this day. Sergeant Binder can't ignore the work I've done on that string of armed-robbery cases. He'll have to put me in charge of the team when we serve the warrants and make the arrests."

"Please be careful, Laura. I know you and Winchell are a hot team, but the guns those thieves used in the jewelry-store robberies don't shoot water, you know."

Laura jumped out of the shower and threw a towel around her head. "Harry Winchell and I are not a hot team. I'm hot. He's an idiot. If we were closing in on Jack the Ripper, Winchell would pull out his football trophies and expect the Ripper to be so impressed, he would immediately confess his crimes and surrender."

"Then why don't you request a transfer to police headquarters? You could still be in the detective division, and you'd be rid of Harry Winchell and Sergeant Binder."

"I can't do that, Darryl. I was only promoted to detective two months ago, and I was lucky to be assigned to the Third Precinct. It's the toughest in the city. If I went running back to headquarters because I don't like my partner and Sergeant Binder acts like a horse's backside, it would look like I can't handle the job. It would go on my record that I have an inability to get along with co-workers and that I buckle under pressure."

"I don't think that would happen. I've met the division chief, and he seems like a smart man. He knows what Binder is like. It's the sergeant who can't get along with people. That's why he has been transferred to every precinct in the department over the years. I don't understand why they don't fire the man. They had the perfect opportunity when they proved he roughed up those two teenage boys he arrested last year."

"Unfortunately, Sergeant Greg Binder would have to kill someone before they got rid of him. Teachers have tenure, and we have the good-old-boy system. The department isn't going to fire a man with thirty years on the force, even if he does think the only thing the rule book is for is to beat prisoners over the head."

"But you've told me yourself the judges are always throwing cases out of court because he screws things up."

"I know, but the only way we're going to get rid of Sergeant Binder is if he chokes to death on one of his cigars."

"Are you determined not to ask for a transfer, Laura?"

"Absolutely."

Laura headed for the bedroom and began pulling on slacks and a blazer. As a detective she no longer wore the traditional blue police uniform, but her work clothes were tailored to hide her natural femininity. She wanted to be accepted because she could handle a demanding job, not because she looked good in tight sweaters.

At five feet six inches and 115 pounds, Laura Bernhardt had the girl-next-door looks that men found attractive, but which did not threaten other women. An unusual combination of honey-blond hair and chocolate-brown eyes offset the fact that her nose was a little too large and her cheekbones not quite pronounced enough for her to be considered beautiful.

Darryl came into the bedroom behind her and picked up the conversation. "Okay, Laura, I haven't been married to you for five years without figuring out that once your mind is made up, there's no changing it. But will you do one favor for me?" he asked, pulling her close and running his fingers through her curly hair. "I know it's not your fault that you aren't getting along with Binder, but will you make an effort to get along with Harry Winchell? He is your partner, and you never know when your life may depend on him. Besides, he doesn't seem like a bad guy."

"He's a jerk. He was in my class at the police academy, and we didn't get along even then. He was furious because I made higher scores than he did." Laura smiled smugly at the memory of Winchell's condescending attitude when he offered to give her tips on shooting, then his shocked expression when she aced the test and he failed.

"And you're peeved because he was promoted to detective four months before you were."

"I wouldn't mind if he didn't keep rubbing it in. He acts like he's the old pro and I'm the rookie."

"The world would not come to a screeching halt if for once you weren't a star," Darryl snapped in exasperation. "There's a reason people are taught teamwork from kindergarten on up, but you act like it's a foreign phrase."

"Just because I don't like Harry Winchell doesn't mean I always have to be a star; and I do so work well with a team."

"Sure, Laura. Look at the sports you like: tennis, but never doubles; swimming; and jogging. You're competitive, but you only participate in activities where you don't have to share the glory. That's fine in sports, but in your job, the cost of being a star could be your life. I don't want to fight with you. I only want to make sure you will be alive tonight."

Laura winced because, difficult as it was to admit it even to herself, she recognized an element of truth in what Darryl was saying. She had always felt if she wasn't number one, she was a failure.

"There's nothing wrong with liking singles in tennis," she said to save her pride, "but I guess you've got a point about Harry Winchell. I'll try harder, for you. How could I refuse when you look so sexy in those carpenter pants?" she said with a conciliatory grin. "I promise not to egg Winchell on today."

"Good, and speaking of eggs, I'll cook this morning while you warm up your car," Darryl said, patting Laura's backside as they headed for the kitchen.

"Give me your keys, sweetie. I'll warm up your truck too. But don't worry about cooking eggs for me. I'm too excited to eat. Until now the assignments Sergeant Binder has given me would make being a school-crossing guard look exciting."

"I can't have my wife running around the city chasing criminals on an empty stomach.

"And here, drink this glass of orange juice before you go. A little vitamin C never hurt anyone."

"I wish you would stop worrying about me, Darryl. You're acting like a mother hen. I can take care of myself." After gulping down the juice Laura said, "What's going on, Darryl? You've always seemed proud that I'm a cop. I've seen you concerned about my safety before, but not like this. Have you lost your confidence in me?"

"Of course not, and I am proud of you. I know you've been in tight spots before. I guess I'm a little worried because you've been off the streets for a couple of months, and you said yourself the guys you're going after have ties with organized crime. If you add those things together with the fact that you aren't getting along with your partner, you come up with potential trouble."

"You can relax," she said, reaching up and putting her arms around his neck and kissing him. "I give you my word that I won't take any chances, but right now I'd

three-piece suits and women in high-heel shoes hurried among the city's poor, where the old and the new stood side by side in stark comparisons of life-styles. Shiny metallic office buildings with hundreds of tinted-glass windows loomed skyward amid the decayed buildings of an earlier age. As she passed the central business district, the new buildings were left behind. Winos huddled in doorways while men and women in tattered coats hunched forward.

It was eight-seventeen by the time Laura pulled into the precinct house and parked next to the long row of official black-and-white patrol cars.

A cloud moved in front of the sun, and Laura felt as though the bleak sky were penetrating her bones with a subtle warning. She ignored it and pushed through the frigid wind to the old brick building. Normally she gave more credence to her intuitions. She had never considered herself psychic, but she had an uncanny knack for answering a question a friend was about to ask, and for instinctively knowing when people were telling the truth —a talent that proved useful in her job and would likely be instrumental in solving the jewelry-store robberies. Today she thought she was only nervous and in a hurry.

"How are you this morning, Adam?" Laura asked, hurrying by the janitor on her way to the detectives' office. She usually arrived promptly at seven fifty-five, five minutes before the official starting time. She liked to give herself plenty of time to go over the offense reports, that day's work assignments, before the informal meeting at eight-thirty when all the detectives gathered in the break room for a cup of coffee and to exchange information about their cases. Laura felt her presence was about as welcome as that of a woman at an exclusive men's club. Sergeant Binder's openly hostile attitude toward her made her dread the morning get-togethers even more. The sergeant had a chip on his shoulder and seemed determined to catch her making a mistake.

Binder was standing in his office door puffing on a cigar when Laura rushed by.

"Good afternoon, Detective Bernhardt," he said sarcastically, looking from her to the clock and back to her.

"I hope your job here isn't upsetting your feminine routine."

Laura flushed. "I'm sorry I'm late, sir. It won't happen again. There was an accident that held up traffic, and—"

"We aren't concerned with your little problems, Bernhardt," the sergeant said, cutting her off. "All the men managed to get here on time, despite the traffic." He turned abruptly back into his office and shut the door behind him.

That bastard, she thought. I'm a few minutes late and he turns it into a case against women's lib. One of these days I'm going to be his boss, then we'll see what he has to say about feminine routine. I don't see how his daughter can stand it. It's too bad a bright girl like Tracy is stuck with a man like him for a father. Well, regardless of how Binder feels about me personally, today is mine.

She checked her in basket excitedly, looking for the warrants she would serve on the jewelry-store robbers.

Good grief. Binder has given me the dregs. Look at all these new offense reports, and not one of them is likely to ever be solved. And what's this note about a shoplifting detail? There must be some mistake.

Laura ran through the basket again, her heart sinking, then she headed for the meeting.

"It's the Miss America of the Third Precinct," Winchell bellowed across the room.

Laura winced, started to respond snidely, then remembered her promise to Darryl and poured a cup of coffee instead.

"Clark, what's up with the liquor-store burglaries? Any suspects yet?" Binder asked.

"The only information I have so far is that the guy has a scar on his left cheek."

"I bet that's the Levitan kid," Fred Phelps said, pouring sugar into his coffee. "We've picked him up a hundred times, and he's always been identified by that scar. He hangs out down at the 7-Eleven. When he's not behind the building, breaking beer bottles against the Dumpster, he's inside pumping quarters into the Asteroids game. I'll go have a little talk with him today."

"Just remember, there's no such thing as a bad kid— only disadvantaged ones," Binder smirked.

The detectives laughed, as if on cue.

"Does anyone have any leads on that prostitute assault last night? Someone really did a number on Sally's face. The streets won't seem the same without her," Carl Livingston said.

"Bet you'd like a piece of that action yourself," leered Roy Spark. "You might have a talk with Big John Lavender, though. I noticed he's back on the streets."

"They paroled Lavender?" groaned José Martínez. "God, we'll have to all start working double shifts just to keep up with the workload. I thought we got rid of him for good."

Laura sat quietly in a corner, waiting for someone to bring up her big case. Finally she asked Binder, "Are we going to serve the warrants on the jewelry-store robberies today? I didn't see them in my basket."

"Winchell, Clark, and Hammond are going out with two teams of officers to make the arrests later this morning," Binder said calmly. "If you had paid attention to the work I put in your basket, you would have noticed I assigned you to shoplifting detail today, Bernhardt."

Winchell's mood brightened like a Christmas tree in full glory on Christmas Eve, while Bob Clark and Gerald Hammond looked down at the floor in embarrassment. The other detectives sat back in stunned surprise, but said nothing.

Laura's face turned beet-red. She couldn't believe what she was hearing. "Sarge, I spearheaded this case from the beginning. I have a right make those arrests. I've earned it. There's no reason to take it away from me now."

"If I want your opinion, Bernhardt, I'll ask for it."

"But, Sergeant . . ."

"Detective Bernhardt, I haven't adjourned this meeting yet, and I would thank you to keep your opinions to yourself. Is that clear?"

"Just tell me why you are removing me from the case at this point, sir," Laura said, emphasizing the "sir" sarcastically. "The detectives who have worked on a case from the beginning always are in on the arrests."

The men shuffled nervously and gave each other uncomfortable looks.

"Bernhardt, if you don't like the way things operate in this precinct, feel free to request a transfer."

Harry Winchell appeared on the verge of open glee.

Laura held her tongue.

"Are there any more questions or comments on the cases you all have been assigned?"

You could have heard a pin drop after Binder's question.

"Then get to work. This isn't a church social."

So that's it, Laura thought. He thinks he can push me far enough to get me out of his hair altogether. Don't hold your breath, Binder, baby. It's not going to work.

Most frustrating for Laura was that she knew good and well that Binder knew what a good opportunity it was for her to have a chance to work at the Third Precinct. The career potential, and sheer stubbornness, kept her from requesting the transfer Binder was pushing her to ask for.

Laura stormed out of the room, almost tripping over the janitor, who was intent on scraping something off the apparently spotless floor.

She checked her shoulder holster, threw on her hat and gloves, and stomped by the growing number of people in the lobby of the precinct. There were bleary-eyed drunks who had just been released after sleeping it off in the holding tanks, a bail bondsman, a couple of attorneys, a pimp in a full-length mink coat, and a woman who was crying and pleading with the duty officer. It was the usual motley crew that could be seen any day at the Third Precinct.

Laura pushed one of the oak doors with all her might.

Binder, if you were struck dead, I'd spit on your grave, she thought.

A blast of cold air hit her, but she didn't feel it. It wasn't the winter wind or her temper that made her suddenly shiver violently. She felt flushed and broke out in a sweat. Laura decided to be extra careful for a few days. Her feeling of violence on the verge of release was getting to her. It wasn't like the game she sometimes played with

her friends, picking up the phone before the first ring and
saying hi and the person's name. This was more like the
day she'd rushed out of class her junior year in college
and made an emergency call home, getting through just
before the ambulance left to take her father to the hospital with a heart attack.

3

Adam weaved his way like smoke through the bustle of
people in the lobby, gliding his freshly oiled mop bucket
beside him. He had perfected the art of observing while
he cleaned, without drawing attention to himself.

He turned to survey his work. The room was spotless,
or would be, at least until the parade of people arrived to
deposit mud on the floor as swiftly as their fear perme-
ated the air. He had polished to a deep shine the heavy
oak doors that gave the illusion of a fortress to some, and
stood more formidable than the cell bars to others. The
glass that separated the detectives' office from the lobby
sparkled under the glaring lights.

The janitor wiped sweat from his brow.

It's been quite a day; most exciting day I've seen
around here in years, he thought.

He looked critically at the floor leading down the corridor to the holding cells, then at the worn walls. He
pulled a rag out of his back pocket and carefully wiped a
smudge from the wall and headed for the rest rooms. It
was three P.M. Adam usually finished cleaning the rest
rooms before lunch, but today he stayed around the
lobby and detectives' office so he wouldn't miss the turmoil that unfolded in rapid succession.

First Miss Laura was late. I knew something was up
when she wasn't here by seven fifty-seven. She always
walks through the big doors between seven fifty-four and
seven fifty-six, sure as clockwork. It was wrong for Sergeant Binder to yell at her. Why, Miss Laura even said
hello to me when she was late and worried about getting

in trouble. I heard the sergeant make fun of her in front
of the other detectives. I pretended to be scraping something off the floor so I could hear. Binder better watch his
step, yelling at Miss Laura like that, and for no good
reason either. It wasn't her fault the traffic was bad. He'd
better watch it, or I'll teach him a thing or two.

Adam rubbed his throbbing temples, then rolled his
mop bucket to the utility closet, where he kept his cleaning supplies. He proudly lifted his keys from the end of a
chain attached to his leather belt. Though there were
only two keys on the oversized ring, one to the utility
closet and one to his apartment, he fingered them with
satisfaction. He was in a position of trust, guardian of the
keys. He turned the key in the lock, reveling in the power
of the tiny clicking sound. With brushes and cleaners in
hand he carefully relocked the door and headed for the
rest rooms. He needed to hurry. He had to leave
promptly today.

I don't remember when there was so much going on,
he thought. Miss Laura came trailing back into the precinct cool as a cucumber around eleven with a man in
handcuffs. Quick as a flash a bunch of people were rushing in behind her, all of them talking at once. A lady was
yelling and crying about how Miss Laura had saved her
baby from the bank robber, and her little kid was crying
because his mom was upset.

The janitor's eyes stung from the ammonia as he
scrubbed the urinals. He polished the mirrors with a torn
rag, just glancing at his reflection, then concentrating
only on the smudges and water stains on the surface of
the mirror, without looking deeper, to his reflection,
which stared back intently.

Miss Laura turned the bank robber over to be booked,
and while the officer was reading him his rights, those
people were all talking at once. Miss Laura talked to
them low and soothing-like and before long everyone was
quiet, even the baby. The little fellow couldn't have been
more than three years old. He was smiling and his mama
was smiling and everyone was waiting in line to give their
statements. All the while, Binder was standing back looking at Miss Laura like he hated her.

Adam scrubbed the floor of the rest room and, without flinching, cleaned the dried vomit where a drunk had missed the toilet. He gathered his supplies and headed for the women's rest room. He stood outside and knocked, then shouted self-consciously to make sure no one was inside. He didn't like to clean the women's rest room. He felt nervous cleaning the same toilets the prostitutes used, knowing he was touching where their bodies had been, their private parts pressed against the seats. He put it out of his mind and continued reliving the day.

When things finally calmed down and I thought it was going to be like any other afternoon, a call came in on the radio and Winchell's crew was in trouble. Miss Laura looked over at Sergeant Binder but didn't say a word. Binder looked around, and Miss Laura and Detective O'Reilly were the only cops in the room. He cursed under his breath, then said, "Okay, Bernhardt, go lend them a hand. O'Reilly, get off your backside and go with her."

They were out of here in a flash. It was only forty-five minutes before they all were back with the three jewelry-store robbers, but it seemed like hours. Miss Laura's pants were torn and Harry Winchell was limping around acting like a whipped dog. All the officers were talking about how Miss Laura had saved that baby from the bank robber, then had gone out and nearly flown over a brick wall after one of the jewelry-store robbers. They said Harry Winchell tried to follow and help, but tripped over a garbage can and sprained his ankle. That gave me a laugh, but the best part of the day was seeing how Miss Laura handled that baby. She sure would be a good mama.

He carefully locked his cleaning supplies back in the closet, fingering the keys lovingly, before he put on his coat and headed for the doors precisely at four P.M.

"Good night, Adam," Laura said as she passed him in the lobby.

Adam looked down at his scuffed work boots and muttered, "Night, ma'am," and rushed out the door. He ran the first three blocks from the precinct, partly from his nervousness over Laura's attention and partly because it was Tuesday. That was one of the days he walked by the grade school a few blocks from the precinct house. The final bell rang at three fifty-five. If he hurried, some of the children still would be around when he got there.

Adam hurried around a group of young men throwing dice on the street and turned down the alley between Twenty-second and Twenty-third streets.

He came out at Birch Street and slowed his pace to a casual stroll. In fact, he made it a point to walk as slowly as possible without looking suspicious. The slower he walked, the longer he could see and hear the children. He wished he could walk by the school every afternoon, but he was afraid of attracting attention.

It was only four and a half blocks from the Third Precinct to Adam's apartment, but he never went directly there from work. Instead, he walked along carefully chosen routes that took him by the places where the children played. He hoped people didn't notice he was watching the children—not that anyone paid attention to what he did. So few people even glanced his way that sometimes he stopped and weighed himself on the penny scale in front of Jones's Mercantile so he could glance furtively in the mirror long enough to assure himself he hadn't become invisible.

Laura Bernhardt notices me, he thought. I don't understand why a classy lady like her wants to go around arresting people when she would be such a good mama. I don't like most women, only Miss Laura and Marie. Other women flaunt their bodies at you, then walk by like you aren't there. Women are mean too. At the orphanage, Sister Mary Xavier—

An exploding pain in his head warned him he was treading on dangerous mental territory.

Miss Laura isn't like Sister Mary Xavier. She's always nice to me. Marie is nice too. We're going to get married and have a family when she comes back.

He started hearing the children's laughing voices and pretended he was going to school to pick up his boy. A group of children walked by him, singing. They played "Step on a crack and break your mother's back" on the uneven sidewalk, hopping a little too close to the street, which was crowded with rush-hour traffic. They darted between fat women carrying heavy sacks and a prostitute talking seductively to a soldier.

Adam pretended he didn't notice the children. He didn't want them to complain to their parents about the man who stared at them. If they complained, he would lose his job, and they might even lock him up again.

Hi, kids. Hi, John and Joe. Hi, Larry. Pretty cold today, isn't it? I'm going to pick up my boy. Have you seen my son, Jeremy?

It's Mr. Smith. Hi, Mr. Smith. Gee, it sure is nice seeing you, Mr. Smith.

Hey, Mr. Smith, are you coming to the football game on Saturday? It wouldn't seem right if you weren't there.

Yeah, Mr. Smith, please come.

You can bet I'll be there, kids. I wouldn't miss it for anything. You know I never miss a game. My boy is playing in it.

Jeremy is the best player in the whole school, Mr. Smith. He said you taught him. I wish you were my father. My dad never plays football with me.

Well, then, why don't Jeremy and I come around on Sunday and pick you boys up in our new car? We can go to the park and throw some passes. Afterward, I think we could talk Mrs. Smith into whipping up some homemade peanut-butter cookies and hot chocolate.

Wow, Mr. Smith. That would be great. We love going to your house.

Adam was in front of the grade school now. Children were milling around the imposing two-story faded brick structure. The date on the front said 1920. The yard was asphalt, surrounded by a six-foot chain-link fence. It reminded him of the orphanage. He rubbed his temples.

They should build these kids a new school, one of those fancy ones like they have in the suburbs with lots of grass and big playing fields, he thought. I heard on the TV that some of the new schools even have carpet on the floors. That's what these kids need. It's not right they have to go to this old place just because they live in the city and their folks don't have money.

He remembered scuffing across the hot asphalt at the orphanage on a summer day while the other children played Red Rover. He had stopped by the fence and looked way up to the top, where the barbed wire was, and wondered what it would be like to live where there were trees and grass, like in the cool green park they went to on special occasions. The pain in his head brought him back to the present.

He walked in front of the school, stopped, took off his worn leather gloves, and set them on the sidewalk beside him. His hands hurt from the cold, but he carefully retied his left shoelace, checked it to make sure it was secure, and started to work on his right shoelace. His shoes didn't need to be tied. It was a way to linger, to hear the children, and to dream.

Daddy, Daddy. Hi, Daddy. Gosh, I love you.

Hi, Jeremy. How about a big hug for your dad?

Don't hug me so hard, son. You're going to squeeze the stuffing right out of me. You sure are growing up to be a strong one.

I'm going to be just like you, Dad.

You're a fine boy. Did you learn anything in school today?

I got an A on my math test. I was the only one in the whole class who got a star.

That's my good boy. What do you say we stop at the candy store on the way home and celebrate, but don't tell your mom. She's fixing fried chicken for dinner, and she'll have my neck if I make you lose your appetite.

I won't tell. You're the best dad in the whole wide world.

Adam put his gloves on and reluctantly walked on by the school. He turned left at the corner of Twenty-sixth Street, carefully ignoring the women's foundations on the mannequins in Helga's Boutique, and continued down the street, where he stopped in front of Grandma's Baby Furnishings. He looked pensively at the display in the window, although it hadn't changed in over a year.

Now, Adam. We don't need all this stuff you keep bringing home. When the baby comes, he can sleep in the same bassinet your mother rocked you to sleep in. I'd like that better, anyway. With all the love your mama gave you, and all the love we'll give our baby, the old bassinet is the best way to start his new little life.

At the candy store he stood in line behind a group of children who were trying to decide between gumdrops and jelly beans. Adam bought a quarter pound of chocolates, ate one on the way out of the store, and threw the rest in a garbage can he passed on the way to the park.

Don't you be taking any candy from strangers, Jeremy. Strangers aren't to be trusted, and I wouldn't want anything to happen to my boy.

Though the wind had penetrated his coat and gloves, Adam walked slowly through the park, where children were ice-skating on the lake. Then he headed to the football field and tied his shoes again. This time his procrastination was real, as his frostbitten fingers protested against the tedious chore of maneuvering the slippery strings.

He was in front of the King Super a few blocks from his apartment when the sun stole away, throwing dark shadows, which played between the streetlights and the storefronts that the children had abandoned for cozy homes and hot dinners.

Adam carefully examined the selection in the frozen-food department while the Muzak droned monotonously. He picked up a family-sized box of fried chicken and laboriously read the label, then checked a package of roast-beef-for-four in a pouch of gravy.

He checked his watch: six-ten. He would have to hurry if he was going to make it back to the apartment in time for the reruns of *Leave It to Beaver.* He sadly grabbed a couple of generic turkey pies and made his way through the crowd of evening shoppers. The family dinners were just a dream. He winced when he walked by a father and son talking happily.

I want someone to devote my entire being to, Adam thought miserably. I want someone who will give me a purpose for living. I want a boy of my own.

He jerked at an electrical charge that seemed to go right through him. He looked around, but no one else appeared to be affected. Something tugged in his memory, leaving him momentarily nervous and queasy, but he didn't know what it meant. He shrugged his feelings off and thought about going shopping that weekend for a new TV.

He hurried to beat another customer to the quick-check line. *Leave It to Beaver* would be starting soon. Then he would watch *The Brady Bunch, Eight Is Enough,* and *Little House on the Prairie.*

The cash register made an electronic beeping sound when the clerk ran his selection across the computer. The top three buttons of the woman's uniform were open, revealing ample cleavage and a roll of fat above her arm-pit. "That'll be seventy-two cents," she said without looking up or missing a beat with her chewing gum.

Adam winced when his hand touched hers. He grabbed his sack and rushed out, rubbing the shooting pain in his temples as he stumbled into the night air.

It was pitch-black when he turned into the alley and huffed up the three flights of stairs to his apartment. He always thought of it as the apartment, never as home. Homes had children and mothers.

He nearly slipped on a patch of ice on the fire escape, then held on to the railing with his free hand to keep his balance.

And he was so intent on watching for patches of ice, he didn't see the box made visible by the neon lights from the bar on the corner until he'd almost reached the landing.

"What the heck is this?" he said in surprise when he finally saw it. "Someone sure went to a lot of trouble to deliver this to the wrong place. I didn't order anything."

Still, he was excited. In all his life no one had left a box outside his door, not even by mistake. Adam set down his sack and prepared to heave the box out of the way so he could get to the door and was surprised to find it amazingly light for its size, about four feet high and two feet wide.

"Well, I'll be. That sucker couldn't weigh more than ten pounds. I wonder what's in it."

As soon as he had the door open and the light on, he carried the box inside.

"No harm in seeing what this is all about. After all, this is my apartment, and it was outside my door."

4

"Darryl, I called to tell you I'm going to be about an hour late. I have some paperwork to finish."

"Laura, I was getting ready to call you. I heard about you and the bank robbery on the five o'clock news. Are you all right? What happened, anyway? How did you get involved with a bank robber when you were supposed to be picking up those jewelry-store thieves?"

"They mentioned me on the news? I wonder how the TV station found out about it."

"I don't know, but they interviewed a lady who said you saved her kid. The way she was talking about you, I got the feeling it was all she could do to keep from saying 'saint' in front of your name instead of 'detective'—which shows she's an excellent judge of character. But, jeez, what a start. I'm not used to hearing about my wife on the news. Are you sure you're okay?"

"It really wasn't that big a deal. I'll tell you all about it when I get home," Laura said. Nevertheless, her voice showed she was pleased by Darryl's enthusiasm and concern. "I'm pretty tired. How 'bout if I pick up a pizza and a six-pack on my way home? The last thing I feel like doing is cooking tonight."

"Carry-out food? No way. I'm marinating a couple of steaks in my secret sauce and chilling a bottle of wine. Couldn't you do your paperwork tomorrow? I'm anxious to see you."

"As far as the paperwork is concerned, twist my arm some more. I'll come in a little early tomorrow and finish it. I don't want you to worry about cooking, though. I'm sure you had a hard day too. It couldn't have been easy working outside in this cold weather."

"I feel like cooking tonight, and I hardly feel like an abused husband. But I will if you don't hurry home."

Laura was barely conscious of the road as she drove. The part of her mind that handled routine mechanical chores took over and operated efficiently while the rest of her consciousness whirled through memories of the day.

The strain that she had held in check for hours began to catch up with her in the privacy of her car. She wanted desperately for chasing bank robbers, scaling fences, and holding bad guys at gunpoint to be no big deal. She imagined that the other detectives took such things in stride. So when her hands began to shake slightly and her mood swung dangerously in the direction of hysteria, she considered it a personal failure. Her disappointment in herself added an aura of gloom to her growing nervousness.

She glanced up at the sky and was surprised to see that the clouds that had hovered over the city most of the day had disappeared. It was the type of brilliantly clear night the Midwest gets only during the winter. Normally she would have found the thousands of stars comforting. Tonight she felt they were her judge and jury.

You'd think the guys could have been a little more supportive this afternoon, she thought. Oh, well, they're just jealous.

The hurt she felt when the detectives all left for a drink after work without inviting her still stung. Not that she would have gone anyway. She just wanted to be invited. She was disgusted when an unexpected sob escaped from her throat, followed by another and another until she was openly crying while she drove down the road.

"My reaction is totally out of proportion to the situation," she said aloud to add emphasis to the thought. "I've had a hard day, and I'm tired. That doesn't mean I'm an incompetent person."

Nevertheless, she felt as if the clouds were gone from the sky because they had entered her. As she pulled into her driveway, Laura tried to get herself under control.

I'll act nonchalant. There's no reason to get so worked up and to have Darryl think I've lost my mind.

She sat in the car and took a few deep breaths, but as soon as she went inside and saw Darryl, her best intentions of being the composed professional were gone. She was in his arms laughing and crying and talking a mile a minute.

A hot bubble-bath and a glass of wine did Laura a world of good, but she could feel herself swinging like a pendulum to a point at the bottom of the emotional scale. She fidgeted with her dinner while she talked to Darryl.

"I was so frustrated with Binder this morning, but when I was out on the street and the action started, nothing was on my mind but the job at hand. On the way back to the precinct house after the robbery attempt, I was thinking how professionally I handled the situation. Then later, when the call came in that Harry's team was in trouble and I was waiting for Binder to decide who would go help, I felt like a little girl hoping for an approving look from her daddy. As for the rest of the detectives, I don't think anything short of a sex change would make them accept me. I can't even get along with my own partner. Am I all that obnoxious? I know there aren't many women in the division, but Jan Garlich and Sara Burns downtown don't seem to have the trouble I do."

She finally took a bite of steak, but her throat was so dry, she felt as if she were chewing leather.

"Of course you're not obnoxious, sweetheart," Darryl said, reaching across the table and squeezing her hand. "It's hard for them to accept changes. For most of them the concept of women detectives is new."

"I'm not so sure. I've been there two months and they still act like they have chips on their shoulders."

"That reminds me of an old friend I ran into today, Laura. We worked on our first construction crew together. He didn't fit in with the other carpenters. He had just graduated from college and the other guys made fun of him. They said things like, 'Hey, college boy, did you nail your thumb to the wall yet?' "

"What jerks."

"Oh, not really. The kid was trying so hard to prove he was good enough to work with them that to the others it seemed like he thought he was better."

"What's he doing now?"

"He's a contractor with fifteen men working for him, and he realized he didn't have to be just like the other men to be good. I hear he married a gorgeous police detective who has the whole town praising her on television."

"You set me up. It was you."

"Yes."

"No wonder you understand me so well, Darryl. I didn't realize myself until now how jealous I am of them."

"Well, now you've proven yourself. You know you can do the job. You don't have to be a man to be a good detective. You only have to be you. That doesn't mean, though, that your gender isn't important in your work. Everyone brings a different perspective to their job, from their backgrounds, their natural talents and interests, and from their sex."

"Did that first construction crew ever get so they accepted you?"

"Yes, and it really didn't take all that long either."

"After you relaxed, did they stop teasing you?"

"I think they probably teased me more than ever, but there was a different tone to it. I could tell they were doing it because they liked me. I got so I could throw it back at them pretty good."

Laura began to feel better about her job. She knew she couldn't change overnight, but for the first time she could see hope. If it weren't for a gnawing unease, she could have been in a terrific mood. She had the feeling she was being watched and reached to overlap the already closed curtains by the dining-room table.

Darryl and her conversation moved to the greenhouse they planned to build in the spring, then to the routine details of daily living. Throughout it all Laura felt a tension that didn't seem related to her day at work or anything she could put her finger on.

While they loaded the dishwasher, she kept looking over her shoulder. She felt like a trapped animal as her feeling of being watched grew irrationally.

"I think I'll sew for a little while, Darryl," she said absentmindedly.

Laura always enjoyed the break sewing gave her. It required a precision and attention to detail she found rewarding, and it gave her an opportunity to express the feminine side she hid at work. The tailored suits that were her trademark at the precinct were a far cry from

the soft materials and swirling designs she created for off-
duty hours. She had a talent for original designs that
were demure, but sexy in their subtlety.

Tonight her desire to get to the sewing machine was
different. It bordered on obsession. During dinner her
mind kept wandering to the sewing machine; not her
usual machine, though. She walked right by her comput-
erized machine and headed for the spare bedroom to set
up the battered portable machine she had picked up on
an impulse the week before at a secondhand store. After
she got it home, she wondered what had possessed her to
buy it. Now it seemed to be calling to her.

As she walked down the hall, she felt as if she were
walking into a nightmare. Only the picture she had taken
of a lion at the zoo last summer stood out clearly, but
instead of the gentle, relaxed pose that she had caught on
film, the lion was crouched, ready to attack. The frame
no longer was a frame. It was an opening the lion could
leap through with ease, into her home, its teeth sinking
into her neck.

Laura did not want to go on. She didn't want to pass
the lion. Worse was the prospect of confronting the sewing machine. Although her mind was rebelling against
moving forward, her legs continued to move her down
the hall, apparently urgent to reach a destination she
dreaded. She fought to remain upright on a floor that no
longer had substance, and still she inched on.

She was even with the lion. She could feel its hunger as
it eagerly eyed her jugular vein. Its rancid breath gagged
her. She tried to scream, but the sound died in her constricted throat.

"No, no, pussycat, I want to play with the lady," a
voice said.

The lion pulled back, snarling its disappointment.

Laura didn't hear the voice externally. It filled her
head like a thought transplant, a loud idea spoken in a
child's voice—taunting, evil. She hovered near the lion,
more willing to confront its jaws than to face the source
of that voice. But she couldn't stay where she was. She
felt as if she were engaged in a tug-of-war, with the power

of the universe pulling her forward. She was hot and dizzy. The world was fading away.

The next thing she knew, she was sitting at the portable sewing machine. She didn't know how long she had been there sewing. She was using an embroidery stitch, forming crimson letters on material the color of dense fog.

She gasped when she saw what she had sewn, not understanding its meaning, only that it foretold terror and danger previously felt only in her darkest nightmares.

The engine of the sewing machine whirred to a feverish pitch, the young voice combining with it in a whine of delight. Laura tried to pull her hands back as the footfeed inched her fingers nearer the needle, which wasn't a needle but the lion's jaws. Thunder roared outside. Lightning flashed in celebration of her fear.

The needle plunged into her finger. The scream that had been locked in her throat burst free, but was swallowed by deafening thunder. The needle yanked itself loose and plunged higher toward her knuckle, impaling her finger against the metal below.

Laura fainted, her blood spreading like an exclamation mark at the end of the mysterious embroidered phrase.

Darryl jerked his head up with a start at the sudden thunder. At first he thought it was a series of explosions and feared the oil refinery a few miles away had blown. He called out to Laura as he rushed to the door to look out.

"My God, it's thunder and lightning. It can't be."

He stood in awe and watched the aerial explosions. Between long flashes of lightning he could see the perfectly clear sky. He had never seen so many stars. They twinkled as though pleased with their view of a phenomenon always before hidden from them through dense clouds.

"Laura, come here and look at this," Darryl yelled, still standing at the door. His voice was lost in another explosion.

She's probably looking out a window at the other end

of the house, he thought, reluctant to pull himself away
from the door.

As suddenly as it began, it was over. Darryl continued
to stand at the door, looking at the stars and doubting
what he had seen. The cold finally forced him back inside.

"Hey, Laura. Have you ever seen anything like that?"
he yelled as he walked down the hall looking for his wife.
She wasn't at her sewing machine in the family room.

Maybe she went to bed, he thought, puzzled. He didn't
really think she would go to bed without coming to get
him, or at least saying good-night. Even if she had, he
didn't see how she could have slept through the storm.

He smiled when he saw the door was open to the spare
bedroom, until he looked in and saw his wife lying limp
over the battered portable sewing machine, her finger still
trapped by the needle.

She didn't gain consciousness again until he had freed
her finger and carried her to bed. She obviously was in
shock. She kept mumbling something about a child letting the lion attack her. He held her gently, kissing her
feverish forehead. He shuddered and thought about the
strip of material that still had been in the sewing machine
when he found her. In a sprawling, childlike print, she
had embroidered, *Beware the Child.*

5

Adam kept his eyes on the box in the middle of his apartment as he pulled off his gloves and automatically
reached to the end of the bed to turn on the television. He
sat on the bed, for once ignoring the TV. Instead, his
complete attention was focused on the cardboard box. He
sat and looked at it and shivered with excitement, watching it as if he expected it to disappear.

The weatherman blabbered meaningless conversation
with the newscaster, then turned to the weather map and

cheerfully predicted more polar weather as another cold
front moved in from the arctic.

"Will you look at the size of that box, buddy," Adam
said, gawking at the box as if he could see right through
the cardboard if he ogled it long enough.

He stood up and walked around it. His curiosity was
like that of a virgin groom on his wedding night who
savors his bride's curves before allowing himself the hidden secrets he longs to enjoy.

Adam hadn't opened a surprise package since he was a
child. At the orphanage the Salvation Army Santa Claus
had given him a candy cane and a shiny red car tightly
wrapped in red paper.

Now he lit a cigarette and stood back by the heater,
just looking and wondering. Then he moved to the sink
for another view. He leaned against the drainboard that
stood precariously on four spindly legs next to the deep,
square sink. His turkey pies were melting and the thin
crust was soggy inside the limp boxes, but Adam didn't
care.

Finally, he stubbed out his cigarette in the sink, took a
deep breath, and walked over to the box, which was held
securely together with industrial staples, the kind they
put on in factories to let you know you are getting something new.

There was a brown envelope attached to the top of the
box. He hated to look at it. When he did, he would know
the box wasn't for him and the adventure would be over.
He couldn't stand the suspense anymore and pulled the
envelope off and read, *Adam Smith, 300 B, Arms Apartments.*

"Well, I'll be. I'll be darned," he exclaimed in disbelief.
The envelope was completely plain except for his name
and address. The box also was plain, betraying no hint of
its contents.

"Now, who would send me a box that size—or any
box, for that matter?"

He searched his mind for a clue, but there was none.
He had no friends, no relatives. The only one there had
ever been was Marie, and she had been dead for thirty
years, hadn't she? Adam rubbed his temples.

What should he do first, read the contents of the envelope or open the box? He didn't remember when he had
been so happy, except when Marie told him . . .

*What did she say? She came in from outside glowing
and smelling of fresh air and told him . . . something.*

Adam rubbed his throbbing head, then opened the envelope as if it were delicate crystal. He pulled out the
card and looked at it diligently. Reading was never easy
for him, and since his stay in the institution it had grown
even harder. He read aloud:

> *Congratulations, Adam Smith.*
> *You are the winner of a unique new Home Entertain-*
> *ment Center and three-dimensional viewing experience.*

"I'm not sure what those fancy words mean, but it
sounds like it might be a new TV. Wouldn't that be something if it was one of those new color sets?"

His whole body tingled in anticipation. He laughed
and ran his hand across the top of the box, then his expression changed to caution and doubt.

"It couldn't be. That box is too tall, and way too
skinny. I think I've looked at every television in the
stores that's ever been made, and I've never seen one that
size and shape."

He was afraid even to hope. He knew from hard experience that dreams might come true for other people, but
not for Adam Smith.

"Funny it doesn't say what contest I won. You'd think
someone that was giving something away would want
credit for it, but it doesn't say anything on the card about
where it came from. And I don't remember entering any
contest. I'd remember something important like that,
wouldn't I? Besides, I never enter contests. If you enter a
contest, you get yourself all worked up for nothing and
end up being disappointed.

"Maybe it's the wrong Adam Smith; but it has my
name and address on the envelope," he said protectively.
"Maybe I should ask Miss Laura tomorrow if I can keep
it. But what if she says no? What if someone sees it and
thinks I stole it? Then again, no one ever comes up here.

better hurry or the bad guys will die of old age before I make it to work."

She threw on her coat and pulled the matching cap tightly over her head. A blast of frigid air met her as she opened the door and hurried carefully across a thin layer of ice to coax her reluctant car to life in the subzero weather.

After she started Darryl's truck, she headed back to the house to kiss her husband good-bye. He met her at the door with an egg-and-sausage sandwich to go. She was pleased when she checked her watch and saw she was ten minutes early.

"If the rest of the day goes as well as this morning, I'll be ready to tackle Jack the Ripper tonight," she said, but her comment left her with an uneasy feeling.

"Lucky fellow," Darryl joked, missing the shadow that momentarily crossed his wife's expression.

Her Dodge was warm by the time Laura wound her way through a couple of miles of suburban streets and headed up the entrance ramp to the freeway. It was only January fifteenth and already she longed for spring.

As she drove, she wondered if her success even on this difficult case would be enough to force Sergeant Binder to give her a chance on other challenging cases. She longed for the opportunity to work up to her potential. She knew she had less experience than the other detectives, but it was humiliating when Binder temporarily assigned Harry to another partner when an interesting case was involved, then sent her to the school to talk to a kid whose bicycle had been stolen.

A woman trying to get ahead in the police department of this city is bucking the same odds as a private in the Army trying to become a general during peacetime, she mused. What I need is the equivalent of war.

She shuddered and looked over her shoulder. She shook off her uneasiness, attributing it to guilt for considering personal advancement at the cost of others, and to the long winter.

She turned her attention to maneuvering her Dodge through the rush-hour traffic that inched like blood clots through the decaying arteries of the city. Businessmen in

No one could see it. And how could I give it back when I don't know where it came from? Here I am talking about giving it back, and I don't even know for sure what it is."

He pulled his knife from his pocket and gingerly slit the box all the way around the top.

"It's too light to be a television, unless maybe it's one of those new electronic circuitry things. What do they mean by three-dimensional viewing experience?"

He pulled the top off the box. Whatever was inside was covered with air-filled packing material. He lifted handfuls of plastic out of the box until he saw the top of a curved, shiny object.

"What on earth is that thing?" he asked, popping a piece of plastic between his fingers.

He slit a panel of the box from the top to the floor. It fell over, scattering packing material from the bed to the bathroom and unveiling the contents of the box. Adam stared at a round object supported by a rectangular base. It looked as if someone had turned an oil drum on its side, cut it off so it was little more than a foot thick, and painted it a shiny metallic black. An electrical cord extended from the base like an invitation.

Adam was more confused than ever. He pulled the object out of what remained of the box, turned it around, and gasped. The opposite side was covered with thick, concave glass, giving the gadget the appearance of a huge, sunken eye. It looked like a child's science project.

"Well, I'll be. It must be a television, but I've never seen anything like it in the stores. Whoever heard of a round television? And that glass must be thirty-six inches in diameter."

The news was over and blurry images of Adam's favorite show, *Leave It to Beaver,* flashed on his black-and-white set while Adam caressed and explored every incomprehensible inch of the cool black eye. He walked around the oddity, checking it carefully for a brand name . . . no name, no registration number, just sleek metal and a sunken glass front. The only writing was below two knobs on the flat base. One said ON/VOLUME. The other said CHANNEL SELECTOR.

He searched the packing material in the box and on the

floor for some kind of explanation, instructions, or even
an inspection sticker. There was nothing.

"Have you ever seen anything like that, Beaver?"
Adam said to the blurry child in the old set. Beaver kept
right on talking to Wally.

"It must be a television," Adam said. He was so elated,
he pulled the plug on his old set, cutting Beaver off right
in the middle of a crisis he was discussing with Wally
while they played catch; a gesture Adam Smith, concerned father, wouldn't have considered possible a few
hours earlier. He plugged the eye, which seemed to smile
at him, into the apartment's only electrical outlet. He
pulled the on knob, and it burst to life.

Adam bolted back at what he saw. There was Beaver
talking to Wally in living color, but more than that . . .
their images were standing out, giving them the appearance of almost being in the room with him.

"So that's what the card meant by three-dimensional
viewing experience," he murmured in amazement.

Wally was in the background playing catch with the
Beaver. When he threw the ball, Adam ducked, sure it
would fly out of the TV. It was like looking at a kid's
View-Master, but the pictures moved. It was real life
brought to him right there in his own apartment. Any
thought of asking Laura Bernhardt for advice was completely and forever forgotten.

Adam moved his old TV from its honored spot at the
end of the bed and set it in the corner. He replaced it with
the new television, then flopped down in his customary
position on his stomach with his head at the end of the
bed. From his perch less than two feet from the screen,
the sunken glass gave him the illusion of being surrounded by the picture. Combined with the three-dimensional effect, he felt he was part of the action.

Two powerful little stereo speakers were built into each
side of the unit. When Wally spoke, his voice came out
one side. When Beaver spoke, his voice came out the
other. Adam lay on his bed, right in the middle of the
conversation, just as their dad might be.

"You listen to your brother, now, Beaver. If you do

what that Eddie Haskell said, you're going to get yourself into big trouble."

He stayed on the bed all evening, propped up on his elbows as he laughed and talked to his favorite television characters. As usual, he watched the channel that specialized in reruns of old situation comedies and family shows. Around nine P.M. he was jolted from the beginning of *Eight Is Enough* by a series of sudden explosions. Adam ran to the door and watched the lightning display.

With his attention drawn outside he didn't see the toilet-paper commercial vanish, briefly replaced by Laura Bernhardt's anguished image as a sewing-machine needle ripped through her finger.

When the sky returned to normal, Adam wondered about the weird storm. Though thunderstorms weren't unheard of in January, he had never seen one in subzero temperatures, and certainly not with clear skies. He soon forgot about the freak storm as the television grabbed his interest. He watched it until the early hours of the morning. Eventually his eyes began to droop. He yawned and tried to stay awake, but realizing he was fighting a losing battle, reluctantly pushed the knob on his new friend to off. The picture instantaneously fizzled to a tiny red retina, in the middle of the screen, that lingered, then disappeared.

Adam fell asleep at the end of the bed. Soon the dreams sucked him in, twisting and flashing the terrors of the past and giving him no avenue of escape. Marie was staggering toward him. She was crying. Her face was white in sharp contrast to the deep red blood that covered her dress, her hands, her legs. Adam reached out to her, to comfort her. Then he was furious about . . . the blood? He reached out, but she collapsed lifeless at his feet in a red puddle, which grew to rivers raging across the uneven floor.

The blood was on his hands and clothes. It spread around the huddled mass that had been the woman he was to marry. The blood was warm on his hands. He started screaming. He still was screaming when the blood cooled, then turned cold. By the time it caked and dried, the screaming was deep inside of him, welling up from a demon that took over and refused to release him.

In his nightmare Marie's lifeless face changed to the familiar face of Sister Mary Xavier. The nun grew from Marie's inert body and towered above him, shouting accusations and threats.

You're a bad boy, Adam Smith; a bad apple. I'll show you a thing or two. I'll show you what happens to boys who sin.

He didn't find out what Sister Mary Xavier had in mind. In the distance he heard a friendly voice calling.

"Adaaaaam. Where are you, my love?"

The voice brought him back into the world of the apartment. He opened his eyes cautiously, expecting to discover that he still was deep within the dream and, instead of seeing his apartment resting peacefully around him, would find the snakes darting at his face.

He was curled in a fetal ball with the light from the neon sign throwing shadows on the blanket gripped tightly in his hands . . . and from the light of the smiling television eye.

"I thought I turned the television off. I must have turned it on in my sleep," he said. His confused, half-awake voice broke through the apartment like a hardball splintering a plate-glass window.

He turned toward the television and stretched his legs to the top of the bed. The eye was filled with scenes of a city park, green beneath a blue sky partly obscured by fluffy white clouds. A lunch was carefully arranged on a picnic table in the foreground. A swing at one side of the picture swayed in a light breeze.

Adam thought he must still be dreaming. The picture was familiar. He was sure he had been to that place. He remembered laying the lunch on the table, then arranging and rearranging it in between nervous glances at his watch.

The television speaker sprang to life as a woman appeared deep within the set, familiar but too distant to identify.

"Adaaaam."

"Marie!" he gasped from his bird's-eye perch on the bed.

She came springing lightly toward him, stopping occasionally to pick flowers. She appeared to float across the plush carpet of grass, her features sharp as she drew near the front of the screen.

"Marie! I'm here, Marie. I knew you weren't dead. Don't go away."

Marie laughed and ran to the front of the three-dimensional screen. She was no farther away from Adam than she had been on the day of the picnic more than thirty years before. Her face was young and glowing with affection as she held up the flowers she had picked. She raised her lips to be kissed.

Adam reached out to take Marie into his arms, but met the solid resistance of cold glass.

"I'm sorry I'm late, Adam," Marie said, her voice flowing out of the television speakers like a symphony. "I finally had to tell old Mrs. Finch I was sick so I could get away from work. I don't think she believed me, but I don't care. I love you, Adam."

She ran to the swing, where she could soar through the air with her joy.

"I love you, too, Marie. I'm here," Adam cried to the lifelike image.

The electronic eye moved to a closeup of Marie on the swing, focusing on her legs as the air pushed up her skirt, revealing the shape of her thighs. Then the picture flickered and turned to white snow.

"Marie, come back," Adam pleaded frantically.

The white snow disappeared, but instead of seeing Marie, Adam saw a man deep within the set at the end of a foggy tunnel. The man was too far away for Adam to see him clearly, but he heard his desperate screams and saw his hands beating in vain against some kind of wall or door. Adam flinched at the vaguely familiar voice and terrifying screams, but his concern for getting Marie to return overpowered his fear.

"Don't leave me again, Marie. Please come back," he begged as he shook the giant eye, whose benevolent smile seemed to have turned into a sneer.

The man continued screaming from his foggy prison
while Adam flicked the channels. When Adam finally
gave up and sat crying in terror and frustration, the white
snow returned briefly. It cleared, revealing Marie once
again in the foreground next to the picnic table. He gratefully pulled himself forward, dangling off the bed, their
faces separated only by the glass.

"I love you, Adam. I'll always love you."

The picture faded to the tiny retina, flickered, and disappeared. Adam shook the TV, trying to bring Marie
back. Black silence. He checked the plug, but it was still
securely in the wall.

"Maybe if I turn it off, then back on, it will work
again."

But the knob didn't yield under his touch. The television *was* turned off. He jerked his hand back, then cautiously reached out and pulled the television to the on
position. Jimmy Stewart and Katharine Hepburn burst
onto the screen in three dimensions. He checked every
channel but found only the scheduled programing. He
was confused and disappointed as he reached out and
turned the television off. Long after the retina disappeared, Adam continued to look at the black eye, which
seemed to be smiling mischievously at him in the glow of
the neon lights at the end of the alley.

The plain card with its typewritten message sat on the
nightstand next to the ticking alarm clock.

6

Wednesday, January 16
Robin says there's going to be a layoff at the grain mill,"
Martha Gibbons said as she filled her husband's bowl
with oatmeal.

Harold took a gulp of his coffee and ignored his wife's
comment.

"Is it true, Harold? Robin said the drought for the past
couple of years has got the wheat surplus way down and

that there isn't enough work to keep you guys busy. Do you think you'll get laid off?"

"I think it's too bad Robin's brain isn't as big as her mouth," Harold replied, spooning sugar onto the hot cereal. "How about some more coffee?"

Martha refilled her husband's cup while watching his expression carefully to see if he was worried. He was a stoic man who was raised to believe you don't bother women with money troubles. He thought a man who bellyached to his wife about his job wasn't a man at all. Martha couldn't read anything out of the ordinary in his expression this morning, but she had noticed that he seemed uncharacteristically tense and short-tempered lately.

She walked behind him, rubbed his shoulders, and kissed him lightly on the head. Harold acted as if he hadn't noticed, but she knew he had. She grinned inwardly at how embarrassed he would be if she ever did something like that in public.

She started to refill his oatmeal bowl, but he held his hand over the dish.

"No, thanks. I'm not very hungry today, and don't pack such a big lunch. You send me enough food to feed an army."

She gave him a surprised look and pulled some of the food out of his lunch pail. Her husband had the appetite of a horse and was skinny as a rail from hard work.

So it's true, then, she thought. I know he is hungry, so he must be worried about saving food because he knows he is going to be laid off.

She turned away so he wouldn't see her concern. It would only make him worry more.

He wolfed down his breakfast, then gave her a quick kiss as she walked him to the door of their mobile home. Martha watched him walk down the gravel road toward Taylorsville a half mile away. He never drove their old pickup truck to work. He said it was a waste of gasoline, when he needed the exercise anyway.

Martha saw the sun creeping over the horizon in front of him and she smiled sadly, thinking that it, like her,

was moving slowly because it simply was too tired to face
another winter day.

She was jolted out of her thoughts by the sound of a
sleepy voice. She turned expectantly and saw Jeff tod-
dling into the living room, rubbing his eyes. His diaper
was sagging around his knees. By the time she removed
the diaper and helped him put on his training pants, her
youngest son was wide awake and full of enthusiasm. She
looked at him fondly and gave him a big kiss and hug
before putting him in his high chair and handing him a
spoon and bowl of oatmeal.

"I a big boy, aren't I, Mommy? I this many," he said,
proudly holding up two chubby little fingers.

"You sure are, sweetie. Before long you'll be sitting at
the table to eat, just like Mommy and Daddy and the
other kids."

Jeff glowed from ear to ear. He grabbed his spoon in
his fist and managed to get most of a bite of oatmeal from
the bowl to his mouth.

The sounds of scuffling at the back of the trailer told
her the other children were up. She wearily set three
bowls and spoons on the table.

"Just because you're in first grade doesn't mean you
know everything," she heard Karen yelling indignantly
from the bedroom, where her fight with Harold junior
was growing louder by the minute.

"You kids had better get ready for school and stop that
fighting, or your dad is going to take the belt to you when
he gets home," Martha shouted halfheartedly. She filled
the bowls with oatmeal, trying to concentrate on completing the task at hand and pushing from her mind the
impossible list of chores she needed to finish that day.

"Nah-nah, nah-nah nah-nah," Harold sang after his
sister as she ran down the hall. His voice held the notes
and changed syllables expertly.

Martha thought this must be the first song all children
with siblings learned, even before the advertising jingles
perpetually repeated on the television and radio.

Karen seemed unaware of the taunt or the victory it
implied for her in the recent struggle.

"There's a knot in my shoestring, Mommy," she said,

confident in her mother's ability to solve any problem that might arise.

"I'll fix it, honey. You sit down and eat your breakfast or you're going to be late for school."

This, at least, was one problem Martha could handle. She hoped she would be able to live up to the more important issues that the family would face if Harold lost his job.

"Where's Sandy?" Martha asked Karen, her fingers still working on the knot.

"She won't get up, Mommy. She says her stomach hurts."

Martha's head jerked up, the small lines on her forehead momentarily deepening to creases. She looked back to the shoestring and hastened her efforts, feeling guilty that the second thought that flashed through her head was concern for her four-year-old's health. The first thought had been dread of another unpayable doctor bill.

Thank goodness Harold made me throw away the charge card that came in the mail before Christmas, she thought. He wasn't being pigheaded after all. He must have been worried even then about getting laid off. I wish he would talk to me about money. I'm not some fragile little thing who has to be protected.

She sighed. She might as well try to move the moon and stars as to change Harold. She wondered what her life would have been like now if she had taken the art scholarship she was offered when she and Harold graduated from high school, or if she had married Arnold Noble. He always did have a crush on her, and Robin said Arnold was a lawyer now. It wasn't him she fell in love with, though.

While Martha knelt down and slid the small tennis shoe on Karen's foot and tied the untangled shoestring, her daughter spontaneously reached out and wrapped her arms around her neck and planted a big kiss on the top of her cheek.

"I love you, Mommy."

"I love you, too, Karen," she said, her voice choking with emotion.

"Are you crying?" her bewildered daughter asked.

"No, of course not," Martha replied, smiling reassuringly. "Now, you finish your breakfast. I'll help you with your hair later."

Harold junior thundered through the living room with the self-confidence of the eldest son. Martha noted with amusement that he didn't even slow down as he ran past the television, flicking it on. He was in the kitchen wolfing down his oatmeal when he realized the television was turned to the morning news, not cartoons. He started to dash from the table to correct his error.

"Wait," Martha ordered. She listened intently while the newscaster announced that a freak electrical storm had startled residents of the city the night before, lighting up a clear sky, then disappearing as suddenly as it had come.

She shuddered at an emotion she couldn't quite name, and was glad they lived in the country. After all, the city was 150 miles from them. What happened there had no effect on her or her family. She hadn't been there in two years, and she had no plans to go back.

"You come right home after kindergarten this morning, Karen," she said, her voice edgier than she had intended.

"Okay, Mommy," Karen replied cheerfully. "We're going to finger-paint today. Mrs. Ives said so. I'll bring you a picture."

Martha started down the hall to check on Sandy, but a crash and Jeff's cries delayed her. She sent Harold junior to check on her daughter while she took care of the bowl of oatmeal Jeff had dropped. She was cleaning the mess off the floor when Harold came running back.

"She threw up, Mom."

"Oh, dear. Harold, you finish your breakfast while I take care of Sandy." She tossed the oatmeal-filled rag in the sink to be rinsed out later and rushed off to take care of her sick daughter.

"What's the matter, Sandy pumpkin?" she asked, feeling the child's forehead and noting that she was feverish. She gently stripped Sandy of her soiled clothes and wiped away the vomit that had splashed onto the child's face and arms.

"I don't feel good, Mommy."

"I know, honey. I'm going to put you in Karen's bed for a minute. I'll be back soon to take care of you."

Martha hurried into the kitchen, where Jeff was crying to be let out of the high chair and Harold had spilled his milk.

"I can't find my other glove, Mommy," Karen complained.

"It's on top of the TV," Martha said, not pausing in zipping Harold's coat and pulling his cap over his ears. She deftly maneuvered Jeff around the spilled milk, then allowed him to run into the living room to turn on *Sesame Street.* She kissed Harold and Karen good-bye and walked down the hall to take care of Sandy. The tiredness and queasy feeling she had had since she woke up overwhelmed her.

Oh, great, she thought. This is really what I need today. Sandy is sick, I'm sick, and I have a million things to do. There must be a flu bug going around. I sure hope the other kids don't get it.

Later she trudged through her morning chores while Sandy slept peacefully and Jeff played with his toys and watched television. Her stomach was feeling better by the time she flopped down in a chair to watch the noon news. The anchorman reported that scientists were attributing the freak storm of the night before to sunspot activity. Martha was certain they were wrong without knowing how or why, only that the knowledge left her with a nagging fear.

7

"Good grief, Laura, what happened to your finger?" Harry asked as he hobbled down the hall toward his partner. "It's swollen up like a boiled hot-dog." His feigned concern didn't quite hide an undercurrent of pleasure.

"I had a little run-in with my sewing machine, and the machine won."

"So you're practicing the domestic arts these days.
Does that mean you are thinking about turning in your
badge and taking up a career as a woman?" he said, looking like a grade-school boy who'd made a smart-aleck
remark that had the class snickering.

Laura was surprised that his sarcasm had no effect on
her. Her finger was throbbing, and she didn't have the
energy or the desire to play Harry's game.

"How is your foot today, Harry?" she asked, her face
reflecting the lack of emotion she felt. When she saw him
wince, then stammer in embarrassment, she realized that
without trying, she had hit his weak point, reminding
him that he had failed the day before. The victory meant
nothing to her. She was too caught up in her own problems.

She remembered eating dinner with Darryl the night
before. After that—nothing. She woke up in the middle
of the night frightened, and confused by the throbbing
pain in her finger. When Darryl told her about the sewing
machine and showed her the strange embroidered phrase,
then told her about the electrical storm, it was like being
told about a movie she had missed, except it obviously
had happened to her. The bloody strip of material and
her swollen finger were proof.

It was weird, but I don't need an appointment with a
neurologist, like Darryl said, she thought. No, there's
nothing wrong with me. They'd probably stick me in the
hospital and poke and probe for days, then decide I was
just tired. I'm sure it will never happen again.

Darryl's description of the electrical storm seemed almost as eerie to her as the incident with the sewing machine.

Just because I've never seen lightning and clear skies
doesn't mean there is anything sinister about it, she told
herself while she rolled paper into her typewriter. It was
probably a meteorological disturbance caused by sunspots, like the news said.

She forced herself to concentrate on her work, and by
the time the rest of the day-shift detectives arrived, she
was attempting to type her reports with one hand. When
a couple of the detectives teased her about her finger, she

remembered what Darryl had said at dinner and laughed with them. The teasing stopped when Binder came into the detectives' office.

"The morning meeting will start a half hour late so Chief MacNamara can attend," he announced gruffly. "Everyone is to arrange their schedules to allow for a longer meeting."

Laura wondered what was up. The chief of detectives occasionally visited the precinct, but something in Binder's tone made her think this would be more than a routine visit. The buzz of voices in the office indicated the others were curious too.

The premeeting banter in the coffee room ended abruptly when Binder walked in puffing on his cigar. The chief of detectives came in with him, but stopped in the middle of the room to shake hands with a few of the detectives.

"Harry, good to see you again," MacNamara said.

"You, too, Chief."

"José, how's that little boy of yours?"

"Getting bigger every day, sir."

"Glad to hear it." The chief then turned to Laura and said, "Congratulations on your promotion. I hope you are enjoying your new job. I'm sure you will be a fine addition to the department."

"Thank you, sir," Laura replied, happy that he had made the comment in front of the others. Laura thought Patrick MacNamara looked like a movie star playing the role of the top detective in the city. His silver hair, trim body, and intelligent eyes emphasized an aura of command. The chief's perfectly tailored suit contrasted sharply with Sergeant Binder's sloppy uniform and stained shirt.

Binder made a few announcements, then turned the meeting over to Chief MacNamara. Laura wished she were working for him, rather than for Binder. It was MacNamara who had convinced her to go into police work. He'd spoken at a recruiting seminar at her college when she was a senior. He'd been professional but practical in his attitude toward police work. She had been impressed by his sincerity after twenty-five years on the

force, and pleased that he emphasized the importance of
the job without painting a false picture of glamor. He
hadn't pulled any punches, but warned the audience that
recruits would face a career of long hours, hard work,
and very little thanks from the public. They would be
expected to deal with the dregs of society without losing
their respect for all individuals. They would be expected
to keep their cool in the most trying situations, and not
rely on their weapons except in life-threatening circumstances.

Laura had been intrigued by the challenge, and en-
rolled in the police academy as soon as she graduated
with a B.S. in psychology.

Laura pulled herself from the past and listened when
Chief MacNamara began speaking.

"As you are aware, men, the current structure of the
Detective Division has been under review for some time.
Presently the majority of the detectives work out of the
downtown office. Each is assigned to one major crime
division, such as homicide, vice, and so forth. The detectives cooperate with, but are separate from, the uni-
formed officers throughout the city.

"When we put detective units in each of the four precincts, we maintained that autonomy, so that you men
answer directly to Sergeant Binder, who answers to me."

Laura noticed that the chief's generic use of the word
men didn't have the sexist connotation it did when
Binder used it. Since he accepted her, he didn't need to
refer to her as being apart from the others.

"Our original idea in sending detectives to the precincts was to have you work in conjunction with the rob-
bery/burglary division downtown, which you have been
doing. Consequently, when crimes such as rapes, homi-
cides, or assault occur in your area, those investigations
have been handled through the downtown office by detectives assigned to and trained in those specialized fields.
Therefore, each of you has limited your investigations to
robberies and burglaries. We stationed you here for that
purpose, with the idea that if you were in the neighborhood every day, you would have a better grasp of what
was happening.

"This system has worked well. However, we have found that you know far more about your areas than just who is committing robberies and burglaries. We want to take fuller advantage of your inside information, so effective immediately we are implementing a pilot program in your precinct. If it works well, we will expand it to the other three precincts. Each of you will continue doing the types of investigations you have handled in the past, but in addition, when other offenses occur in your area, you will also work on them. Detectives from the downtown office will be available to assist you and give you advice."

Laura was only vaguely aware of the questions the detectives were asking the chief. MacNamara's announcement seemed too good to be true. With the expansion of her scope of duties, she would have more chance to prove herself, and probably would be promoted several years sooner than she would have been under the old system. Best of all, she would learn a lot from her increased contact with the detectives downtown. Her throbbing finger reminded her that despite her determination to shape her own successful future, there were forces at work that she didn't currently understand. She noticed goose bumps were standing out on her arms, though the room was too hot.

"Sergeant Binder will provide me with regular reports on how the system is working," MacNamara said. "And, although I will make regular visits to your precinct to monitor the new program, you still will receive your assignments from, and be answerable to, Sergeant Binder."

Every silver lining has a cloud, Laura thought at the prospect of continuing to work for Binder. She started to leave with the other detectives, but MacNamara stopped her.

"Bernhardt and Winchell, stick around for a minute, please."

She and Harry looked at each other nervously. It wasn't often that the chief of detectives sought private audiences with individual detectives. Protocol required that anything he had to say to them went through Binder, but the sergeant didn't look surprised and left the room with the other detectives.

"You two look like battle casualties," MacNamara said
when everyone else had gone. "I heard you were stabbed
by a sewing-machine needle, Bernhardt. You'd better get
that finger looked at today. When was the last time you
had a tetanus shot?" Before Laura had a chance to respond, he continued, "But I didn't ask to talk to you to
play mother hen. Sit down, both of you. You don't have
to look as if you are waiting for a firing squad. First, I
want to congratulate you both on a job well done yesterday. Laura, I understand you distinguished yourself
twice. Of course, part of it was luck—being in the right
place at the right time—but you showed skill in thwart-
ing that bank robbery. Next time, however, I don't want
heroics. A dead heroine is useless to everyone. Call for
help, understand?"

"There really wasn't time, sir."

"Make time, Bernhardt," MacNamara said firmly.

"Yes, sir."

"You both did well yesterday, but don't get too comfortable in this praise yet," MacNamara said sternly. "We
seem to have a problem that needs to be worked out.
Normally I don't interfere in personnel problems with
the detectives, but this time I'm making an exception.
Bernhardt and Winchell, you are good detectives, or I'd
see you both kicked out of this precinct and back on the
streets giving traffic tickets. I'm going to give you one
chance to clear up the personal problem between you.
Partners don't compete, they work together. Your personality conflict is setting the entire precinct on edge. I
have a report here from Sergeant Binder recommending
that you two be assigned to different partners for the sake
of the precinct," MacNamara said, holding up a form.
"We don't make new assignments after only two
months."

Laura and Harry glanced at each other guiltily.

"The sergeant listed incompatibility as the reason for
the request. I'm not a divorce judge and you aren't a
squabbling married couple, though you've been acting
like it. You are professionals who should be mature
enough to work out your problems. It's not as if you were
patrolmen stuck in the same car eight hours a day. As

detectives you have a lot of autonomy. You should both enjoy this new system, because you will be together even less. But when you are working together, you must cooperate with each other. The alternative is putting yourselves and others in danger, and that is a situation that I will not tolerate."

"Yes, sir," Laura and Harry replied in subdued voices.

"Good. Now get out of here," MacNamara said, tossing the request form in the trash can.

Laura and Harry walked down the hall in silence. Harry finally broke the silence. "What's on the agenda today, partner?"

"Stake out our friendly neighborhood fence. Look, Harry, I'm sorry. It's my fault we got in trouble."

"No, it's my fault."

"I'm telling you, it's my fault."

"Don't be so stubborn, Laura. You know good and well it's my fault."

They looked at each other and burst out laughing.

"Partners?" Laura asked, extending her good hand.

"Okay, but it would be a lot easier if you weren't so good-looking," Harry said, shaking her hand.

"Pretend my face looks like my finger."

"It's a good thing you didn't hurt your right hand. I'll do anything for my partner but fill out her paperwork."

"You should talk, Hopalong. If we have another chase, I'll have to carry you on my back."

"Does your finger feel as lousy as my foot?" Harry asked as they grabbed their coats and headed for the door.

"No. It's fine."

"There you go being a martyr again. From the looks of that finger, it's got to hurt like the blue blazes."

"You're right. Do you happen to have some aspirin on you?"

"I was going to ask you the same thing. Let's stop at the drugstore and pick some up. By the way, when was the last time you had a tetanus shot?"

"Why does everyone insist on mothering me? We're partners, Harry, equals."

"Yeah, just as I suspected. I can tell by the look on your face you haven't had one of those shots since you were a kid. We can stop at the hospital on the way back this afternoon."

"I'm not getting a shot."

"Bernhardt," Sergeant Binder yelled just before Harry and Laura got to the door. "I hear you hurt your finger last night."

"It was nothing, Sarge."

"Nevertheless, stop by the emergency room today and get a tetanus shot."

"I don't need one, Sergeant. It was a stainless-steel needle."

"Bernhardt, don't you ever do anything you are told without arguing?"

"Okay, I'll get the shot."

"Harry, if you don't stop that snickering, I'm going to step on your sore foot," Laura threatened as they hurried across the parking lot.

"Detectives don't snicker," Harry said, breaking into open laughter.

Laura joined him. She got into the driver's side of the stakeout van. Thanks to Harry's foot, at least they wouldn't be fighting about who was going to drive for the next couple of days.

The weather forecast for cold, dreary weather seemed to be wrong. The temperature was rising and a cool January sun shone across the city. Harry was talking about the Super Bowl. Laura was only pretending to listen, and she didn't have to put much effort into that. When Harry started talking football, all she had to do was insert a grunt occasionally and he was satisfied. While she drove, she tried in vain to remember what had happened after dinner the night before.

Maybe the storm was what made me act so strange, then forget, she thought. Nature definitely has more of an effect on us than we realize. For years the Police Department has automatically assigned more officers during the full moon. If that storm was an unusual electrical disturbance, who knows what temporary personality changes it might have caused? And, since I was very tired and emotional last night, anyway, I was a prime target.

But, I was acting pretty strange this morning, too, she thought.

She hadn't seen Tracy Binder since the last Students Against Drunk Driving meeting two weeks ago. Laura had become pretty close to the sergeant's daughter during the past year, since she took over the adult advisor position for Tracy's high school SADD group. Tracy had often talked to her about her frustration with her father. It was awkward for Laura, since she couldn't stand the man but had to be careful what she said to Tracy. The girl loved and respected her father.

At about ten o'clock Laura had picked up the telephone and said, "Hi, Tracy." She didn't realize the phone hadn't even rung until she was sitting there with a dial tone in her ear. She was glad no one had been around. Maybe I do need a vacation, she thought.

8

Tracy Binder sat in the booth at the TG & Y soda fountain. She pushed the button on her digital watch for the fifth time in five minutes: five-fifteen P.M. She felt as if she had been waiting for Mark for fifteen days, not fifteen minutes. She had to talk to him tonight and be home by six or her dad would have her neck.

I wouldn't wish being a cop's daughter on my worst enemy, she thought, checking her watch again. I can't breathe without him monitoring it. And Mom is no help. She goes along with anything Dad says. Maybe if he hadn't been so strict, I wouldn't be in this mess now. No, that isn't fair. I have no one to blame but myself—not even Mark. But, what am I going to do? I'm only sixteen, I have a year and a half left of high school, and I'm in trouble with a capital *T*.

Tracy had thought about calling Laura Bernhardt for advice. She'd even picked up the phone that morning and

started to dial the number, then hung up. Laura certainly
would be able to understand her problem with her dad
and why she couldn't talk to him. Working as a woman
detective in his department must be almost as bad as
being his daughter. It wasn't that he meant to be mean
and stubborn. He was only trying to protect the women
around him. His father had died when he was only four-
teen and his last words to Greg Binder were "Take care
of your mother and sisters." Her dad threw everything
into living up to his father's last wish. Thirty-six years
later he still was trying to take care of his mother, his
three married sisters, his wife, and Tracy.

Tracy knew her dad couldn't stand Laura. Ambitious
women did not fit into his view of the world.

Tracy wished she could talk to her dad about her problem, but there was no way.

She couldn't talk to her mother either. On something
as important as this, her mom would feel obligated to tell
her dad, and she would do anything to keep him from
finding out.

She put her head close to the big picture window by
the booth and searched the street for a sign of Mark. She
realized with bitter irony that she was a woman now. Her
carefree girlhood was gone forever.

Maybe she shouldn't even tell Mark. Maybe she should
get up and call Laura Bernhardt right now, before Mark
came. No, she didn't know Laura well enough. She didn't
think Laura would tell her dad, but you never knew
about grown-ups. They usually stuck together at the
most inopportune times. Just because Laura was encour-
aging when Tracy had told her she wanted to join the
police force when she graduated from college didn't mean
she could be trusted with this kind of news.

She thought about her dad again. He would kill Mark
if he found out. She didn't know what he would do to
her, but she had visions of being locked in her room for
the rest of her life.

What's going to happen to my college education now,
and my chances of becoming a police officer?

Tracy checked her watch again: five twenty-five. She

looked out the window and saw Mark coming down the sidewalk.

Oh, God, what am I going to tell him?

Mark walked as if he owned the world, with his easy gait, and his hands stuck loosely in the pockets of his football letter jacket. Tracy thought she loved him, but she wasn't ready to marry him. She wished the tiny new life growing inside her would disappear and let her be the child again. But it wasn't going to go away. The doctor said the test was positive. She was pregnant.

Mark walked into the store and looked around. When he saw Tracy, he smiled and walked toward her. Tracy tried to keep from crying. Mark wanted to be an engineer. His grade-point average was the highest in his class, and he already had a couple of colleges talking to him about football scholarships.

They had been going steady for a little more than a year, though her parents knew nothing about it. Her dad said high school girls had no business going out on dates, that there was plenty of time for boys later. So Tracy's girlfriend Sally would come by on weekends and pick Tracy up in her folks' car. They would drive a few blocks to where Mark was waiting with Sally's boyfriend. Tracy would go with Mark, and Jim would go with Sally. They would meet again about eleven forty-five and Sally would drop Tracy off in front of her house just before her midnight curfew.

"Hi, Tracy. What's up?" Mark asked, sliding into the seat across from her. "You look like you lost your best friend. Your eyes are almost as red as your hair. What did you do, fail your geometry test?"

In spite of herself Tracy's eyes were filling with tears. She looked around and saw a couple of kids sitting down in the booth behind them.

Mark was concerned now. He wrapped both her hands in one of his and said, "Do you want to go someplace more private?"

Tracy nodded.

Mark took a big gulp of the Coke Tracy hadn't touched and put his arm around her as they walked out the door onto the tree-lined boulevard.

"I've got Dad's car down the street. We can sit there."

When they reached the car, Tracy couldn't hold back anymore. All the tears that had been welling up inside of her since she'd gone to the doctor came flooding out. Mark held her tightly and stroked her long, copper-colored hair while she sobbed against his chest.

"What is it, honey? Trouble with your dad again?"

Tracy wiped the tears from the freckles Mark swore were cute, but that she hated. She looked down at her hands, took a deep breath, and said: "Oh, Mark, I'm—I'm pregnant."

"Oh, shit. Are you sure?"

"I went to the doctor. I'm sure."

"Oh, shit."

She burst out crying again and he put his arms around her and held her.

"I'm sorry, Mark."

"Don't worry, honey. It will be okay. I promise it will." He held her back a little way so he could look at her and said, "What do you want to do, Tracy? Do you want to get married? I always figured I'd marry you someday. It might as well be now as later."

"How can we get married, Mark? Even if we graduated early, we still would have a full year of high school left. And if we dropped out, we'd end up hating each other."

Tracy thought she saw relief in his eyes.

"Do you want to have an abortion?" he asked.

Tracy shuddered. The word had been on her mind all day, but hearing it out loud brought the reality of the situation into the open like a slap in the face.

"It looks like it's the only thing I can do, Mark, but I'd have to have my parents' permission because I'm under eighteen. I'd die if my dad found out. I don't know how I could pull it off without telling my parents. An abortion costs two hundred fifty dollars, and you have to pay in advance. I only get a five-dollar-a-week allowance. The baby would be born before I could scrape together the money. Even if I got a part-time job, my dad would never let me work enough hours to earn that kind of money."

"How far along are you?"

"About six weeks. I have to have the abortion in the next two months or they won't do it."

"Don't worry, Tracy. I'll think of something. I promise."

9

The day poked by for Adam. When he woke up Wednesday morning, he expected to find his old television at the end of the bed. Surely the events of the night before had been another dream.

The strange new television was there this morning. Did I really see Marie last night? he wondered. It must have been one of the dreams, but, oh, it seemed so real with her reaching out to me, laughing and smiling.

He had flicked on the television as soon as the alarm rang, hoping Marie's image would burst forward—but only the regular programs with the strange three-dimensional figures appeared.

If that was a dream about Marie, it was a new one. I don't remember ever having a good dream.

During the day Adam avoided all the detectives and officers as much as possible, including Laura. Every time he walked by one of them, he thought: They know. They are going to come and take the TV away.

Then he would tell himself there was no way they could know, and he would rub his temples, which were throbbing more than usual.

By quitting time he had convinced himself that he had dreamed of Marie and the screaming man. When he left the precinct, he started to turn left and walk straight home to watch the new television, then halted and turned right for his evening ritual.

I can't let my boy walk home alone in a neighborhood like this. Jeremy will be expecting me. Besides, I want to tell all the kids about our new television set.

He paused at the edge of the school grounds and retied his shoes. He scraped his fingers on the concrete and

nearly toppled over when he heard a chorus of children's
voices screaming, "We're gonna tell. We're gonna tell."

He relaxed when he realized they were yelling at one of
their classmates, not at him.

*What's all this fighting, boys? You should learn to get
along. You make up and when Jeremy gets here, we'll all
go back to our house and watch our new television set.
You're in for a real treat. You've never seen anything like
it, but only the best is good enough for my family.*

The children walked by, oblivious to the janitor's
thoughts. Adam followed them to the corner.

*Don't forget about our football game this weekend.
You'll know our car when I come by. It's a shiny red Cad-
illac.*

The children turned right on Twenty-fourth Street,
with Adam following at a discreet distance. When they
turned left on Grand, only two blocks from the precinct,
he was afraid to follow any farther and kept going
straight until he reached Spear. He turned into the alley
between Spear and Parkway Boulevard and soon was
heading up the steep stairs to his apartment.

When he unlocked the door, he grinned jubilantly at
the round eye, which smiled its silent welcome.

The three-dimensional shows fascinated him as much
as they had the night before. He marveled at the technol-
ogy that allowed him to see the figures stand out, even
without the help of the glasses they gave you at 3-D movies. He had been to one of those movies a few months
before, and noted it seemed childish in comparison to his
lifelike television.

All too soon it was past midnight and Adam kept doz-
ing off. He reluctantly turned off the television and sank
into his troubled sleep. He didn't know how long he had
been asleep when he heard a child's voice calling to him
in his dream. The voice sounded desperate as it cried,
"Help me, Daddy! Help me!"

Still sleeping, Adam twisted and mumbled in response,
"Beaver? Is that you? I told you what would happen if
you did what Eddie told you to do. I told you what
would happen if you sinned."

"Stop her, Daddy. Help me!" the young voice called

more urgently. The frightened cry grew louder until it
snapped through the apartment like the shrill ring of a
telephone. "Help me!"

"Who's there?" Adam cried out as his eyes flew open.
He looked around, confused by the silent emptiness. He
had decided it was another of the dreams when, at the
end of the bed, the concave eye burst into life by itself.

"Marie?" Adam called hopefully as a woman walked
toward the front of the screen on an unfamiliar street.
There were overflowing garbage cans and litter blowing
down the street. He saw that some of the buildings were
boarded up, while others had broken windows and glass
lying on the windowsills and sidewalk. His breath came
in uneven spasms as he watched the screen and waited
for the woman to come near.

"Answer me, Marie. Tell me you hear me," he groaned
in a near whisper.

Now he could see her clearly. She continued to walk
toward the foreground, but there was nothing of her
happy attitude from the scene the television had shown
him the night before. Snow was beginning to fall, and he
could see the wind whipping it at her face like darts. Her
small frame seemed to shrink in her battered coat as she
wrapped her blue wool scarf more tightly around her
neck.

"I knew you were alive, Marie. I knew I didn't kill
you. They said I strangled you with that scarf, but I
couldn't have. There you are, still wearing it. Please answer me, Marie. Tell me you hear me."

The figure in the television was oblivious to the anguished cries of the man on the other side of the screen.
Adam's head and arms dangled off the end of the bed as
he attempted to get as close as possible to the woman he
loved.

Marie stopped in front of a deserted building and
looked up at a boarded-over window on the second floor.
She seemed to be trying to make up her mind about
whether to go up there. She wiped tears from her eyes,
but they were immediately replaced by new ones, which
flowed unnoticed as she stood clutching the scarf.

"My darling, why are you crying? You must hear me. I'm here," he called to her.

She seemed to gather her courage, walked to the door, and was swallowed by the building.

Just as the door closed behind her, the television speaker sprang into action.

"Help me, Daddy!" shouted the child's voice that Adam thought he had dreamed. The child continued to scream, his dire cry filling the apartment while the screen showed only the building that had engulfed Marie.

Adam slowly began pushing farther back on his bed. He was shaking. He knew he was awake, but he also knew he couldn't be. He didn't know how long he lay there, his body convulsing involuntarily while the child pleaded for help. Finally the voice faded and the picture began to roll and fill with lines, then was replaced by white static. The static cleared to the fog of the night before and the man deep in the set, still screaming and pounding.

By now Adam was sitting up on the bed, hugging his pillow, his knees drawn protectively to his chest. Beads of sweat had formed on his forehead.

"It's part of the dreams. The dreams are taking over again. The men in white are going to come and lock me up. They will take my new TV. They'll take the key to my janitor's closet."

The hypnotic pull of madness gave way to greater horrors as the scene changed again. Sister Mary Xavier stood before him in three dimensions. He gasped at the familiarity of her body. . . . She was naked. The gold ring that signified her marriage to Christ glistened on her finger.

"Come here, Adam Smith," she demanded. "Come here right now. I'll show you what happens to boys who spy, who sin."

He remembered. This was one of the nightmares that plagued him during the dreams but kept its answers beyond the horizon during his waking hours. Adam wasn't dreaming now. He was wide awake. The television seemed to have reached into his head while he slept and filmed the tormented pictures in order to flash them back at him in Technicolor.

"Come here, Adam," Sister Mary Xavier demanded.

Adam lunged at the television and slammed his fist against the off button to erase the nun's image. The knob didn't yield because the TV wasn't turned on. He turned it on and off in rapid succession, turned the channels, but nothing had any effect. Sister Mary Xavier didn't go away. He had thought he wanted to remember. Now he knew he had been wrong. Now he had no choice.

As he pushed himself back on the bed, as far from the television as possible, he once again was sixteen years old. He had sneaked into her room when she was at evening prayers and hidden behind the heavy draperies when he heard her return and turn the doorknob. He was trapped. He tried to hold perfectly still while he heard her undressing.

Then she saw him.

"Come here, Adam," she demanded.

"I didn't mean to spy. I only wanted to look at your room," he pleaded from his curled position on his bed.

He felt his adult life slip away as once again he relived the memory from his adolescence.

"You know why you came, Adam. Come here and I'll show you what happens to boys who sin." Her voice was alluring, with an undercurrent of cruelty as she spoke to him and walked toward the front of the screen, caressing her breasts, running her hands along the inside of her thighs.

Adam shrank back on the bed in his apartment, whimpering, while Sister Mary Xavier spoke. She didn't seem to see Adam Smith, the janitor, crouching frightened in his apartment. It was as though she were looking at the boy he had been thirty-four years ago, the boy who had never been the same after that visit to her room. The lens that projected the picture on the strange TV seemed to be that boy's eyes. The audio seemed to be what that boy heard. But to Adam he was a boy again, and he was appalled when his genitals involuntarily stirred at the sight of her lean, angular body. He reached furtively

down his boxer shorts to untangle the uncomfortable
swelling trapped in the folds of material.

Sister Mary Xavier stood out of reach on the inside of
the television, talking to him. "Do you want to see what
happens to boys who lust after nuns?"

"No," Adam whispered, but he inched forward on the
bed.

The screen blinked suddenly to blackness, leaving only
the shrinking retina and Sister Mary Xavier's laughter
fading slowly.

Adam realized in horror that the arousal he had been
unable to stop had released itself, equally out of his control.

He pulled himself farther back on the bed, creeping
backward until he felt the cold resistance of the wall
against his back. There, huddled in a fetal ball, he stared
wide-eyed at the blank set.

"This isn't real. It's one of the dreams I never remember. In the morning it will all be gone. But I remember
now. She made me do things to her, and she did things to
me that hurt and felt good too. They weren't the things
that make babies. They were abominable things. Oh,
God, I'm so ashamed. I liked it. I went to her room over
and over again, until one night the Mother Superior
caught us. That's why I had to leave the orphanage."

If not remembering had been as frustrating to Adam as
a mirage just out of reach, remembering was like finally
reaching the middle of that illusory lake only to have its
unpalatable water drag him into endless suffocation.

"But I won't remember in the morning. It's just one of
the dreams," he repeated like a chant until sleep finally
released him from his anguish.

When the alarm clock rang, he woke still huddled
against the wall, grasping his pillow . . . and he remembered. But the memory seemed to be only partially right.
He felt something important was missing.

He reached toward the end of the bed to turn on the
television, afraid of what the picture would show him but
unable to stop himself. He gave an audible sigh of relief at
the friendly faces and voices on *Good Morning America.*

Only then did he notice the gold ring on top of the

television set. He picked it up gingerly and turned it over in his hands. The inscription hidden on the inner side read: SISTER MARY XAVIER.

On Thursday and Friday the television only came on when Adam turned it on and went off when he turned it off. He would have thought he'd dreamt of Marie and Sister Mary Xavier if it weren't for the ring that still adorned the top of the television. Sometimes he picked it up and held it gently in his hand, seeing it as proof he had been forgiven. Other times he thought the metallic symbol of godliness was as close as he would ever come to heaven because, in reality, he was cursed. He became obsessed with the ring and finally decided he had to get it out of his sight. He put it in his pocket on Sunday when he went to the park to watch the children play football and ice-skate. He was determined to come home without it. He paused at every garbage can and Dumpster but couldn't force himself to reach his hand into his pocket, lift out the ring, and throw it away. He strolled through the park all day having imaginary conversations with the children, their parents, and most of all with Marie.

I'm so happy you came back, my darling. I always knew you would. The nightmares have gone away too. Maybe the ring has brought me this good luck. I'd better keep it, just in case.

He looked around, confused that Marie was not standing beside him, then smiled and thought, She must have stopped to get popcorn. She'll catch up.

When Adam returned home at dusk, he carefully set the ring in an empty shoe box and put the box at the top of his closet. He slept so well that night that, when the alarm went off Monday morning, he was filled with an unaccustomed sense of well-being. It was all he could do to keep from humming while he mopped the floors at the precinct.

"Good morning, Adam," Laura said as she rushed by him to her office.

She spoke to me, and she smiled too. I wouldn't have imagined it. She even said my name. He set about his work with a vengeance, determined that not a speck of

dust was going to contaminate the area where Laura
Bernhardt worked. He even replaced her trash can with a
new one from the storeroom.

When he carried his cleaning supplies to the women's
rest room and knocked self-consciously, a woman came
out. Adam glared at her as she walked down the hall.

*It's one of that kind of women. I saw her looking at me
and wiggling her body. All women are like that, except of
course for Marie and Miss Laura. That whore was bounc-
ing her breasts and shaking her rear on purpose. She
wanted me to look at her. She's like Sister Mary Xavier.
They're both bad. Sister Mary Xavier made me do those
things to her. It wasn't my fault.*

That evening on his long route home, it seemed to
Adam that all the women were flirting with him and
trying to get his attention.

*They'd better watch themselves or they'll find out what
happens to women who sin.*

When he finally arrived home, he settled down happily
to watch his new friend, the TV. He noticed that Beaver's
mom wasn't as perfect as he once had imagined.

"You'd better keep an eye on your wife, Mr. Cleaver,"
he sadly advised the television character, who was in the
garage putting together a bicycle for the Beaver's birthday. "You didn't see the way she was looking at Whitey's
dad, but I did. Yes, indeed, I saw it. I bet that kind of
thing has been going on all along, but I didn't notice
because I couldn't see things as clearly on the old television. I can see real good now, Mr. Cleaver, and your wife
is like all the others."

He couldn't understand why Mr. Cleaver wasn't listening to him. He'd regret it. He'd find out about his wife
too late.

"It's a good thing Beaver and Wally can count on me,
Mr. Cleaver. I know how to protect them from the likes
of their mom."

A pain stabbed him between his temples. He moaned
and grabbed his head. When the pain subsided he looked
back at the television. He didn't understand what had

happened. The late news was on, although it seemed to him only a couple of minutes had passed since he had watched *Leave It to Beaver*. He had lost four hours.

10

Monday, January 21

"I'm a little tired, Darryl. I think I'll go take a nap," Laura said.

"Are you sick? I've never seen you take a nap at six in the evening, and you look really pale."

"Sick? Not likely," she said, with more bravado than she felt. "It's been a long day, and when it is time to go to bed, I don't want to fall asleep right away," she said, running her hands seductively over his hips.

"I have to look over these blueprints. Then I think I'll take a shower and join you."

He kissed her neck and Laura could tell by the slight shivering of his body that he mistook her moan for passion. In reality what she felt was pain. Darryl went into the den to finish his work and Laura staggered down the hall to the bedroom. She collapsed on the bed, feeling as if someone had stabbed a hot knitting needle through her temples. Almost immediately she was lost in the nightmares that had plagued her for the past week. She was running down a dim corridor. She had to hide from the evil thing chasing her. She could hear a child's laughter in the distance, as though this were nothing but a fun game of hide-and-seek, but she knew if he ever caught her she would die.

The laughter was closer.

She grabbed frantically at a door and slid quietly inside to hide. The pounding of her heart sounded like drums in an echo chamber, drowning out all other noise. . . . It covered the sounds of a woman screaming as a man pulled something tight around her neck and squeezed on the other side of the room.

"No," Laura whispered, torn between her natural desire to help and her paralyzing fear. She could see the woman's agonized face clearly, but the man was turned away from her.

Laura's only thought now was to escape. She inched slowly to the door, afraid the loud beating of her heart would give away her presence. In spite of legs like rubber she finally reached the door, but as she held her hand out to the doorknob, she saw it turning. The thing that had been pursuing her was outside. In indecision she looked desperately from the door to the murder scene. Outside, the child's voice rose merrily, creating such a chill of dread in Laura that she quickly bolted the door—locking herself inside with the murderer.

While Laura crawled back to the corner, she watched helplessly as the murderer snuffed the life from his victim. To Laura's horror the woman's face changed. First she was blond, then brunette. Brown eyes appeared to pop from their sockets, then blue eyes, as the man tightened his weapon around a parade of changing faces.

The last woman crumpled to the floor and disappeared as though she had never existed. Laura inched closer to the wall, willing herself to become invisible.

The man turned deliberately, as though he had known all along that he had an audience. He began to walk in her direction. She screamed when she saw he had no face. He started shaking her and her screams became more frantic.

"Laura, wake up. You're having a nightmare. Laura!"

She started to fight the man's grip on her, then saw Darryl's face and began to sob and melted gratefully into his safe embrace.

When his comforting strokes turned to passion, she responded eagerly, willing the nightmare from her mind; but long after her husband's even breathing told her he was sleeping soundly, she lay awake. The nights are bad, she thought, but the days aren't much better. I keep feeling as if I'm being watched, and every time I hear a child laugh, I jump. I can't let Darryl know, though. He already wants to drag me off to the doctor. Whatever is wrong, I'm sure I can get it under control myself.

She rolled over and looked at the clock. It was only ten P.M. and she realized with relief that her blinding head-ache was gone.

11

Wednesday, January 23

"Sure, I can finish this drink. I can finish this one and five more if I want to," Rhonda Hackman bragged. Most of the patrons in the bar were from Metro College across the street, but the men sitting across from her in the dimly lit booth were older, in their thirties. They looked as if the closest they had come to college was selling drugs outside the gates. Their friend, sitting beside her in the booth, moved his hand from her knee to midthigh. She didn't care. Nothing mattered except who was going to buy the next round. The leg the man was caressing wasn't hers. It was as though she were looking at the scene in the booth from somewhere on the ceiling.

Rhonda was vaguely aware that the voice of the girl in the booth was getting louder and that people were staring at her. It didn't matter. It wasn't Rhonda Hackman, business student with a shaky C average, they were look-ing at. It wasn't the Rhonda who came to this bar every night and tried to fight off her loneliness by sitting for hours staring from her drink to the unpainted walls cov-ered with crude graffiti. She didn't even know the chubby woman with coarse, bleached blond hair and heavy eye makeup. Why should she care if people stared?

"How's your headache, girlie?" one of the men on the other side of the booth asked with a sneer. Rhonda thought his name was John or Jim.

"I don't have a headache, because I don't have a head." She giggled. She remembered that the Rhonda who had walked into the bar four hours ago had a head, and it hurt. Then the men came in and sat at her booth and started buying her drinks. They gave her some pills that weren't aspirin. Before long her head didn't hurt

anymore, and she stopped noticing that the men looked
dirty. Later they slipped a small vial into her hand. It had
a tiny spoon attached to the top by a thin silver chain.
They said if she went into the ladies' room and sniffed
some of the white powder, her head would feel really
good. She knew it was cocaine, but she didn't want to
admit she had never tried it, so she did what they said.
When they gave her a tiny square of paper with Mickey
Mouse's picture printed on it and told her to hold it under her tongue, it seemed like the most natural thing in
the world to do. Sometime after that Rhonda's head left.
It was floating above the booth, looking down at the
strange woman who was slouched in the seat talking too
loudly.

She felt wonderful until her head came crashing from
the ceiling and landed heavily on her shoulders. The
room was hot and smoky, and she felt sick to her stomach.

"I wanna go home. I don't feel good," she whined. The
man beside her made no effort to let her out of the booth.
His fingers were fumbling to reach under her panties. She
suddenly was aware it was her body he was touching. She
jerked away.

"There's no reason to get unfriendly now, girlie. That's
no way to treat us after we made your headache go
away."

His face was distorted and Rhonda was afraid. "I've
got to go home. I have classes tomorrow," she pleaded.

"We'll take you home, baby. We'll take good care of
you. We know how to take care of pretty little college
girls, don't we, guys?" The men on the other side of the
booth laughed.

"We'll give you a ride straight to your front door,
girlie."

She started to cry. "I wanna walk home." She was
dizzy and wanted out of the booth, but the man beside
her didn't move. Even if he had, she didn't remember
how to make her legs move.

"You can't be wandering around a neighborhood like
this after dark. Something might happen to you," one of
them said. Their voices were so far away, she wasn't sure

which one spoke. Now they were all laughing. Rhonda was vaguely aware that she was on her feet and they were leading her out of the bar. Her stomach was churning and her head was too heavy for her body.

Her perception jolted back to normal when they walked outside and she was hit with a blast of cold air. "Let go of me," she shouted. "I don't want to go with you." She struggled to free herself from the grip two of the men had on her arms. They grabbed her more firmly. A couple walked by and looked at her with disgust, but kept on walking.

Reality began to slip again. The real Rhonda saw them pushing a girl who looked like her into the back of a van. The girl was struggling and screaming. One of them hit her and pulled the door of the van closed. They were pulling away from the curb. Rhonda was back in her body, her face hurting from the blow. Two of the men were leaning over her, yanking off her clothes, while the third drove the van. She was screaming. They hit her again and stuffed a rag in her mouth. It tasted like motor oil and dirt. Then one of the men was on top of her, but she didn't see him anymore. She was twelve years old and at her mother's funeral. Everyone else was crying. She wasn't crying. She was mad at her mother for going away and leaving her alone. Now she was back in the van looking at the other man climb on top of the gagged, struggling woman. She was crying for her mother. She wanted forgiveness for the anger she'd felt at her mother's death.

She heard a voice saying, "Hey, Joe, you'd better take that gag out of her mouth for a minute. She's not breathing right. We don't want this bitch to die on us." He yanked the rag out of her mouth and she vomited on him. The man named Joe cursed and hit her. Rhonda didn't feel it. She was seeing it from the top of the van.

Both Rhondas lost consciousness.

12

Thursday, January 24

There's nothing sinister about this place, Laura told herself. It's only a hospital corridor. I've never been here before, and I'd never heard of Rhonda Hackman until this morning. This is an unpleasant assignment, but not mysterious in any way. She kept repeating it to herself as she walked down the hall, but she couldn't shake the feeling of having taken these same steps before, hundreds of trips to room 414 E, thousands of steps that repeated themselves without end in a world she had but glimpsed. Her denial was as familiar to her as the corridor. It didn't resemble the corridor in her dream, but her terror was nearly as intense. Her throat tightened and her mouth felt like cotton.

When I turn the corner, I'll stop at the water fountain, then I'll feel better. She shivered when she realized what she had thought. What water fountain?

You're losing it, Laura, she told herself. There won't be a drinking fountain. You only thought there would be because you are thirsty.

She turned the corner and walked to the fountain. The scene was more familiar than the pictures on her wall at home. She felt caught in the groove of a broken record with no one to come and release it so it could reach its natural conclusion.

"Detective Bernhardt, are you okay?"

Laura whirled around. "I'm fine, Bob," she replied edgily between coughs. "I choked. The water went down the wrong pipe." She was rambling, and Joe was looking at her strangely. She flushed under his scrutiny. She felt silly and moved the conversation to more neutral ground. "Are you the officer who brought in Rhonda Hackman?" she asked.

"Yes. She's pretty messed up."

While the officer talked, Laura felt herself returning to normal. The overpowering sense of déjà vu had passed. She asked questions and made notes, already considering the course of action she would follow on the investigation.

"Officer Johnson and I found her in the alley across the street from the Science Building at Metro College at 0800 hours while we were on routine patrol," Bob said. "She was unconscious and her clothes were in a heap beside her in a manner that suggested they had been thrown there rather than removed at the spot. Her purse was under her clothing. Her billfold was still intact, along with five dollars and some loose change. Though she had dried blood on her body and clothes, there was no sign of a struggle at the scene."

"Do you think someone raped her, then dumped her there?" Laura asked, already drawing her own conclusions.

"It appears that way," Bob said. "We're waiting for the results from the lab samples. They are checking the usual —vaginal fluids, pubic hairs, fingernail scrapings, and so forth."

"Good," Laura said, jotting down a few words in her notebook. "What is her medical condition?" she asked as they walked to the girl's room.

"It was touch and go for a while. By the time we got her here, she was suffering from acute hypothermia. She has been officially reclassified now from critical to serious condition. The doctor said she has a concussion, several broken ribs, numerous cuts and abrasions, and possible internal injuries. She appears to be suffering from shock, and they are monitoring her closely for further complications."

"I want to get the bastard who did this," Laura said, surprised by her own vehemence.

Bob shook his head slowly in agreement, but his eyes maintained a more impersonal expression. "There may be more than one perpetrator involved in this case, though we won't know for sure until we get the report back from the lab," he said. "The initial examination of the pubic-hair samples indicated she might have been attacked by two or even three men."

Laura sighed and asked, "Have you taken a statement from her?"

"So far she hasn't talked to anyone. When she regained consciousness, she started screaming and fighting. The doctor had to sedate her. Now she lies and stares at the ceiling. She doesn't seem to be aware of people in the room with her. The doctor said you can try to talk to her, but only for a few minutes. He doesn't think she will respond, though, and he said not to push her."

"Has her family been notified?"

"We don't know who to contact. Her name was on her driver's license, and she had a Metro College ID card. We checked with Metro, but they don't have a next of kin listed in their files. She lives off campus. Apparently she doesn't have a roommate."

As the officer continued filling her in on the particulars of the case, Laura felt her indignation growing. This was one case she would solve. She braced herself and turned to walk into room 414 E.

When she walked through the door, Laura was barely able to repress a gasp. It wasn't Rhonda's battered appearance that shocked her, though it was bad; it was the certain knowledge that she had seen this woman before, in this hospital bed, in this condition.

Rhonda Hackman lay on her bed, her unfocused eyes toward the ceiling. Her face was swollen almost beyond the point that allowed immediate recognition that she was of the human species. Her arms extended limply from the short-sleeved hospital gown in a mass of bruises. The only indication that this woman should be in a bed instead of a drawer in the morgue was the sound of shallow breathing.

Laura walked over to the bed and took one of the girl's flaccid hands in both of hers. "Rhonda, I'm Detective Bernhardt. I know you are feeling really bad right now, but I need your help. Can you answer a few questions for me so we can catch whoever did this to you?"

Rhonda's eyes flickered with recognition. She turned her head slightly toward Laura and closed her eyes. Laura stroked the girl's hand gently. The girl on the bed opened her eyes again and spoke, hesitantly, as if each word took its toll in physical agony. "I've been expecting you. You're going to tell me to call you Laura. You're going to say you want to help me. That's what you always say in the dreams."

Laura wasn't surprised by Rhonda's comments. She wasn't frightened as she had been when she was walking down the corridor. It suddenly seemed perfectly natural that this young woman would know, as she had, that their fates were somehow intermingled.

"I want to help you, Rhonda, but in order to do that, I need you to tell me who did this to you."

"I started having the dreams about a month ago," Rhonda said, as though she hadn't heard Laura's question. "You were pretty in the dreams too. I didn't think you were real until today. When I woke up in the hospital, I knew you would come. In the dreams you said you wanted to help me, but no one can help me, Laura. I knew that even in the dreams. I've got to escape from something. I don't know what it is, only that there is no escape."

"You're wrong, Rhonda. You have escaped," Laura said intensely. "You're safe now, and we're going to find whoever did this to you."

"There were three of them," Rhonda said. Her voice was strained from the effort of talking, but her eyes remained passive.

"I remember part of the evening. Other parts are a complete blank."

Laura gently held the girl's hand while she relayed what she remembered about the previous evening. Laura watched her intently as she spoke, her rage increasing at the trickery and brutality the girl had suffered. When Rhonda finished her story, all Laura could say was "I'm so sorry." They sat quietly for a few minutes while the girl stared at the ceiling. Finally Laura said, "Rhonda, we need to notify your family. Can you give me the name of someone to call?"

"No," Rhonda gasped frantically. "There's no one. Promise me you won't call anyone. Please, promise me," she pleaded.

"Rhonda, isn't there someone who will be worried about you?"

Rhonda chuckled, but the sound that escaped her

throat was mirthless and filled with irony. "I'll tell you about my family," she said, "but only if you give me your solemn word that you won't make any attempt to contact anyone."

"I promise, Rhonda. I won't tell anyone you don't want me to." Laura was still hearing the echo of the bitter hiss Rhonda had used when she said "family."

"My father is a minister. Some of my earliest memories are of his passionate sermons proclaiming there is no such thing as rape, only women who lead men on and put ideas into their heads. Even when I was a little girl, I wasn't allowed to wear sweaters because sweaters put ideas into boys' heads. My skirts had to be several inches longer than the other girls' because my father said if you showed your knees, you were putting ideas into boys' heads. I wasn't allowed to wear patent leather shoes. My father said they would reflect my underwear under my clothes. He used to say that the greatest invention ever made was the chastity belt, and it was a sign of the devil working in the world that they weren't still made today. When I was eight, my father saw me talking to a boy in my class on the way home from school. He beat me until I had black-and-blue welts all over my buttocks and thighs, then he made me write a thousand times, *My body is an agent of the devil.*"

Laura listened to the story, appalled that a person like Rhonda's father could be allowed to shape the mind of a child. "What about your mother?" she asked.

Rhonda smiled. "My mother was wonderful. When my father was gone, she would laugh and play with me. When he was home, we had to be quiet and study the Bible. Sometimes when he wasn't looking she would wink at me. She was my friend."

"What happened to her?"

"When I was twelve, I went to the grocery store with her one evening. When we got back in the car, a man was hiding in the backseat. He had a gun and made my mom drive to a deserted road. He raped her, then made her drive him back to town. He got out of the car like nothing had happened and walked away. My mom couldn't face my dad. That night she blew her head off."

"Oh, God," Laura groaned. She was thinking of her own wonderful parents, who always made her feel as if she were the most special, intelligent girl in the world. "I don't know what to say."

"There's nothing to say, but I think you can understand why I can't call my father."

"Yes, but I'm going to get the men who did this to you."

"Why bother, Laura? People will react like my father. They'll say I asked for it. I'm not exactly a virgin, you know. When I was sixteen, I ran away from home. I guess my father was right about me. I go to the bars and I sleep around. Society says there is no such thing as rape when a woman does those things. I didn't want to. I'd tell myself, 'Tonight I'm not going out.' Then eight or nine o'clock would roll around and my apartment would be so quiet, and I was so lonely. I'd end up going out. Society will say I got what I deserved."

"No! You didn't deserve this. No one had the right to do this to you, Rhonda. Sure, you didn't use the best judgment in the world, but that didn't give those men the right to do this to you. If loneliness were a punishable crime, everyone would be in prison at one time or another. The perverts who left you in that alley to die are the ones who have to be punished. We've got to catch them and lock them up. They've got to pay for what they did, and they have to be stopped before they do it to someone else." Laura was pacing the floor, gesturing emphatically at Rhonda and trying to make her understand. Rhonda was looking at her as if it were Laura who didn't understand.

"Even if you find them, I won't press charges. I won't go to court and testify."

"You must, Rhonda. I know it will be hard, but it's important. You can't let them get by with this."

"It's not what you and I think that matters, Laura. It's what the court will think. Can you honestly say that if I press charges and go to court that I won't come out looking like the guilty party while the men go free?"

Laura started to deny it, but she couldn't. "You know I can't promise, but we've got to try. Times are changing.

Women aren't considered the guilty ones in rape cases anymore. Sure, the system still isn't perfect, but it's the only one we've got to work with right now. We are getting convictions on rape charges."

"No, Laura. I don't want to go through it. I only want to forget. Don't even bother to try to find them. I won't identify them. I won't press charges."

Laura felt like smashing her fist through a wall. She knew Rhonda was right, but she had to keep trying. What good was her badge if she gave up? "I'll come to see you again, Rhonda. Maybe you will change your mind."

"I won't change my mind, and please don't come back. I'll tell the doctor I don't want to see you."

Laura picked up her purse and walked toward the door. She didn't know what else to say.

"Laura, in the dreams I had, you did see me again, but not regarding this case. I'm sure of that. It was later, and I could never tell what it was about."

The sense of déjà vu cloaked Laura again like a tightly bound shroud. She wanted to bolt from the room in a desperate attempt to negate what she knew Rhonda was going to say. She felt if she could escape hearing the words, it would erase their reality, but she was rooted in the doorway.

"I don't know why," Rhonda said, "or under what circumstances, but when I see you again, I know my pain will be over . . . and yours will be just beginning."

Laura realized, in horror, that the expression on Rhonda's face was pity, not for herself lying battered in a hospital bed, but for the detective standing healthy in the doorway. She ran from the room in a frantic attempt to flee the moment. In that instant she saw the scene as an illusion in a carnival house of mirrors. She realized with certainty that her real image was not in the first mirror, but somewhere in the middle, with the picture stretching to infinity in both directions.

13

Friday, January 25

"Look at you. Why don't you wash your hair?" Harold Gibbons angrily asked his wife.

Martha said nothing, only huddled further in the corner of the couch.

"And look at this house. It's a bigger mess than you are. I go out and work my tail off all day, and you won't get off your backside long enough to clean things up a little around here. I can't even have my friends over for a beer. I'd be too embarrassed. This place smells like dirty diapers."

Martha began to cry. Sandy, Karen, Jeff, and Harold junior were sitting at the kitchen table crying. Karen came running into the living room and grabbed hold of her father's leg. "Please don't yell at Mommy. You're scaring me, Daddy."

"Get in there and finish your breakfast," Harold bellowed, pushing Karen away. Jeff's bowl crashed to the floor and he started crying even louder.

"A man can't even get any peace in his own home. Go take care of your children, Martha. That's the least you can do around here," Harold screamed as he stormed out the door.

Martha couldn't move from the couch. She sat sobbing and trying not to throw up. She was sick. She had been sick for more than a week, but she dared not tell Harold. He would want her to go to the doctor, and they couldn't afford it. Besides, her husband never got sick, and he had little patience with anyone who did. He considered it a sign of weakness, tolerated only in children. If adults got sick, he felt they were trying for sympathy, or plain goofing off. No, Martha couldn't tell Harold that she looked a mess because she was too ill to fix herself up, and that the house was dirty for the same reason.

She sobbed at the thought of his outburst. He had never yelled at her like that. There had to be more on his mind than the house and her hair. He must really be

afraid of being laid off at the grain mill, a prospect that
upset Martha even more than the tongue lashing.

The kids were all hanging on her, crying. They were
trying to comfort her and be comforted at the same time.
She gently pushed them aside and half wobbled, half ran
down the hall to the bathroom. Once again she was unable to keep her meal down. Later, when she leaned,
dizzy, over the bathroom sink and held a damp cloth to
her forehead, she thought the real shame was that she
was wasting food. Lord knew, they couldn't afford to
waste anything if they planned to make ends meet.

Harold junior and Karen came into the bathroom and
looked with worried expressions at their mother.

"Darlings, can you get yourselves ready for school
without my help this morning? Mommy isn't feeling very
well."

"It's Daddy's fault for yelling at you," Harold junior
said, his little hands clinched into fists.

"I don't want to hear you talk about your father that
way. He didn't mean to yell. He's tired from working so
hard, that's all. He loves us and we love him."

"Don't you work hard, too, Mommy?" Karen asked
with wide eyes. "Daddy said you don't."

"Of course I work hard, sweetheart. You know that.
Daddy doesn't understand what is involved in taking care
of a family. He didn't mean to yell."

"We can get ourselves ready for school, Mommy.
We're not babies," Harold junior said.

"I can change Jeff's diaper for you, Mommy," Karen
said.

"And I'll get Sandy dressed," Harold added.

"I can dress myself," Sandy said from the bathroom
door. "Tell him I can, Mommy. I'm not a baby like Jeff.
I'm almost as big as Karen."

Martha forced a little smile and patted them all on
their heads as she walked to the bedroom to lie down.
She hoped she could make it without fainting. She had
fainted three times in the past week.

Before long she heard Harold junior and Karen leaving
for school. She could hear Jeff and Sandy playing in the
living room and watching television.

I'd like to run away from home, she thought. Her mind drifted to lost dreams. In her daydream she was single and pretty. She was a successful commercial artist living in the city, dating intelligent and rich men who bought her presents. Her pleasant daydream became a nightmare as the picture changed. She was in the city, but she was poor. She was alone and afraid, but worse, something was stalking her.

She didn't realize she had drifted off to sleep until Jeff was pulling at the sleeve of her nightgown crying, "I'm hungry, Mommy."

14

The television howled merrily, as if it were delighted with its game; or was it only a child's voice in the distance that Adam heard? He didn't ponder the source of the sound. He was intently watching the screen and a woman walking down a city street. Though he couldn't see her face, he felt he should know her. It definitely wasn't Marie, but something about the way the woman walked was familiar. He could see that she was holding a bulky object in her arms, but he couldn't tell what it was. He had the feeling she was young, but he couldn't tell for sure. The picture blurred, turned to white snow, then the Andy Griffith show came back on the screen in three dimensions.

It was a familiar routine for Adam now. Sometimes the television came on by itself in the middle of the night, releasing him from the nightmares and posing more questions than answers. Sometimes the regular shows would blur in the evening and he would see Marie or Sister Mary Xavier, or the man screaming in the fog. Yesterday it started showing the woman walking down the street. Six times during the evening her image flashed briefly on the screen. He never saw her face, only her back, as she awkwardly carried her package.

It was Friday and Adam didn't know whether to feel

excited or frightened at the prospect of three nights and
two days at home with the television. The prize had arrived at his door ten days ago, but normal measurement
of time didn't seem appropriate. He felt the TV had arrived only yesterday, and that it always had been there.
Every day when he returned home from work, he unconsciously held his breath while unlocking the door, until
he saw the television sitting at the end of the bed. He
wasn't sure if his anxiety was from his strong desire for it
still to be there, or a nagging dread that it might be.

The TV showed him good scenes of Marie sometimes,
and he lived for those moments. Other times it showed
him the things he didn't want to see: Marie unhappy,
Sister Mary Xavier, and more. So he nervously unlocked
his door each day and came home to he knew not what
pleasures or terrors. He did believe, however, that
whether he wanted it or not, the TV was there to stay.
He'd originally set it at the end of the bed because that
was a place of honor and importance to him. Now when
he looked at it, he had the feeling it owned that spot.

Since the moment Sister Mary Xavier's ring had appeared on top of the set, a thought had been germinating
in Adam's head, one that made him so nervous, his hands
now trembled slightly day and night. Regardless of where
he was or what he was doing, the thought remained. If
the television could release objects from its depths into
the world, could it also release people into his apartment?
If it could, would it return Marie . . . or would it unleash Sister Mary Xavier? The hope and terror of the
situation ate at Adam like maggots working their way
from the interior of his stomach to his flesh.

It used to be the nights that blurred together in meaningless sameness. Now it was the days that lacked reality,
brought into focus only briefly by his occasional en-
counters with Laura Bernhardt, who had been in the office less often than usual since the day the chief came and
held a meeting with all the detectives.

Even the scary things the TV showed Adam had a
special clarity. The television was helping him put together a giant jigsaw puzzle that would forever end the
nightmares. It was like having an abscessed tooth and

going to a dentist who doesn't believe in using novocaine. Sometimes the pain of the cure seemed worse than the problem.

The television reached into Adam's head again and projected a picture of his apartment on the screen, but it wasn't the apartment where he lived now. It was where he'd been living when he met Marie. That apartment had been on the bottom floor. She had lived next door to him. He had seen her on numerous occasions, but they both had been too shy to do more than nod at each other or smile before rushing their separate ways.

He heard Marie crying through the thin walls of their apartments. "No, Mama. I don't want to. Please don't ask me to do that."

"You've got to do this for me, Marie," a woman said. "It's just this once, baby. He's waiting outside. It won't mean anything to you, and it'll mean your mama can eat this week. You don't want your mama to go hungry, do you?"

Adam's rage grew as he remembered the scene from thirty years before. A man's voice came through the television speaker. "Hey, in there," his slurred voice yelled, "I don't have all night. Do we have a deal or not?"

"I can't go to bed with him, Mama. I've never even slept with a man before. It's wrong, Mama."

Adam remembered his feeling of impotence. He felt like going into the hall and punching the man out, or telling him he was married to the girl in the apartment. He didn't have the nerve to do either. Finally, in desperation, he bolted into the hall, yelling fire, and pulled the alarm. The man outside Marie's door ran out of the building, cursing. Adam ran out behind him and watched him disappear down the street. Before the fire engines arrived, Marie's mother left, complaining about ungrateful daughters. The next day Adam got up the nerve to talk to Marie. If she knew who set off the false fire alarm, she never mentioned it.

Now the television showed Marie outside the abandoned building. He didn't understand why she couldn't hear him call to her. Marie had always understood him. In fact, they used to laugh at their uncanny ability to

communicate with each other. One day they realized that
for months they had been talking in half sentences during
their lively conversations. It wasn't necessary to complete
thoughts because the other one already had grasped it.
Now he couldn't understand her misery or why a child
was screaming for help in the background.

"Why can't you hear me, Marie, and why doesn't that
child's daddy help him? Oh, I get it. I bet you are going
to help that little boy. You never could stand to see children suffering. When we have children, then—" He
grabbed his temples to stop the burst of pain that deto-
nated through his head. Outside the sky lit up in a fiery
explosion of lightning and thunder. Adam barely noticed.
He shut his eyes tightly and held on to his head to try to
control the pain. It seemed as if the storm were originat-
ing in his head and were so intense, it took over the city.

15

The weekend stretched before Laura like the smile of a
new moon. Several times she had considered telling Darryl about her conversation with Rhonda Hackman, but
finally decided some things were better left unsaid. Besides, the whole episode at the hospital seemed unreal
now, and she felt silly for having overreacted. She vowed
to put work completely out of her mind for two glorious
days, and she was succeeding wonderfully. She was in her
husband's arms, dancing in perfect rhythm to the live
band at the country club. She felt beautiful, pampered,
and loved. Darryl and Laura enjoyed coming to the club.
It was modest compared to the ones in the more exclusive
neighborhoods, and the people were friendly and unpre-
tentious.

"You look so sexy, we may have to leave early," Darryl
whispered in her ear. She looked up at him with her most
seductive smile and pushed her breasts teasingly against
his chest.

Darryl whirled her around the room with the dips and

flourishes of an accomplished ballroom dancer. When the song ended, they breathlessly returned to their table to join their friends Ben and Sharon.

"I bet Darryl and Laura will agree with me," Ben bellowed in his usual exuberant style. "What do you guys think—isn't it true that he who has the most toys when he dies wins the game of life?"

"Oh, wrong, Money Breath," Sharon retorted.

"What is it this time?" Laura laughed, "a new rifle, a new boat, or a Windsurfer?"

"All three, and the list is growing," Sharon explained. "I think he's getting anxious for summer."

"I'll second that," Darryl added. "I vote for the Windsurfer, Ben. We can go out to the lake, do some windsurfing and fishing, have some barbecues, get a suntan, and generally behave like the privileged class. Laura and I might buy a few toys ourselves. I signed a contract today to renovate a hundred-unit apartment complex so they can turn them into condominiums."

Laura looked at her husband with a mixture of surprise and pride. "Why didn't you tell me?"

"I wanted to break the news when I could order champagne. I've always had a flair for the dramatic."

"Hey, buddy, congratulations," Ben said, pumping Darryl's hand. "Now you can get the Windsurfer, and I'll get a fishing boat and we'll have twice the toys for half the money."

A waiter appeared at the table, as if on cue, carrying a bottle of champagne in a bucket of ice.

"You really did have your timing planned perfectly, didn't you, darling?" Laura said.

"Wait until I get you home," Darryl whispered in her ear. "I'll show you perfect timing."

The waiter filled their glasses and left with a generous tip.

"A toast to friendship and success," Sharon said as they raised their glasses.

It didn't take them long to finish off the bottle of champagne, and Darryl had Laura back on the dance floor. After several dances in a row Laura said, "I've got to take a break. I'm getting dizzy. I think I'll get my purse

and make a trip to the ladies' lounge. Don't pick up any
pretty girls while I'm gone."

"I promise to try to fight off the hordes of eager beau-
ties, but only if you hurry. A man only has so much
willpower, you know."

I've never been able to handle champagne, Laura
thought as she made her way across the stuffy, crowded
ballroom.

Inside the lounge she gratefully sat down on one of the
chairs before a long line of mirrors and took deep
breaths, noticing the light scent of pine deodorizer. For
once the lounge was empty, and Laura was grateful for
the temporary solitude and cool air. She shut her eyes for
a moment, feeling content and slightly tipsy.

Her eyes darted open when she felt someone staring at
her. She looked nervously around the room. At first she
tried to ignore the feeling of being watched, since the
room was obviously empty. The feeling increased rather
than diminished, however, and Laura's police instincts
took over. She automatically reached for her shoulder,
where she usually carried her gun in a holster, and felt
naked in its absence. The department encouraged the
detectives to carry their weapon even when off duty, but
it wasn't mandated. Laura normally did keep it with her,
but there was no discreet place to carry a gun when she
was wearing an evening gown. She couldn't carry it in
her purse because she had to leave it unattended at the
table while they danced.

The air in the room was changing from pleasantly cool
to cold, and goose bumps stood out on Laura's arms like
a warning. In a moment of panic she considered running
from the room, but whether or not she had her gun, she
was a police officer. She was the one others called on
when they were afraid. She certainly wasn't going to go
rushing in terror from an empty lounge at the country
club. Her eyes darted about nervously, then she took a
deep breath and looked at the floor inside the stalls for
feet. Nothing. Still, she was certain someone was watching her; and whoever it was posed a threat. Even without
her gun she was confident she could defend herself with a
well-placed karate kick. She stood with as much determi-

nation as she could muster and, one by one, kicked open the stalls. They were all empty.

"You fool, Laura," she said aloud to break the tension. "You've got to stop behaving like the hysterical heroine in a gothic novel. You came here to fix your makeup, and that is what you are going to do."

She forced herself to sit on one of the chairs again and pull her lipstick from her purse, but her hands were shaking so badly, she couldn't apply it. Her fear at the hospital and her recent overall feeling of dread was back in full force and growing. Her throat constricted and she heard her breathing come in short wheezes. Her hands and feet were tingling and cold. Her terror was growing to the proportions of her nightmares, but this time she was wide awake. As her breathing became more labored, she was overcome by a wave of dizziness and nausea. She was sitting still, but the room was spinning around her. She grabbed the counter in front of her to keep her balance while the mirror spun her agonized reflection in rapid circles around the room. She held frantically to the table-top as her one contact with reality, closed her eyes, and felt as if she were trapped on a spinning amusement-park ride.

Suddenly the room bolted to a stop, lurching Laura forward in her chair. Her head and stomach took longer to become stationary and a sharp pain in her head forced her to keep her eyes closed.

It was the smell that finally forced her cautiously to rejoin the world, though it wasn't the world she was familiar with. The odor of pine was gone, replaced by the pungent rot of decaying bodies. The taste of champagne turned sour in Laura's mouth as she looked through the mirror, which no longer reflected the innocent room under bright fluorescent lights. The room was shrouded in bone-chilling black. The only light came from the scene in the mirror, as though it were real and she and the room were nonexistent. She was drawn to the mirror to escape the nothingness around her. She could feel herself being pulled toward it, to where a row of coffins stood, waiting, open.

From deep within the mirror she could hear women

weeping. The last coffin in the row slammed shut and the women's weeping seemed to decrease slightly. Slowly, one by one, the coffins closed. Each time, a sobbing voice was silenced—until only one coffin was left open and the only sobs were her own. She stared, hypnotized by the scene, then stood passively to meet her fate. She could disappear within the mirror now and find peace. It would be easy. It would be right. Her will was like a physical entity dissolving just out of her reach.

"No!" she shouted, drawing on a core of inner strength.

From above her, all around her, a child's voice laughed loudly. She covered her ears, trying to block the evil sound, which bounced off the walls and was absorbed in the mirror.

"Laura, Laura, answer me. What's wrong?" Sharon was shaking her frantically. "Are you okay? The door was locked. I couldn't get in. There was another one of those weird electrical storms. Darryl—all of us—were worried about you when you didn't come back. What happened in here? Geez, it's cold. It feels like a freezer."

Laura looked at her friend, the glassy expression in her eyes replaced by recognition. She looked cautiously into the mirror. It was only a normal mirror in the familiar lounge of their neighborhood country club. A light odor of pine filled the air.

Tracy Binder sat huddled against the door of the car, crying. She and Mark had been fighting. It wasn't her fault she didn't feel romantic; how could she, under the circumstances? And he was totally unfair to blame the baby on her carelessness. He was the one who had kept telling her if she loved him, she would show him. She felt sick to her stomach, and she felt guilty because he had to work at the Conoco station to earn money for an abortion.

"Come back over here," he pleaded. "I only want to hold you. I won't try anything. I'll meet you halfway," he said, moving toward the middle of the car.

Tracy looked at his impish grin and couldn't stay mad.

She moved toward him slightly and let him pull her into his arms.

"It's not just that I feel sick all the time, Mark. I keep having these nightmares that are really getting to me. I dream about a row of coffins. They are all open, but I know they are waiting to be filled. I wake up in a cold sweat every night."

"It's because you feel guilty about the abortion. There's no need to, Tracy. It's not bad. What is inside of you isn't a baby yet. It's nothing more than a little blob. You are thinking of yourself as a murderess, but you're not."

"I wish I could be so sure about it, Mark. How can we know when a fetus actually becomes a person and develops a soul?"

"Jeez, Tracy, if you fix fried eggs for breakfast and one of them has a little red dot on it, you know it's been fertilized. Do you say you had fried chicken for breakfast?"

"That's gross, Mark. A baby isn't like a chicken," she said vehemently, as she pulled away from him again. "There's something else about the dreams," she added in a low, frightened voice. "It's not little coffins that I see. It's big ones that you would bury an adult in. I always wake up feeling like someone or something is waiting to put me in one of those coffins and close the lid; and sometimes I feel like I'm being watched, even when I know no one is around. It's like something awful is going to happen and I have to wait around for it. I'm scared, Mark."

"It's your subconscious working on you, that's all. Nothing is going to happen to you. In a month it will all be over."

"That's what I'm afraid of."

16

Adam whistled as he trotted up the fire escape to his apartment. It was clear and warm for a January Sunday, and he had been walking in the park all morning talking to the children. It had been one of the best weekends he could remember in years. He had shared it with Marie and the television. Marie was still locked in the TV, but Adam knew now that she was still alive, otherwise she wouldn't have been able to talk to him.

He fingered Sister Mary Xavier's ring as he bolted around the landing of the fire escape. He had taken it from the shoe box and now carried it everywhere, because it was a sign that he was forgiven, proof that Marie was going to come back to him. He didn't know when, but he felt it would be soon.

He had spent Saturday with Marie, reliving their good memories via the eye of the wonderful three-dimensional television.

He put Sister Mary Xavier's ring in his pocket when he reached his apartment and unlocked the door. As he closed the door behind him, the television sprang to life. Adam smiled broadly and threw himself on the bed, with his face close to the screen, and waited.

There she was, coming through the door of that long-ago apartment. She glowed from fresh air and happiness. This was one of the scenes the television had started to show him many times, then cut off moments before he found out what it meant. Adam leaned closer to the screen and willed Marie to stay. He had never seen her so happy.

"Adam, darling, I have wonderful news. You'd better sit down first."

"I'm sitting down. I'm lying down," Adam cried from his perch inches away from Marie. He held his breath. The television was going farther than it had before with this scene.

"How would you like to move up the date of the wedding?" Marie asked, her eyes twinkling, "—because, darling, in about seven months, there will be three of us. The doctor just called me at work and confirmed it. I'm pregnant."

"Yahoo!" Adam bolted from the bed in his excitement. Marie was coming back, and she would have his child. His dreams were going to be fulfilled.

Marie was laughing and holding her stomach. "Meet little Adam."

"No, Marie, we'll call him Jeremy. Adam is too plain a name for our child." He was reaching out to the screen to hold her, but the glass interfered. Soon, though, it would be different.

"I've got to get back to work now, darling. I only sneaked away to tell you the news. I'll see you tonight, and we can celebrate." Then she was gone.

Marie was coming back that evening, and she was going to have their baby. He had to get ready for her. He rushed around the apartment cleaning and straightening. Marie liked for things to be neat. He scrubbed the floors and cleaned the counters. He polished the bathroom until the old shower shone. When everything was spotless, he still had several hours before Marie got off work.

"I think I'll go out and buy food for a special dinner and window-shop for baby things. Tomorrow after I get off work, Marie and I can go out and buy everything we need. If I sit around here waiting now, I'll go crazy."

Adam hurried back from the supermarket. He wanted to have plenty of time to finish preparing for Marie's homecoming. He swung the sack of steaks beside him and held on to the milk protectively, almost as though it were the baby. When he entered his apartment, breathless from running up the steep fire escape, he started automatically to turn on the television, then hesitated.

"I'm not quite ready for Marie yet. If she's going to come through the TV, maybe I should wait until I'm ready to turn it on. Then again, the TV always shows me Marie when it is ready." He reached for the knob again, pulled his hand back, reached, and finally decided not to turn on his friend. If Marie was there, he wasn't ready for her. If she wasn't, he would be disappointed.

Adam put the milk and steaks in the refrigerator and the roses in a glass of water, then laid out his best clothes. He hummed while he undressed, and showered carefully. He paused in the middle of shaving and looked quizzically at his reflection in the mirror. Who was the old man staring back? It couldn't be his face.

"Will Marie recognize me? It's been so long. Will she love an old man? Of course she loves me. She said so this afternoon. She saw me today. I know she did. It was me she was looking at when she said she was going to have our baby."

Adam was so nervous when he got dressed, it was all he could do to steady his hands enough to button his shirt. For once he wished he were a drinking man.

Outside the sun had stolen unceremoniously away from the city, leaving the deep shadows of early evening.

"Marie should be off work now," Adam said, staring out the window at the deepening twilight. "Anytime now, my love, we'll be together again."

He could feel a shadow of doubt enter him, in the way that night slowly engulfed day. He shook it off and started the steaks. "She will come," he said firmly while he put the steaks into a frying pan and turned the fire on low.

The aroma of the steaks filled the apartment as Adam paced nervously across the old floor. His stomach grumbled from hunger, reminding him that he had forgotten to eat when he came home at lunch and saw Marie in the television.

"I'd better turn the television on. She might be waiting for me to turn it on to release her." He sat formally at the end of the bed and carefully pulled the knob, willing Marie's image to appear in glorious three-dimension.

"The score is tied with three minutes left in the game," a sports announcer said while football players pounded into each other like sardines fighting for a spot in a can.

Adam's face dropped; then he turned the channel selector. One station after another came and went with the steady click of the channel changes: football, more football, evening news, an old movie. No Marie.

He turned the television back to the news and waited. The news ended and still he waited. *The Jeffersons* ended. He waited. He put the shriveled steaks in the oven on warm and resumed his pacing between the door and the television. He stood on the landing of the fire escape to see if Marie was coming down the street. Finally, he went inside and resumed his vigil by the television. Eight o'clock. Nine. Ten. After the late news he drifted off into a troubled sleep.

"Daddy, help me, Daddy. Help me." The voice was inside his dream and out of his dream. Adam mumbled and turned over. "Help me," came the more urgent call.

Groggy, Adam began to wake up. "Marie?" he called quietly, hopefully.

"Daddy, help me," a child's voice cried. He sounded about the same age as the grade-school boys Adam followed, about seven or eight.

Marie was standing before the deserted building, her blue scarf pulled high on her neck to block the blowing snow.

Adam heard the child screaming frantically, and Adam knew, finally, the meaning of the nightmare scene. "Marie, don't do it. Stop, Marie." He pounded on the sunken glass of the television eye and pleaded with Marie while she disappeared within the walls of the sinister building. He shook the set as though he could shake her out of the building like shaking a doll from a doll house.

"Stop, Marie, stop. You can't do this. Why, Marie?"

The child's screaming ceased, and Adam knew it was too late. And he knew that, now, Marie would come to him. He sobbed.

Adam saw the door to his apartment within the television. He could hear Marie's steps as she trudged up the stairs, faltering, then continuing slowly. He held his breath. Maybe he was wrong about the recurring television scene. He had to be wrong.

With his face inches from the screen he waited for Marie to come through the door. Slowly it opened and she stumbled through. Her face was white and grimacing in pain above her blue scarf. Blood covered her skirt and her hands and arms where she had tried in vain to keep her life's fluids from escaping.

"Help me, Adam," she pleaded. "I need a doctor."

"What have you done, Marie?" Adam asked coldly, because he had seen the building and had known.

"I had to do it, Adam. I had to have the abortion. Let me explain, darling, but first I've got to get to the hospital. He stuck a coat hanger into me. I'm dying."

"What about our baby? You murdered our baby," Adam screamed. He felt the rage growing, exploding inside of him. He heard Marie pleading with him to let her explain, but his head was on fire with rage at her betrayal.

The glass that had separated him from Marie was gone as he reached out and grabbed her and tightened the scarf around her neck, as he had twenty years before. He was screaming and tightening the scarf. The blood, Marie's blood, which had been unleashed by the butcher abortionist, rolled down her legs into a pool on the floor.

Marie stopped struggling. Adam released his grip on her, and she fell lifeless to the floor. The apartment reeked of burned steaks and blood.

He screamed and covered his eyes with his hands. When he let his arms fall limply to his sides, Marie was gone. The blood was gone. The heavy concave glass protected the sunken eye that revealed its terrors at will. There was no picture on the set, only the shrinking red retina.

But in his hands Adam held Marie's blue scarf.

"No," he wailed. He ripped the television from the wall socket and threw it across the room. Its heavy glass shattered into thousands of tiny pieces. He charged toward it to rip out its evil electronic guts—there were none. There was nothing but broken glass and an empty metal shell; and a blue scarf that lay crumpled on his bed.

"Next, the screams will come," he said passively. "They'll lock me up and give me the pills. I won't have to deal with this at all." He waited eagerly for madness to release him from his pain. The screams remained locked in his throat. The men in white did not come with their merciful pills.

In frustration Adam grabbed Marie's scarf from the bed and tried to tear it to shreds with his bare hands. The strong wool would not yield. He gingerly walked around the broken glass and pulled a butcher knife from the kitchen drawer. He plunged the knife into the scarf, slicing, shredding, mutilating it until it was nothing more than a pile of threads on the kitchen table. He gathered the remains in his hands and took them outside on the landing and threw them into the brisk wind. He stood on the metal landing in shirtsleeves and bare feet and watched the wind grab the tiny pieces of scarf, which swirled together like a hive of angry yellow-jackets, then scattered and fell toward the dirty alley. Adam watched until his feet stuck painfully to the icy metal. He went inside to the tiny bathroom and splashed hot water on his face, then leaned over the sink, his breath coming in shallow gasps. He dried his face roughly and walked out to—

"Oh, my God."

The television sat unscathed at the end of his bed. Marie's scarf lay draped across the top of it.

Adam felt dizzy and supported himself against the wall. "No," he rasped in a barely audible voice. "I got rid of you. I destroyed you. I destroyed the scarf. I don't want you anymore. I don't want to know anything else about the nightmares. I liked it better before. You can't still be here. You can't toy with me anymore. Find someone else to torment. Leave me in peace."

Adam looked at the television and the scarf on top and wondered if he were awake or asleep. He must only have dreamed he smashed it against the wall. He looked at the wall. The plaster was gouged and ripped from the impact of the TV. He turned, his eyes wide and blank, and walked toward the bed. Pain brought the room back into focus. He had stepped on a piece of thick, slightly rounded glass. The sunken eye on the television seemed to smile a sweet invitation to more games.

Adam sat at the top of the bed, as far from the television as possible, and stared at it suspiciously. The eye came to life while he watched. He was looking at the shadow of a child on a swing, lazily moving back and forth. The child wasn't visible, just his shadow growing long and short as the swing moved.

"I love you, Daddy." A sweet child's voice rang clearly through the speakers.

"Jeremy?" Adam whispered in disbelief.

"Of course, Daddy. Who else would I be? You were right to punish Mommy. You always were the only one who loved me. Mommy was evil, like Sister Mary Xavier. They're all like that, Daddy. You know. You've seen how they flaunt their bodies at you."

Adam didn't say anything. He sat and looked warily at the shadow child. Too much had happened. He couldn't absorb it all.

"We're going to be great friends, Daddy."

The shadow child was replaced by the shrinking retina.

Adam looked nervously at the television. The shadow child had talked to him. He had insisted he was Jeremy, but he couldn't be. His son was dead. Marie was dead.

Adam's eyes appeared as glassy and unseeing as the blank electronic screen, though he knew now the television was not electronic. It was an empty metal case filled with the ghosts of his nightmares.

He wanted to cry and scream, but his grief was too intense. It was true. Marie was dead and he had killed her. The things they had said at the trial so many years ago were true. Now he had nothing.

"Marie, Marie." He kept repeating her name until it was a monotone chant. "I'm sorry, Marie. I didn't mean to hurt you. I didn't know what I was doing. It was an accident."

He began rocking on the bed with steady, even movements. Unconsciously he resumed his futile chant. For the past fifteen years he had tried to remember what happened the night Marie died. Like the knowledge of his behavior with Sister Mary Xavier, his memory of killing Marie, once remembered, would not go away. Tears began to sneak out of his eyes. They came individually and unnoticed. Their volume increased to a slow trickle, then to a steady stream. Soon they were like the river of blood that had erupted from Marie's body. His vision was blinded by the torrent of tears. When he wiped his hands across his face, he was surprised by the clear, thin liquid. It should have been red and thick.

"Why, Marie? Why did you do it? You seemed to want our child as much as I did. It doesn't make any sense. Nothing makes any sense anymore."

Before, he had at least had half a life, waiting for it to blossom to fullness when Marie came back. How could he go on each day when he knew with certainty he was a murderer who had sucked away his love's life as surely as the abortionist had killed his son?

He retreated to the deep recesses of his mind, to the days of Sister Teresa and his early childhood. In his mind's eye he was sitting on her lap with his head cushioned by her soft breasts. She was comforting him, and he felt himself enfolded in the safety of her bulk. He began to relax. He closed his eyes and drifted in Sister Teresa's secure love.

He gave a start. The kind nun's arms and lap were gone. He was falling into a deep hole. At the bottom was Sister Teresa's coffin. He was picking up speed, flying toward her open, unseeing eyes and her rigid body. They were going to bury him with her because he had killed her with his flu.

Adam jerked awake. There was no comfort in Sister Teresa's memory, only the knowledge that he had committed two murders. Even as a child he had been a killer.

The shadow child swung back and forth within the television and giggled. The man couldn't see him now, but he could see the man. This was a good game, and oh, so much fun. He liked games where he made the rules.

"Daddy, Daddy, Daddy. I'm going to play with Daddy," he sang. "Aren't you having fun, Daddy?" he asked as he jumped from the swing and stuck his nose against the glass. "Oh, poor Daddy can't hear me." He giggled as though someone were tickling him, or as if he knew a joke that no one else knew.

17

"I don't know why you insist on ruining a perfectly good Sunday evening by bringing this up again. I'm not going to the doctor, so you can forget it," Laura shouted as she stormed down the hall.

"Damn it, Laura, you are the most stubborn woman I've ever met. If you are right and there really isn't anything the matter with you, then the trip to the doctor's office won't hurt you a bit; and if there is something wrong, you will find out and you can get it taken care of."

Laura stopped in midstep and swung around, looking up angrily at her husband. "I'm not going to take time off from work and throw away good money to have some pompous doctor tell me I'm tired. I already know I'm tired, and this conversation is making me exhausted."

"The way Sharon found you in the ladies' lounge Friday is a little more than tired, I'd say."

"Right. I was tired and I drank too much champagne. You're making a big deal out of nothing."

"Okay, then, what about the night with the sewing machine? I've seen tired people plenty of times, but I've never seen anyone lose it like that from simple overwork."

Laura hesitated. Darryl had hit on an area she was too concerned about to acknowledge. She was glad she hadn't told him what had really happened Friday night, or about the incident with Rhonda at the hospital. That would put him in such a state, he'd probably use her handcuffs on her and personally deliver her to the doctor.

"You think I'm going crazy?" she screamed defensively.

"I didn't say that, but, sweetheart, you need to go to the doctor and find out what is going on. You're probably anemic or something simple like that," he said softly, pulling her rigid body next to his. "Maybe your blood sugar level is messed up. There's any number of explana-

tions. Come on, let's go in the bedroom and I'll give you
a back rub."

"It won't do any good. I still won't go to the doctor,"
Laura said, the tension easing in her body as Darryl
rubbed her shoulders.

Laura allowed Darryl to lead her into the bedroom,
but she knew she would not give in about going to the
doctor. What could she say to him—that she saw coffins
in mirrors and imagined she had been places she could
not possibly have seen before? How about "Oh, yes, doctor, and I have blackouts and impale myself with sewing-
machine needles after embroidering gibberish on cloth. I
pick up telephones that haven't rung and start to talk to
people who aren't there; that's when I'm not imagining
that storm clouds are filling my body and invisible people
are staring at me."

"Maybe tomorrow you could call in sick, Laura, so
you could get some extra sleep."

"You know I don't have the kind of job where I can
call in sick just because I'm a little tired. In fact, I can't
even call in sick when I am sick. The motto around the
precinct is that you don't call in sick, you crawl in sick.
I'm right in the middle of investigating a rape. Leads get
cold. If I miss work, we may never find the men who
attacked that woman."

"Tracy, wake up. It's okay, angel. Daddy's here," Greg
Binder said as he sat on the side of his daughter's bed,
rocking her. Her mother stood behind him, clutching her
furry pink bathrobe around her and looking worried in
the pale light that filtered through the gingham curtains
from the street.

Tracy began to wake up and glanced with relief around
her familiar bedroom with its mountains of stuffed animals, football banners, and cheerleading pom-poms.
"Oh, Daddy, I had the most awful dream," she said,
burying her head in his shoulder as she used to do when
she was a little girl.

Her father held her more firmly and rubbed her back,
trying to rub away the shudders that kept going through
her body even now that she was awake. "Everything is

okay now, baby. You're awake and it's over. That must have been quite a dream. You were screaming. You scared your mom and me half to death."

"Mama?"

"Yes, Tracy. I'm here, darling." Mrs. Binder stroked her daughter's hair.

"Oh, Mama and Daddy, it was terrible. It seemed so real. There was a man after me and he was going to kill me. I was running and I couldn't get away. My feet would hardly move. He caught me and was trying to strangle me."

"It was only a dream, Tracy," Greg said. "You're safe now."

In a little farm town 150 miles from the city, Harold Gibbons was holding his wife and comforting her. He couldn't understand why recently she had started having severe nightmares. It wasn't like her at all. He'd been trying to be more considerate since the day he lost his temper and yelled at her in front of the children, but he vowed to treat her even better. It wasn't her fault he was worried about getting laid off from his job. He knew she had to stay home and take care of the kids, so she couldn't get a job even if there was a job available for her in town.

"It's okay, Martha," he whispered. "I'll take care of you."

18

Monday, January 28
The damp cloth slipped off Laura's forehead as she moaned and turned over in bed. She hadn't taken her temperature since Darryl had insisted in the morning, but she felt as if it still were at least 102 degrees. Her husband had gotten his wish from Sunday; she had no choice but to stay home from work. She wasn't getting any rest, though.

As she drifted in and out of fitful bouts of sleep, she
didn't know what was real, what was a dream, and what
was a hallucination. Sometimes she heard a child laughing. Another time she was walking alongside the row of
open coffins, and she had returned to her nightmare of
the faceless man strangling a series of women. Even when
she realized she was home in bed, she was frightened.
The only good thing that had come from the day so far
was that she'd convinced Darryl that the incident at the
country club Friday evening was the result of her coming
down with the flu.

Adam was nervous and jumpy all day Monday. He
tried to concentrate on his work, but his mind kept going
back to the television and Marie's scarf. He knew he had
shattered the TV and torn up Marie's scarf, but they were
intact again. It didn't make any more sense than the
shadow child who insisted he was Jeremy. To make
things worse, Miss Laura was gone sick. He felt as if
seeing her was the only thing that could anchor him to
reality.

He had been too frightened to go home after work,
until the cold forced him to face his fears.

Now Jeremy was talking to him soothingly from the
television, and Adam was beginning to calm down and
understand. Things were clearer than they ever had been
for Adam Smith.

19

Tuesday, January 29

Adam walked purposefully toward the grade school. It
was Tuesday, and he had more reason than ever to see
the children. He had to warn the boys about growing up.

On Monday he had been confused about women. He
felt guilty for having killed Marie, and he was frightened
of the television set. He knew better now. Jeremy had
explained it all to him last night. He had wanted to talk

to Miss Laura about it today, because she was the only
good woman and also the only person he could trust. She
had been home sick again, though, so he would have to
warn the boys instead.

A couple of children on roller skates came zooming
down the street. As they passed Adam, they ran into a
woman who, in turn, bumped into Adam. "Excuse me,"
she said, and hurried on her way without looking at him.

It was shameful the way that woman pressed against
me, pretending it was those boys' fault. Women are like
that, Adam thought. They press their bodies against you
and get you worked up, then they kill your babies. Jeremy told me. I have a smart boy. I didn't really murder
his mama. I only gave her the punishment she needed.
You have to punish women sometimes. After I punished
Marie again Sunday, I didn't think I wanted to remember
any of it. Jeremy told me it was important to remember.
He said I have a job to do, and I have to remember for
the job.

Adam stayed about five feet behind three little girls he
was following.

You boys stay away from them, he thought when he
passed the grade school and heard a group of boys teasing the girls. They will get you in trouble. They'll grow
up and use you and make you do bad things to them.
They'll do bad things to you too. Then the trouble will
really start because you'll like it and you'll believe their
lies.

Adam stayed a discreet distance behind the girls and
wondered if they would stay together or split up. Maybe
if you started training a girl young enough, you could
raise her properly and she wouldn't be sinful. She could
be like Miss Laura. He would be doing one of those girls
a favor if he took her home and taught her how to behave
and what happened if she sinned.

"Sara," a lady yelled from down the street. The girls
saw the woman, waved, and ran toward her. Adam
ducked quickly into the alley.

The rest of the way home, Adam noticed the women
flaunting their bodies at him. Even though they wore

heavy winter coats, he could tell they were sticking out their breasts and wiggling their backsides.

When he walked into his apartment, Jeremy's shadow was in the television waiting for him.

"Daddy! Daddy's home."

"Were you a good boy today, Jeremy?"

"Yes, Daddy."

"You won't leave me, will you, Jeremy?" Adam pleaded. "You're all I have. If I lost you, I wouldn't be able to stand it."

"No, Daddy, I'll never leave, but you were bad on Sunday when you tried to get rid of me. You shouldn't have done that," Jeremy said threateningly.

"I didn't mean to," Adam said. "I didn't understand then."

"If you try that again, Daddy, you will have to be punished. You know that, don't you?"

"I love you, Jeremy. I wouldn't do anything to hurt you, but when can I see you, son?" he asked the shadow.

"When the time is right, Daddy. First, you have to prove you really love me."

"I'll do anything you say, if we can be together."

Adam fidgeted nervously before the set. Jeremy called him daddy, but sometimes he felt like a puppet with the shadow child pulling the strings. Besides, the television had played so many tricks on him, he couldn't help but worry a little that this child was another trick, not his Jeremy at all.

"Who is the man who keeps screaming in the fog, Jeremy?"

"You'll know all about it before long, Daddy dear."

Jeremy's shadow faded from the screen and was replaced by a man and woman in an office. The woman was closing the blinds at the window. When she turned, Adam saw she was wearing a tight sweater.

"Please stay a little late tonight, baby," she said, running her fingers along the man's spine.

"You know it's my kid's birthday, Ann. I'd like to stay, but I can't."

"You'll be home in plenty of time for the party."

The man smiled lustily. "You're probably right," he

said. He drew her sweater up and began pulling it over her head.

The television switched to a closeup of the woman's gold earring rolling across the floor by a Christmas tree. At first Adam was confused by the tree, since it was the end of January. Then he realized he was seeing something that had happened before. Throughout the next hour Adam watched the woman seduce the man. He was disgusted by her evil acts and her moans of pleasure, but his eyes remained glued to the television.

It was only when the screen went blank and the tiny red retina disappeared that he noticed the gold earring on top of the television set. He carefully picked it up and put it in the shoe box with Sister Mary Xavier's ring and Marie's scarf.

20

Wednesday, January 30

"Here comes the bus, Mommy," Karen shouted excitedly as she dashed down the street to her mother and father.

"I saw it first. I should have been the one to tell her," Harold junior complained, pushing his sister in revenge. Karen started to cry but shut up quickly when their dad threatened to pull off his belt and whip them right there on Main Street.

Martha was taking the early bus so the children would have time to see her off before school, and because she had an important appointment to keep.

"Bus," piped in Jeff proudly as he pulled at his mother's skirt.

"I want to go on the bus, too, Mommy. I want to go see Grandma," cried Sandy, holding more tightly to her mother's hand.

"It's okay, darling. Mommy will only be gone a few days. Mrs. Jones will take good care of you. I'll be home before you know it."

"I don't know what has gotten into you, Martha, taking off like this and leaving me with all these kids. What kind of wife deserts her family like this?"

Martha looked nervously at Harold's belligerent stare. He couldn't change his mind now about letting her go. Too much was at stake. "What can I do, Harold? You know I don't want to leave, but Mother is sick. She needs me. I'll be back in less than a week. Mrs. Jones will be there during the day to take care of the kids and to fix supper for you."

Harold reached down and swatted Jeff, who was playing with a cigarette butt, then stuffed his hands in his pockets moodily.

Martha gave a sigh of relief when the bus pulled in front of Lathe's Mercantile, its air brakes screeching and exhaust fumes filling the small-town air.

"Give Mommy a kiss good-bye, and you be good for your dad, you hear?" She knelt down and was surrounded by hugs from her four children.

Martha stood up and tried to kiss her husband goodbye. He looked furtively around, then kissed her on the cheek.

"Watch out when you change buses at the city. You never know what kind of weirdo you might run into at a place like that. I'd feel better if your mom had a phone so you could call when you got there."

"I'll call from the pay phone at the drugstore." She started toward the bus, turned around quickly, and said, "I love you, Harold." Then she disappeared past the driver and soon was waving to the children from a window seat.

Tears filled Martha's eyes as the bus took off. She had never before lied to Harold. She felt as if she didn't have any choice this time. They had four kids, only two of them in school, and hardly enough money to make ends meet. She couldn't tell her husband where she really was going, or why. Thank goodness her mother didn't have a telephone, so he couldn't check up on her.

When she called Harold, it wouldn't be from the drugstore in the small town where they grew up. Martha Gibbons was only twenty-four years old, but she felt old and defeated as the bus took off for the 150-mile journey to the city.

Several hours later Martha was at the Mid-City Family Planning Clinic.

"Speak up, miss. We can't help you if you don't tell us your name, now, can we," Ms. White droned as a statement, rather than a question, in her nasal voice.

"I already told you my name. It's Martha Gibbons." Martha squirmed in the straight chair while the administrator gave her a condescending smile.

"We've found that some of the women who come to us have a habit of changing their names every time we speak to them. We must establish that you are who you say you are, now, mustn't we?"

"I've already shown you my social security card, and I told you I don't have a driver's license. I don't know what else I can do, Mrs. White." Martha fought back her anger. She was determined she wouldn't give this woman the satisfaction of seeing her break down. She longed to be back home baking bread and taking care of her babies. "I would have brought my birth certificate if I had known I needed it, Mrs. White."

"You may call me Ms. White." The administrator sniffed indignantly. "Well, I guess we'll have to take your word about who you are, though anyone can steal a social security card." She sighed. "We know what some types are like, don't we?"

"I'm not a thief," Martha replied evenly. Her hands were clenched into fists in her lap. She had to resist the urge to tell off the dried-up woman across from her, then walk out.

"Of course you aren't, miss. None of them ever are."

"It's Mrs. Gibbons, not Miss."

"According to our records, Miss Gibbons, most of our clients are married, but if we had a dime for every one of them who could produce that husband if they had to, we wouldn't have much money."

"We have four children," Martha replied, emphasizing the *we* as proof she was indeed married.

"And how many abortions have you had?"

"I've never had an abortion," Martha nearly shouted.

"You don't need to get snippy, miss," Ms. White sniffed, the sweet edge of her voice more sarcastic than ever. "After all, we didn't call you. You called us."

"I know," Martha murmured. She unconsciously stretched her hands protectively over her stomach and the still indistinguishable life growing there. Then she thought about Karen, Harold junior, Sandy, and little Jeff, all counting on her, all needing shoes, clothes, and winter coats. She thought about the food that was in too short supply and the doctor bills that never ran out. Harold did the best he could for them, but you could only stretch a dollar so far, and their budget was at the breaking point. Martha reluctantly pulled her hands away from her stomach and reestablished her loyalty to the children she already was responsible for.

"You do receive ADC, of course," Miss White said.

"What?"

"Aid to Dependent Children. You are on welfare, aren't you? Most of our clients are."

"Harold and I have never taken charity. We've always taken care of our own," Martha replied, outraged.

"If you don't receive ADC, you can't receive Medicaid. If you don't receive Medicaid, you will have to pay for the abortion in advance. You realize it is two hundred fifty dollars, don't you?"

"I know," Martha said miserably. For the past three years she had been scraping and saving to surprise Harold with a chain saw. She had just put aside the last of the $350 she needed when she discovered she was pregnant. Between the fee for the abortion, the bus fare, her room at the YWCA, and food, every penny would be gone when she went back home. She hated to think of Harold spending every free minute, year round, scrounging for scraps of wood and sawing them by hand for the stove, but there wasn't any choice.

"Okay, miss, go back to the waiting room until the nurse calls your name. Then the doctor will examine you. We can set up the abortion for a week from today."

"A week? I can't wait that long. I've got to get back home. I thought you would be able to do it in a couple of days." Harold would have a fit if she called and said she would be gone that long. He might even call her mother's neighbor and check up on her. She couldn't go home and come back to the city again. He had barely let her leave this time.

"We can't schedule you any faster than that. Take it or leave it."

Martha was desperate now. "Please, Ms. White. I don't have enough money for a place to stay for a week and for food too."

Ms. White looked at her coldly, then turned her back and walked to the door that opened into the crowded waiting room. Only after she opened the door did she speak, loudly saying, "Miss Gibbons, we are not running a one-day trash removal service. You'll have to wait in line for an appointment like everyone else."

Martha turned bright red and stumbled, humiliated, into the lobby, trying to avoid the staring eyes.

Finally the nurse called her name and led her to a private examination room and handed her a paper gown. Martha put on the gown and waited, alone and shivering, while the antiseptic walls seemed to stare at her accusingly.

After the exam she paid in advance the $250 fee for the abortion, then walked back to the Y and paid for a room for a week. She had six dollars and fifty cents and a return bus ticket. If she talked to Harold for three minutes this evening, she would have five dollars left for food for the entire week.

She picked up a loaf of bread on the way to the Y, then sat in the park and ate part of it, carefully considering how many slices she should eat now and how many to save for later in order to stretch her money through the entire week. I can buy a loaf of bread a day while I'm here, she thought as she watched the children play in the dim winter-afternoon sun. It might not be the most balanced diet in the world, but I can stand it for a few days.

When the temperature began to drop, it was still too early to call Harold, so Martha started walking, exploring the city streets. What do you do to kill time when you are waiting for an abortion? she wondered, then gave a humorless chuckle at her appropriate choice of words.

Ahead of her a cathedral seemed to beckon with its safe, sturdy walls.

She sat in a pew at the back of the impressive cathedral, tears running down her face. "Oh, dear Father, how can it be a sin to protect the children I already have? I try to be a good person, to follow the rules of the Church, but where did it get me and my family? The Church says I can't use birth control, and the Church says I can't have an abortion. How can those things be more of a sin than bringing a child into the world which I can't feed and clothe? How can it be virtuous to condemn not only this unborn child, but also the children I now have? Isn't it a sin to let my children go hungry when I have a way to prevent it?"

Martha felt the church should shake on its foundation with her sacrilege. She was frightened, angry with God, and angry with the Church. "I feel so guilty and frustrated," she prayed. "If what I'm planning to do is wrong, let the walls come down around me, swallow me, and carry me to hell." The church remained silent, massive, and unyielding. Martha sighed and walked out into the cold night.

On her way back to the Y she halted suddenly in front of a bar with neon lights flashing overhead. She looked in terror down an alley across the street and at a metal fire escape. The alley and staircase were empty, but she was terrified. She felt rooted to the ground, expecting some evil to sweep her away. A drunk couple pushed by her, laughing, and Martha broke free of her paralyzing fear and ran. She didn't stop until she was safely in the YWCA, the door to her room bolted behind her.

21

"Welcome back, Laura," Harry said as he met his partner coming down the hall of the precinct. "You must have been really sick to take two days off work."

"I'm fine now," she replied, but she felt weak and disoriented from two days of fever and nightmares.

"What have you got going today, partner?" Harry asked. Since the chief's restructuring of the precinct Harry and Laura hadn't seen much of each other and Laura was surprised to note that Harry had actually seemed to miss her.

"I'm going to see what information I can round up on the Rhonda Hackman case," Laura said. She hadn't told anyone Rhonda didn't want to press charges. She was still hoping to change the girl's mind. She was frustrated that the flu had put her a couple of days behind on the investigation.

"I heard those guys beat her up pretty badly," Harry said. "The lab report came in yesterday afternoon. I think Sergeant Binder put it on your desk."

Laura checked the report thoroughly. It confirmed Rhonda's story of three perpetrators. She called the bar at which Rhonda said she had met the men and learned that the bartender who had been on duty that night would be in at noon. After the morning meeting she quickly caught up on some paperwork, then drove to Metro College to see what information she could get from the administration.

Unlike the branch campuses in the suburbs with their stark architecture, the main campus of Metro College had massive columns and ivy-covered walls. Laura walked up the wide staircase and into the hundred-year-old administration building. An administrative assistant led her to a small office.

"Rhonda Hackman, yes, that was a terrible thing, just terrible," the matronly assistant told Laura as she searched through one of the numerous file cabinets for Rhonda's records. "We girls were talking about it this morning at our coffee break. I've been working at Metro for thirty years, and I can't tell you how I've seen this neighborhood go downhill. There was a time I wouldn't have been the least bit frightened walking by myself at night. Now it makes me nervous going to my car in broad daylight. We all carry Mace. You have to these days, you know. It's a shame, a real shame. Ah, here's her file. No wonder I couldn't find it. It was misfiled. Imagine that. My eyes must not be what they used to be. I never used to make filing mistakes."

She laid the file on her desk. "Now, what do you want to know about Rhonda Hackman? There's not much we can tell you, Detective Bernhardt. We have twenty-five thousand students here. We couldn't possibly get to know them all. It's not at all like the old days."

The clerk was not able to give Laura much helpful information, but she really hadn't expected her to. She did, however, give her the picture from the girl's file, reluctantly, and only after Laura faithfully promised to return it when she completed her investigation.

Laura sat in her car a few minutes, staring at Rhonda's picture. She knew she had bleached-blond hair, but she really had no idea what she looked like. When they had met, the girl's face had been too swollen to tell anything. It seemed eerie that she did not recognize Rhonda from her picture after their precognition at the hospital. Although college identification pictures were always horrible, Laura could tell that Rhonda had the potential to be pretty if she lost a little weight and learned how to fix her hair and makeup. If the case ever went to court, she would have to talk to her. It wouldn't help her cause to come in made up like a hooker. The girl's heavy makeup was apparent even in the picture.

Laura put Rhonda's picture in her purse. She reached the bar shortly after noon. Wooden tables filled the center of the poorly lit room and booths lined the walls. The lunch crowd was there in full force and the aroma of Reuben sandwiches and hamburgers engulfed Laura when she walked inside, reminding her she hadn't eaten. She took one of the few empty seats at the bar and ordered a Reuben on rye. She decided to eat and to get the feel of the place before she talked to the bartender. He obviously did not have time to talk then, anyway.

The bartender reminded Laura of a younger Harry Winchell. He was tall and muscular and kept snatching glances at himself in the mirror. He was wearing a tight T-shirt that read HINEY WINE on the front and ASK ME ABOUT MY HINEY on the back. For the most part the lunch crowd was pretty quiet, but Laura didn't doubt the place hopped during the evening. She could visualize Rhonda sitting at the bar talking too loud in her attempts to fit in, and not fitting in at all. Laura was hopeful the bartender would remember her and the men she was with that night. They must have stuck out like sore thumbs.

By the time she finished her sandwich, the crowd had thinned out. Laura showed her badge to the bartender, then Rhonda's picture.

"Yeah, I remember her. What a weird chick. She comes in here all the time."

The bartender glanced admiringly at himself in the mirror again and began pulling plates and glasses off the bar into a bus tray.

"Were you working Wednesday, January twenty-third?" she asked while he wiped the counter.

"Maybe I was. Maybe I wasn't. Why do you want to know?"

"Three of your customers decided to rough this girl up some that night. I think you might be able to help us find them."

"That girl was asking for trouble. She's always in here making an ass of herself and trying to get laid."

"That sounds a bit sanctimonious coming from someone who wears a T-shirt like yours," Laura replied sarcastically. "Do you remember seeing this girl on January twenty-third? That was last Wednesday, the last time you worked nights. I already checked your schedule."

"A lot of people come in here. My job is to fix them drinks, not to baby-sit for them. If I went around giving out information to the police, this place would be empty in no time. People around here don't like cops much."

Laura met his belligerent stare and replied cheerfully "Is that so, buddy? I don't think that's true. I think your customers would love to have a cop assigned especially to this bar. I bet they'd think it was fun to have a man in blue in here most of the night. He could chat with them, and maybe shake them down for drugs. Your boss would appreciate you a lot, too, when he found out he owed all that personal attention to you."

"I think my memory is getting better."

"I thought it might."

"The broad you're talking about may have been in here last Wednesday. She can guzzle the drinks pretty fast, but she isn't real big on tipping."

"Did she have any friends that she drank with?"

"Nah. Sometimes she would pick someone up and leave with him. She's a weird bird. She wears enough makeup to plaster a wall and her hair always looks like she's just seen a ghost."

"What about the men she was with the last time you saw her?"

"These three fellows came in and started buying her drinks. They were real scum bags. One of the men had his hands all over her. She was enjoying every minute of it."

"What did the men look like?"

"They were about average height. They all had brown hair. And they were dirty. They looked like they were in their early thirties."

"Your description doesn't narrow it down much."

"I can't help it if they weren't seven feet tall with bright red hair and scars down their faces. You asked me what they looked like, and I told you. Are you about finished? I have work to do."

Laura pulled out a stack of mug shots of known rapists she had brought with her. "Take a look at these and tell me if you recognize any of them. And, buddy, I don't need any more memory lapses. If I find out later Rhonda Hackman was with one of these guys that night and you don't point him out to me, I'll be back to see you."

The bartender glared at her and grabbed the pictures. He sullenly looked at them, then said, "I've never seen any of these guys."

"Okay, that's all for now. I'll let you know if I need any more information."

Laura was disappointed. She'd been hoping for a good lead from the bartender. She'd have to come back that night and talk to some customers. It would help if she had a better picture of Rhonda. She would go to the hospital and talk to her. Maybe she had a picture, and maybe she could remember something else about the men. Rhonda might be feeling a little more cooperative now that she'd had a few days to think about what those men had done to her.

"What do you mean, she's gone?" Laura asked the nurse in disbelief. "She couldn't possibly have been discharged yet. In her condition she should have been here for weeks."

"I know, Detective Bernhardt, but there wasn't anything we could do about it," the nurse replied defensively. "It wasn't our fault. We told her she shouldn't leave, but she wouldn't listen. Her doctor warned her against it. This isn't a prison, though, and patients can check themselves out if they want to."

"When did she leave?"

"Monday morning."

"Where is her doctor? I want to talk to him."

Laura sat across from the doctor in his office, tapping her foot in frustration.

"It's as the nurse told you. We advised Miss Hackman against leaving, but we couldn't hold her against her will."

"Damn," Laura muttered under her breath. "What was her condition when she left?"

"She was improving, but she still needed treatment. She was more responsive than when she was admitted, but there still were definite signs of shock."

"How can you let a woman who is in shock and badly injured just walk out of here?"

"If we had tried to keep her against her will, we would have faced a lawsuit. The only time we can legally hold a person is if he is a minor. Then we can get a court order if the parents refuse to cooperate."

"Okay, Doctor. If she shows up again, please call me at once," Laura said, handing him her card.

Laura drove to Rhonda's apartment. She had to talk her into checking back into the hospital. If only she had not been sick Monday and Tuesday, she could have gotten to the hospital in time.

"Yes, I saw her a couple of days ago," Rhonda's landlady said. "She looked as if she had been in a bad accident. Is that what you are here for? She's not in any kind of trouble, is she?"

"Can you let me into her apartment, Mrs. Henderson?" Laura asked. "No one answered when I knocked, and as you know, she is injured."

"Well, I don't know. That's highly irregular. But you being a policewoman and all, I guess it will be okay—but only for a minute," Mrs. Henderson volunteered, after only a slight hesitation.

Rhonda's clothes and personal belongings were gone from the apartment.

"Will you look at this. She packed up and moved out without paying the rent she owes me. I didn't think she was that kind of girl. It only goes to show, you can never tell about people."

Laura was looking around the drab furnished apartment for some clue as to where Rhonda might have gone, a receipt, a piece of paper with an address, anything.

"Wouldn't you have heard a tenant moving out?" she asked.

"Not necessarily. Rhonda didn't have very many personal belongings—not that I snooped around her apartment, mind you. I don't do that sort of thing."

"Of course not," Laura said, though she was certain this woman probably snooped around her tenants' apartments at every opportunity. She had more important things to worry about than Mrs. Henderson's ethics. She was wondering, What now? A case without a victim is no case at all. Anyway, that probably was the way Binder would see it. When she returned to the precinct house, she found out she had correctly guessed her supervisor's reaction.

"But, Sergeant, why would she rush out of the hospital if she wasn't afraid, or if someone wasn't threatening her? You didn't see how badly she was injured. I'm surprised she was well enough to leave without fainting in the hall. It doesn't make any sense that she would leave her apartment too. She could barely breathe. She had four broken ribs, for heaven's sakes. Ribs don't mend overnight, you know. She had a bad concussion. Her whole body was bruised and swollen. She could barely talk, and she was

in a great deal of pain. I think she has met with foul play.
It is vital we continue to investigate this case," Laura said
adamantly.

Binder puffed furiously on his cigar and glared at her.
The ashes from his cigar dropped on his shirt next to a
red food stain and burned a small hole in the fabric.
"We've been through this already, Bernhardt," he said
angrily. "The hospital confirmed the Hackman woman
didn't have any visitors, and you didn't find any sign of
foul play at her apartment. There is nothing to justify
further investigation. The woman obviously wants to be
left alone. The hospital called here while you were out
and told me the Hackman woman told them she had told
you she didn't want to press charges against the men.
You should have dropped the case then. I ought to bring
disciplinary action against you for not reporting it."

"She was in shock at the time, Sergeant. I was the first
person she talked to after the attack. I couldn't go by
what she said under those circumstances."

"The investigation is over, Bernhardt. Drop it. That is
an order. We have too much to do around here without
wasting time and taxpayers' money on wild-goose
chases."

"I'll make a deal with you, Sergeant Binder," Laura
said desperately. "Give me one more day to investigate
the Hackman case. If I don't turn up a substantial lead by
tomorrow afternoon, I promise to drop it and never mention it again."

"This is not open for negotiation, Bernhardt. You have
at least ten other cases piled up in your basket that need
attention, and I expect you to get on them. Good God,
downtown at headquarters all they have to deal with is
asbestos. I have you. I'd be willing to trade at this point,
Bernhardt. You are pushing your luck."

"Asbestos? What do you mean?"

"When they started remodeling, they discovered that
headquarters was insulated with asbestos. The mayor is
about to have a coronary over it. It's going to cost hundreds of thousands of bucks to remove it. I guess they
unleashed quite a bit of it in the air before they discovered what they were working with. And, Bernhardt, if

you don't get out of my office and get to work, I'm going to personally get you transferred to whatever department down there has the most of the stuff flying around."

22

Whimpering, Adam crawled backward across the cold linoleum. He resembled a dog too intimidated to fend off the kicks of an irate master.

"I don't want to," he whined.

In contrast Jeremy's voice rang from the television speakers in sweet innocence. "But you promised, Daddy. You said you loved me and would do anything to help me. You are the only person who can punish the baby killers. You have to do it, like you punished Mommy."

"I didn't mean to kill her. It was an accident," Adam pleaded. "I never said I would be a murderer. I didn't know what you meant when you said I had a job to do."

"You knew what I meant, Daddy." A mean tone began to form around the edges of the shadow child's voice. "Yesterday you were glad you killed Mommy, weren't you?" he snapped waspishly.

Adam was confused because Jeremy was right. He remembered thinking that Marie was evil like the others and it was good that he punished her. Now he wasn't sure. Killing Marie had been an accident. What his son wanted him to do was cold-blooded murder.

"They'll catch me, Jeremy, and lock me up. I'll never see you again. They always catch murderers. They caught me before. You don't know what it was like," Adam implored. He covered his head as though fighting off invisible blows.

"Look at me, Daddy," Jeremy threatened. His voice was still young, but it had lost its childlike quality. "If you don't do what I say, I will have to punish you."

Adam peered hesitantly from under his arm, without moving it from its protective position. The room was distorted. It stretched before him, long and narrow, with no

avenue of escape. The refrigerator's hum changed to a
growl and bent toward him like a rabid grizzly bear. The
steam heater in the dark shadows of the apartment was a
hissing leopard.

"I don't want to hurt you, Daddy," Jeremy warned.

The television loomed before Adam, growing larger
until it dwarfed him. It was the giant detached eyeball of
a monster that could erase him with one blink of its lid.
The walls of the apartment breathed as the television
reached into his memory and surrounded him with the
shadowy fears of his childhood.

"But I'd be killing the baby too," he beseeched.

"You aren't thinking straight, Daddy. The mamas are
the baby killers. You are acting like a crazy person again.
Look around you. Do you see what a sane person would
see?" Jeremy asked through diabolical laughter.

Adam moved his eyes furtively around the apartment.
Every corner was filled with demons. A wild boar peered
from under his bed. The refrigerator inched forward to
attack.

Jeremy's voice changed again to that of a blameless
child. "You're not well, Daddy. I'll help you to see things
clearly again."

Adam's head exploded in agony. He writhed uncon-
trollably on the floor, unaware of anything but the excru-
ciating pain. He fainted.

When the janitor regained consciousness, the shadow
child was there to help him feel better and to help him
understand.

Thank God for my sweet Jeremy, Adam thought as he
sat on the bed, fingering the gold earring. He had had a
close call earlier and had almost drifted back into the
depths of madness. Fortunately his son had been there to
save him. He rolled the earring around the palm of his
hand. The Ann woman was a sinner, like Sister Mary
Xavier and Marie. He had seen her rolling and thrashing
around the floor, tempting that man, making him miss
his baby's birthday party. She was no better than a com-
mon slut. Now she planned to be really bad. She was a
baby killer. Jeremy had shown him. Jeremy was right.
She had to be punished, as he had punished Marie. Ma-

rie's blue scarf lay over his knee. He had to do it. He had to make the world good enough for Laura Bernhardt. The baby killer couldn't stay in the same city with Miss Laura.

Jeremy had made his headache go away. Then he had shown him Sister Mary Xavier. Adam grinned. He didn't have to worry about the nun ever again. He saw her in the television hanging from a rope in her room. He watched her swinging there. Her face was blue. Her eyes bugged out. Her mouth hung open and she had soiled herself. At first he felt sick at the sight, but Jeremy explained that the nun had known she was bad and had punished herself.

There was a time, when Jeremy was young, when he had thought Sister Mary Xavier was the purest of all women. He had seen her aloofness as superiority, and the stories that circulated about her at the orphanage added to her mystery. The children whispered that she had actually helped a priest with an exorcism. Only the most holy of women could do such a thing without being contaminated herself.

Sister Mary Xavier was dead now, but not all the women would punish themselves. The baby killers kept on living.

Tonight Jeremy had shown him the Ann woman at the baby-killing place. It wasn't like the place Marie had gone. Women walked into a shiny building, as bold as they could be, to kill the babies. Some of them smiled and talked to their friends while they waited. Adam hadn't known there was a special baby-killing place before Jeremy showed it to him. Jeremy said the police didn't do anything to stop it. He said it was perfectly legal for women to kill the babies. Jeremy said that was why he had to punish the Ann woman. It made sense. The baby killers must have been why Miss Laura was so upset when she came out of the sergeant's office today. She probably found out about the baby-killing place and wanted the sergeant to stop them. She couldn't rely on Binder to help her, but she could count on him, Adam Smith.

He rubbed his temples and carefully put the earring in

the shoe box with Sister Mary Xavier's ring. The pain in
his head throbbed dully while he put on his coat and
stuffed Marie's scarf in his pocket. At ten-thirty P.M. he
walked through his door for the short walk to the park.

Rhonda Hackman woke up screaming from a nightmare. At first she was disoriented by her strange surroundings; then she remembered. She had been frightened at the hospital. Someone or something was out to
get her and she had to escape. She barely remembered
rushing back to her apartment and putting her few belongings into her suitcase and leaving without telling anyone where she was going. The medication they had given
her at the hospital had dulled her senses, but it hadn't
eliminated the pain. It was all she could do to carry the
suitcase. Her ribs and lungs were on fire with the pain,
but she knew, as surely as she had known that Laura
Bernhardt was going to walk into her room that day at
the hospital, that she was now being stalked by a killer.
She had wandered through the streets not knowing where
to hide. Finally the pain was so bad she had to stop. Her
new furnished room on the bottom floor of the Arms
Apartments was hideous but cheap. She struggled out of
bed to close her curtains and block out the neon lights
from the bar across the street.

The pain from her injuries was barely tolerable, but she
was more upset by the dream. She was soaked in sweat
and she sobbed quietly. It had started. The lid on one of
the coffins had slammed shut.

23

Thursday, January 31
They know, Adam thought as he walked down the city
street. His eyes darted nervously at the people he passed.
His arms were tight across his chest, his gloved hands
squeezing the opposite arms as though in a protective
self-embrace.

When he woke up, he remembered little of the night before. He recalled walking home from work, then having a nightmare. Jeremy was mad at him and his head hurt. He dreamed he was crouched in a tree at the park. A woman came and he dreamed he jumped on her and strangled her with Marie's scarf. She was so startled, she didn't even struggle. There had been a look of surprise in her eyes before they became blank and unseeing.

Then he heard the morning news on the television. It had not been a dream. He had killed that woman, the Ann from the television.

A half block from the precinct he noticed the cars. The parking lot was filled with them. Strange people were walking into the precinct, official-looking people. He stopped dead in his tracks. Adam's heart was pounding. His palms were sweaty.

Run, he heard an internal voice tell him. They are after you.

He couldn't run. His feet were rooted to the sidewalk.

There was no escape. He had been bad again. A lifetime of experience told him there was no avoiding the punishment. If he ran, they would track him down like a wild animal.

Adam picked up his leg to move it forward. It was lead weight. He inched toward the precinct house. His body seemed caught in slow motion while his heart fluttered weakly.

"Freeze!"

He heard the command from all directions as guns were pulled and pointed toward him. He stood dead-still and opened his eyes. Everyone was ignoring him, as usual. He had only imagined the voices and the guns.

Chaos was reigning in the building. Strange people milled in groups. Voices were louder than usual. Adam stuffed his hands into his pockets so his shaking would not betray him.

"Police are investigating the murder of a thirty-year-old woman at Mid-City Park last night," the announcer said. Laura turned up the volume on Danny Dodge's radio so she wouldn't miss anything. In her mind she heard the coffin slam shut from her nightmare the night before.

"It couldn't be related to my dream," she said aloud, as though the sound of her voice would help to convince her.

"An official spokesman has set the time of death at somewhere between ten P.M. and midnight," the announcer continued.

Laura shuddered. She had wakened with the nightmare at exactly three minutes after eleven. She had been so badly frightened that she got up and watched the late movie on television.

"At this time no one knows why the woman was at the park, which apparently is several miles from her home. The victim's name is being withheld pending notification of relatives."

Laura's first thought was of Rhonda Hackman, but Rhonda was only in her early twenties. When she pulled into the parking lot of the precinct, she got the last parking spot and wondered who the additional cars belonged to.

"Hey, what's going on around here?" she asked Bob Clark after she had entered through the doors of the precinct house to find an unaccustomed crowd. Some were strangers and some she knew as detectives from downtown.

"Didn't you hear about the murder last night?"

"I just picked up something about it on the radio."

"The investigation is going to be handled from here because the contractor is removing asbestos from the homicide division downtown."

"Bernhardt," Binder shouted from his office, "get in here."

"Yes, sir," Laura said, walking toward him.

"Effective immediately, you are on special assignment to the Homicide Division. There's a meeting in the conference room in five minutes. I've reassigned your other cases." He turned and walked off in his usual abrupt style.

Laura stood in the hall in a state of semishock. A few weeks ago she would have been thrilled at the chance to

work on a murder investigation. If she did well, it could
be the break she had been waiting for in her career. She
still was interested in her advancement, but now she had
a more personal stake in the case. For the first time she
was certain she wasn't having a breakdown as Darryl
suspected. She must be experiencing some kind of precognition.

At first she was astonished that Binder had assigned
her to the case. Maybe her stubbornness had paid off. As
he'd said yesterday, he was anxious to get her off his back
for a while. Then she realized that with the events of the
past two or three weeks, it was inevitable she would be
involved in the investigation. She grabbed her coffee and
nervously headed for the meeting.

"Good morning, Adam," she said absently as she
passed the janitor.

Most of the detectives in the conference room were
from the downtown Homicide Division, but Laura was
glad to see that Bob Clark was going to be working on
the case, as well as José Martínez. She grimaced when
Harry Winchell walked in as though it were his personal
case.

Murders certainly weren't unusual in the city, but it
was a break for Laura to be involved in the investigation,
and her intuition and her bizarre experiences of the past
few weeks told her this case was not going to fall into one
of the more routine categories of murder by a family
member or lover.

Laura noted with surprise that the chief of detectives
himself was heading the meeting.

"The victim's name is Ann Locke," Patrick MacNamara said to the gathered detectives. "A jogger found her
by the ball diamond at the Mid-City Park at five-thirty
A.M. Her vehicle was found locked in the parking lot at
Twenty-eighth Street and Parkway Boulevard. She had
been strangled with an unknown object. Robbery was not
the motive. Her purse was found intact next to her."

The hairs on Laura's arms were standing on end and a
barely perceptible line of perspiration had formed above
her upper lip. Again she heard the thud of the coffin
slamming shut in her dream.

"The area has been sealed and a team of investigators is currently at the scene," MacNamara continued. "According to her driver's license she lived five miles from the park. Besides approximately seven dollars, she had a few credit cards, an electric bill, and an unemployment card in her purse, plus the usual makeup and keys."

Why? Laura wondered. What motivated that woman to drive five miles to one of the most dangerous parks in the city at that time of night. If she could figure it out, maybe she could end the unreal quality that was engulfing her own life.

An hour later Laura and her old partner Harry Winchell entered the victim's apartment. The police photographer, José, took pictures of Ann Locke's apartment while Laura and Harry looked around. Laura noted the apartment was perfectly neat, as though she had just cleaned it for company. There definitely was no sign of a struggle.

"Look at this, Harry," Laura said. A bottle of champagne sat on the dining-room table in a bucket of melted ice. Two clean glasses sat beside it. "It looks like Miss Locke was expecting company."

Laura found only women's clothing in the closets, but there were two toothbrushes in the bathroom, and a man's electric razor. They searched the apartment thoroughly but found no sign of drugs. Laura confiscated an address book. Maybe one of the woman's friends would be able to give them a clue.

While Harry finished examining the apartment and Martínez took more pictures, Laura went across the hall to the return address on the electric bill found in Ann's purse.

"Come on in. The door's unlocked," a woman yelled from the apartment when Laura knocked. She knocked again.

"Did you sleep in this morning?" a woman asked as she opened the door, then looked at Laura in surprise. "Oh, I'm sorry. I thought you were my friend. May I help you?" She saw the electric bill envelope in Laura's hand and looked at it quizzically. "What's going on?

That's my electric payment. I gave it to my friend to mail yesterday. Who are you?"

"I'm Detective Bernhardt with the police department. May I come in for a minute?" She showed Susie Price her identification.

Susie sat at the kitchen table, crying. "I still can't believe it. Ann dead? It isn't possible." She shakily lit a cigarette while Laura looked at her kindly.

"Can you think of anyone who would want to kill your friend?" Laura asked.

"No one." Susie hiccuped. "Ann didn't have an enemy in the world. Everyone liked her. There must be some mistake." She began to sob. "Any minute now Ann is going to walk through the door and we'll all have a big laugh. Maybe someone stole her purse. It couldn't have been Ann." Susie lit a cigarette, stubbed it out, then lit another.

"The victim matched the picture and description on her driver's license," Laura said gently. "We checked her apartment. It appears she hasn't been home since yesterday. Do you know if Ann was expecting company last night?"

"I'm certain she wasn't expecting anyone. I was over there around eight last night and got her out of bed. She had been feeling kind of depressed, and she specifically said she wasn't even going to answer the telephone. She was going to lie in bed and eat peanuts and she wasn't even going to bother to put the dishes in the dishwasher or pick her dirty clothes up off the floor," Susie said as she paced the kitchen.

"Mrs. Price, when we checked her apartment, it looked like she had just cleaned it. The bed was neatly made and there was a pair of sheets in the top of the clothes hamper, like she had changed them before she went out. There wasn't a peanut jar by the bed. The dishes were washed, and there was a bottle of champagne sitting in a bucket of melted ice with two clean glasses next to it. Can you think of any reason your friend would lie to you about her plans?"

"This is crazy. I don't believe you. I was there. I talked to her. I saw her in her old flannel nightgown. She had a

handful of peanuts. She offered me some. I walked into
the kitchen and got myself a beer. The dinner dishes were
lying on the counter. Ann never did care about a clean
house. She was extremely relaxed about housework.
When I went to the bathroom, I saw the bed unmade.
She had been reading before I came over. When I left, she
was walking down the hall to go back to bed again. I
didn't hear her go out later." She absentmindedly filled
the tea kettle and lit the stove, then burst into tears.

"Apparently after you left, she got up, cleaned the
apartment, changed the sheets, got dressed, set a bottle of
champagne in a bucket of ice, and drove to the Mid-City
Park."

"That's impossible. She wouldn't have done that," Susie said firmly. She stopped suddenly as though preoccu-
pied by a mental picture. "Michael," she whispered suspiciously.

"Michael? Was that her boyfriend?"

"It couldn't be Michael," Susie said. "He is in Seattle."

"Maybe you'd better tell me about this Michael."

Susie looked at the detective doubtfully.

"Mrs. Price, your friend has been murdered. If you
know anything at all, it could help us find her killer."

Through her tears Susie told Laura about Ann's boss
and the upcoming abortion.

"Could she have had a date with another man?"

"I'm sure she didn't. She was bitter about Michael."

"One more question, Mrs. Price. Did Ann ever do any
drugs?"

"Never," Susie said. "She hated them."

"People change, and she was under a strain. If she was
picking up drugs, it could explain why she was in the
park."

"Ann Locke was my best friend for ten years. I don't
know why she was in the park, but I assure you it was
not to get drugs."

Susie gave Laura Ann's parents' names and address, as
well as the names of a few other close friends.

"Thank you for the information, Mrs. Price. We'll contact Ann's parents," she said as she pulled on her coat.

"If you think of anything else that might shed light on the case, please call me."

The case didn't make any more sense to Laura than it did to the victim's friend. The fingerprint crew would check Ann's apartment. It was possible she'd been killed there and the killer cleaned up afterward to get rid of the evidence, but Laura didn't think so. Over and over she heard the dull thud of the coffin closing in her dream. There was something wrong in the city. Someone, or something, evil had been unleashed. Her fears for Rhonda increased. At the door of Susie's apartment Laura turned back and on impulse asked, "Mrs. Price, did Ann mention anything about bad dreams lately?" Only a fraction of a second passed between the question and the answer, but to Laura time seemed suspended in slow motion. It was a silly question. The woman probably thought she had lost her mind, but she feared the answer.

"Why, yes. She was quite upset by them. She kept dreaming about a row of coffins."

24

Friday, February 1
"Someone must have seen something. There is no such thing as a perfect murder. If you people step up your interviews, you're bound to turn up a lead."

Adam heard Chief MacNamara's voice drifting down the hall. He was mopping as close to the door as possible so he could hear the detectives' conference. They had found the Ann woman's body yesterday. He gave a shaky sigh of relief as he listened. They apparently did not have any clues.

"The only good lead we have is Michael Statler," Adam heard MacNamara say.

"I've checked it out, Chief. We've confirmed that he was in Seattle at the time of the murder," Laura said. "So far he is the only person with a motive. We've checked

with her friends and family. They all say the same thing,
that Ann Locke was well liked by everyone and that she
never did drugs."

"Well, someone sure didn't like her," MacNamara retorted. "And as far as the drugs go, we'll know more
when the autopsy report is complete. She wouldn't be the
first person who fooled her family and friends."

"Michael Statler's alibi seems a little too pat for me,"
Bob Clark said. "What did the detective say who talked
to him in Seattle?"

"He reported that Statler appeared genuinely surprised
by Locke's murder. He also was very nervous that his
wife might find out he was having an affair with her,"
Laura said.

"I bet he was," Winchell piped in.

"His plane ticket confirmed he was in Seattle at the
time of the murder," Laura added.

"Could he have flown back here, murdered Locke,
then made it back to Seattle before he was missed?" Mac-
Namara asked.

"No way, and the Seattle Police Department confirmed through dozens of witnesses Statler's whereabouts
on January thirtieth," Clark said. "Their cooperation has
been very helpful."

Adam remained in the hall, mopping vigorously.

"I still want Statler's bank account checked, his personal and his business accounts. I wouldn't be at all surprised if he withdrew a large sum of money recently. He
might have hired a hit man to get rid of a talkative lover.
Maybe she was threatening to go to his wife. Clark, take
care of it. Bernhardt, you go have a talk with Statler's
new secretary. I want to know every person he talked to
during the past two weeks. Winchell, see what you can
find out about Susie Price. We only have her word that
she and Locke were best of buddies and that Locke
planned to stay at home the night she was murdered.
Jealous and angry friends have been known to commit
murders, and the lab says the fibers around Locke's neck
could have come from a woman's scarf. What did the lab
say about fingerprints at her apartment?"

"They found nothing to indicate that anyone had tried

to remove fingerprints or that anyone other than Locke had cleaned the apartment on the thirtieth. Her fingerprints were on the vacuum and the other cleaning supplies," Laura said.

"Were there any signs of fibers in the apartment that could be matched with the murder weapon?" MacNamara asked.

Adam jerked at the reference to the scarf. He would have to keep it well hidden. He looked nervously at the secretary who walked by him into the conference room. Did she notice that he was hanging around? Was she going to report him? He listened carefully but could not hear what she was whispering to the chief. He moved his mop closer to the door and glanced inside furtively, then quickly carried his mop bucket to the men's rest room. He had to get away from the detectives. He couldn't take a chance of them noticing him in the hall.

He began to calm down while he cleaned the bathroom windows. There's no reason for me to be nervous, he thought. He smiled slightly. Jeremy told me they would never think of me, and he was right. Why should they? They don't know about Jeremy and the television. Besides, the Ann woman deserved to be punished. Jeremy showed me. She was going to kill her baby.

His genitals stirred when he remembered the things he had seen her do with the man in the television. His lips curled with satisfaction at the memory of the scarf pulled tight around her neck. Too bad she didn't struggle more, he thought.

It didn't occur to Adam to wonder how Jeremy got Ann Locke to come to the park. Jeremy was all-powerful. Adam wanted to be enfolded in his apartment and watch more women on the television.

I only watch them so I will know which ones are evil, so I can make the world good enough for Miss Laura, he thought piously, but he licked his lips as he thought of their erect nipples and their moans as they thrust to meet the men they taunted with their bodies.

They are evil sinners, Adam thought as he cleaned the mirrors. They need to be punished. Maybe they will struggle more than the Ann woman.

He caught his reflection in the mirror and started, as though out of a hypnotic state. His retinas were small and bright, like the television eye when it went off at night. He felt as if he were looking at a stranger, and that the stranger was planting the bad thoughts in his head. He stood looking at his reflection. It was his face, but it couldn't be his thoughts coming from his head.

Suddenly the memory of Ann Locke at the park came flooding back, but he saw it from the perspective of the old Adam Smith, a man who could never intentionally hurt anyone.

What have I done? he wondered in horror. He remembered his satisfaction when he killed that woman, but it was like seeing inside someone else's head. I don't want to punish anyone, even if they are bad. I'm not a murderer. What happened to Marie was an accident. I loved her.

Then he thought about Jeremy and could hear the boy's words in his head, telling him he had to punish the baby killers, that he was the only one who could do it— who would do it.

Mixed in with Jeremy's words was an image of Marie begging for his help and the nuns at the orphanage warning him what happened to sinners.

If I do what Jeremy wants, I'm bad. If I don't do what he wants, I'm bad.

I'm bad.

I'm bad.

I'm bad.

Bad people must be punished.

Adam knew what he must do.

25

"Up, up I go, and where I stop, nobody knows," Jeremy sang as he swung higher. Jeremy was feeling wonderful. Adam's anger and the Ann woman's fear had been the best meal he had absorbed since the master created him for the daddy person. The master was feeling well fed, too, and pleased with Jeremy's progress in bringing Adam to him.

Jeremy was ready for the daddy person to come home so they could play more games.

"Daddy shouldn't keep me waiting. I don't like to play alone. Daddy is being naughty. He is being naughtier than he has been since he tried to break the television. He promised he wouldn't be bad anymore, but he lied. Shame on Daddy." His eyes squinted in petulant anger. Adam was defying him, and Jeremy liked to get his own way. He insisted on it.

"You shouldn't get that gun, Daddy," Jeremy said. "It's dangerous to play with guns. Isn't that what good daddies say to their sons? Well, good sons must keep their daddies from playing with guns too. I'm a very good son, an excellent boy. I'll keep the daddy person from playing with the gun. If daddy hurts himself, I won't have any fun. I won't have anyone to play with. Daddy promised he would never leave me. Now he is at a pawnshop buying a gun so he can kill himself. That would make me very angry; and that would make the master very, very angry."

Jeremy laughed and slowed the swing. "I'll have to punish daddy when he gets home. He wants to be punished. He doesn't really want to die. Silly daddy. He doesn't know what he wants. He's lucky to have me to help him. He's going to bring the gun right back here. If he really wanted to kill himself, he wouldn't do that. He knows I won't let him leave me until he's ready to join the master.

"I'm bored. I've been alone all day with no one to play with. When Daddy comes home, I'll play a game with him. I'll play a punish-Daddy game."

The round eye had been ominously still since Adam made his way up the shadowy fire escape. Now he sat caressing the gun. Six bullets waited in front of him in a neat row. He looked anxiously at the silent television but eventually turned his full attention to the gun and bullets.

The television remained blank.

One by one Adam loaded the bullets into the gun until every chamber was filled. He wondered if the women the television showed him were as evil as he. He decided it didn't matter anymore. He tried to think of what it would be like in hell, but the images eluded him. He tried to visualize his life continuing, getting up in the morning each day and going to work, going by the school to see the children, coming home to the apartment. There used to be a certain amount of comfort in the sameness of his life, but that had changed. When he went to work, he was terrified of being discovered. The precinct had always been crowded and hectic, but he had been able to fade into the surroundings. Now the people were elbow to elbow. Worse, they were all looking for him. Soon they would know. All those homicide detectives couldn't be fooled for long. Miss Laura was looking for him too. What would she think of him when she found out, after she had been kind to him?

She'll hate me. I couldn't stand for her to hate me, he thought.

The television remained lifeless.

He used to enjoy seeing the children, but since the night he punished Ann Locke, when he walked through the streets to see them, he felt as if his thoughts were transparent and everyone knew his guilt.

Other things had changed about seeing the children. It used to be his special time. Now he was constantly aware of the little girls. He hated them because of their power. They must be born with that power, Adam thought.

Then there was his apartment, Jeremy, and the television.

"My Jeremy," Adam whispered sadly. Sometimes the boy was a comfort to him. Other times he was afraid of him. The ache in Adam's head was more constant than ever from wondering what Jeremy would show him next in the television.

He looked at the TV and wondered what Jeremy looked like and why he always saw only his shadow. His back stiffened in fear, though he didn't understand why. He only knew the idea of the shadow child suddenly springing into his apartment was more terrifying than the homicide detectives, or even hell.

His legs were asleep and tingling from sitting perfectly still and cross-legged for too long. The gun felt heavy in his hand. He put the barrel in his mouth and closed his lips around the cool metal. He angled the barrel of the gun upward, toward the top of his head, and prayed for the first time since he had left the orphanage. He entreated God to forgive him. He continued his prayer at length, asking forgiveness for every bad thought and deed he could think of that he had committed. He prayed in order to delay pulling the trigger.

He jumped at the sound of static in the television and held the gun more firmly in his mouth. Jeremy was going to be furious with him. He had to decide immediately whether to face Jeremy or God.

He chose God.

He squeezed his eyes tightly closed . . . and pulled the trigger.

There was no explosion from the gun.

There was no gun.

Adam was holding a lollipop in his mouth.

He gasped and pulled the candy from his mouth and looked at it in disbelief, his tastebuds stinging from the mixture of sweet cherry and the sour contents of his stomach. He dropped the candy, which stuck to the fuzz on the blanket.

In the television Jeremy's shadow loomed large, frightfully near in three dimensions, as the swing moved toward Adam's bed. The child's voice rang clear and sweet from the speakers, as any other child's might, as he sang "On the Good Ship Lollipop."

Adam's mouth formed the word *no,* but only a squeak escaped. Again he formed a *no.* This time it came out as a wail, one long syllable that he wasn't aware of beginning and that he didn't know how to end.

The shadow shrank long and narrow into the recesses of the television as the swing made its pendulum movement backward, only too quickly to swing toward the room while Jeremy continued to sing the children's song.

Each time the swing came forward, it inched out of the

glass, casting its shadow across Adam's bed. Still, the child could not be seen, but the shadow moved across Adam's legs as cold as dry ice. He tried to jump from the bed, but his legs had lost all feeling from sitting in the awkward position. He rolled onto the floor to escape, crying from the pain when he stretched his legs.

"Please, Jeremy, stop," Adam begged, but Jeremy continued to sing.

The swing came forward again and half filled the apartment while Adam crawled across the floor to escape a cold so intense, it burned his skin.

"God, please save me," Adam cried. "Forgive me. Take me now." He pulled himself to his feet, his legs like pincushions, and took a couple of steps before he collapsed. His heart beat so rapidly, he felt it would explode from his chest.

The shadow filled the entire apartment, coating it with a thick layer of frost as Adam managed to escape into the tiny bathroom and slam the door.

He leaned over the sink, gasping for air, his bronchial tubes so constricted that, painfully, he was able to suck in barely enough air to keep from suffocating. His breathing was loud, but not loud enough to drown out Jeremy's song from the adjoining room. Adam was covered with perspiration from the effort of breathing and fell against the door. The intense cold, like metal in the arctic, jolted him forward, ripping the back of his shirt as he pulled himself free.

Desperate now, he reached for the door of the medicine cabinet and pulled out a new package of single-edge razor blades. They dropped from his shaking hands, and he had to try several times to pick them up. Jeremy's song didn't sound as if it were coming from the television twelve feet away. It had moved closer. It was right outside the bathroom door. Adam fumbled frantically with the secure wrapping on the razor blades. He finally was able to open the package, and dropped it in the sink when he heard the doorknob to the bathroom start to turn. He fumbled for the bolt, his hands unable to accomplish the simple movement.

The bathroom knob was turning slowly. On the other

side Jeremy was singing with a cheerfulness that chilled Adam more than the physical blast of cold from the expanding shadow.

With one last effort he jerked the bolt. It broke free and slid into place with a click. Only then was he aware of the pain in his fingers as he tried to move them from the lock. They were frozen to it. He jerked them away, leaving behind the top layer of skin from his fingertips.

He sat back on the stool and sobbed, his heart continuing to flutter uncertainly, but mercifully refusing to stop beating. Outside, Jeremy's song was changing to an eerie minor key while the doorknob turned back and forth determinedly.

There was only one door to the bathroom and no windows. Adam's only hope of escape was to use one of the razor blades in the sink. He reached into the sink, and he sobbed. It was filled with chocolate bars.

Outside the door Jeremy taunted him with his singing.

Adam didn't remember passing out. When he came to he was huddled at the back of the shower. He listened carefully. There were no sounds from the apartment. As quietly as possible he got out of the shower and stood by the bathroom door, holding his breath while he listened.

Nothing.

He stood in the bathroom for what seemed like hours before he gingerly touched the door. It was no longer cold. Slowly he pulled back the bolt and turned the knob. He opened the door hesitantly, still listening, and walked into the room. His eyes clouded with fear when he saw Jeremy's shadow swinging gently in the television.

"Say thank you, Daddy. You must always say thank you when someone gives you candy. Isn't that right? Didn't you like the lollipop and the chocolate, Daddy? I like them. I like them better than peanuts and popcorn. Don't you?"

Adam was beyond fear. His eyes started to go blank as he retreated into the safety of madness, until Jeremy said, "Candy is sweet, like Laura Bernhardt. Do you want to see what happens to sweet Laura when you are bad?"

"Run, Laura. Run, my love," Adam screamed when he saw Laura Bernhardt's image spring onto the screen. She was sitting in a restaurant, smiling at the person across from her. Smiling at Adam.

She continued eating dinner and talking. He couldn't hear what she was saying. Why didn't she listen to him? She had to escape.

"Run, Laura! Run, my love!"

Darryl jerked his head in the direction of the voice. No one seemed to notice the screamed warning but him. Laura and the other patrons of the restaurant were enjoying their dinners.

Run, my love!

His emotions were a jumbled mass of jealousy, confusion, and disbelief. Someone was calling out to his wife, and he was the only person hearing it.

"Darryl, what's the matter, sweetheart?"

Run, Laura love!

Darryl could feel the electricity growing in the air around them. The warning was real. They had to get out, now. He bolted from his chair and grabbed Laura, yanking her roughly to her feet.

"Move," he yelled, pushing her in the direction of the door. Laura looked at him as if he were crazy. The other patrons moved quietly out of his way. "Run, Laura," he screamed, grabbing her hand and pulling her behind him as he rushed to the exit.

"What's wrong?"

"We've got to get out of here."

The electricity in the air was growing stronger. Other people felt it and began bolting for the exit. They were screaming and falling in their desperate attempts to flee.

Darryl held tight to Laura's arm and propelled her forcibly toward the door. He heard thunder and nearly lost his balance when a series of lightning bolts struck.

Flames engulfed the restaurant, quickly catching the bamboo chairs and paper lanterns. People were screaming and running in panic. In front of them a woman's hair was on fire. Laura threw her coat over the woman's head and extinguished the flame while Darryl fought to keep them from being trampled. He pulled the three of them through the door and to safety.

Darryl and Laura stood in the parking lot, holding each other and watching the inferno. They heard screams from within the restaurant until the sound of sirens filled the air.

The brief storm that wrought its destruction on the restaurant consolidated in Adam's head. Tiny lightning bolts struck behind his eyes. He clutched his temples and his mouth stretched in a silent scream.

In the television the shadow moved on the swing. "Poor Daddy doesn't feel well. You'll feel better tomorrow. Then we can play another game."

26

Saturday, February 2

The autopsy report on Ann Locke confirmed she was pregnant at the time of her death. There were no drugs in her system, which made it unlikely she was at the park for a drug deal. They were continuing to check out leads, but each one brought them to a dead end.

Laura didn't mind the weekend shift. She was more determined than ever to solve the Locke case, and she appreciated the relative peace and quiet of the precinct on Saturday. Working also helped keep her mind off the pain of her burns. The doctor had offered to prescribe pain pills, but she didn't want to dull her reasoning processes. She already was tired after waiting half the night at the emergency room.

Despite the horror of the evening before, she couldn't think of a time she and Darryl had felt closer.

God, I was frightened, she thought. I was sure we would be trampled. If Darryl hadn't headed us for the door before the lightning struck, we would have been killed. A lot more people would have been killed if it hadn't been for his warning.

She gave a puzzled frown when she thought about Darryl's explanation. He said he'd heard thunder, then felt a buildup of energy that reminded him of the way he had felt in Vietnam before lightning struck his building. She put the doubts from her mind. She was grateful they were alive.

The poor people who died, she thought. I'm going to live with their agonized screams, and the smell, for the rest of my life. Thank you, God, for not letting Darryl be hurt badly. His shoulder and leg may have a few scars, but that is nothing.

She shuddered at how close they had come to being among the casualties. Twenty people had died, the biggest fire disaster in the city's history.

The primary topic of conversation around the precinct was the freak electrical storm. In fact, it was the talk of the town. Laura had been bombarded with questions since she came in with her hands in bandages. The doctor said she would be fine in a few days. The bandages were mainly to decrease the chance of infection.

"I hear they are calling in meteorologists from around the country," Fred Phelps said, eyeing Laura's bandages sympathetically. "Those storms are weird. That's the third one in less than a month. My wife is totally freaked out by them. I guess everyone is. What did you think when lightning hit the restaurant?"

"I don't know. I really don't remember."

"You're taking this coolly. I'd think you would be jumpy today after being in that fire. What a way to die. Those poor people."

"Yeah," Laura said. In her mind's eye she heard the screaming and smelled the charred flesh. She saw the woman's hair go up in flames, and herself and Darryl pushing through the crowd.

"They said the restaurant was hit five times," Fred said authoritatively. "I've never heard of lightning doing that before. You know the old saying, it never strikes twice in the same place."

"Excuse me, Fred. I've got some work to do."

"Oh, sure. Was I being a clod? You seemed so under control, I didn't think it would bother you to talk about it. My wife says that sometimes it takes a couple of minutes for my brain to catch up with my mouth. I didn't even think about what it must have been like for you to be there and see those people burning up. My wife thinks it's the Russians."

"What?"

"The Russians. She thinks the Russians are experimenting with weather control. What do you think about the way the sky fills up with lightning without a cloud in sight? Have you ever seen anything like it?"

"I don't know. Excuse me." As she walked away, she heard him discussing his theory with Harry.

Laura lied when she told Fred she hadn't given the storms much thought, but she didn't believe any of the theories that people were discussing: Russians, sunspots, a change in weather patterns resulting from aerosol sprays deteriorating the ozone.

Everyone in the city has seen at least one of those storms; everyone but me, that is. Every time they happen, I'm involved in some new terror.

27

The cathedral ceilings and marble staircases at the art museum made Martha feel as if she were in a palace. This was her third afternoon of exploring the massive building, and she finally had seen most of the exhibits. She was awed by the talent: Rembrandt, Michelangelo, Picasso, Van Gogh, El Greco, and so many other famous names, her head was spinning with them.

Her abortion was still four days away and she was fighting a growing sense of depression. She felt there was no world in which she fit, neither Taylorsville with Harold and her children nor the city that she had dreamed about for years. She couldn't help contrast the little paintings she had been proud of completing in high school to the work of the great masters, and she felt silly for ever considering she could be a real artist. She also couldn't help but compare Harold and herself to the men and women she had watched almost as carefully as she

examined the paintings. The people were so different
from her family and friends in Taylorsville, she felt she
had ventured into a foreign country, not just a city 150
miles from home.

Martha sat on one of the benches to rest her feet and
give her stomach a chance to calm down. Her morning
sickness had stretched into the afternoon. She also was
suffering from a lack of sleep.

A woman who was so beautiful, Martha thought she
should be in one of the paintings stopped in front of a
painting near her. Her clothes reminded Martha of the
ones she looked at in *Vogue* while waiting in the checkout
line at the supermarket. Even her hair was perfect.
Martha pulled her old coat closer around her to hide the
old-fashioned dress she had made when Harold junior
was a baby. She kept planning to make herself a couple of
new dresses, but the kids always needed something and
month by month she put off her own needs until the
months turned into years.

"I really don't think it was one of his better periods,"
Martha heard the woman's companion say. She was with
a man who also looked as if he had stepped off the cover
of a magazine. "Compare the colors and strokes of this
work to the subtlety of his earlier paintings."

"I think you are missing the point, darling. Here he
has achieved an existential realism. It isn't a lack of subtlety, it is a boldness of spirit."

Martha tried to imagine having such a conversation
with Harold. The sharing of ideas was what she missed
most in her marriage. If she could force Harold into a
museum, she knew he would walk sullenly ten steps behind her, and if she pressed for an opinion on a painting,
she would be lucky to get a response at all. His standard
answer for anything besides the price of grain and football was "It's okay, I guess." She sometimes thought she
could have a more meaningful conversation with a brick
wall. But what was her option? She didn't fit in with the
people she had seen in the city any more than Harold did.
If ever there had been a chance that she could have, it
was gone.

As the man and woman walked away arm in arm,

Martha looked enviously at the woman's slim figure. You can tell she hasn't lived through four pregnancies, she thought, not to mention too many meals of macaroni and potatoes. Poverty may not broaden your mind, but it sure spreads your backside.

She sat staring intently at one of the paintings, but what she was seeing was herself as she might have been with the man she might have married.

When the lights blinked on and off twice, she knew it was almost five and the museum would close in a few minutes. Her first reaction was panic. She felt safe here among the art. It was different on the streets. The sense of foreboding that had plagued her since the middle of January had grown when she came to the city, and the freak electrical storm the night before really set her on edge. As a devout Catholic she didn't doubt there were evil forces afoot in the world, but they were only concepts to her. She never had any direct contact with them, though she knew a couple of people who claimed to have seen spirits. That was different. It was like kids telling ghost stories. Now, for the first time in her life, she believed with all her soul and intuition that she was on the verge of coming face-to-face with an unfriendly supernatural power.

Martha walked reluctantly toward the exit, dreading the shadowy walk back to her room. In front of her was the couple she had seen earlier. Martha was shocked that they were arguing. She had imagined that their relationship was perfect.

"If you are worried about the living room, paint it yourself," the man was saying.

"It wouldn't hurt you to help. If we both work on it, we can finish it in a couple of hours tomorrow. If I have to do it myself, it will take all day."

"I don't need you to organize and direct my weekends, Brenda. Get off my back."

"I don't need to wait on you hand and foot either. You like to have a nice home, but you aren't willing to lift a finger to make it that way. I bring in half the money, but when was the last time you washed a dish or put a load of laundry in the washing machine?"

Martha hurried by the couple and out of earshot. She
was embarrassed by their public display. She had thought
that people who wore expensive clothes and talked
knowledgeably about art had class. She realized now she
was wrong. Her picture of their homelife had been of
champagne in front of a fireplace. She hadn't even considered that the well-coiffured woman worried about
coming home after a day at work and doing the cooking,
cleaning, and laundry.

Harold would never talk to me that way in public,
Martha thought as she walked down the stairs to the
main level of the museum. She never even had to mention
household repairs to Harold. He automatically fixed the
things that broke and painted when they could afford the
paint.

She hesitated at the exit, afraid to walk out into the
growing darkness. She resolutely pushed through the
door, pretending Harold was with her. She couldn't remember ever feeling anything less than totally safe when
she was with her quiet husband.

Her eyes darted from side to side as she hurried down
the street. There were more people on the sidewalks than
she saw in a month at home, but she felt alone and ex-
posed. Something lurked in the shadows of these streets,
and it knew her name. It caused storms to brew from
nothing and filled her nights with dreams that left her
covered in a cold sweat. She didn't realize that her
breathing was shallow and jerky until she reached the
YWCA and inhaled deeply.

With the door of her room securely bolted Martha finally calmed down and slowly ate the bread she had
saved for dinner. She smiled as she thought about the day
Harold brought her home from the hospital with Sandy.
She had been surprised and confused when they came in
the driveway and one whole end of it was filled with large
rocks and fill dirt.

"I figured I'd build some flower gardens," Harold had
said.

Martha had known the flower beds were for her. Harold couldn't care less about flowers. He had so much
other work to do after he got off at the mill, he didn't

have much time to work on the flower garden, but every day for several months he devoted an hour to placing rocks and hauling the fill dirt until finally Martha had the prettiest flower garden in all of Taylorsville.

How shallow the man at the museum is in comparison, she thought.

She turned out the light and hugged her pillow, wishing it were her husband. She clung to her thoughts of Harold, but as she drifted into a fitful sleep, *it* took over. *It* was stronger and nearer, and *it* wanted her.

28

Sunday, February 3

The refrains of an organ and choir singing a familiar hymn punctured Rhonda's dream enough to admit the outside world into her subconscious. She was ten years old and had fallen asleep in church. Now the congregation would watch while her father punished her.

"No, Father, please don't. I won't fall asleep again. I promise," she pleaded, but he had her by the hair and was dragging her to a boiling pit. She jerked awake and discovered she was in the Arms Apartments. The choir continued to sing from her clock radio as she looked around to get her bearings. The impression of a child on a swing flashed across her subconscious, then was lost in the pain from her broken ribs.

Rhonda tried to shake her feeling of disorientation. Why are they playing church hymns? she wondered. Isn't it Friday? When I went to sleep, it was Thursday. I was out of food and thought I'd have to go to the store when I woke up.

She looked at the clock. It was noon, and there was a gnawing hunger in her stomach. She struggled from the bed and nearly fainted. She slowly made her way across the room, hanging on to furniture and stopping when she felt dizzy.

She splashed her face with cold water. The dizziness

subsided, but the hunger and disorientation did not as she
made her way back to the bed and looked at the digital
clock more carefully. The luminous dial read Sunday,
February third.

"Could I have slept through two and a half days?" she
asked in amazement. "No wonder I'm hungry."

She knew she had to get dressed and go buy food, but
she dreaded leaving the safety of the apartment. She had
checked into the Arms Apartments on the previous Monday, and her only recollections of the week were of pain
and danger. Her hunger became more urgent than her
fear, and she pulled on the jeans and shirt she had thrown
over a chair.

The sunlight in her face blinded her after a week in the
darkened room. She squinted, put on her sunglasses, and
looked around curiously. She had been drugged and in so
much pain when she checked into the apartment, she
realized now that she had no idea where she was. This
part of the city was not familiar to her. She watched the
landmarks and street signs carefully so she would be able
to find her way back to the apartment. There were few
people on the streets, and those she did pass reminded
her of her loneliness and isolation. She found a café and
gratefully went inside.

"Hey, Charlie, where the heck is that order of eggs?" a
waitress yelled good-naturedly through the window that
opened into the kitchen.

"When it comes time to leave the tip, keep in mind it
ain't my fault your eggs are taking so long, Sam," she
yelled across the diner to a man sitting in one of the
booths, but her eyes were on Rhonda. She took a drag off
her cigarette, which now was nothing more than a stub in
the ashtray, and left it smoldering a brown hole into the
filter of one of a dozen butts that threatened to overflow
into the tray of uncovered sweet rolls next to it. She
grabbed a glass of water, coffeepot, and menu in one
smooth motion and hurried over to Rhonda's booth.

"Hi, hon. I'm Ethyl. Coffee?" she asked, turning up
Rhonda's cup.

"You gonna let these eggs sit here all day and rot, or
are you gonna take them over there and give 'em to

Sam?" Charlie yelled as he slammed a plate of eggs and hash browns under the warming light.

"That man thinks his whole day is a flop unless he's giving me a bad time," Ethyl said as she filled Rhonda's cup. "Here's your menu. I'll be back in a jiffy to take your order."

She grabbed Sam's eggs, lit a cigarette, took a puff, and left it in the ashtray without missing a step.

"What kind of soup do you have?" Rhonda asked when the waitress returned to the table.

"We've got some nice homemade chicken noodle soup. I made it fresh this morning. Charlie don't touch the soup. If you don't get it from a can or fry it, he wouldn't know what to do with it."

Rhonda smiled a little, though it had an unpracticed feeling. "I'll try some of it."

Ethyl stopped at the cash register and took a customer's money, then brought back the soup and a tall glass of milk.

"Hope you'll help me out with this milk. There's no charge. Charlie ordered too much again. It's gonna spoil if I can't find someone to drink it." Ethyl rambled on casually, not giving Rhonda a chance to get a word in edgewise.

Even so, Rhonda noticed the woman was watching her closely.

"Mind if I sit down?" she asked as she set the soup on the table. "We don't get many women in here, just these darned old men with their snide remarks. A girl gets lonely not having another woman to talk to."

Ethyl sat across from Rhonda before she had a chance to respond, and lit a cigarette that she pulled from her uniform pocket.

Rhonda listened to the waitress chatter and soon was smiling in spite of herself. She was so starved for a friend that this outgoing woman seemed like a gift from heaven. After she finished her soup and milk, Ethyl insisted in bringing her a piece of cherry pie with ice cream. Rhonda barely touched it.

"Do you know of a supermarket close by?" Rhonda asked after she'd finished her third cup of coffee.

"There's one two blocks from here. Go left outside the
restaurant, then turn right at the corner. You'll run right
into it."

"Hey, Ethyl," Charlie shouted from the kitchen. "You
working here or not? Sam needs you to get up and take
his money."

"I'm coming, Sam," Ethyl said, jumping from her seat.
"You just got up there, didn't you? See, I told you, Charlie. I've never left a customer waiting in my life. You
know that, but you aren't happy unless you're on my
case," she said without malice.

Adam handed his money to the waitress. He didn't
know why the silly woman and fat cook called him Sam.
He didn't bother to correct them. He was too busy looking at the woman the waitress had been talking to.

She's one of them, he thought. She's one of the women
from the television. Jeremy showed me how she goes to
the bars and teases the men.

He fumbled with some change, bought a paper in the
middle of the block, and waited for the woman to come
out of the restaurant. When she did, he followed and saw
her go into the supermarket. He waited, then followed
her from a distance as she carried her groceries down the
street. It came naturally to him after the years of following the children. He chuckled when she went into the
lower level of the Arms Apartments, then he ducked into
the alley and whistled as he walked up the fire escape to
his own apartment.

Jeremy would be very pleased with him. Jeremy would
never have reason to punish him again.

29

Jeremy had been pleased with him. He told Adam he had
lured the woman to the building as a special treat, but
that was before he had been bad. Now he would have to
prove himself before he could have her.

Jeremy had faded from the screen, and Adam was leering at the image of a woman in the television. Although she was older than most of the women Jeremy had shown him, she still was good-looking. He inched closer to the screen as she stripped in the examining room at her doctor's office. The television zoomed in for a closeup of her chart. Her name was Joyce Jenkins.

"She's tan," Adam whispered in amazement. "Even her breasts are tan. She must be one of those hotsy-totsy suburban women who sit under the lights in those tanning salons at the shopping centers. I've seen them advertised. Well, rich suburban bitch, you've got enough money for a year-round tan, but not enough for your baby, huh?"

Adam laughed when Joyce looked around the examining room nervously. "Feel like someone is watching you, Mrs. Rich Bitch? I see you, but you don't see me." His breathing became quick and shallow when she took off her skimpy underwear. Her stomach was smooth and flat, without a trace of the baby she was carrying.

"You wouldn't want to get that pretty little stomach all fat from a baby, would you," Adam sneered. "No, of course not. You couldn't play tennis at your fancy country club with a fat tummy. Wait until you find out what happens to baby killers. We'll see how you like to be killed, Mrs. Rich Lady. Will you try to scream? Will you kick and fight?" He grinned, looking at Joyce's neck. It was long and slender, just right to wrap a scarf around and squeeze.

Adam toyed with Marie's scarf while he watched Joyce in the three-dimensional screen. "You look like you are standing naked here in my apartment. You shouldn't do that in front of strange men. Something might happen to you. Someone might punish you." He made a loop in the scarf and snapped it tight, then drew back nervously when the doctor entered the room, afraid the man could see him. He relaxed, realizing he was safe from discovery, and watched with fascination as the doctor performed the examination.

When the screen finally turned to white snow, he looked at the clock eagerly. "It won't be long now.

Should I snap the scarf hard and break that pretty neck, or should I squeeze it slowly and watch her struggle?"

He picked up a locket, which he had found on top of the television when he came back from following Rhonda Hackman, and looked at the pictures of a teenage boy and girl inside. "You'll be better off without her," he told the smiling faces.

Joyce Jenkins was exhausted. Spending the morning at the doctor's office was tiring enough without getting the distressing news that she was pregnant. Then she got into a fight with her teenage daughter, Irene, and had to ground her. By then she just wanted to take a nap, but she had the cleaning to do and groceries to buy.

When she returned from shopping, Irene was gone. It was ten P.M. and she still wasn't home. Joyce's husband, Bud, was at a lodge meeting and her son, Larry, was studying with a friend, so Joyce was sitting in the living room, alone, fuming because Irene had disobeyed her.

She's probably with that juvenile delinquent boyfriend of hers, Joyce thought bitterly. She automatically reached to her neck to play with the locket she always wore. The kids had given it to her for Mother's Day, and it had their pictures in it. The locket was gone. I must have left it at the doctor's office, she thought, making a mental note to call tomorrow.

Irene Jenkins sat in the living room of her boyfriend's apartment. She took another hit of pot and laughed with her friends about how she had shown her mom she couldn't ground her like a little kid.

As Irene was opening a fresh beer, on the other side of town her mom responded to a telephone call by jumping into her car and rushing to Mid-City Park. A voice that sounded like Irene's had said she was in trouble.

At the Arms Apartments, Adam put on his coat and walked deliberately toward the park.

30

Bud Jenkins sat across from Laura in the Jenkinses' den. His son, Larry, sat beside him on the verge of tears.

"Are you sure you don't want the tranquilizer the doctor left you?" Laura asked kindly.

Bud jerked his head from side to side. "Not until I find my daughter. I won't take anything until my little girl is back."

Laura hated this assignment. The man's and the boy's grief and frustration were almost more than she could bear. Not only had his wife been murdered, but his daughter was missing. "We'll find her, Mr. Jenkins. Every officer in the city is looking. We have her picture on television and in the newspaper." What Laura did not say was that if the girl had been with her mom, the chances were good that she was dead too.

"I know this is very difficult for you, Mr. Jenkins, but do you think you can answer a few more questions? It's important."

Bud looked at her as if she were speaking a foreign language. Then, slowly, his eyes began to show comprehension. "I don't know what I can tell you. I came home at midnight and Joyce and Irene were both gone. Joyce's car was gone too."

"Do you have any idea why they might have gone out?"

"None. It doesn't make sense, especially Joyce going to Mid-City Park. She wouldn't do a thing like that. Joyce won't even drive through this neighborhood without the windows up and the doors locked. She had absolutely no reason to be where she was found."

Laura felt goose bumps forming on her arms. She had no doubt that Bud Jenkins was right, but there were no signs in the Jenkinses' home that anyone had forcibly entered, or that anyone had made the woman drive to the park. The doors and windows had all been securely locked, and Bud said his wife would not have opened the door to a stranger at night. It didn't make any more sense

than the scene they had found at Ann Locke's apartment.
It wasn't any more logical than the electrical storms.

"Are you sure, Mr. Jenkins, that your daughter was
with your wife last night? Could she have gone to spend
the night at a friend's house?"

"I'm certain they were together. Irene was grounded
for coming in late last week, and my wife was sticking to
her guns about not letting her off the hook for two full
weeks. She had one more week to go."

"What about you, Larry—do you have any idea why
your mom and Irene might have gone to the park?"

"Dad's right. Mom wouldn't have gone downtown.
She's always lecturing us on staying out of parks at night
and learning self-defense, and not opening the door to
strangers, and stuff like that."

"Before you went to your friend's house to study, did
she say anything about going anywhere yesterday?"

"She was going to the supermarket, but that was early
in the afternoon."

Laura looked up, interested. Perhaps she and the girl
went to do the shopping and someone cornered them in
the parking lot and forced them to drive to the park.

"Was Irene going to the store with your mom?"

"No. Mom left before I did, and Irene still was here.
She was in her room pouting because Mom wouldn't
change her mind about grounding her."

"If you looked in the refrigerator and the cabinets,
would you be able to tell if your mom ever came back
from the store? If your mom was abducted at the supermarket, and Irene wasn't with her, maybe your sister just
sneaked out of the house and went to stay at a friend's
because she was mad."

Laura watched while Bud and Larry pored through
the kitchen cabinets and refrigerator.

"All the things I asked her to pick up for me are here,"
Larry announced. The tears that had threatened to overflow since Laura arrived broke loose. Laura turned discreetly away while Bud held him tightly and they cried
on each other's shoulders. Laura wished she could leave
them alone with their grief, but she needed more information, both to find Irene and to catch Joyce's murderer.

"Where did Joyce usually shop?" she asked Bud. "It won't hurt to check around and see if anyone saw your wife talking to anyone there yesterday."

"I don't even know. I always took our meals for granted. Joyce was such an efficient homemaker, I never considered asking where she bought things."

"I'm sure she was, Mr. Jenkins."

"She always shopped at Circle Super," Larry said. "She saved the stamps they give."

Laura made a note in her notebook, then asked if Irene had an address book they could borrow to check with her friends. "I'll also need both of you to give me a list of her friends who may not be in the book."

Larry left to look for the address book, but stopped and answered the telephone. "It's for you, Detective Bernhardt."

Laura talked to Harry Winchell quietly for a few minutes, then hung up and asked Bud, "What color coat does your daughter have, Mr. Jenkins?"

"It's one of those short down ski jackets. It's kind of purple, and it has a hood."

"A girl was seen at a 7-Eleven store downtown a few minutes ago who matches your daughter's description. Apparently someone was in the store with a portable radio and this girl heard the newscast about your wife. She was visibly upset and ran out. The clerk didn't see where she went, but we have officers searching the area."

"Oh, thank God. Please let it be my baby. I don't think I could stand to lose them both."

31

It took Laura forty-five minutes to drive from the Jenkinses' house to Mid-City Park, but Laura thought Joyce could have made it in half the time late Sunday night, especially if she was speeding. The rubber marks in the driveway indicated she had peeled out in a hurry.

At least the daughter had shown up safe and sound.

Laura wanted a chance to question the girl carefully, but the family needed some time to themselves now. Perhaps Irene was telling the truth about not having seen her mother since Sunday afternoon and having no idea why she went to the park, but her story about spending the night at a girlfriend's house didn't ring true.

Laura showed her identification and was admitted through the police blockade. MacNamara was personally heading the investigation at the crime scene. He told Laura the routine police patrol must have found Jenkins's body shortly after the murder. The puzzling part was that Joyce apparently was in a rush to meet someone. The car had been found running, her purse was in the seat, and the driver's door was open.

"From what I learned this morning about the victim, such behavior is totally out of character, Chief," Laura said.

"Do you have any ideas?"

"I want to ask the family more questions before I speculate."

A member of the fingerprint crew came up and asked MacNamara a question, and Laura left to look around and sort through what she knew about the murders, and what she suspected.

That woman would not have come to this park and acted as she had unless she'd felt she had urgent reason, of that I am sure, Laura thought. From the information I have so far, I'd guess the only thing that would drag her out here would be fear for a member of her family. She'd been found next to the phone booth. Could a member of her family have called her from there and said they were in trouble? They were all gone last night, so any of them could have done it, but why? We'll have to check all of their stories, but I'm inclined to think if anyone called, it was Irene. She looked more than upset this morning. She looked guilty.

I doubt that the girl killed her mother, though. Perhaps she got in trouble, called for her mom's help, then left, and her mother was killed by the same person who killed Ann Locke.

But what caused Ann Locke to come here? Did some-

one call her from that phone booth? Is there some connection between the two women? So far the MO indicates
it was the same killer, but was it bizarre coincidence that
they apparently came rushing into his grasp?

Laura sat on a park bench and considered the aspects
of the case only she knew. I wonder if Joyce had been
having nightmares? I'll have to ask her husband. There is
no denying that Ann Locke's dreams were similar to
mine. Could these strange electrical storms somehow be
increasing our ESP? If so, are we picking up each other's
thoughts, or the murderer's thoughts? She shuddered at
the possibilities.

She made a mental list of leads to check while she
made the short drive back to the precinct.

One thing is certain, she thought while she walked into
her office, a real person is killing women. She was shaken
from her thoughts by the janitor.

"I'm sorry about your hands, ma'am."

"Thank you, Adam. They're fine. The bandages make
them look worse than they are." She smiled. The man
seemed genuinely upset about her burns. He was so shy,
he could barely get the sentence out. Laura realized it
was the first time she had ever heard him say a complete
sentence.

What a sweet man, she thought, then forgot him as she
immersed herself in the investigations.

Don't worry about being hurt by the lightning again,
Laura darling, Adam thought as the detective walked
away. Adam wasn't sure if he caused the lightning, or if
Jeremy caused it when he disobeyed the boy. He believed
he could control the storms, though, by doing what Jeremy told him to do.

He rather liked the idea that he was able to cause the
sky to explode, though the power frightened him. Plus,
lately when the storms came, it meant pain for him.
That's why he believed he might be causing them, rather
than Jeremy. The pain was so intense, it made sense to
him that it couldn't be contained in his head and exploded across the city. That was over now. He wouldn't
defy Jeremy again. He couldn't understand why he had

ever fought his son. Jeremy wasn't asking him to be a
murderer. He was allowing him to be an avenger, like the
superhero in comic books.

The precinct was in chaos. In addition to the extra
people who had been brought in to help investigate Joyce
Jenkins's death, there were news crews from the three
television stations and from both newspapers. Adam had
to repress a smile. The detectives were bustling around
acting as if they knew what they were doing, and Chief
MacNamara had just strolled in and assured the reporters everything was under control and the murderer
would be apprehended soon.

You're not such a big deal, Mr. Hotshot, Adam
thought. Go ahead and tell the reporters about your
promising leads. You and I know you are lying through
your teeth.

Adam felt as if he were seeing the personnel at the
precinct for the first time. For fifteen years he had felt
inferior to them.

You're pretty dumb, boys. Here you are looking all
over the city for me, but you are so blind, you can't see
what is right under your nose.

Adam lowered his head and covered his mouth to hide
his smile. He wished he could hold Laura in his arms and
tell her what he had done for her. She might not understand at first. After all, she was only a woman, but she
would come around. He wanted to shout to the reporters
that he was the one. For the first time in his life he was a
celebrity, and no one knew. It wasn't fair. On the other
hand he wasn't ready to be discovered. He had more
work to do for Jeremy, for Laura, and for the babies.

He remembered the sense of power he had felt Sunday
when he avenged Joyce Jenkins's baby, and the week before when he had avenged Ann Locke's baby. He could
hardly wait to feel the exhilaration again and hoped Jeremy would send him out on another "errand" very soon.
Maybe someday the city would know what he had done,
and his name would be spoken with awe and respect.

*Mr. Smith, on behalf of the mayor, we would like to
present you with a small token of our esteem. You have*

single-handedly rid our city of its most dangerous element —the baby killers.

Mr. Smith, could you please smile for the camera? Mr. Smith, there is a telephone call for you. Quiet, everyone. It is the President. We are going to put the call on the speaker phone so the whole world can share this momentous occasion.

Adam, the First Lady and I want to thank you for your unerring devotion to duty. You have accomplished in your city what many of us at the nation's capital have been unsuccessful at for years. But because of your example, we are sure we can get legislation passed that will enforce a mandatory death sentence for women who have abortions. You have acted with courage and without thought for your own safety. The name Adam Smith will go down in history as a synonym for social justice, and I am pleased to announce that Congress voted unanimously today to set aside February fourth as a new national holiday—Adam Smith Day.

Oh, Adam, the children and I are so proud of you.

It was nothing, Laura. I did it all for you.

"Hey, Janitor, are you going to stand there in the middle of the floor all day daydreaming, or are you going to get over here and empty my wastepaper basket?"

"Yes sir, Sergeant. I was on my way."

Binder's phone rang for the hundredth time that day, and he missed Adam's look of surprise, then the glint in his eye when he saw a shiny new photograph of Tracy on the sergeant's desk.

32

"Perhaps Tracy can tell us what causes thunder and lightning," Mrs. Hendricks said with her knack for calling on the person who wasn't paying attention. The students were as curious about the recent unusual storms as the rest of the city, and science teachers across the district had changed their lesson plans to move the weather section forward.

"Tracy, I asked you a question. Please answer it."

Tracy looked up in a daze. The child had been singing again. It wasn't as if she thought the song, or even remembered the voice of someone singing it. It was as if the child were in her head. He was singing his favorite song: "On the Good Ship Lollipop." Tracy wondered how such a happy song could sound so sinister. The teacher's glare brought her back to the reality of the classroom. "I'm sorry, Mrs. Hendricks. Would you repeat the question?"

"I asked you what causes thunder and lightning."

"He's angry," Tracy said with a shudder before she knew the words were coming out of her mouth.

The class laughed and Tracy blushed.

"I expected a more sophisticated answer than a preschooler's view of God," Mrs. Hendricks replied sarcastically. "Glen, can you enlighten Tracy for us?"

Tracy sank down in her chair, wishing it would swallow her. She hadn't meant God. She had meant the child. She certainly couldn't explain herself and gave an audible sigh of relief when Mrs. Hendricks moved on.

Despite her fear of Mrs. Hendricks, one of the toughest teachers in the school, Tracy was drifting away again. Glen's explanation of lightning was an incomprehensible drone in the background. The child was singing again. This time "The worms crawl in, the worms crawl out, the worms crawl into Tracy's mouth."

Tracy suppressed a scream at the vivid image. She wasn't aware of the bell ringing and became confused by Mrs. Hendricks's soft shaking of her shoulders.

"Tracy, Tracy."

Tracy looked around the room. The seats were empty, as if the child had greedily gobbled up all the kids in his greed.

"Are you ill, Tracy?"

"No, I'm fine. I'm sorry."

"That's what you told me last week, Tracy," the teacher said, looking suspiciously at the girl's eyes. "You know I will not tolerate students on drugs in my class. I think it's about time I had a talk with you parents."

"Drugs? I'm not on drugs, honest. I've never even tried them."

"I'm not a fool, Tracy. Do you think I've taught for twenty years without recognizing when someone is stoned? You are either ill or on drugs. Either way, it is time your parents were notified. I'll call your mother this afternoon."

"Please, Mrs. Hendricks. Don't do that. I'm not on drugs, and I'm not sick. I'm just a little tired. I haven't been sleeping well lately."

"Whatever the reason for the change in your behavior and attitude during the past few weeks, it has got to stop. You used to be one of my best students. Now you are a mess. Look at yourself. You've even become untidy in your personal appearance. Your hair is greasy. Your blouse is wrinkled. Your shoes aren't polished."

"Don't call my parents. I will do better. You'll see."

"I have no choice," Mrs. Hendricks said, though more sympathetically this time. "Now go on to lunch. You are already late. Here, wipe your eyes and nose first," she said, handing her a tissue.

Tracy blew her nose and walked as fast as she could to the nearest rest room. When she stood in front of the mirror, she saw herself as her teacher was seeing her. She looked terrible. She wished she could hide in one of the stalls for the rest of the day. She finally forced herself to go to the lunchroom. She came to a sudden halt ten feet from the door. Mark was leaning against a locker in animated conversation with Becky. He was twirling a strand of her perfect blond hair in his fingers. Becky looked up. She smiled smugly at Tracy, which caused Mark to look up. Mark's embarrassment said it all for Tracy. She heard him calling to her as she turned and ran back to the rest room to hide. She stayed there until she heard the bell for the next class; then she quietly grabbed her coat. She had never skipped school in her life, but today she couldn't stay another minute.

As she walked outside for the long walk home, she shuddered at the feeling that someone was watching her and enjoying her troubles.

* * *

"I want my mommy," Jeff whined.

"She's not here, so you'll have to cope for a couple more days," Harold snapped. He also missed Martha, though he wouldn't admit it to the children.

"We could call her, Daddy," Harold junior suggested.

"You know your grandma doesn't have a telephone."

"We could call Mrs. Anderson next door to Grandma. She could get Mommy."

"I don't know her telephone number, and I don't remember her first name, so I can't get the number from the operator."

"Mommy has her number in her address book," Harold junior said hopefully.

"Are you sure?"

Harold junior looked pleased that he knew something his dad didn't know. "I'm sure. She always calls Mrs. Anderson when she needs to talk to Grandma."

It hadn't occurred to Harold that he could call his wife. Not only had he not known about Mrs. Anderson's number, but long-distance calls were a luxury they couldn't afford. After five days without his wife the expense of a phone call was looking pretty minimal.

At least it would calm the kids down, he thought, not admitting, even to himself, it would also make him feel better. If someone walked up to Harold Gibbons and asked him what his relationship was with Martha, he would stare as if the person had lost his mind and reply, "She's my wife." No one in Taylorsville would ever consider asking such a question, though, and Harold wasn't the type of man to sit around and explore the complexities of human emotions. Nevertheless, he had gained respect for Martha during the five days she had been gone. He had always taken for granted that he worked harder than she did. Not that he resented it. It was the way he saw the structure of the world. On Thursday and Friday Mrs. Jones had taken care of the children, but for the first time in his life Harold had total responsibility for them over the weekend. Trying to keep up with the kids had left him far more exhausted than working at the grain mill ever had. He also discovered that Martha's absence from his bed left him with an emptiness that couldn't be explained solely by the lack of sex.

"If you kids are real good, maybe we could call your mom after you take your baths," he told the anxious children.

By the time he had helped the children finish their baths, they had worked themselves into a state of feverish excitement. One threat from Harold that if they didn't calm down the deal was off turned them into instant angels. They knew from experience that their dad did not make empty threats.

All four children stood around him, trying not to bounce up and down after Harold junior produced Martha's address book and Harold dialed the number.

"Mrs. Anderson, this is Harold Gibbons," he shouted into the phone. He remembered the woman was hard of hearing and a little senile. "I'm sorry to bother you, but I was wondering if you could go next door and get my wife. The kids want to talk to her."

"Who did you say this is?" the woman asked.

"It's Harold Gibbons," he shouted louder.

"Why, hello, Harold. You don't have to shout. I'm not deaf, you know. Did you want to talk to your mother-in-law? I'm afraid she isn't home."

"No, I want to talk to my wife."

"If you want to talk to Martha, why are you calling me?"

"I was wondering if you could go next door and get her. Martha is there visiting her mother and we want to talk to her."

"Martha is here in town? Oh, I don't think so, Harold. I would have heard about it if she was. No one comes to visit without me knowing. Besides, your mother-in-law isn't even here. She's been away visiting her sister for ten days now. She won't be back until Friday."

"You must be mistaken."

"I know when my own neighbor and best friend for fifty years is out of town, sonny. I should. She left me the key to her place and I've been over there every day checking on things and taking care of her plants. I don't know where your wife is, but she's not at her mother's house."

The kids were beginning to get impatient and had begun jumping up and down asking if their mother was going to come to the phone soon. All four of them began to cry when Harold hung up.

"Your mom and Grandma have gone out visiting, and they aren't expected back until after your bedtime," he lied.

"Couldn't we stay up and wait for them?" Karen pleaded.

"You know better than to ask, especially on a school night. Besides, Mommy will be home in a couple of days," he said, taking all four of his children into his big arms and hugging them; but he wondered if she would be home. His mind was in a whirl of confusion. "I'll tell you what," he said to his restless children, "—if you promise to be good, I'll let you have some ice cream before you go to bed."

The unexpected treat pacified the children and Harold was relieved when they went to bed with very little grumbling. While they slept, Harold paced the living room, cursing quietly. His imagination was running wild. He was certain Martha had run off with another man. It was the only explanation, and the thought of her in someone else's bed made him crazy with jealousy. His anger was so intense, he rammed his fist through the cheap paneling in the living room.

"So that's why she has been acting guilty and nervous lately," he muttered vehemently. "It explains why the house has been a mess too. While I've been working my tail off at the grain mill every day, she has been screwing around." At that moment he could easily have killed her and her lover.

"I have to go," Harold said sarcastically, parroting what Martha had told him the week before. "My mother needs me.

"It wasn't your mother who needed you. It was some cocksucker who wanted to put his dirty dick in my wife. If you think I'll take you back after this, Martha, you're crazy." But when he tried to imagine his life without her, he couldn't.

For the first time since he was ten years old, Harold Gibbons broke down and cried.

33

Tuesday, February 5
Laura cross-checked the names on the two lists for the fourth time. It did no more good than the first three times she had examined them. A score of detectives were interviewing everyone who knew either Ann Locke or Joyce Jenkins. The only person who seemed to have a motive to murder Locke was her former employer and lover, Michael Statler, and he had an airtight alibi. So far no one seemed to have a motive to murder Joyce Jenkins, and the detectives had been unsuccessful in making a connection between Statler and Jenkins or Locke and Jenkins. There still were people to interview concerning both women, and Laura hoped one of them could provide a lead.

Laura had found but one similarity, and it was information she was keeping to herself for the time being. She had called Bud Jenkins Monday evening and he confirmed that his wife had been suffering from nightmares about a row of coffins during the past couple of weeks. She deleted the information from her reports. She didn't know how to explain even having asked the question. She would have to come up with something far more concrete as evidence; and evidence of any kind seemed nonexistent in both cases.

The media was having a field day with the cases. Fortunately the news reports had made the public more curious than frightened. Panic typically set in with random murders, and these cases appeared anything but random, even if they were mysterious. Nevertheless, the media attention was putting additional pressure on the department to solve the cases quickly. Laura saw the police

pathologist walking down the hall with a report in his
hand which she thought probably was Joyce Jenkins's
autopsy report.

"Hey, John, wait up," she yelled as she ran after him.
"Did you find anything interesting?"

"Laura, you know I'm supposed to hand-deliver this
report to MacNamara. He'll fill you in on anything he
wants you to know."

"Come on, John. Give me a break. You owe me one.
Remember when your car broke down and I drove you to
the garage, then picked up your wife at work and gave
her a lift home?"

"Okay, I remember," he said, still walking, but slowing
his pace. We've confirmed what everyone suspected: the
same person killed both women. We positively identified
the fibers on Jenkins's neck as the same as those found on
Locke's neck. I'm sure that doesn't come as any surprise,
but did you know Joyce Jenkins also was about two
months pregnant?"

"No, I didn't," Laura said, stopping dead in her
tracks. "Her husband didn't mention it, which seems
strange. Thanks, John." She turned to go back to her
office, her mind in a whirl, and nearly tripped over the
janitor and his mop bucket. "Hello, Adam," she said automatically, without actually diverting her attention from
her thoughts.

Why didn't Mr. Jenkins mention that Joyce was pregnant? she mused as she hurried toward her office. Is it
possible he didn't know? It could be a coincidence that
both women were a couple of months pregnant, or this
could be the break we've been waiting for.

After talking to Jenkins on the telephone Laura went
rushing back down the hall, this time to MacNamara's
office.

"Laura, just the person I wanted to see," he said as she
knocked on his door. "I'd like for you to call Bud Jenkins
and see if he knew his wife was pregnant."

"I already did, Chief, and we've got the connection
we've been looking for between Locke and Jenkins. Bud
Jenkins said Joyce was scheduled to have an abortion,

and at the same clinic Ann Locke went to the day of her death."

"Good work, Bernhardt. I won't ask you how you found out she was pregnant."

"Lucky guess, sir," she replied with a sheepish grin.

"Sure it was," he replied with an expression that let her know he knew she was lying but wasn't going to make an issue of it. "Let's see if you can come up with some more lucky guesses today. I have another long list of Joyce Jenkins's friends and acquaintances I want you and Winchell to wade through. One solid lead doesn't mean we can drop all the other avenues of investigation."

Laura looked disappointed. "I thought you might want me to help with the interviews at the clinic. After all, I am the only woman assigned to the case, and the women at the clinic might be more likely to open up to me."

"Equality of the sexes works both ways, Bernhardt. I think we men will muddle through the interviews somehow."

Laura gave a chagrined smile. "I did sound pretty sexist, didn't I? I'll get right on this list of names," she said, taking the papers MacNamara handed her.

"Track these people down wherever they are, Bernhardt. We haven't got a minute to lose. If they aren't at home or at work, look for them at church or the bars, if necessary."

"Yes, sir," she said, then nearly tripped on the wet floor outside MacNamara's office as she left.

"Sorry, Miss Laura. Just doing my job."

"Well, you certainly do it well. You seem to be everywhere today, Adam."

The connecting link! Patrick MacNamara thought excitedly. *That Bernhardt is a good detective. I suppose I should have let her conduct the interviews at the clinic, since she came up with the lead. But I want to do it personally.*

The chief wouldn't have admitted it to anyone, but he had been feeling stifled in his administrative position. He was glad the asbestos at headquarters had chased him out of his sterile office. Actively working on an interesting case at one of the precincts made him feel ten years younger. He was in the best of two worlds: coordinating the overall efforts of the investigations, plus taking an active part in solving the crimes. He began to jot notes to himself as he thought of the many things that needed to be done and checked.

I need a complete list of employees at that clinic, as well as any who might have quit recently, he thought. I also need a list of clients from the past twelve months. I'll need a court order for that. I'll send Martínez over to pick it up as soon as the judge signs it. I think we are onto something here, and I don't like the smell of it. If a psycho is working at that clinic, other women's lives might be in danger.

He buzzed his secretary and had her send for the detectives who weren't already working on another aspect of the case. After barking quick orders he headed for the clinic.

Patrick took an immediate dislike to Priscilla White. If the woman hadn't looked like an undernourished sparrow, he could easily have envisioned her cheerfully murdering clients. He could not imagine someone so sanctimonious working at a family planning clinic.

"I'm sure none of our employees are responsible for those women's deaths," Ms. White said. Her voice was so sugary sweet that Patrick wondered how she kept from gagging on the falseness of it. "Of course, most of the women who come in here are trollops. Heaven only knows what sort of men they have associated with. I've known all along those women were bound to come to an unpleasant end. People who live their kind of life should expect it." She sniffed haughtily.

"I'm surprised you work here if that is the way you feel, Ms. White." Patrick made a mental note to check out everyone associated with the woman. Maybe she had a large friend with similar attitudes.

"With my skills and background, I could work anywhere"—she sighed—"but Dr. Morgan would be lost without me. I've worked for him for years, long before he came to this awful place."

"It must be difficult for you," he said sympathetically.

He thought it best to play the woman's game at this point, and possibly catch her off guard. "I can tell you are a good Christian woman, Ms. White. I imagine discussing the clinic with your friends is the only way you endure."

"I would never do that, Chief MacNamara. We simply don't discuss the clients outside the office. Our services are strictly confidential, though I suspect the women themselves talk quite freely about their"—sniff—"abortions."

Patrick stood to leave and was repulsed when Ms. White batted her eyelashes and asked, "Are you married, Chief?"

"Yes," he lied.

At nine P.M. Laura was still at the precinct, typing her reports, though it seemed a waste of time. No one she talked to provided any useful information.

The connecting clue between the two victims had made the detectives more optimistic, but Laura still felt anxious. There still were the nightmares and electrical storms to consider. There had to be some reason she was having the same nightmares as the victims, and she was certain she wasn't pregnant. She winced guiltily when she realized she hadn't made love to her husband in two weeks. She and Darryl had barely even talked to each other. When she finally did get home at night, she was so exhausted, she fell asleep immediately after a hot bath. She knew Darryl was getting upset, but she had chosen to ignore it, since she didn't see any way to remedy the situation. She vowed to make love to him tonight, but instead of feeling enthusiastic about it, she dreaded the idea of staying awake an extra hour.

A couple of hours later she heard Harry still typing, the clicking of the keys in perpetual disharmony to the country-western music that blared from the radio on his filing cabinet. Laura was trying to gather enough energy to stand up and go home. If nothing else Harry's music would force her out. She cringed at the twangy song of another drunk who was in trouble for not keeping his pants zipped. The drunk's maudlin tale of his wife's leaving him ended, followed by a child singing a rhyme she remembered from grade school—or at least the first line was the rhyme she remembered.

Laura sat up, startled and frightened. A feeling of unreality gripped her. She looked at Harry, who was still typing, but it was as though he were in another dimension.

The air in the room seemed to grow thick and menacing while she listened to the rhyme on the radio. Why couldn't Harry hear it? She recognized the voice. It was the same one she had heard the night the sewing machine stabbed her. It was the voice she had heard in the ladies' room at the club, the voice that had caused her to wake up screaming in the middle of the night.

I'm dreaming now, she thought. This can't be happening, not here at the precinct with Harry sitting across from me. Soon he'll wake me up and tell me to go home.

But she knew she wasn't dreaming.

The child's voice rang through the office, audible only to her:

> School's out, school's out
> The hospital let the girl run out
> The girl did play
> Now she must pay
> For getting in the family way.

Laura's eyes were wide with fear. She gulped, then rubbed her arms where goose bumps were standing out in warning of danger. She looked at Harry, who was still typing, oblivious that anything out of the ordinary was happening. She felt as if Rod Serling's voice should be in the background, saying, "Laura Bernhardt doesn't know it, but she has stepped into the Twilight Zone."

She gripped the edge of her desk firmly, relieved by its comforting solid feel, but she felt if she tried to cross the room to Harry, she would run into an invisible wall that separated her from the real world.

The air in her private, desperate world seemed to be running out. Her throat felt as if it were collapsing from the effort of trying to suck in the precious life-giving gases. The room was spinning, and she called out for Harry, not expecting him to hear her.

Harry looked up. "Did you say something, Laura?"

She was so relieved he had heard her, she felt like crying. She could breathe again, but the rhyme kept repeating itself on the radio. If Harry could hear her, he must be able to hear the child too. "I was wondering what that song is on the radio," she said, trying to sound nonchalant despite the loud beating of her heart.

"I know you aren't a big country-western fan, but everyone knows the 'Cannonball Express.' "

He doesn't hear it, she thought shakily. Does that mean I'm crazy? She started frantically writing down the rhyme, which played again and again without pausing.

"What are you writing?" Harry asked.

"The lyrics. They're interesting. I thought I'd write them down so I wouldn't forget them."

"Are you okay, Laura?" he asked suspiciously.

"Sure, why do you ask?"

"The song is an instrumental. There aren't any words."

Laura stuttered and stalled for time. "Of course, uh, I was kidding. I was writing out a shopping list."

The child's voice was louder now. Why couldn't Harry hear it?

I'm losing my mind, Laura thought. The voice has escaped from the radio. It's filling the whole room. She tried to keep her hands from shaking. It was impossible, so she hid them in her lap.

"Are you sure you're okay? You don't look so hot."

Laura could barely hear him over the loud singing, but she couldn't tell Harry what was happening. She had to get out of there.

"I think I'll go home. See you in the morning," she said, grabbing her coat and rushing out the door.

Harry followed her and yelled down the hall, "Do you want me to give you a ride home?"

She ignored him and rushed out of the building. Her hands were shaking so badly, she had difficulty unlocking the car door. When she finally got in and started the

engine, she screeched out of the parking lot and drove
blindly for several miles, unaware of where she was heading or of traffic signals. Twice she barely missed another
vehicle when she ran red lights. Her only thought was to
get away from that voice. Finally she pulled to the curb
and put the car in park, letting the engine idle. She didn't
know how long she sat there shaking and trying to calm
down.

It wouldn't have been necessary for her to write down
the childish lyrics. The words were indelibly etched in
her brain:

> School's out, school's out
> The hospital let the girl run out
> The girl did play
> Now she must pay
> For getting in the family way.

"What does it mean?" Laura whispered. The heater
was blasting hot air, but she was freezing. She kept thinking of the rhyme and trying to make sense of it.

School?

Hospital?

Rhonda! He's going to kill Rhonda; but she isn't pregnant, Laura thought. She beat her hands in frustration on
the steering wheel. She realized she had no idea if
Rhonda was pregnant or not. She had to find her and
warn her. She started sobbing, as much from frustration
as from fear. In a city of a million people she didn't have
a prayer of locating someone who didn't want to be
found, at least not without the aid of an all-points bulletin, and she was powerless to file one. How would she
explain it to the chief and to Sergeant Binder?

The memory of Rhonda's voice at the hospital came
back to her: "When I see you again, my pain will be over
. . . and yours will be just beginning."

"No," Laura shouted, certain Rhonda had been referring to her own death. And if that was what Rhonda's
dreams meant, and those of the other victims, what did
her own dreams mean?

It was midnight by the time Laura turned onto her

sleepy residential street. Her car engine and the distant barking of a dog were the only sounds. She glanced at her reflection in the rearview mirror when she drove under the streetlight at the corner of her block. She grimaced at her tear-streaked face and prayed Darryl would be asleep. Her home, like the others on the block, was dark. She turned off her car lights and engine and coasted quietly into the driveway. She did not turn on the lights in the house when she let herself in. Instead, she tiptoed down the dark hall to the bedroom. As soon as she walked over the threshold Darryl turned on the lamp on his nightstand. She jumped guiltily.

"Welcome home, stranger," Darryl said testily. Then he saw her red eyes and distraught expression. "Don't you think it is about time you told me what is going on, Laura?"

"Nothing is going on. I've just been working late again. Things will be better when this case is solved," she said, sitting next to him on the bed and kissing him lightly on the forehead.

"Come on, Laura. Don't treat me like I'm an idiot. You've been crying tonight, and you've been behaving strangely for the past month."

"You're right. Everything isn't fine. This is my first murder investigation, and there is a lot of pressure on me. Two women are dead and we are afraid more will die before we catch the murderer. Everyone at the precinct is on edge. All of us are working long hours."

"I'm sick of you patronizing me, Laura. I'm your husband. I know there's more involved here than what you're telling me. How would you like it if the tables were turned and it was me being secretive with you?"

"I'm telling you the truth," Laura said, averting her eyes.

"Yeah, and I'm the pope. I want you to go to the doctor."

"We've been through this at least half a dozen times, Darryl."

"That's right, and I'm getting tired of sounding like a broken record. Since I can't get you to go voluntarily, I will make the appointment for you tomorrow and personally drive you to it."

"I don't have time, and I'm not sick."

"Make up your mind, Laura. Either I take you to the doctor tomorrow, or I march down to the precinct and have a little conference with Sergeant Binder and Chief MacNamara."

"You wouldn't dare," Laura said angrily. "That would be an inexcusable violation of my rights. I'm not a little kid you can order around. I'm an adult."

"Then act like one, and start treating me like I'm your husband. You used to trust me. If you value what is left of our relationship, you'll level with me."

Laura winced at his words. She hadn't realized things had deteriorated that far. Besides, the weight of her secret was suffocating her. At some point she would have to confide in someone. Who better than her husband?

"You're right. There is something bothering me, but if I tell you, you will think I'm crazy. I swear I'm not crazy. It's real."

"I won't think you're crazy," Darryl said, pulling her next to him.

"You'd better reserve judgment on that until you hear what I have to say."

Laura talked for the next two hours. She started with the incident with the sewing machine and ended with the rhyme on Harry's radio. When she'd finished, Darryl held her tightly while she cried.

"My poor baby. I had no idea."

"Do you think I'm losing my mind?" Laura asked, pulling herself away far enough to look into his eyes.

Darryl didn't say anything at first. Finally he spoke. "I don't know what to think. I said you could trust me, and you can. I would prefer to think you were having some kind of breakdown, because if you aren't, your life could be in serious danger. I guess I do believe you, because if I had my way, I'd whisk you out of the country and not let you out of my sight until whatever maniac is responsible for these crimes is locked up and the key thrown away."

Laura looked at him gratefully. "I don't think I could stand it if you thought I was crazy."

"I'm still taking you to the doctor tomorrow."

"A psychiatrist?" she asked suspiciously.

"No, our friendly M.D. You are going to need to be strong and healthy to get through the next few weeks, unless you will let me take you away for a while. There will be other cases for you. I don't think you should be involved in this one. I'm afraid for you, sweetheart; and I'm afraid for myself. I don't know what I would do without you."

"I can't run away, Darryl. I already am involved in this case."

"That's the whole point. You are too involved."

"I won't run away."

"Then you will have to start approaching it differently."

"How?"

"First let me take you to the doctor tomorrow for a checkup. We can go during your lunch hour."

"Okay."

"Then, if this Rhonda Hackman doesn't turn up dead, I think you should see a psychiatrist."

Laura looked at him angrily. "You do think I'm crazy."

"No, and maybe we both should go to a psychiatrist. I've heard something too. That's why we weren't killed the night of the fire. I heard a man calling out to warn you. He called you 'Laura darling.' No one seemed to hear it but me. Afterward I convinced myself I'd imagined it. At first I was jealous, then I was frightened, because I could feel that the warning was real. Now I'm a little jealous again. Is someone in love with you?"

"Not anyone I know of. You're the only one who calls me darling, and I didn't hear anyone calling to me that night."

"Maybe you know the murderer, Laura."

She looked amazed, then skeptical. "No. That would mean there would have to be a connection between me and the murder victims, and I'd never heard of them before their deaths. The only connection we've made between them is through the Mid-City Family Planning Clinic, and I've never been there."

"Then who did I hear warning you at the restaurant?"

"I don't know, but you are assuming there is a connection between the lightning and the murders. We don't know that. Lightning is a natural phenomenon, and those women did not die of natural causes. The only reason I brought up the lightning is because the strange incidents that happen during the storms might be explained by increased psychic powers."

"Then you must have a secret admirer who can communicate telepathically, at least during the storms."

Laura shivered and laughed nervously. "He seems to have a crossed connection, since you heard him and I didn't. At least you know how I feel. It's a relief not being the only one this is happening to."

"I don't like the idea of some man in love with you and talking telepathically."

"Neither do I. It gives me the willies. There are enough unexplained things going on."

"If this Rhonda Hackman woman does turn up dead, Laura, there's something else you have got to do, and you aren't going to like it."

"What's that?" she asked warily.

"You have to go to MacNamara and tell him your story."

"I can't do that, Darryl. You know me and love me, and you've had one of these incidents happen to you, too, and you still think I might need to talk to a psychiatrist. What do you think MacNamara is going to think?"

"If Rhonda Hackman is murdered, MacNamara is going to think your little visions, or whatever they are, are the best leads he has so far. Besides, what choice do you have? If you really are getting psychic information in advance, you might be able to save someone's life, but only if you tell. Is your ego more important than human lives? In fact, maybe you should talk to him first thing tomorrow. If he believes you, maybe you could save the Hackman woman."

"He wouldn't believe me yet. I don't have any concrete evidence."

"What have you got to lose by trying?"

"Only my whole career?"

"If you don't get some help, you may lose your life."

"I don't think that's likely. Only pregnant women are being murdered."

"You talked a lot about a child's voice, Laura. Where does that fit in?"

"I wish I knew."

34

Rhonda Hackman cursed the results of the early pregnancy test. When she picked up the kit at the supermarket, she really expected the results to be negative. She had assumed her period was late because of the trauma from her injuries. She had been wrong. Now she was trying to figure out who the father might be.

How long had she been hiding at the Arms Apartments? Time had become meaningless. She slept except on those occasions when she was forced to buy food. The swelling had gone from her face, and her bruises had turned from purple to black and were slowly fading. Her ribs still ached, but the pain was more tolerable.

Her total isolation, which at first she had welcomed, had become oppressive. She started talking to herself for the comfort of a human voice.

"When was I raped? *Rape,* there's an interesting word. It implies so much, and says so little. It was the day I took my accounting exam. That would have made it January twentieth—no, January twenty-third. Has it been long enough that this baby could belong to one of those men?" She shuddered at the thought. Try as she might, she couldn't remember whether she had had a period between the time she slept with someone and the night of the rape.

"I won't have a baby fathered by one of them," she said vehemently. "I'd rather die first."

It was highly unlikely the baby was conceived the night of the rape, but the slightest possibility made Rhonda want to rip the child from her stomach. She felt as if she were growing a monster within her. In her mind she had no options. She had to have an abortion.

She couldn't stay hidden at the Arms Apartments much longer. With the money needed for an abortion deducted from her meager savings, soon she wouldn't be able to pay rent or buy food.

"How long have I been out of school? I wonder if I could catch up again? Damn, I wish I knew the date. When my clock radio broke, I lost track of time."

Rhonda felt as if she had been in a dream for the past few weeks and that the pregnancy test had plunged her into icy reality. She looked nervously out the window at the dark street. Images of the nightmares that still plagued her sleep flashed through her head. She associated the darkness with the nightmares. She was terrified that if she left the apartment, she would meet those dreams head-on.

"Dreams aren't real," she told herself. "I'm perfectly safe. I've got to stop being afraid sometime. It might as well be now."

In her mind's eye she could see the newsstand in front of the supermarket a few blocks away.

"I could get a paper and be back in fifteen minutes. Nothing is going to happen to me if I walk three little blocks. I could find out the date and check the want ads for a job."

Part of her cried out to wait until morning. She wanted to pull the covers way over her head until the sun was high. Another part of her berated her cowardice. It said if she didn't face her fears now, she would never be able to face them. She finally gathered her courage and dressed to go out.

She walked down the street with determined steps. She didn't know what time it was, but even the bars were quiet and deserted.

After she had walked a block, she thought she heard footsteps behind her. Her heart was pounding when she spun around to face her pursuer. The street was empty and she gave a sigh of relief.

It suddenly occurred to her that this time of night, the newsstand might be empty. Once again she considered

going back to the apartment. She hesitated, then forced
herself to move forward.

If it's empty, I'll come back tomorrow. The walk will
do me good, she thought, trying to generate enthusiasm
she did not feel.

Weren't those footsteps and a child's laughter behind
her? She jerked around again and saw the street was
empty, then ran the rest of the way to the supermarket.

There were lights on in front of the market. She stood
under them, gasping for air, the pain in her ribs partially
replacing her fear.

Then she heard the voice. Someone was calling to her
from somewhere in the parking lot.

"Rhonda, thank goodness I found you. Why did you
leave the hospital like that? I've been worried sick."

"Laura? Detective Bernhardt?" Rhonda said in disbelief.

"Yes, it's me, and am I ever glad to see you. Come on.
I'll give you a ride home. You shouldn't be wandering
around this time of night. It's dangerous."

"How did you know where to find me?" Rhonda
asked, squinting suspiciously in the dark.

"I didn't. I'm here on a stakeout. We heard someone
was planning to rob this store tonight. I need to get you
out of here. Remember the talk we had at the hospital?
I'm happy to say I told you so. Here we are together
again, and we are both fine."

Rhonda's laugh of relief verged on hysteria. It really
was Laura. For the first time in weeks she felt safe. She
walked eagerly into the darkness . . .

. . . where Adam waited with Marie's scarf.

Rhonda tried to scream when he jumped out and
grabbed her, but the scarf that he deftly twisted around
her throat cut off the sound. At first she expected Laura
to run to her rescue; then she realized the woman's voice
had been a trick. She tried to fight and kick, but her
efforts only wound the scarf tighter around her neck. Her
ribs were on fire with pain. Her lungs felt as if they were
going to explode.

As darkness descended, she saw her father high on his
pulpit proclaiming that women get what they deserve.

Then the pain was gone. Her mother stood before her with open arms. Rhonda was home.

Darryl shook Laura gently. "Wake up, darling. It's okay. You're having another bad dream."

"Oh, Darryl. It's too late. She's dead."

"Who's dead?"

"Rhonda. I failed her."

"It was only a dream. People often dream about the last thing they talk about at night."

Laura was breathing evenly again, and Darryl realized she had been talking in her sleep. He held his wife gently for a while and looked up at the skylight, praying that it had only been a dream.

35

Wednesday, February 6

Darryl rolled over and checked the clock radio for what seemed like the hundredth time. After Laura's nightmare he had bolted awake at her every movement. She was sleeping peacefully now, but he was wide awake. Although the sky was pitch-black, it finally was morning. The luminated face on the clock read five A.M. There was no sense trying to go back to sleep. His head was spinning with the things his wife had told him the night before. He turned and looked at her sleeping soundly and wanted to reach out and hold her in his arms.

Was the woman he loved having a nervous breakdown? Darryl couldn't imagine it. Laura had always been level-headed, but the stories she had told him seemed so bizarre, they couldn't possibly be real. On the other hand, she had verified that she and the murder victims suffered from similar nightmares, and he could no longer deny that he had heard a warning the night of the fire. He also knew that Laura was prone to pick up on psychic energy. He had seen it often enough. She frequently would walk up to him and start rubbing his head in the exact spot it was aching, or she would begin to massage a sore muscle in his back or arm, even though he hadn't told her he had strained it. Her actions were so automatic, she didn't realize she was doing it unless he brought it to her attention. There also were times she rushed around straightening the house because she felt they were about to have unannounced company. She would put away the last dish or pick up the last newspaper and the doorbell would ring.

What she had said last night, though, was in a totally different category. The incidents she described involving the child she had never seen smacked dangerously of insanity, or of the supernatural. Darryl didn't believe in evil supernatural forces wandering the planet, wreaking havoc. That was the province of screenwriters.

Darryl hugged Laura protectively. Whatever the explanation, one thing was undeniably real. Women were dying. What if Rhonda Hackman had died last night? If his wife was experiencing precognition or a pyschic bond with the killer, she was in great danger.

She looked beautiful lying next to him, and he desperately wanted to make love to her, but he didn't want to wake her. He knew she needed to sleep, and he didn't want to face her rejection. Recently when he approached her sexually, she backed away. He knew if he stayed in bed, he wouldn't be able to resist her. He was about to get up and fix breakfast when she turned to face him and snuggled her face in his chest. Darryl kissed her, then he kissed her again and again. Laura did not turn away.

Later, while Laura was in the shower and he was dressing, Darryl wondered if he should mention her nightmare. He was pretty sure she didn't remember the dream, and he hated to spoil this peaceful morning. He realized, sadly, that such mornings had become very rare and he marveled that it was only a month ago that he had taken their happiness for granted. It seemed like an eternity.

She just had a bad dream, he thought while he buttoned his shirt. He wasn't certain, though. When Laura walked into the bedroom smelling of soap and perfume and dressed only in a towel she had wrapped around her

hair, he made up his mind. If Rhonda Hackman had
been murdered during the night, she would find out soon
enough. If it was only a nightmare, there was no sense
worrying her.

Darryl grinned at his wife and pulled her back into
bed.

"We're going to be late for work," Laura murmured,
but her hands told him she didn't care.

Laura forced herself to hurry from the parking lot to
the precinct house, despite the dread that welled up inside her like a malignant cancer. It was eight twenty-five
and she expected Binder to greet her with sarcasm. That
was the least of her problems. She had slept only a few
hours the night before, but she wasn't tired. She was running on nervous energy.

Her emotions had been a mass of contradictions while
she was driving to work. She was relieved that the fright-
ening incidents that haunted her days and nights were no
longer her secret alone, but she worried that Darryl
thought she was crazy. She couldn't blame him if he did.
Her own nagging thoughts shouted that she was, indeed,
out of her mind. When she heard voices that were not
there or saw images that could not possibly exist, they
were nevertheless as real to her as her own body. Later,
the unlikelihood of the experiences made her doubt her
senses, and she remembered from her college psychology
classes that the delusions of the mentally ill were real to
them in every way.

On the other hand, didn't the dreams she shared with
the victims prove that something inexplicable was happening? Her proof didn't seem very convincing as she
faced the door of the precinct house. Even Darryl was
reserving judgment on her sanity until they found out if
Rhonda Hackman had been murdered.

Laura's thoughts of Rhonda were laced with guilt. She
not only liked Rhonda and felt a kinship because of their
precognition at the hospital, she felt responsible for her.
Nevertheless, she dreaded putting her career on the line
for a person she barely knew. The only hope of finding

the young woman was an all-points bulletin, and she couldn't get one without talking to MacNamara.

"Let's go, Laura. There's been another murder," Harry said, popping quickly in and out of the office where Laura was hanging up her coat.

Her guilt and dread increased with each step. She had no doubt who the latest victim was, and she held herself personally responsible. She should have looked harder for Rhonda when she disappeared from the hospital. She should have told MacNamara about her dreams.

"We've got the same MO as the others," MacNamara told the gloomy detectives, "but this time the murder took place in the parking lot at the Circle Supermarket a few blocks from the park. So far the victim hasn't been identified, and we have no idea what she was doing wandering around in a dark parking lot in the middle of the night. Get the lights, Clark."

Laura steeled herself while Bob turned off the lights and the chief fiddled with a slide projector. Her knuckles turned white from the force of her fingers as they dug into the edge of the chair.

I can handle this, she told herself. She squinted when the blinding white light of the empty slide projector burst through the room. Then MacNamara flicked a button and the first slide covered the wall. Rhonda Hackman's dead face loomed before the detectives larger than life. Laura's head felt light. She sat perfectly still, grasping the chair, while the room rotated around her. Then darkness enveloped her.

Laura's first sensation when she regained consciousness was a blinding pain in her head.

"Are you feeling better?" MacNamara asked, then said over his shoulder to the group of detectives surrounding her, "Get back, you ghouls. Give her some space."

"I'm so embarrassed," Laura muttered.

"Don't worry about it, Bernhardt," the chief said reassuringly. "I've done the same thing, only it was at my first autopsy."

Laura managed a weak smile and started to sit up.

"Take it slow."

"I'm okay now."

"The rest of you can sit down. The show is over," MacNamara said while he helped Laura to her chair.

"I can identify the victim," Laura said. She was trying to choke back the tears that threatened to further humiliate her. "Her name is Rhonda Hackman. She was raped a few weeks ago. I was investigating the case when she checked herself out of the hospital and disappeared."

MacNamara looked at her with surprise, then turned to the staring men. "Okay, guys, you heard the detective. We've got a positive ID, so let's get to work. Martínez, pull the file on Rhonda Hackman and bring it back in here. Bernhardt, go lie down for a few minutes, then you can fill me in on any information you have on this woman. The file will give us enough to get started. Go on, get out of here."

Laura headed for the employees' workout room and lounge while MacNamara barked orders at the detectives.

A half hour later she woke up with a jerk and looked at her watch. She continued to lie on the chaise for a minute while her mind cleared. She had to get up and talk to MacNamara. The question was, what should she tell him? She repaired her makeup and when she was confident she looked composed, if not terrific, she headed for MacNamara's office.

"Hey, Laura, wait up."

Laura stopped, determined to take the ribbing with good grace. "Hi, José."

"A few of us guys are going out for a beer after work, Laura. We were wondering if you would like to come along?"

Laura couldn't believe her ears. She looked at José to see if he was putting her on, but his expression didn't show that he considered there to be anything strange about the invitation. She smiled and said, "I'd like that."

"Good. We'll catch you later."

The other detectives Laura passed also were friendlier than usual, and none mentioned her fainting episode. She saw Harry off by himself and walked up to him.

"Have you got any ideas on the connection between

Rhonda Hackman and the other victims, partner?" he asked when she approached him.

Laura was stunned. Harry was actually asking her opinion. She could have understood the change in the men if their friendliness had been twinged with pity. She would have hated it worse than being ribbed, but she would have understood it. She hadn't seen any signs of pity, though.

"How come everyone is being so nice to me all of a sudden, Harry? That's the last thing I expected after my little spectacle."

"Oh, is that what it was? It looked like a pretty human reaction to us. There wasn't a person in the room who didn't feel a little sick and light-headed when MacNamara flashed that slide on, and none of us had met the woman."

"I still don't understand."

"It's hard working with someone who is perfect, Laura, especially when that person is a pretty lady."

"If you only knew how far from perfect I am." She shocked him by giving him a quick hug, and left him standing staring after her with a lopsided grin as she purposefully walked to MacNamara's office.

She told the chief about Rhonda's saying she had dreamt about her. She also told him that she and the victims had experienced similar nightmares. Instead of going into detail about the incident with Harry's radio, she said only that she had had a premonition that Rhonda Hackman was going to be killed. She purposely deleted reference to the child and the more damaging experiences that could not be verified. Being removed from the force on psychiatric grounds would not bring Rhonda back to life.

"Why didn't you come to me sooner with this information, Laura?"

"I was afraid you wouldn't believe me."

He put his hands on his temples and silently rubbed his head. Finally he looked up and said, "I don't know what to think at this point."

"At least you aren't patronizing me. Are you going to take me off the investigation?"

"I'm not going to decide anything right now. I want to think about what you've told me and, frankly, check out your story. How long has it been since you took a day off? You look terrible."

"Thanks."

"You didn't answer my question."

"It's been a while. A couple of weeks, I guess."

"I want you to go home, and I don't want to see you around here until Friday. You are to get some sleep. That is an order. And, Laura, if you have any more of these premonitions or dreams, call me immediately. I don't care what time of day or night it is."

36

Martha stood in front of the shopwindow and stared at the display without really seeing it. She was too nervous to concentrate. In two hours she would walk into the Family Planning Clinic, be escorted to one of the cold examining rooms, and have an abortion.

She had been walking for an hour. She was tired and hungry, but moving made the time pass more quickly. As she paced the crowded city streets, loneliness welled up inside her. She walked faster to keep her mind off her problems, but when she came to a café, she paused. A customer opened the door and the smell of pancakes and bacon floated into the street. Martha's stomach growled longingly as she stared in the window. She hadn't eaten a real meal since she'd left home, and she was getting weaker by the day.

There's no sense torturing myself, she thought, and continued walking. Tomorrow I will be home and this rotten experience will be over. Someday I may even look back and laugh about how silly I was to be afraid.

Martha didn't feel like laughing, though, and she couldn't imagine ever laughing about the past week and what would be coming up today. That was only what people said to help themselves get through a bad experience. Today she wished she could run back home and hold her children so tightly they'd say, "Mom, jeez, you weren't gone that long." Anyway, that is what Harold junior would say. He thought he was getting too old to be hugged. Her eyes were far away and longing. We named our first son correctly, she thought. He is exactly like his father.

The thought of Harold brought tears to her eyes, but no one she passed paid any attention. She noticed on her first day in the city that people did not look her in the eye as they did in Taylorsville. Here people wrapped themselves in a protective cocoon of indifference. She winced when she realized these people were much like her husband, masking their feelings behind robot exteriors. She wondered if they took the mask off when they got home, or if, like Harold, they wore it constantly.

Does he miss me? Will he be glad to see me tomorrow, or will he be angry because he had to take care of the children while I was gone? she wondered. She longed to be home, but she dreaded the tension she was afraid would be between her and her husband the first couple of days.

At least I didn't have nightmares last night. That was a relief, wasn't it? She didn't feel more secure in the absence of the dreams, though. She felt as she did in the spring when tornado season was at its peak. The dreams were like the winds that blew across the plains when a tornado was still safely in the distance. People who live in tornado country know that when the wind dies down and the sky becomes deathly still, it is time to run for shelter. Martha had that feeling today, but there was no shelter for her, so she walked resolutely to the Family Planning Clinic, hoping the procedure would not be painful, but believing she deserved the pain.

When she walked into the waiting room, she was surprised that all the seats were empty. The only sound came from Ms. White's typewriter. Martha walked up to her and stood quietly in front of her desk. When the tiny woman did not acknowledge her presence, she cleared her throat and waited expectantly. Martha was sure the woman had heard her and dreaded another scene. Finally, she said, "Ms. White, I have an appointment."

The woman looked up through her bifocals with an expression of irritation. "Your name?" she asked coldly.

"Mrs. Harold Gibbons, Martha."

"All appointments have been canceled for the remainder of the week, Miss Gibbons," she said, running her finger down the appointment calendar. "We have rescheduled you for ten A.M. Monday." She returned immediately to her typing, letting Martha know the conversation was finished.

Martha couldn't believe her ears. She continued to stand by the desk, trying to absorb the woman's words. Ms. White ignored her. "But you said it would be today," Martha finally pleaded. "I can't stay in the city until Monday. I have to go back home."

"That is your problem, Miss Gibbons, not mine," the woman replied without pausing in her typing.

"Isn't there some way I can see the doctor today?"

"We seem to be repeating ourselves, miss. I've already told you that all appointments have been canceled. Do you want the appointment on Monday or not? If you don't, there are plenty of other women who will be happy to fill that time slot."

Martha didn't know what to do. She did not have enough money to stay at the YWCA until Monday. She didn't have the money for food. On the other hand, she had to have the abortion. "Monday will have to be okay, I guess," she said, then walked dejectedly out of the clinic and back to her room. She had no idea what she was going to do. She locked her door, flopped on the bed, and cried herself to sleep.

Patrick MacNamara hunched low in a seat at the back of the bar, nursing a Scotch and trying to decide what to do about Laura Bernhardt. Normally if one of his detectives came to him with a story like hers, he would put him on leave and refer him to the department's psychiatric program. The research he had done today, and his gut feeling, indicated that Bernhardt wasn't crazy. What was crazy, he decided, were these murders. MacNamara had asked the pathologist to do a pregnancy test on Rhonda Hackman. He'd called back a few hours later and said the woman had been pregnant. Although he hadn't received the complete autopsy report, it was obvious from looking at the body that the results would come out similar to the other murders. Three women had now been strangled, all three of them pregnant.

The picture of Rhonda that Laura had picked up from the college had been helpful. They had found a waitress who recognized her and said she thought the girl had been living at the Arms Apartments, not a particularly good place for a young college woman to hang out, MacNamara thought. Bernhardt had told him she suspected Hackman was pregnant, but there was no way she could have found that out during the rape investigation. First, the girl's doctor said he hadn't done a pregnancy test. Secondly, the pathologist said she was in such early stages of her pregnancy that a test would not have turned out positive two weeks ago.

MacNamara gulped down the rest of his drink. It's got to be someone from the Family Planning Clinic, he thought, unconsciously running his finger around the edge of his glass. He had talked the judge into closing the clinic for a few days, but next week it was going to be open again. That only gave them Thursday through Sunday to try to find the murderer.

Rhonda didn't quite fit into the pattern of the other women. Her name was not listed on the clinic's appointment calendar, and there wasn't a file on her. Her file could have been removed by someone who didn't want the police to know she was a client, or she could have given a false name. He had a team of experts going over the appointment calendar with a fine-tooth comb. If Hackman's name had been on it, then was erased or whited out, they would find it.

The waitress returned with his lunch. He was a regular customer and knew the help by name. Normally he liked to flirt with the waitresses. This afternoon he barely noticed that Sally's new blouse showed even more cleavage than usual.

The case didn't add up. When the landlord at the

Arms let them into Hackman's apartment, they found an early pregnancy kit in the bathroom. It was positive, and the crime lab said it had been used within the past twenty-four hours.

"Why would a woman go to a clinic and find out she was pregnant, then go to the supermarket and buy a pregnancy test? And if Hackman had been a client at the clinic, it would have had to be in the last week or so. Everyone in the place couldn't be involved in the murders, so if she had been there recently, why didn't anyone recognize her picture? Even if they didn't recognize her, they would surely remember a woman coming in with her ribs taped and still showing injuries from an assault.

He took another gulp of his drink. If the alcohol didn't help him think more clearly, maybe it would take the edge off his frustration.

Then there is Laura Bernhardt, he thought, scratching his head. In his years on the force he had been involved in a few cases where clairvoyants had been called in. It usually was a total waste of time, and MacNamara thought it plummeted police science into the dark ages. There was one case, though, when he was a young street cop, in which a woman had come up with some remarkable evidence on a murder. She not only was able to locate the body, she contributed important information about the killer.

He had personally read every word in Bernhardt's file and she never had shown any signs of psychic ability before. He had to admit, however, that she had uncanny luck in solving her cases.

MacNamara's talk with Milner about her hadn't helped much either. Her main fault seemed to be that she was too eager to prove herself. She certainly hadn't shown signs of insanity.

He thought back over the conversations he'd had earlier with Bud Jenkins and Susie Locke. They both confirmed Laura's story about the nightmares. Even if Bernhardt had fabricated her own nightmares, it didn't explain why Jenkins and Locke had shared nearly identical dreams.

I've got to make a decision, he thought. If Bernhardt is
on the level, she might be the best lead we've got. She
might also be in serious danger. He dropped his swizzle
stick and paled at a sudden thought. Tomorrow I'm ordering that woman to have a pregnancy test. If it is positive, I'm assigning her office duty until after the kid is
born. If she stays on the case, I don't want her going
anywhere by herself. I don't like the idea of her having
the same dream as the victims. I don't like it at all. I hope
she and Winchell are getting along better, because they
are about to become constant companions.

A child's laughter penetrated Martha's heavy sleep. In
her dream a lady detective was warning her about something. The woman was attractive and had the professional look Martha imagined she would have if she had
moved to the city instead of getting married. The warning apparently had something to do with the laughing
child. In her dream Martha smiled. Oh, I see. I have to
wake up now. The kids are home from school. She struggled to bring herself back to consciousness. She had to
give her children their snack. Her eyes slowly opened. At
first she thought she was still dreaming. She should be in
her familiar bedroom. She remembered she wasn't at
home. She was at the YWCA. She felt like crying but
forced herself to stay in control. This was no time to fall
apart. She had to make some decisions, even if all the
choices seemed impossible at the moment.

Is it morning? Did I sleep straight through the night?
She looked out the tiny bar-covered window. It was light,
but she couldn't tell the time of day. She went into the
hall to look at the clock. It was only two P.M. She was
amazed she had slept only an hour, and gave a sigh of
relief. Harold was expecting her to call this evening to tell
him which bus she would arrive on. She was going to
have enough explaining to do without her call coming in
twenty-four hours late. He might even try to get hold of
her at her mom's house if she was late. She would have to
expand her lies when she talked to him. It seemed the
longer she stayed in the city, the more deeply entrenched
she became in deceit.

Several women were standing in a cluster, talking loudly about a notice on the bulletin board. Martha had noticed them around the Y during the past week and had been amazed at their boisterous exuberance. She paused to see what they were looking at.

"Are you interested in a temporary job?" one of the women boomed.

Martha suddenly was wide awake. "I sure am," she said excitedly.

"There was a fire at the United Foods warehouse yesterday. They are hiring temporary help to clean up the place. They want people who can work ten to twelve hours a day through the weekend. It's going to be dirty work, but it pays eight bucks an hour. They're calling it contract labor, so they won't even take taxes out. And they are paying cash at the end of each day."

It sounded so perfect, Martha dared not even hope. She did some quick calculations in her head. If she got the job, she could bring in enough money to pay for her room until the abortion, to eat real meals, and to take a couple of hundred dollars back home with her. Maybe it was too good to be true.

"Is it close to a bus line?" she asked doubtfully. "I don't have a car."

"No, but I have a car. You can ride with us. By the way, my name is Judy, and this is Jan and Cynthia."

They were leaving in half an hour, so Martha hurried to get ready. On the spur of the moment she put her last fifty cents in a vending machine for a package of cheese and crackers.

It was nearly six by the time the women got back to the Y. All four of them had been hired and were to report to work at six A.M. The others invited her to join them for dinner, but she declined, saying she had a phone call to make. That was true, but she also didn't want to admit she had no money for dinner.

Martha dreaded going out by herself at night, but the pay phone hanging on the wall at the Y offered no privacy, so she walked to the booth at the end of the block. She dialed zero and asked the operator to reverse the charges. She started crying at the sound of Harold junior's voice.

"Yes, we'll accept the charges," he told the operator in his most grown-up voice, then yelled, "It's Mommy. Mommy's on the phone."

She talked to each of her four excited children, assuring them she would be home soon and that she loved them. Only Jeff was quiet on the other end of the line. He still was young enough that he didn't quite know what to do with the receiver Sandy was holding to his ear, but Martha knew he was grinning and shaking his head at the other end while she told him what a good boy he was.

Sandy said Daddy wanted to talk to her, and Martha heard Harold tell the kids to go finish their dinner. She tried to keep her hands from shaking while she waited for him to get on the phone. She heard a door close and knew he had stretched the cord into the girls' room so he could talk to her privately.

"Hello, Martha."

She winced when his voice rang cold and impersonal across the miles. She tried to sound normal. "It's good to talk to you, sweetheart." They spoke the words people always said on the telephone, but the conversation was far from normal. The silence of what wasn't being said crashed through the wires.

"Is your mother feeling better?"

Martha visualized his words as blocks of ice. She could imagine them freezing a critical crossline between Taylorsville and the city, cutting off communications to several states.

"She's a little better, but I'm afraid I'll have to stay here until next Tuesday. She can't get around on her own yet."

Then he was yelling at her. "Do you think I'm a fool, Martha? I know you aren't at your mother's house. Who is he? Do you think you can take off with some man for a couple of weeks, then come back here and expect me to take you back?"

Martha's mind bolted in several directions at once while her heart flip-flopped. She mentally kicked herself for not having realized that Harold would find out she had lied and would assume she was having an affair. How could she tell him that yes, she was breaking one of the ten commandments, but when she went astray, she went right to the top of the list—Thou shalt not kill. Like an animal trapped in a forest fire, her mind darted to and fro looking for an escape. She had to come up with an explanation Harold would accept, and she had to do it quickly, but she had started this fire herself, and unknowingly had nurtured the flames until they formed a complete circle around her. Her deceit was closing in and engulfing her. Harold was saying she could never come home. She had dreamt so often of being single, childless, and living in the city; now her dream was catapulting into a real-life nightmare worse than any she had suffered during the past week.

The deception was over. If she had told Harold she was pregnant before, she might have been able to talk him into agreeing to an abortion. Now it was too late. She didn't think the truth would do any good at this point, but it was the only thing she had. If he wouldn't take her back, at least she could let him know that she had not been unfaithful and that she loved him and their children more than anything in the world.

She heard Harold yell to the kids that everything was okay and that they were to go take their baths. She could imagine them outside the bedroom door, frightened and crying because their dad was screaming at her.

"Haven't you got anything to say for yourself?" he hissed quietly so the children wouldn't hear.

"It's true that I'm not at my mother's house, but I'm not having an affair," Martha sobbed. "I know you don't have any reason to believe me, but I can prove it. Would someone who was having an affair be staying at the YWCA? I've never been unfaithful to you. I love you, Harold."

"You have a funny way of showing it. You abandon me and your children and take off with some man, then tell me a story about the YWCA. Where are you?"

"I'm in the city, and I am staying at the Y. I did not come here to meet a man, and I didn't abandon you or the kids."

"The city? What are you doing in the city if you didn't go there to meet your lover?"

"I'll explain it all, but first, call the Y and verify my story. Ask to talk to me. They'll say that I'm out now. I'm calling from a phone booth on the corner. Verify when I checked in. You'll see I've been here all along." She wanted to prove she wasn't having an affair, but she also wanted to buy a little time before she told her husband about the abortion.

Harold paused, then said, "Okay, I'll call, but your story had better be good. What is the number there?"

"I don't remember it. The operator will have to give it to you, but I'll give you the number here at the phone booth so you can call me back." She squinted to read the number on the telephone. She hadn't noticed how dark this end of the street was. She was barely able to make out the number for Harold, and waited anxiously for him to call her back. While she stood looking at the shadows along the shabby street, she was painfully aware of the darkness and her vulnerability. Had the streetlight burned out while she was talking to Harold? She hadn't noticed, but it was possible. She didn't remember having any trouble seeing the numbers on the dial when she called him, but if she tried to telephone someone now, she wouldn't be able to see.

Her eyes darted up and down the street while she waited for the phone to ring. Anything could happen to a woman alone in this neighborhood. The memories of her nightmares assaulted her in vivid clarity. She felt like running to safety as fast as her legs would carry her, but she had to wait for Harold's call. Her marriage depended on it.

When the phone finally rang, she grabbed the receiver gratefully.

"Okay, Martha, I believe you are staying at the Y, but what are you up to?" Harold asked, his voice not quite as hostile as before.

"I don't know how to tell you this. Do you remember how I was tired and sick the last few weeks?"

"Are you ill?" His voice showed real concern. "You haven't got cancer or something like that, have you?"

"No, I'm not sick. I'm pregnant." She rushed on and told him the story before she lost her nerve. When she finished talking, Harold said nothing. Finally Martha asked if he was still there.

"I'm here. I just don't know what to say. Why didn't you tell me you were pregnant?"

"I was afraid you would say no to an abortion." Her voice was calmer now, but tears were streaming down her cheeks. "I told myself I was doing it for the kids, because we can't afford another child and the ones we already have would suffer. I told myself I was doing it for you, because you have enough responsibilities. I told myself I was doing it for the baby, because it isn't fair to bring it into a life of poverty. I'm beginning to realize that most of all, I'm doing it for myself. I don't want another child, Harold. I'm tired. I don't have the energy to get through another pregnancy and take care of Harold junior, Sandy, Jeff, and Karen, then start all over with two o'clock feedings and diapers."

"You could have at least told me. Do you think I'm an ogre? What do you think I would have done, beat you?"

"You don't exactly encourage me to talk to you, Harold. You don't tell me anything about what is going on with your job or our finances, and when I ask you, you either ignore me or make me feel like it is none of my business. You never seem to want to talk to me about anything."

"But an abortion, Martha? How could you consider killing our baby?"

"And what about my life, Harold? Don't I have a right to a life? Don't I have a right to have enough energy to be a wife to you?"

"Come home, Martha. Forget this whole thing."

"Pregnancy isn't something that goes away if you ignore it."

"Then come home for a few days, and if you still want to have the abortion, you can go back to the city and keep that appointment on Monday."

"I can't do that either," she said, and told him about the job.

"Are you sure you want to come home at all?" he

replied angrily. "You always wanted to live in the city. Maybe you aren't planning on ever coming back. Maybe you have met another man there."

"How can you say that?" She sobbed. "I've hated every minute of this. I want to be home more than anything. I didn't know how lonely life could be without you and the kids. I would love to hop on the next bus out of this godforsaken place, but we need that money."

"It looks to me like you spent one week in the city and turned into a bra-burning women's libber. I've never let you and the kids go hungry. Now you don't trust me to support you anymore."

"Why can't you see that it isn't an insult to you for me to help out a little? Are you willing to deny our children what that money will buy for them because of your male pride? I'll only be gone five more days."

"You say that today, but what about Monday? How do I know you won't call again and say you aren't coming back, that you've found another job?"

"I won't. I promise. You seem to think I'm having one big party here. I'm not. I hate it. I'm hungry, I'm tired, I'm sick, and I'm lonely, but I have to do this. I love you, Harold. I wish I could come home this very minute."

Harold hesitated then said, "I love you, too, Martha. These past few days I've been afraid I'd lost you."

"There will never be anyone else for me, Harold. I've loved you since we were kids. I promised to keep loving you until death do us part. I'll keep that promise."

"Till death do us part, Martha."

She reluctantly hung up the phone but made no effort to leave the booth. Her emotions were too jumbled to go back to the Y right away. She was filled with relief and sadness, love and confusion; but everything was going to be all right. Harold loved her and wanted her back, and the deceit was over. She vowed never to lie to him again.

When she was talking to Harold, she was so nervous she didn't notice the cold. Now she realized she was freezing. She looked anxiously down the dark street toward the Y. Not only was the streetlight burned out, but while she had talked to Harold, a fog had settled over the city, securely hiding anyone who might be lurking in a

corner or alley. The normally busy street was abandoned.
She jumped at the unexpected sound of the telphone ringing.

"Harold?" she said nervously into the receiver.

A child's laughter burst through the earpiece, paralyzing her with fear. She slammed the phone down.

"It's only a kid playing a game," she said, her voice
sounding alien as it bounced off the walls of the small
phone booth, but even as she spoke, the child's laughter
was back. It wasn't coming through the lifeless telephone
this time. It was descending on her in the darkness. She
recognized it as the voice from her dreams. She squinted
to see through the patchy fog. The voice was clearer now.
It seemed to come from everywhere and nowhere.

Martha's panic grew. She had to make it back to the Y.
As she bolted from the telephone booth, she spotted a
figure lurking in the shadows across the street. She
couldn't make out his face, but it was obvious from his
size that it was a man. She was certain he was watching
her, waiting for her. Her heart palpitated wildly as she
backed slowly into the phone booth and shut the door
behind her. She dug frantically through her purse, looking for twenty cents so she could call the police. Even as
she felt in the darkness for loose change, she knew it was
futile. She had spent her last fifty cents on cheese and
crackers.

She picked up the receiver. Maybe she could make an
emergency call without money. The line was dead.

"This is one of the nightmares," she whispered. "I'll
wake up in a minute." But even as she whispered, the
man started to walk slowly across the street toward her.

Her only chance was to make it back to the Y. She had
to outrace him. She yanked the door of the phone booth.
It wouldn't budge.

The man was halfway across the street when she felt
the presence. She began screaming. She could see nothing, but she felt the child with her in the booth. He was
keeping her from escaping. His laughter reverberated
through the phone booth. His evil assaulted her like a
physical blow, and she gagged on the smell of decaying
flesh.

The man was stepping onto the sidewalk, but she couldn't see his face through the fog. The child's laughter penetrated her screams. She covered her ears, but the child's voice welled up inside her head.

The man's hand reached for the handle of the phone booth.

Martha was still screaming. The world should be dark, but a light was blinding her. The child's laughter was replaced by another sound. It was a car honking. Martha continued to scream while the man ran away. The car was following him. It was Judy and her friends. They were right behind her would-be assaulter, honking and yelling at him. She heard Judy and Cynthia shouting and calling him a pervert.

"When we catch you, we're going to cut your balls off and stuff them in your mouth, you asshole," Jan yelled. Their car screeched into an alley after him.

The child wasn't in Martha's head anymore, or in the phone booth, but she could sense his anger and knew he could—and would—come back for her. She felt the lightning welling up in the sky like an angry fist. The premonition she felt when she first heard about the electrical storms flashed through her head like a primitive warning, unlike any thought pattern she had ever before experienced. She charged blindly into the street. As she leapt over the curb, the electricity made her hair stand on end. She felt the force of the lightning hit the phone booth. In the same instant she was airborne.

She woke up on the sidewalk on the other side of the street. Judy, Cynthia, and Jan were leaning over her. The sky was quiet and the fog had lifted. Bright streetlights illuminated the darkness.

When the women were certain Martha was okay, Judy bellowed, "That's one creep who won't bother you again. You should have seen him bolt over the wall at the end of the alley. He was scared shitless."

"It's a good thing we came along when we did," Cynthia interjected. "Lady, you could give lessons on getting into trouble. That storm was weird. It was just one bolt of lightning that hit the phone booth. You're lucky to be alive."

Martha shook her head in the affirmative and started to sob.

"It's okay. You go ahead and cry. Say, we brought you a hamburger and some fries."

Martha looked at the bag her new friend held up and started laughing hysterically. For the first time in a week she was looking at a meal, and she couldn't eat it if her life depended on it. She did gratefully take a sip of hot coffee Jan held to her lips. Martha's hands were shaking too badly to hold the cup.

"Come on. We'll give you a ride back to the Y," Judy said.

Later in the evening Martha felt well enough to eat the cold hamburger and fries. She didn't mention the child, or the nightmares, to her friends. She didn't even allow herself to think about them, because if she acknowledged them, she would have to admit the danger wasn't over.

37

Adam bolted blindly down the dark alley and tripped over a garbage can. The lid banged loudly on the pavement as he struggled to his feet and continued running. He didn't know how far he had run or where he was. His only measurement of time since the women chased him was the increasing pain in his lungs and ribs. He was gasping for air and limping, but he continued to run. It wasn't the women he feared now. He had lost them almost immediately. He was trying to escape from Jeremy's wrath. The boy screamed inside Adam's head, blocking all other sounds. Adam could feel the rage behind him, in him, around him. Then, suddenly, it was gone.

Adam fell to the ground, wheezing and clutching his chest. When his breathing became less labored, he rolled into a fetal ball and made no effort to get up. He waited helplessly for Jeremy to finish him off, but the only sound was the loud beating of his heart. The only sensation was the pain in his lungs and muscles. His son had given him a job to do, and he had failed him. Jeremy didn't like to be disappointed. Jeremy said a good father never let his son down. Adam knew he was right. His son was God's agent, and he was his son's agent. He had failed his boy and his God, so he waited for the inevitable punishment.

He continued to wait, but he felt only emptiness. His fear of the punishment was replaced by terror of the emptiness. Recently he had felt Jeremy's presence even when he wasn't watching the television. He felt him when he was at work or walking by the grade school, but tonight the boy had abandoned him, leaving a burned-out shell, not a person.

"I'm sorry," he whined. "Please don't leave me. I'm nothing without you. I'll get the woman next time, just don't go away, Jeremy."

He blubbered and begged, but Jeremy was not with him. Adam whimpered and sucked his thumb until the sweat covering his body turned to ice, and still there was no Jeremy. The cold forced him to stand up and get his bearings.

He was a long way from home, but finally he heaved his way up the dark fire escape. He dreaded reaching the door, because he feared the television would be gone, taking with it his only reason for living. As he turned the key in the lock, he wondered how he ever could have considered taking his own life when he had Jeremy to live for; now he didn't have Jeremy and he had lost the courage to end his miserable existence.

When he walked inside, he felt the boy before he saw his shadow in the round eye. He stumbled across the room, fell prostrate before the metal box, and hugged the base of the television. He had to get the child within to forgive him.

Adam cowered while the boy calmly chastised him. "How can I trust you, Daddy, when you keep letting me down? I don't ask much, do I? Maybe I should find a better daddy."

"I won't let you down again, son. You've got to believe me. Please, don't leave me."

"You've broken your promises before, Daddy."

"I won't again. You'll see. I'll get that woman. I'll do anything you say."

"Anything? Anything at all?"

"Yes, you have my word. Stay with me, and I'll be a good father."

"If I stay, I'll remember your oath. Will you be ready when I call on you, even if what I ask is difficult?"

"There isn't anything I wouldn't do for my boy."

"Then I'll give you one more chance."

The shadow child faded from the screen, replaced by the shrinking red retina. Adam smiled and curled up on the bed with his shoe box. Everything was okay. Jeremy was still there. He lovingly fingered the growing number of souvenirs. There was Marie's scarf and, of course, Sister Mary Xavier's ring. He picked up the Ann woman's earring. He had a special fondness for it because she was the first woman he had punished for Jeremy. Then there was the bleached blond's pink gloves. He tried putting them on his hands, but they were way too small. He remembered how spooky she'd acted before he punished her. When she'd started acting as if she were talking to Laura Bernhardt, it had frightened him. For a minute he'd thought maybe Miss Laura was really there, before he realized Jeremy was making her think Laura was there. He laughed when he thought of the way she had walked right into his waiting arms. All the women had come eagerly to him. Jeremy had explained to him that he had made the Ann woman think she was going to pick up her boyfriend at the park, and that Joyce had thought she was going to rescue her daughter, who had really run away to spend the night at her boyfriend's house.

He frowned at the necklace belonging to the woman from the phone booth and put the box away. When he reached out to turn on the television, he noticed a woman's ring on top. "Jeremy really has forgiven me," he muttered aloud, then gently kissed the new souvenir. The ring could only mean that Jeremy was going to let him punish another woman, and Adam was as excited as a child waiting to go to a carnival.

38

Thursday, February 7

Laura pulled her knees under her on the couch and wrapped an afghan snugly around her shoulders. She silently thanked MacNamara for ordering her to take some time off work. She knew the tensions of the past months were taking their toll. Darryl also was relieved she was home for a couple of days, though he couldn't hide his continued concern about her nightmares and premonitions. She was sorry she had been forced to discuss them with her husband and boss. On the other hand, she felt as if she had been struggling under an oppressive burden. The burden wasn't gone, but at least now she had help carrying it. She leaned against the end of the couch and smiled at the luxury of spending a day alone at home. The doctor had confirmed she was in perfect health after Darryl firmly escorted her to the appointment he'd made for her yesterday. He did lecture her on getting more sleep and eating regular meals, though. She started following his advice immediately. On the way home she and Darryl stopped at their favorite Italian restaurant and stuffed themselves on a late lunch of lasagna and garlic bread. They were home by three, and Laura gladly went straight to the bedroom and fell into a deep sleep for several hours.

She frowned at the memory of the nightmare that had awakened her. She had been tempted to call MacNamara but decided against it. She knew all her dreams weren't premonitions and if she bothered the chief at home, she wanted to have more substantial information to give him. By nine she was back in bed again, and if she had any dreams during the remainder of the night, she didn't remember them.

I'm not going to think about the dreams or the murders today, she told herself firmly. This is my day off. I'm not going to think about anything more serious than when to start my next nap and what sexy negligee I'm going to have on when my husband walks through the door tonight.

She took a sip of the coffee she had placed on the end table, then picked up the morning newspaper and rolled the rubber band off. Despite her determination not to think about work, she looked at the paper apprehensively. No headlines shouted that another woman had been mysteriously murdered, so she relaxed and began glancing through the stories.

When she reached page five, her eyes grew wide and she paled. She stared at a picture of an unrecognizable molten heap. The caption and story said it was a telephone booth that had been hit last night by a freak bolt of lightning. The paper said no one was near the booth at the time and no injuries had been reported.

It was her nightmare yesterday afternoon, but in the dream a woman had been using the telephone and someone was coming across the street to kill her. Laura had cried out to warn her, but the lady didn't hear. According to the paper the lightning had hit around the time Laura woke up in a cold sweat.

Now she would have to call MacNamara, and she dreaded the prospect. She still didn't know if the chief believed her or if he had decided she was crazy.

I should have called him last night before I had a chance to read the paper, she thought. Since I didn't, he will probably think I made it up. I didn't even mention the dream to Darryl because I didn't want to worry him. Oh, well, there's nothing I can do about it.

"Bernhardt, I was just getting ready to call you," MacNamara said when his secretary transferred her call to him. "I want you to go to the doctor today and get a complete physical, and while you are at it, have him give you a pregnancy test."

"I did that yesterday, sir, right after I left the office. He says I'm as healthy as a horse."

"And the pregnancy test?"

"The official results won't be back until tomorrow, but I can assure you I am not pregnant. I only had the test because, under the circumstances, I knew you would order it."

"When the report comes in, I'd like to talk to your doctor personally."

"If you are satisfied with his report, are you going to keep me on the case?"

"Yes, if you are healthy and the pregnancy test is negative. Why did you call, Laura? Did something else happen?"

She told him about the nightmare and the picture in the paper, but added that she didn't remember what the man and woman looked like.

"Why didn't you call me last night? Never mind that now. I want you to get down to headquarters right away. I'll meet you there in an hour. I'm going to set up an appointment for you with Jerry Farmington and Andy Carpenter."

"Oh, I see. The police department's artist and hypnotist. Jerry can hypnotize me and have me relive the dream and Andy can draw the people I describe."

"Don't get your hopes up, Laura. You know as well as I do that hypnosis doesn't always work, and your dream might have been just a bizarre coincidence; but it's worth a try."

An hour later she walked nervously into headquarters and pushed the elevator button.

The chief walked into Jerry's office a few seconds after she arrived, followed immediately by Andy. He offered Andy and Jerry no explanation, and they knew better than to ask for one.

The hypnosis was nothing like the way it was portrayed on television. Jerry didn't swing a pendant in front of her face and tell her she was falling into a deep sleep. Instead, it reminded Laura of her meditation tape. Jerry quietly talked her into a deeper and deeper state of meditation. She didn't believe at first that she was hypnotized, but when he told her she could now see her dream, it was as vivid in her mind as if it were happening right then. The difference was that, under hypnosis, she didn't feel the fear and frustration that had bolted her awake Wednesday evening. As Jerry led her through the dream, she saw the woman in the telephone booth. Jerry told her the action was going to stop, and she would see the scene

as a photograph rather than a moving picture. Andy
drew rapidly while she described the woman.

Laura's brow knitted into wrinkles and she looked confused.

"What is it, Laura? What do you see?" Jerry asked
calmly.

"There's someone else in the phone booth."

"Can you describe this person?"

"It's not a person. It's a shadow."

Jerry and Andy looked doubtfully at MacNamara. The
chief nodded his head and pointed at Andy's drawing,
indicating he wanted the artist to draw whatever Laura
described.

Suddenly the horror of the dream came rushing back
to her and she began to scream to the woman. "It's the
child. You've got to run. Get out or you'll be killed."

"It's okay, Laura," Jerry coaxed. "You feel no emotion. Do you understand?"

Laura pulled instinctively away from the picture in her
mind, but she was calmer. Jerry talked to her until she
once again was able to detach herself from what she saw.
Andy drew what she described but could not hide his
curiosity over this unexpected assignment.

"Laura, the picture is going to move again, but in slow
motion. Do you see anyone else?"

"I see a man. He's coming across the street."

MacNamara sat up eagerly in his chair.

"What does he look like?"

She squinted at the vision only she was seeing. "I can't
tell. It's very dark, and it's foggy."

"Which way is the man walking?"

"He is going toward the phone booth. The woman is
frightened."

"Is she afraid of the man?"

"Yes, but she is afraid of the shadow too."

"Where is the man now, Laura?"

"He's right outside the phone booth."

"Can you describe him?"

"I'm behind him. I can't see his face. I've got to help
the woman."

"What is he wearing?"

"It's too foggy. I can't tell. I'm too far away. I can't help her. My God, the lightning is coming." Laura jerked, then looked around in relief.

"What's happening now, Laura? Where are you?"

"I'm in my bedroom. I woke up."

"That's it," MacNamara said. "Bring her back."

Later, the chief gripped the steering wheel of his big Oldsmobile firmly and kept his eyes focused straight ahead, even though they still were sitting at the curb and the ignition was off. Laura sat quietly in the passenger's seat, staring at the pictures Andy had drawn. The picture on the left was a composite of the woman's face. The picture on the right epitomized the entire nightmare. The unidentifiable man was walking toward the booth. The woman had her hands over her ears and was screaming, but what Laura was staring at was the shadow. It looked like the smoke of a genie entering its bottle. But there wasn't any bottle. The shadowy figure was suspended partway inside the woman's head.

MacNamara finally cut through the silence. "I don't envy you your dreams."

"Do you believe me, Chief?"

"I believe that is what you dreamed, but I'm not convinced it has anything to do with the murders."

"Are you going to check it out?"

"I might as well. It can't hurt anything."

"Can I help?"

"I don't think that would be a good idea. I'd rather assign it to a more objective person. I'll have Martínez run the woman's picture over to the family planning clinic to see if anyone recognizes her."

"What about the other picture, the one of her in the phone booth?"

"You can have it. I'd just as soon not have it around the precinct."

Laura nodded her head in the affirmative. She wasn't anxious for the other detectives to see the picture either. "If someone recognizes the woman, then what?" Laura asked.

"Then you and I will go have a talk with her."

"Can I go to the office this afternoon?"

"No. Go back home and get some more sleep."

"I'm not tired. I couldn't rest if my life depended on it. I'd rather be working."

"I don't want you back on the case until I talk to your doctor."

"I understand," she said reluctantly. "I guess I'd do the same thing if I were in your shoes." She handed the drawing of the woman's face to MacNamara and looked down at the other picture. "Do you know what is wrong with it?" she asked pensively.

"Could something be wrong? I certainly didn't notice."

Laura ignored his sarcasm. "The problem is, you can't tell if the ghost is going into her head, or coming out." She looked up in time to see the chief shudder.

Darryl stared intently at the picture on the coffee table while Laura watched him anxiously. She had told him about the dream, the newspaper, and the hypnosis. Now she was waiting for him to say something. He didn't know what to say, so he kept looking at the picture. He was wondering if his wife really was crazy. He couldn't tell her that was what he was thinking, though the picture seemed to indicate a sick mind.

"What did MacNamara say?" he finally asked.

"He acted like you, then said he would see if anyone at the clinic recognized the woman. You don't think anyone will, do you, Darryl?"

"I don't know, sweetie. I only know that I love you, and I'm worried about you."

"I shouldn't have shown you the picture," she snapped angrily.

"I'm glad you did. You promised to keep me informed, remember. If you don't tell me what is going on, I'll be even more worried."

"I think I could use a glass of wine," Laura said with a sigh. "How about you?"

"That's the best idea I've heard all evening. Why don't you bring back the whole bottle?"

Laura headed for the kitchen while Darryl continued to stare at the picture. He looked across the room at the rug Laura had hooked last winter, but he didn't see it.

His thoughts still were on the picture, the murders, and his wife's mental health. He looked down at the picture again, then blinked and stared in horror.

"The ghost!" he gasped. He backed away from the coffee table while keeping his eyes on the shadowy figure in the picture. "It was suspended partway inside the woman's head before. I know it was. Laura and I talked about it. I saw it there—so why is it outside the phone booth?"

This is ridiculous, he thought. Laura is so concerned about the picture that her fear is making me hallucinate. He looked at the ceiling and concentrated on being calm and logical. When I look back, I'll see the picture as it really is, he told himself, but when he looked down, the ghost was hovering at the edge of the paper.

He closed his eyes and shook his head, as if trying to shake the crazy hallucination from it. He knew what he thought he had seen couldn't possibly be real, but he couldn't shake the terror that was growing in the pit of his stomach like a malignant tumor. He kept his eyes closed, as though blocking out the impossible would negate it. Then something came at him, like an electrically charged wind. It knocked him off balance and passed through him. His eyes bolted open and he saw that the shadow was gone from the picture. His body felt as though it had been flash-frozen from the inside out, and he staggered and tried to keep his balance.

Laura screamed and he forgot his own fear and rushed to the kitchen. She was huddled in a corner with a wild look in her eyes.

"What is it?" he asked, pulling her to him but afraid of her answer.

"I felt it. It was trying to get into me. It wasn't my imagination, Darryl. It was real."

"I believe you. The shadow is gone from the picture." He pulled her back into the living room and to the picture. He stared at it in disbelief. The shadow was back where it had started, suspended partway inside the woman's head. It was just a picture, a harmless, inanimate object on the coffee table.

Darryl held Laura tightly, as much to comfort himself as to reassure her. "I don't know what is going on around

here, but I want that picture out of this house. Now!" he
said.

Even after he and Laura had carried the drawing two
blocks from their home and burned it, Darryl didn't feel
safe. He tried to tell himself there was a logical explanation for what had happened, but he couldn't shake his
feeling of dread. He had felt something pass through him,
and when Laura screamed, he had felt an evil force in the
air.

"They're going to find the woman in that drawing,"
Laura said with certainty while they held hands and
watched the charred remains of the picture scatter in the
wind. "I only hope they find her alive."

39

Tracy had been grounded since the day she walked out of
school. She didn't care. In fact, she was glad. It gave her
an excuse to turn down Mark and her friends. It did hurt,
though, that Mark seemed relieved that she couldn't go
out with him. She winced when she thought about her
boyfriend. He had started walking her to class again and
eating lunch with her, but their relationship was strained.
She knew he planned to break up with her when the
abortion was over. She could see it in his eyes. The love
had been replaced by a sense of duty.

Her mom and dad had wanted to take her to the doctor after their conference with her science teacher, but
she convinced them she had gotten lazy because she was
tired of winter and anxious for spring vacation. She also
knew that if there were any more complaints about her,
they wouldn't be dissuaded next time, so she was making
a real effort to do better in school and to improve her
grooming. At first it was difficult, but she learned to go
through the motions that were expected of her. She was
amazed she was able to appease her parents and teachers
so easily. They seemed to think that clean hair and completed homework meant a healthy mind. The truth was

that her nightmares had become more severe and more frequent, and she was in the depths of a despair that seemed like an endless black tunnel.

She was supposed to be working on her homework now, but when she heard her dad mention the murders, she pressed her ear against the wall and strained to hear their conversation.

"I wish I was working on the investigation, but someone has to keep up with the routine work around the precinct," her dad grumbled. "MacNamara has taken half my people, but our workload hasn't decreased. We still have the same old burglaries, assaults, family disturbances, and so forth to take care of."

"It must be frustrating for you, dear."

"It's not so bad. As busy as I've been, I still manage to keep up with the scuttlebutt on the murders."

"Do they have any good leads?"

"I shouldn't be telling you this, but everyone is convinced the murderer is someone from the Mid-City Family Planning Clinic. If they could only figure out who. Everyone seems to check out, but it would be too much of a coincidence that all three women were pregnant and two out of three had appointments for an abortion at that clinic."

"Maybe the murderer is a psychopath who just kills pregnant women."

"We've thought of that, but it doesn't fit. Only someone from the clinic would know they were pregnant. None of them were far enough along to show. Also, it appears that the victims were lured to their deaths."

"Maybe they were being blackmailed."

Tracy threw her hand up and bit her finger to keep from crying out, It's the child. Find the child and you'll stop the murders. She couldn't do that, though. Not only would she have to admit she was pregnant, but, when her parents heard her story, they would be convinced she was crazy and have her committed. She couldn't give her dad any useful information anyway. After all, the child was only a figment of her imagination; a loud hallucination that shouted in her head, jarring her with splitting headaches.

"MacNamara got a court order to close the clinic for a few days, and we are going over the list of clients with a fine-tooth comb," her Dad said.

He's going to find out, Tracy thought desperately. But I gave a false name and address. I used the fake ID Mark gave me. There's no way they can trace it back to me, is there?

"Get away from the wall, you little cunt." The voice rang from within her head and jerked her back as though she had been struck. Tracy tried to scream, but her voice stuck in her throat.

"Only whores eavesdrop," the voice taunted.

"Leave me alone," she pleaded, unaware that in her terror, her plea was a silent thought. "I can't take any more."

The child's laughter hammered through her head and beat against the inside of her skull. She staggered to the bed and curled in a fetal position under the covers while the voice taunted and threatened her. The attack seemed endless and she lost awareness of her room. When it was finally over, the house was quiet. She tiptoed to her parents' bedroom and heard the heavy breathing of their sleep. Exhausted, she returned to her own room and pulled the covers over her head, like a small child warding off the boogeyman. She knew she needed help, but she didn't know whom she could turn to.

She fell asleep and dreamt about Laura Bernhardt.

40

Friday, February 8
Darryl had seemed relieved that Laura was going back to work. After the incident with the picture the night before, he didn't like the idea of her being at home alone. Laura also was glad, but for a different reason. The doctor had promised to call MacNamara first thing this morning, so she would be officially back on the cases. She was more determined than ever to solve the murders. She

was certain the chief was convinced the ghost suspended partway inside the woman's head in the picture was only a dream manifestation unrelated to the murders. Laura knew differently. It had to be the child who taunted her and whom her subconscious had warned her about the night she impaled her finger with the sewing machine. So far she didn't understand how the child and the murderer were connected, but she wouldn't rest until she found out.

"I'll stop you, you little brat," she said.

When she said it, she hadn't realized the force was near, so she was caught off guard when evil struck her, doubling her over with nausea.

"You won't do this to me," she shouted defiantly as she struggled to stand straight. "I will not be intimidated by you. I will not be frightened."

The unseen blow barreled at her again, and she sank to her knees, but she held her head high. "You're little and you're evil," she gasped. "I'll beat you. You had me frightened at first, but you went too far, and now I'm mad."

She could feel the force's anger grow. Despite her brave show, she was terrified. Still, she was determined not to give in. "You're nothing but a child," she screamed, "a mean, evil child. I will not be pushed around by a rotten little bully."

The entity's anger filled the house and shook the walls, but through her fear Laura had a flash of understanding. "I'm right, aren't I? You're powerless on your own. You aren't committing the murders. You can't. You have to get someone to do your dirty work for you because you are too weak to do it yourself. I'll find whoever you are using, and I'll stop him, and I'll stop you."

She felt something trying to get into her head. She knew she was lost if it succeeded, but she didn't know how to fight it. In desperation she began chanting, "God loves, God loves," over and over again. Around her, pictures were flying through the air and crashing on the floor, but she continued chanting. The shaking of the house began to subside, but she continued her chant. She could feel the child's anger dissipating in impotence.

When she could no longer feel the force, she continued to chant until she was calm, then she looked up and said, "I am stronger than you. I will win."

She cleaned up the mess, put on her coat, and drove to work. She had a plan.

Laura didn't have a chance to discuss her idea with MacNamara. When she arrived at work, she found him pacing his small, makeshift office.

"We got a positive ID on the woman from your dream, Laura, and I want you to know I don't like this one little bit. Her name is Martha Gibbons and she is scheduled for an abortion on Monday, the day the clinic reopens."

Laura nodded but said nothing.

"I can't deny that your dreams mean something, but that doesn't mean I'm going along with the ghost business. I don't doubt that you dream it, but not everything in your dreams has to be real."

"I agree perfectly, Chief," she lied. She was back on the case and she wasn't going to jeopardize it by revealing too much. Besides, what could she say? By the way, Chief. I had a great morning. I fought off an invisible force that seemed to be the evil spirit of a child. I did pretty well. The confrontation ended in a draw, but if you agree to my suggestions, next time I may beat the devil. No, MacNamara was having enough trouble accepting that she might be having precognitive dreams. She wasn't going to bring up the supernatural aspects of her experiences, not now or ever.

"The secretary at the clinic said Mrs. Gibbons had mentioned she was staying at the YWCA. I suggest we get out there and talk to her," MacNamara said.

Neither of them said much during the drive. When they arrived, the chief automatically took charge.

"Martha Gibbons isn't in any kind of trouble, is she?" the woman behind the counter asked when Patrick and Laura showed their identification. "She seems like a nice lady, but awfully nervous. We don't want any trouble. We work hard to maintain a good reputation. That's pretty difficult nowadays, especially in this neighborhood."

"No, ma'am. Mrs. Gibbons hasn't done anything

wrong. We just want to ask her some questions about something she might have seen."

"Is it about the man who approached her when she was making her telephone call a couple of days ago? I was working that night, and she was pretty upset. It's a good thing her friends came along when they did. The poor woman. I've been telling the manager for months that we need to install a phone booth inside so the women can make private calls. It's too dangerous for them to wander around outside after dark."

Patrick and Laura glanced at each other while the woman behind the counter rambled on. No words were necessary for them each to know they both were thinking about Laura's dream.

"Is Mrs. Gibbons in now?" the chief asked.

"No. She and some of the other girls got temporary jobs at the Food King warehouse, the one that caught fire a few days ago."

They got the address and left. Still another plan was forming in Laura's mind as she buckled her seat belt. She wondered how she was going to talk the chief into going along with it.

"If we find out what we think we are going to find out about Mrs. Gibbons's telephone call, someone will need to be assigned to guard her," Laura said while the chief pulled into the traffic. He clamped his jaw into a stubborn line that reminded Laura of Sergeant Binder, but minus the cigar and surly attitude.

"If the murderer went after her once, he is likely to try again," Laura continued.

"You're considering a lot of ifs, Bernhardt."

"Maybe, but if I'm right, can we afford to take chances with Martha Gibbons's life, or lose an opportunity to catch our man?"

"I understand what you are saying, and I've already thought about it. If she confirms the story about the telephone booth, I plan to assign some men to stake out the Y."

"No offense, Chief, but you might as well hang up a banner telling the murderer we are onto him. Male detectives hanging around the outside of the YWCA will stick out like a sore thumb. On the other hand, if I checked into the Y, no one would notice. I'd be just another woman, and I would be inside, where I could monitor her more closely."

"I won't use you as bait, Laura."

"You wouldn't be. This is totally different. Remember when you accused me of being sexist because I told you as a woman I thought I could get more information from the people at the family planning clinic? You were right then, but don't you think that now you are being a little sexist? You are saying it is okay for men to guard Martha Gibbons, but it is too risky for me. I have the same training as the other detectives. There is no reason why I can't handle the job."

"Laura, I hate having to repeat the obvious. It isn't that you are a woman and the other detectives on the case are men. It is that you are having dreams and other strange experiences that might affect your objectivity in a crisis situation. I can't afford to take that risk."

"I didn't ask to have these dreams, but you act as if the fact that I am makes me a liability in solving these crimes. That isn't true, Chief. If anything, it gives me an advantage. Without my dreams you wouldn't even have known about Martha Gibbons until she turned up dead."

Patrick sighed and rubbed the back of his neck with one hand. "Let's see what Martha Gibbons has to say before you start arguing with me about the next step in the investigation."

Laura looked out the window at the bright February sunshine. Her eerie experiences lately seemed unreal. A few weeks ago, she didn't even believe in the supernatural. Now she was preparing to do battle with a spirit and his helper. She didn't doubt her sanity anymore; rather she doubted the structure of the world as she had spent a lifetime perceiving it.

"Martha Gibbons, report to the front office," an impersonal voice blared through the loudspeaker. Martha looked up in disbelief and discarded the blackened label she had just stripped from a can of peas. She couldn't imagine why she was being paged, but she feared it was not a good sign.

She knocked hesitantly on the door of the office, then entered. "I'm Martha Gibbons," she quietly told the attractive secretary. "Did you want to see me?"

The secretary smiled pleasantly. "There are a couple of police officers here to see you, Martha. They are waiting in the employees' lunchroom."

"Police? Why?" Martha asked, her fear growing. "Nothing has happened to my children, has it?"

"They didn't say what they wanted, but they didn't look like it was anything that serious," the secretary said sympathetically. "You'll need to punch your time card before you talk to them, but don't forget to punch back in before you go back to work."

Martha searched frantically for her time card on the wall outside the office, and fumbled when she finally tried to put it in the clock. If the police were there, something must have happened to one of her children, or to Harold.

She had been panicky in her hurry to find out what was wrong. Now she had the opposite reaction. She walked slowly toward the lunchroom as though not knowing the horrible truth would make it go away, but all too soon she was at the door and opening it. She looked past the man and stared at the woman. Her dream came flooding back. It was the woman who had warned her. Now she was here in person to collapse Martha's world. She had failed her children and something had happened to one of them.

"Mrs. Gibbons, are you all right?" The two police officers had rushed forward and grabbed her. "You looked like you were about to faint," the woman was saying. Though her voice sounded as if it were coming from the end of a tunnel, Martha recognized it from her dream. "It's one of my kids, isn't it? Something has happened to one of my children." They were leading her to a chair, which she fell into heavily.

The man spoke. "No, Mrs. Gibbons. Nothing has happened to your children that we know of. That's not why we are here."

"Is it my husband, then?"

"No," the lady replied, "and we are sorry to have frightened you so. We only want to ask you a few questions about someone we think you might have seen a few days ago. We would like to talk to you concerning a crime we are investigating."

"Oh, thank goodness. They paged me and at first I was sure I was going to be fired, and then when the woman in the office told me the police were here, what was I to think? When I came in and saw you standing here, I remembered—" But Martha didn't finish the sentence. Abruptly she stopped talking, while the lady detective looked at her curiously.

"You were saying, Mrs. Gibbons?"

"Nothing. I was frightened. That's all." Martha obviously was wrong about it being the same woman as in her dream. Still, sitting there and looking at her was spooky.

"I'm Chief MacNamara and this is Detective Bernhardt," the man said. "The desk clerk at the YWCA told us you were accosted by a man this week when you went out to make a telephone call. Is that correct?"

The fear from that evening welled back through the mental hole Martha had shoved it into. In her mind's eye she saw the man approaching her. She heard the child's laughter, and she felt her own panic; but how could she explain that to these two police officers? She glanced at Chief MacNamara, but her eyes went back to Detective Bernhardt. I don't have to explain to this woman, she realized with a start. She knows. She is the woman from the dream, and she is going through it too—the storms, the child's voice, all of it.

The nonverbal communication abruptly broke off and Martha said aloud, "I'm not sure *accosted* is the right word. I was making a phone call, and there was a man who came toward the booth. He didn't actually say anything, I was just frightened."

"Could you give us a description of the man who approached you?" Detective Bernhardt asked.

"I'm sure I couldn't. I never did really see him. It was quite dark and foggy. When he was walking toward me, it was like watching a silhouette. When he got close enough to the booth for me to see him, I was so frightened, I'm afraid I closed my eyes and started screaming. It seems silly telling it now, but it was so dark and shadowy. I panicked. Some friends of mine came along and he got scared and ran away."

"Do you think they got a good look at him?" MacNamara asked hopefully.

"I don't know. They're working here too. You could ask them. They drove up in Judy's car and chased him down the alley, so they had their headlights shining on him for a while."

"Mrs. Gibbons, when this man approached you, it may have been only a random mugging or rape attempt," MacNamara said soothingly. "On the other hand, we have reason to believe there is a chance, only a small one but still a chance, that it wasn't random at all."

"What?" Martha said weakly, but even as she spoke, she knew he was right. The dreams, the child, the feeling of being watched, had all come together in that phone booth. She didn't know who the man was or why he was after her, but she was afraid he would try again.

"Have you heard about the murders of three women in the city recently?" he asked. "The media have been carrying reports stating it appears the same person may be responsible for all three deaths."

"Yes."

"There is some information we have not released to the press, Mrs. Gibbons. All three of the murdered women were in the early stages of pregnancy. We have confirmed that two of them were scheduled for abortions at the Mid-City Family Planning Clinic. We suspect the third woman might have registered at the clinic under a false name.

"We have confirmed that you also have an appointment at that clinic for an abortion, Mrs. Gibbons," MacNamara continued. "As I said before, there is only a slight possibility that the man who approached you at the telephone booth is the same man who killed those women, but I'd like to assign a man to keep an eye on you for a few days. He'll be outside, so he won't disturb you."

Martha felt as if she were the criminal. She was humiliated that these strangers knew about her upcoming abortion and assumed they condemned her. "I don't know," she said. "Since what happened Wednesday, I don't go out alone at night anymore. I'd hate to waste someone's time."

"It's no trouble at all, Mrs. Gibbons, and if the man comes back, we want to be there to catch him."

Martha thought again about the dreams, and the feeling she had that the horror was not yet over. She also wondered how the police had found out about what happened at the phone booth. She couldn't imagine the desk clerk calling the police two days after it happened. She looked at Laura Bernhardt. They knew because of that woman, she realized. She had to have a chance to talk to the lady detective. She was the only person who could help her.

"Okay," she said, "but only if you assign Detective Bernhardt to me."

Chief MacNamara looked at Detective Bernhardt doubtfully, then back at Martha. "I guess that would have some advantages. We could arrange for her to work here with you for the remainder of the weekend, and she could have the room next to yours at the Y, so she would be close by in case of an emergency." He turned to Laura. "You've got it, Detective Bernhardt." Then he asked Martha, "How do you get back to the Y after work?"

"My friends give me a ride."

"Good. When you get back tonight, Laura will be waiting for you."

Martha sensed that the rest of her conversation with the officers was routine, but she didn't really grasp it. Her attention was focused on fighting off a feeling of anger she felt welling up from something, somewhere in the distance.

41

Adam stood quietly in the shadows of the alley, fingering the ring in his pocket and watching the telephone booth. He vowed that this time nothing would go wrong. He wouldn't let his son down again.

It's me and Jeremy, just like Batman and Robin; two caped avengers fighting for justice, he thought.

The temperature had dipped to zero and his breath formed in a frozen cloud around his mouth.

Despite the weather Adam wasn't cold. He was filled with jubilant anticipation. His son had given him what he had always lacked, a sense of power and purpose.

He heard footsteps and let the ring drop back into his pocket, holding firmly, instead, to Marie's scarf. He heard a woman's voice say nervously, "Freddie? Mrs. Young?"

He smiled broadly and waited. When the footsteps reached the alley, he grabbed his prey and dragged her into the darkness. Her startled cry was replaced by the snapping sound of her neck. He decided the sound was close enough to that of a turkey wishbone snapping to permit him to make a wish.

I wish that Jeremy would be with me in person very soon, and that we stay together forever.

Adam glowed under the umbrella of Jeremy's praise. He happily watched the shadow child swinging in the television.

"Will it be soon, Jeremy? Can we be together in person before long? I wished for it tonight. I wished with all my might that you would come to me, and I wouldn't have to see you only as a shadow ever again."

"Yes, Daddy, very soon. I only need you to do a few more little favors for me, then we can be together. First, I've got some bad news for you, Daddy. I'm sorry to have to be the one to tell you, but there isn't anyone else to do it."

Adam looked at the television suspiciously. Jeremy

didn't sound sad about passing on the bad news. His voice had an undercurrent of glee.

"It's about Laura Bernhardt," Jeremy continued. "She has fooled you. She isn't any better than the others."

"No!" Adam shouted angrily. "It isn't true. Miss Laura is a saint."

"I'd say *slut* is a better word for her," Jeremy hissed self-righteously.

His shadow faded from the screen, replaced by Laura Bernhardt with the man Adam had seen at the restaurant. They were in a bedroom and she stood seductively in front of him on the screen. The man was leering at her while she slowly stripped for him. He watched the woman he loved seduce the man on the screen and Adam sobbed from heartbreak and betrayal. The picture of Laura's unfaithfulness continued to unfold through the next several hours. The scene changed from the first man to Laura hugging that partner of hers, Harry Winchell, right in the precinct. Then he saw a younger Laura in the back of a car with a boy. They were kissing and the boy had his hand on her breast. The pictures of her making love went on mercilessly. Periodically Adam became confused and saw himself in the picture as her lover. When the scenes were finally replaced by the shrinking red retina, then blackness, Adam hid in the shower stall and masturbated.

Laura awoke with a start and reached out for Darryl. He wasn't there and she realized she was in her room at the YWCA. It wasn't quite midnight, but this was the third time she had awakened from the dream of Martha Gibbons in the telephone booth. Each time she felt as if she were on the verge of picking up a clue she had missed, but it continued to elude her.

"I've got to remember," she muttered to herself. "Somewhere in that dream is the answer we've been looking for, but even hypnosis didn't help."

She squeezed her eyes shut and concentrated on every detail of the dream, but to no avail. She couldn't remember anything about the man who was walking toward Martha. The fog was so thick, she couldn't possibly have made out more than a shadow, so what was it that kept nagging at her? Laura tossed and turned on the unfamiliar bed, punching the pillows and wiggling in her attempt to find a comfortable position. She fervently wished she were home snuggled next to Darryl, especially in light of the fight they'd had just before she left. She understood his fear for her safety, but she couldn't let that interfere with her job. If this assignment worked out as well as she hoped, the murders would be solved over the weekend and her life with Darryl could get back to normal. If it didn't work, she would have to talk MacNamara into implementing the plan she had thought of that morning.

She drifted into a fitful sleep, still trying to remember what it was she was forgetting.

42

Saturday, February 9
The moon was receding from the sky in anticipation of a new day as Jeremy sat on his swing singing merrily to himself and waiting for Adam to wake up. He was in no hurry. He was having a wonderful time contemplating his next game.

"Things are going like I planned." He giggled. He jumped from his swing and rolled gleefully on the grass, which turned brown under his body. "Now the daddy person has to take care of the Martha Gibbons woman," he said with a smile that stretched across his face without touching his eyes. "When you are playing pickup sticks and drop one, you don't leave it there forever. You go back, and the second time you make sure you don't drop it again."

Laura was in the street, squinting at the telephone booth and at the man who was walking toward it.

"That's it," she cried out. "It was so obvious, I missed it."

Bzzzzzzzz.

The alarm clock shook her into the present. She awoke with an exhilaration that quickly turned to frustration. In the dream she knew the answer, but it had stayed in her subconscious. She flicked off the alarm and concentrated.

Nothing.

She finally gave up and turned the radio on to listen to the five A.M. news. She had set the alarm early because the chief had arranged for her to work at the cannery with Martha.

"A police spokesperson said the latest victim was grade-school teacher Heather Evans," the announcer said. "Although the cause of death has not been released, the spokesperson verified that the crime appears to have been committed by the same person or persons responsible for the death of three other women in the city in the past few weeks."

Laura was wide-awake now, sitting upright on the bed and listening intently. When the announcer began talking about a City Council decision to restrict snowplowing to major city arteries, she jumped out of bed, threw on her robe, and headed for the telephone in the hall to call MacNamara. Despite the early hour she had no doubt he would be at the office.

"It's more important than ever for you to stay there and keep an eye on Martha Gibbons," the chief said when she reached him.

Laura couldn't help noting the exhaustion in his voice and assumed he had been at work since Heather Evans's body was discovered. "Are there any new clues?" she asked.

"Maybe, but they are confusing at this point. The victim's husband had gone out to pick up a pizza. He said he was only gone for twenty minutes. When he returned, his wife was gone, but this time there was a note. She said she was going to pick up a student, Freddie Young, and his mother and transport them to a safehouse for battered women. The child's mother allegedly called and asked Mrs. Evans's help following a family disturbance. We have talked to the student and his parents and verified that none of them could have made that telephone call. They don't have a telephone, and they have six witnesses who say there was no family fight Friday evening and that none of them left their apartment all evening."

Laura pulled her bathrobe around her more tightly, although the temperature at the Y was too warm. What the chief was saying made sense in its own impossible way. If the victims were being fooled into thinking there was a crisis, they could be lured into the murderer's trap. "Is there anything else?" she asked.

"Yes. Heather Evans was pregnant, and yesterday was her first day back to work after a bad case of the measles. Her doctor had recommended an abortion, but, Laura, the woman didn't make a decision until yesterday afternoon. Her husband said she called her doctor from the school yesterday and set up the appointment. The procedure was to have been done in his office next week. He is in no way connected with the family planning clinic, and Ken Evans is certain his wife has never been a patient at the clinic. In fact, he was with his wife at her doctor's office the day she found out she was pregnant. We will be checking today to see if we can make a connection between anyone at his office and anyone at the clinic."

"And if there is no connection?"

"Then our one theory is shot to hell, and Martha Gibbons is our only lead. Don't let her out of your sight."

Laura knew she would never have a better opportunity to suggest her plan. She looked up and down the hall to make sure she was alone. She, too, had been convinced the murderer was someone from the clinic, but even if it wasn't, her plan still might work. She would convince the chief the new development would make it less dangerous for her, though she suspected she would be putting herself in more danger, because if the murderer was not getting the names of his victims from someone at the clinic, he must be getting them from the child.

"I have an idea, Chief. You've cleared the doctor and nurse from the clinic, and I'm sure they would go along with us. You could set up an appointment for me at the clinic on Monday. We can have the doctor fake a pregnancy test and say it is positive, then I'll schedule an abortion. No one there has ever seen me, so if the mur-

derer is someone from the clinic, we might be able to
ferret him out."

"No, Bernhardt. Forget it."

"I'm going to have to be at the clinic with Martha on
Monday, anyway. If the killer is an employee there, once
Martha goes back to Taylorsville, we will have no leads.
If it isn't someone from the clinic, I won't be in any
danger anyway."

"Maybe you're right. Okay, we'll give it a try."

Laura hung up and stood in the hall, thinking. She was
frightened. Whatever the child was, if it was able to know
that totally unrelated women were pregnant and planning
abortions, it had more power than she'd originally
thought. But why did it send the murderer only after
those women? And where did she fit in?

She picked up the phone again and dialed her husband,
forcing her voice to sound normal.

"I heard the news this morning," Darryl said accusingly. "I want you to come home, Laura. This is too
dangerous. Your career is not worth your life."

"I have no intention of dying, sweetheart," she said
quietly, so she wouldn't attract the attention of the handful of women who were beginning to come out of their
rooms and head for the rest room.

"And the four dead women did plan to die, I suppose."

"I understand how you feel, Darryl. If I were in your
shoes, I imagine I would react the same way, but I can't
come home. We are getting close. I know it. Bear with me
a little longer, and I promise I'll make it up to you."

"I'm frightened for you, Laura, and I'm afraid for myself. I don't want to lose you."

"You won't. I promise I'll be careful. I missed you last
night."

"You could be here tonight if you wanted to."

"I can't, Darryl. Please accept that. I'll be home Monday evening. Please don't be angry."

She hung up without mentioning her appointment at
the family planning clinic on Monday.

When she unlocked her room and went in to get
dressed, she noticed that her watch was not on the nightstand.

That's odd, she thought. I would have sworn I had it on yesterday and took it off before I went to bed and laid it right here.

Only a monumental act of self-control enabled Tracy to swallow her soft-boiled eggs without gagging. She tried to eat without looking at the clumps of egg white swimming in the sea of yellow yolk. If she saw what she was putting in her mouth, she would have to run from the table; then her mother would want to know if she was sick. If her mother questioned her, her father would get into the act. Tracy knew there was no way she could hold up this morning under a cross-examination by her dad. Even so, three bites were all she could manage. She stood up nonchalantly and washed the eggs down the drain while her mother pulled the butter from the refrigerator for her dad's toast. Neither of her parents seemed to notice that the garbage disposal got most of her breakfast. She loaded the dishes on the counter into the dishwasher and wiped the stove with the dishrag.

"If you don't need my help this morning, I'd like to go to my room and work on my history paper so I can watch television this evening," she said.

She saw her dad look up from his morning paper and exchange a meaningful pleased-parent look with her mother.

"Go ahead, dear. I can finish up here," her mother said sweetly.

Tracy hurried toward her room, marveling at her parents' gullibility. She closed the door behind her and curled on the bed and waited for her stomach to stop churning. She remained there long after her stomach recovered and stared dry-eyed out her bedroom window at the children playing tag across the street. The tears that a month ago had soaked her pillow each night no longer came. They had decreased in direct proportion to the increase in her depression and fear, until this morning there were no tears left to cry. Tracy felt as if she were poised precariously over a black hole in space and that one false move would send her tumbling endlessly into its interior. She could feel the child's power growing as her sanity and self-control weakened.

She drifted off to sleep with the word *help* frozen in a soundless plea on her lips.

43

"It's such a relief to have someone I can talk to about it," Martha said. "I guess I knew something was wrong as long ago as the first electrical storm, even though I wasn't in the city then. When I heard about it on the television, I felt an inexplicable sense of dread."

She and Laura were talking in hushed voices so the other patrons of McDonald's, where they were eating dinner, wouldn't overhear.

"Even after I came to the city and that man started coming at me when I was in the telephone booth, I still didn't let myself believe anything supernatural was going on. It wasn't until I saw you at the warehouse yesterday that I couldn't deny it anymore. It was more than just having seen you in my dream. When I looked at you, I knew it was happening to you too."

"Everything is going to be okay now," Laura told Martha in a cheery tone that she hoped didn't sound as false to the woman she was supposed to be protecting as it did to her. She was exhausted from the day of working at the warehouse and hardly felt she could save a fly from a spider. Besides, the conversation had taken on an ominously familiar ring. The memory of her telling Rhonda Hackman everything was going to be okay rang guiltily in her memory. Now Rhonda was dead.

"What is the thing that is causing all this?" Martha asked. "There's the man, but there's also the other thing. It's like a child, but it isn't like a child."

"I wish I knew, Martha. Whatever it is, it is sneaky. Promise me that under no circumstances will you go anywhere without talking to me first. Be particularly suspicious of anyone calling on the telephone."

"I will be. One close encounter with that obscenity was enough for me. I only want Monday to come and go as quickly as possible so I can get home to my children and my husband and forget it all. This is the first time I've been by myself in my entire life. I'd heard about loneliness and homesickness, but I never understood how painful it is. Do you have children, Laura?"

"No. Maybe someday we will have a child, but not now."

"I'm sorry that I've taken you away from your husband for the weekend, but I've got to admit, I'm sure glad for the company. It's been awful going through this by myself."

Laura wished she could blurt out everything that had been happening to her. She, too, could use some support; but she was a cop on assignment and she had to maintain her professionalism.

The two women sat quietly for a while, then Martha asked, "Do you really think it will try again, try to kill me?"

"I would be doing you an injustice if I made light of the situation, Martha. We obviously think there is some danger, or I wouldn't be here."

"Does your boss know about the child?"

"No, but he does know about the dreams. It isn't the child we are after. I think whatever the child is, it has someone under his control. If we catch him, I think the child will lose its power."

"But if it can control one person, couldn't it find someone else to control?"

Laura shuddered. She, too, had thought about that possibility. "I don't think so," she said hesitantly. "I think this thing was unleashed by a set of circumstances that happened to come together at the right time and place."

"It's too bad my friends couldn't give you a better description of the man they chased the other night. That was weird. With the car lights shining right on him, you would think they'd have gotten a good look at him, even with the fog."

"A detailed description definitely would help, but we

will find him anyway," Laura said, but secretly she was
troubled by the information the women had given her
and MacNamara. It was as if all three women had been
looking at a different man. Their descriptions not only
didn't match, they were contradictory. One said he was
short, another tall. One said he had on a hat, another said
it was a stocking cap. Among the three of them they
hadn't received one piece of matching information.

"Would you like to play some cards when we get back
to the Y?" Martha asked. "I'd like to do something to
take my mind off this whole mess."

"Maybe. What time is it? I couldn't find my watch this
morning."

"It's eight P.M. I wonder if there is a thief at the Y. My
necklace is missing too. It wasn't expensive, but I'd hate
to lose it. My kids gave it to me for Christmas. It's a gold
chain with a pendant. It has WORLD'S GREATEST MOM
engraved on it."

"We'll probably find it and my watch when we get
back, either in the covers or under the bed. Let's forget
about playing cards. I only want to take a long, hot
shower and sleep until morning. That warehouse job is
exhausting. I'd rather chase criminals any day than stand
for hours stripping labels off cans. My feet are killing
me."

Martha laughed. "I'm glad it isn't just me. I was feeling like a wimp because my feet hurt."

When they finally got back and Laura had a chance to
shower, she scrubbed until her skin felt raw as she tried
to get the smell of smoke off her. She wasn't looking
forward to another day at the warehouse, but if that was
where Martha was going to be, she had to be there too.
Despite a complete search of her room she could not find
her watch.

Unlike the night before, she had no trouble falling
asleep, but too soon after she had slipped into the weight-
less euphoria, she was jarred awake by frantic knocking
at her door. Her grogginess turned to nervous energy
when she heard Martha's voice. This was it, and with
luck, tomorrow this case would be solved.

As soon as Laura opened the door, Martha came rushing in, her voice breathless with fear and excitement that bordered on hysteria. "Oh, thank goodness you and Chief MacNamara found me at the warehouse. I would have gone. Even knowing what I know now, I still almost went."

"Settle down and start from the beginning," Laura said.

"It was a phone call, like you said it would be. I almost went. I would have sworn it was really Harold. It sounded like Harold, and he said things that only Harold and I know. He even mentioned stuff that happened when we were still kids in high school. He said he felt so bad about the fight we had on the phone that he'd dropped the kids off at a neighbor's house and had taken the bus to the city to be with me until the abortion. I was certain it was Harold. It wasn't only his voice and the fact that he knew things that only Harold could know, he talked like Harold would talk and said the things Harold would say. He said he took the bus because the truck broke down again and that I'd better appreciate all the trouble he had gone to in order to get here. He wanted me to meet him at a hotel near the bus station. I was so excited, I forgot all about your warning that this might happen. I went to my room and got dressed and was halfway out the door when I stopped. I thought about waking you up to tell you where I was going, but I didn't want to disturb you, so I was going to leave you a note. Then I remembered what you said about it being able to fool people on the telephone. I was sure that wasn't the case. It was my husband I was talking to. It wasn't like that lady who went out to help her student. I know my own husband; and that is what made me suspicious. I thought about how strange it was that Harold would ask me to walk by myself for fifteen blocks through the city streets. He gets upset if I walk by myself in Taylorsville at night. I decided to call home. I figured if it really was Harold who had called, no one would answer the telephone because the kids would be at the neighbor's house and he would be here. Harold answered the phone! I woke him up. I didn't know what to say, so I told him I called to tell him I love him and was looking forward to seeing him soon. Then I hung up and knocked on your door."

"You were right to check it out, Martha. Where exactly did the person who called want you to meet him?"

After Martha gave her directions, Laura told her to go to her room and not to open it for anyone but her. "I have to make a phone call, then I need to borrow some of your clothes, if that is okay."

"Sure, but be careful. I don't want you to get killed either."

"Don't worry about me. There will be so many cops around that area, he won't have a chance to get within ten feet of me." She escorted Martha to her room, then called MacNamara.

"I'll pick you up personally, Laura. You aren't to go anywhere until I get there. Is that clear? This is no time for heroics. You aren't stepping one foot out of my car until I'm sure every square inch of the area is covered by plainclothes cops."

"It sounds good to me, Chief. The more the merrier, as far as I'm concerned."

Twenty minutes later Laura was rushing through the cold air to MacNamara's car. She had noticed that Martha's coat was threadbare, but she hadn't realized how thin until she felt the blast of cold air whipping through the material.

My middle-class existence would seem like untold wealth to Martha, she thought as she climbed into the chief's warm car. Then she said aloud, "We've got to stop meeting like this, boss. My husband is getting suspicious." She knew how corny she sounded, but it was better than the glum reality of the situation.

"Before you get out of this car, I want the safety off on your revolver," MacNamara said, ignoring her comment. Then he was on the radio, giving orders and checking the location of the various men who had been pulled in on a moment's notice.

"You sure set this up quickly, Chief."

"I had a few fellows on call."

Laura nodded and smiled. With the exception, perhaps, of Superman, she couldn't think of anyone she would rather have in charge.

They drove a couple of blocks with MacNamara giving her instructions. Laura found it difficult to believe that only a few weeks before she had been bitter because she never got exciting assignments. She remembered her mother telling her to be careful what she asked for, because she might get it. She vowed that if she got through this case alive, she would go visit her parents.

Two more blocks and they ran into fog. It was like a wall surrounding the stakeout area. MacNamara gave Laura a worried look, but neither of them said anything about the similarity to Martha's last experience with her would-be assassin.

"I've got so many plainclothesmen in this area, we could hold the policeman's ball, but you're still not to take any chances, Bernhardt. I figure the department has fifty thousand dollars invested in your training, and we owe it to the taxpayers not to throw that money away."

"Hey, Chief, you know me. I'll do anything I can to save the taxpayers money."

He pulled to the curb. "Have you finished connecting the sound system I gave you?"

"I'm all set."

"Are you picking her up, Livingston?" MacNamara asked.

"Every word, Chief."

"I guess this is where you get out, Laura. You're three blocks from the rendezvous point. I'd feel a lot better about it if this damn fog hadn't set in."

Laura didn't think the wall of fog was any more accidental than the electrical storms, but it was too late to back out. "It never bothered Sherlock Holmes, so I'm not going to let it bother me," she said, jumping out of the car. She moved quickly, not because she was in a hurry, but because she might lose her nerve if she sat any longer. It had only been forty-five minutes since Martha had knocked on her door, and she hoped MacNamara had been able to set up his men thoroughly in such a short time.

She pulled the coat collar around her face, partly to

hide her features and partly to block the penetrating cold. She hoped it was doing a better job of hiding her face than it was of keeping her warm.

The sound of her footsteps echoed against the pavement, and the fog grew worse as she neared the point where Martha was to meet the man. She looked around, but she couldn't see two feet in any direction. That meant the men who were supposed to be guarding her wouldn't be able to see her. On the other hand, it wasn't going to make it any easier for the man who was after her either.

Laura heard something a block from the hotel where the fake Harold Gibbons had told Martha to meet him. "Footsteps behind me," she whispered, and prayed that her radio was working. She gripped the gun in her pocket and prepared to use it if necessary. The trouble was, in this fog she wouldn't be able to tell who she was shooting at. If she acted in panic, she could inadvertently kill another officer.

Her heart pounded wildly while she continued to walk. The footsteps were growing nearer. They couldn't be more than a half block away, but the fog was distorting the sound and making it difficult to judge the distance.

Someone grabbed her. At first she thought it must be one of the officers because she was certain the footsteps couldn't have been that close. Then she felt something being wrapped around her neck and knew the murderer had her. She managed to pull the gun from her pocket, but her attacker was behind her and she couldn't twist around and point it at him. She struggled and the cloth tightened around her neck. She was no longer a cop. She was a woman who was being murdered. She dropped her gun and heard it go off, but the sound of the child laughing in her head made the gunshot quiet in comparison.

The fog turned from gray to black and the ground began to shake. She was aware of screaming and shooting and sirens, but she couldn't twist around and free herself from the grip of the murderer. He seemed to thrive on the confusion.

"I've got him," she heard someone shout through the haze of her fading consciousness.

The scarf was no longer around her neck, and the fog

was gone. It didn't lift. It simply disappeared in the blinking of an eye. The ground was still and police officers were running in all directions. She heard a familiar voice say, "What the fuck happened?" and she started laughing. It was Harry Winchell being his usual poetic self, and she thought she had never heard a more pleasant sound in her life. . . . Her life. She was still alive.

MacNamara was barking orders. The man had gotten away, and it didn't take long to discover that not one of the two dozen police officers who were on the scene had gotten a glimpse of him; nor had she. They were no farther along than they had been before, but she was one heck of a lot colder.

"You may think you won because he got away," Laura whispered to the child, "but you didn't. Martha Gibbons is still alive."

She felt the anger build around her and the ground began to shake again. The buildings trembled, then the shaking subsided. Laura's shaking didn't stop for another hour.

She wanted desperately to go home, but she was still on assignment and had to return to the YWCA. She was in her room when it hit her, what she had missed in the dream. She had been concentrating so much on her sense of sight that she had overlooked it. It wasn't something she had seen at all. It was a sound. She had heard it again tonight, but she couldn't remember exactly what it was. Both in the dream about Martha Gibbons and tonight, as she walked through the fog, she had heard footsteps, and something else. She tried to put herself back into those scenes again and focus on the elusive sound. She knew it was somehow familiar, but its recognition dangled teasingly out of reach.

Inside the television in Adam's apartment, bolts of lightning flashed around the shadow child as he lashed out his anger in his mysterious world. As fire raged inside the television, a heavy layer of frost covered every surface of Adam's apartment. The janitor hadn't returned yet, but Jeremy wasn't thinking about his father. He was thinking about Laura Bernhardt.

"I'll get her for this," he vowed. "It's my game. I'll teach her for trying to fool me. She will play by my rules, and then I'll kill her, because in my game, I decide who lives and who dies. No one had better try to fool me again, or they will be sorry. That Laura person is going to be sorry she crossed me. No one crosses me, and no one changes the rules of my game."

His anger subsided somewhat and he snickered because unwittingly the Laura woman was setting a trap for herself and ensuring that the daddy person would cooperate in punishing her when the time was right.

44

Monday, February 11
Laura professionally scoped out the pedestrian and vehicular traffic in front of the Y before allowing Martha to carry her suitcase to her car. Sunday had seemed interminably long, but Monday morning finally had arrived. They were on their way to the clinic, and Laura was painfully aware that if another attempt was made on Martha's life, it probably would occur now. All the victims, with the exception of Rhonda Hackman, had been scheduled for an abortion, and even Rhonda had been pregnant. In no case, though, had any of the women actually had the abortion before they were murdered.

Laura was surprised another attempt had not been made on Martha's life yesterday. After the incident Saturday night, the remainder of the weekend was ominously quiet. She suspected the child realized security would be too tight for his man to get to Martha, but she didn't understand why he didn't cause another storm, like the one that had killed the people at the restaurant. She and Darryl would have been killed, too, if Darryl hadn't heard the warning. Had the warning been heard in spite of the child, or had he wanted her to remain alive at that point? And who was the person who had called her darling and shouted for her to run? She felt as though the more she learned about this mystery, the farther she was from solving it.

When she was certain the coast was clear, she helped Martha load her suitcase into the trunk. After the abortion Laura was going to drive her to the bus station and stay with her until she was safely on her way to Taylorsville.

"I wish I had been able to find my necklace," Martha said sadly. "I don't know what I'm going to tell my kids. They're certain to notice it's gone."

Laura flinched at Martha's mention of the necklace. It was true that nothing unusual had happened Sunday, but this morning was another story. She had not told Martha, nor did she intend to, but when she turned over to turn off her alarm, she had noticed something strange on her nightstand. In a pile next to her clock radio she had found a pile of tiny, twisted pieces of gold-colored metal. At first she didn't know what it was, until she saw the bent and charred pendant. The words WORLD'S GREATEST MOM were barely recognizable on the destroyed necklace. There was no way anyone could have entered her room during the night, but someone, or something, had. It had mutilated Martha's necklace and left it there for her to find. Not a single link in the chain was intact. Each piece looked as if it had exploded from the inside.

"Before you catch your bus, we can stop and pick up another necklace like it," Laura said. "You'll know it isn't the same one, but your kids won't know. It will be my treat."

"That would be wonderful if we could buy another one, but I can pay for it. I have plenty of money from working at the warehouse."

Laura silently fingered the envelope in her pocket that held the remains of Martha's necklace. Martha was so absorbed in her own thoughts, she didn't seem to notice Laura's frown. She planned to have the lab examine what was left of the necklace, but she didn't expect a logical explanation. She was certain it was the work of the child. What frightened her was that she wasn't sure what it meant. Was it a threat against Martha, or a destructive tantrum protesting his defeat? She hoped it was the latter, but she planned to watch Martha very carefully today, just in case.

She was jolted from her thoughts by the sound of Martha crying. "The worst is over. You will be fine," she told her.

"I feel like a criminal." Martha sobbed. "I didn't think I would ever see the day when I would have an abortion."

"If you have doubts, it isn't too late to change your mind."

"I've been through it a million times in the past few weeks. I don't want to do this, but I don't see that I have any choice. I honestly don't have enough energy to take care of another baby, and Harold and I really can't afford to take care of it."

"You have to do what you think is best. I know it won't make it easier for you, but I want you to know that I admire you for the strength you've shown in this difficult situation."

"Thanks. That does help."

"We're here," Laura said, backing into a parking space on the street. "Do you remember what you are supposed to do? You'll go ahead of me, but I won't let you out of my sight. If there is any sign of trouble, I'll be right behind you. After you go into the clinic, I'll come in, but don't show that you recognize me."

"Okay."

"Then you'll leave in front of me, and I'll keep an eye on you until we get back to the car. From there on it is smooth sailing. We'll stop and replace your necklace, then I'll put you on the bus. In a few hours you will be with your husband and kids."

"Oh, Laura, I can hardly wait."

"Then let's get this over with."

Laura locked the car doors while Martha waited. This was the critical time, and all her carefully honed police instincts were in action. She had her gun ready to use at a moment's notice, while her eyes searched the street for any suspicious signs.

"That's Harold," Martha shouted, waving excitedly at

a man in a battered pickup truck. The man waved back with what Laura thought looked like calculated self-control.

"It's really him this time," Martha said, rushing toward the street.

Laura held her back. "Wait a minute. It might be another trap. If the child can make someone sound like your husband on the phone, maybe he can make the killer look similar to him too."

"No, it is my husband."

"At least give him a chance to park. After all you've been through, you don't want to get run over."

Harold slowly parallel-parked the truck while Martha impatiently shuffled from foot to foot and Laura discreetly removed the safety from her revolver and held it ready in case it was a trap. Finally he sauntered across the street with his hands in his work pants while Laura watched him guardedly. As soon as he stepped on the curb, Martha embraced him. Laura noted his pleased and somewhat embarrassed reaction to his wife's reception and decided this was, indeed, the real Harold Gibbons.

"I don't believe you are here," Martha said through tears of happiness. "I've never been so glad to see anyone in my whole life."

"It's not that big a deal," he responded, his neck turning pink as he glanced at Laura self-consciously. "I decided I'd better come up and get you before you started looking for another job. I stopped by the YWCA and they said you had already checked out."

"My friend Laura gave me a ride. She had an appointment for a checkup today," Martha said, giving Laura a surreptitious warning glance.

Laura knew she hadn't told Harold anything about the dreams, murders, or surveillance and played along. "It's nice to meet you, Harold. Martha has said a lot of nice things about you." She was glad for Martha, but she hoped Harold wouldn't blow her cover once they got inside.

Harold nodded his head stiffly at her greeting and stuffed his hands farther into his pockets. Laura sensed he wasn't trying to be rude, but rather was a shy man who felt uncomfortable with the situation.

"I guess I won't be needing that ride to the bus station," Martha said happily.

"Take good care of yourself, Martha," Laura said meaningfully.

"Oh, I will. From now on everything is going to be just fine."

They transferred Martha's suitcase to Harold's truck. Then Laura made an excuse about needing something out of her car so Harold and Martha would arrive at the clinic a few seconds before her.

Laura needn't have worried that Harold would give her away. He was so embarrassed about being at the clinic that he stared at his shoes while he waited for someone to call his wife. Before long the nurse called Martha's name and Harold disappeared with her into the interior of the building. Laura was still waiting an hour later when a pale and shaken Martha emerged, supporting herself on Harold's arm. Laura casually strolled out the door a few seconds behind them and watched while they got into Harold's truck. She ran up to the passenger's door and said, "I know a place where I can get that necklace wholesale. I'll mail it to you, and if you get hungry, I recommend the truck stop halfway between here and Taylorsville. They make a mean hamburger. I wouldn't bother to stop *anyplace* around here. The food in the city is awful."

"Good idea," Martha said, reaching out the window of the cab and squeezing Laura's hand. "The longest stop we'll be making in the city is for red lights."

"Don't forget to lock your car doors."

"We will, and, Laura, thanks for everything."

Laura watched them pull away from the curb and decided her job had its rewards after all. Martha was on her way back home and the child and murderer were temporarily foiled; but she knew the victory wasn't complete yet. A murderer was still at large, and it was her job to find him. She rubbed her wrist where her watch should be. After finding Martha's necklace she no longer thought she had left her watch at home or lost it at the Y.

She held her hand to her chest and felt her gun in its holster. She walked back to the clinic. She not only was about to become an expectant mother in the eyes of the clinic staff; before she left everyone would know loud and clear she wasn't going to have the child. She also knew that if the ploy didn't work any better than the department's botched plan Saturday night, she was in danger of becoming a dead cop.

A pan flew unaided across Adam's apartment. The windup alarm clock followed, shattering on the floor.

Jeremy was in a rage.

"My daddy and I will stop you, you bitch," the shadow screeched from the interior of the television. The janitor was at work and no one was in the apartment to see Jeremy's unleashed fury. "You saved the Martha woman, but you won't save yourself."

Residents throughout the city felt a tremor and noticed that clouds seemed to form from nowhere. Then as quickly as the disturbance started, it ended. The ground stood still and the clouds dissipated harmlessly.

. . . And in Adam's apartment Laura's watch sat on top of the television while Jeremy giggled the laugh of a spoiled child who knows that, in the end, he will get his own way.

45

"No one suspected a thing," Laura told the chief. "My performance as an unhappy mother-to-be could have won an Academy Award."

She had reported to MacNamara's office after she picked up a new necklace for Martha and dropped the old one off at the police lab. She noticed puffy dark circles under the chief's eyes and doubted that he was getting much more sleep than she was lately. She also thought she saw a gleam of excitement and wondered if that was the look Darryl said she got when she was work-

ing on a particularly challenging case. She had felt that
way about this case at first, but now what she felt was
stubborn determination . . . and fear.

"Have you had any more dreams, or is there anything
else going on I should know about?" MacNamara asked.

"No, sir," Laura said, neglecting to mention the necklace. She thought it was better not to mention it until she
had received the lab report. "Martha Gibbons left the
city with her husband after the abortion, so I think she is
going to be okay now." Secretly she wondered if Martha
would be all right. She planned to call Taylorsville tonight, just to make sure. She didn't know how far the
child's power extended.

"If everything is okay, why are you standing around
my office wasting time?" MacNamara asked gruffly. "I
seem to recall Binder saying you have so much unfinished
paperwork on your desk that the insurance company is
threatening to cancel the precinct's fire policy."

"Yes, sir," Laura said with a grin. She thought Mac-
Namara was spending too much time around the sergeant. He was beginning to pick up his mannerisms, but
MacNamara's gruffness came off as a façade. Binder's
was real.

Laura sat down at her desk and groaned at the foot-
high stack of papers covering it. She had just begun wad-
ing through them when she noticed someone standing
quietly in front of her. She glanced up and saw Sergeant
Binder's daughter.

"Hi, Tracy," she said, looking immediately back at her
desk and continuing to sort papers while she talked. "If
you're looking for your dad, you just missed him. When I
came in a few minutes ago, I passed him on his way out.
He was complaining about having to go to the dentist."

Normally Laura would have been happy to stop and
talk to Tracy. Today was not a normal day. Laura hadn't
had a normal day since before the murders had started,
and she didn't have time to entertain the sergeant's
daughter.

"I know my dad isn't here. I came to talk to you, if you
have time."

The tone in Tracy's voice got Laura's attention. She

looked up and thought, Good grief. The girl is petrified. Aloud she said, "Of course I've got time. Why don't we find someplace quiet to talk? This office is like Grand Central Station. Would you mind talking in one of the interrogation rooms? That's the only place around here where we will be sure not to be disturbed."

Laura and Tracy walked silently down the hall, with Laura taking in every detail of Tracy's demeanor. She wouldn't have dreamt that someone could change so much. The confident, bubbly kid she had talked to in December was gone. She looked beaten and intimidated.

"That man gives me the creeps," Tracy whispered, pulling her arms protectively around her chest.

"Oh, that's the janitor. He's a nice man—kind of shy, though. Here we are," she said, holding the door for Tracy.

Laura listened in horror as Tracy spilled out her story. Not this sweet little girl, too, she thought. Damn the murderous, evil thing that is doing this to all of us.

Tracy looked on the verge of a breakdown. "I haven't known what to do." She sobbed. "I've obviously lost my mind, but the child seems so real. I know it is silly, but I feel like all my hope has vanished." Then she added as an afterthought, "Gone as thoroughly as my charm bracelet, which seems to have disappeared into thin air."

An image of Martha's mutilated necklace flashed through Laura's head. She believed Tracy's bracelet was not misplaced, but had been taken by the child. She reached out and gripped Tracy's hand and spoke slowly, weighing each word carefully. She had to make Tracy understand the seriousness of the situation. "You've done the right thing by coming to me, Tracy. First, let me assure you that you are not crazy. The child is real. I have felt him too. So have the women who were murdered. They all had nightmares similar to yours. I've been having the same nightmares."

Tracy looked at her in disbelief. "You aren't just saying that to patronize me, are you? Adults do that to kids all the time, but I came to you because I thought you were different. I've been eavesdropping on my dad and mom's conversations. Dad hasn't mentioned anything about the child."

"That's because he doesn't know about him. Chief MacNamara knows about my dreams, and he knows there was a ghost in one of them, but that is all he knows. My husband knows a little about it, but I haven't completely leveled with him either. The only people who really know about the child are the women who are being terrorized by him. It isn't only you and me. I spent the weekend guarding a woman who has been having experiences similar to yours and mine."

"Then he is real?"

"Yes."

"He's been causing the storms, too, hasn't he?"

"I think so."

"I was less frightened when I thought I was crazy."

"I know what you mean, but down deep, all of us who are involved have known all along it is real."

"I guess you're right, Laura. I wanted to believe I was crazy. That's a lot easier to accept than this."

"Tracy, you know what you have to do, don't you?"

"No, I can't. I won't tell my dad I'm pregnant. I'd rather die first."

Laura took Tracy gently by the chin so the girl had no choice but to look into her eyes. This was no time to mince words. "Tracy, 'I'd rather die' is a colorful phrase, but understand this: That is exactly what the child has planned for you."

Tracy pulled away from her, put her hands over her face, and sobbed convulsively. Laura walked around the table and held her. She vowed to herself, and to the child, that she would stop him.

Finally Tracy's sobbing turned to little hiccups. "Isn't there any other way besides telling my dad?"

"You know there isn't."

The girl nodded solemnly.

"Until we find out who is helping this creature, and how to stop them both, it isn't safe for you to go anywhere by yourself. We know it has the power to sound like someone else on the telephone and to know things it couldn't possibly know, so be particularly suspicious of phone calls."

"Can I wait until tomorrow evening to tell my dad? That way I could at least tell Mark I was going to confide in my parents."

"Absolutely not, Tracy. This isn't just a matter of you being pregnant. Four women are dead. You could easily be next. I imagine the chief will want to assign someone to guard you. That's what he did with the last woman we discovered was in danger. She had her abortion this morning and is on her way safely home—but, Tracy, even with me there guarding her, there were a couple of tense moments. She almost was fooled and nearly walked into the murderer's trap."

"Chief MacNamara is going to know about me?" Tracy asked, horrified. "Everyone is going to know. I couldn't stand it. I'm so ashamed."

"No, everyone is not going to know. It will just be your parents, the chief, and me."

"Not the chief of detectives, Laura. Please. I'd be too humiliated."

"We'll see. The first thing you have to do is to talk to your dad."

"I'll tell him tonight. I promise," Tracy said, walking toward the door.

"Wait a minute, Tracy. Where are you going?"

"I've got to catch the bus back to school."

"Sweetie, you still don't understand. You can't go back to school today. It's too dangerous. You need to stay here at the precinct house until your dad comes."

"You mean I have to tell him about the baby here?"

"You can tell him at home, but you have to stay at the precinct until he comes back. This force, or creature, whatever it is, seems to know when someone is about to slip away, and I think it will pick up its efforts to get you."

The color drained from Tracy's face as she listened.

"You'll be safe if you do what your dad and I ask. You can stay in my office until your dad comes back, then I'll tell him you are here and need a ride home. I'll let him

know you have something important to talk to him
about, but I won't tell him what."

"I can't stay around here all afternoon, Laura. I'm too
upset. I don't want all the guys my dad supervises to see
me like this. Everyone will end up talking, and that
would make it a lot worse for my dad and mom, and for
me too."

Laura looked at Tracy's trembling hands and panic-
stricken eyes. She looked like a caged wild animal. Perhaps it wasn't a good idea for her to stay at the precinct
house. She looked as if she would crack if she was sub-
jected to much more stress. Laura thought she might
even need medical attention, but she couldn't get it for
her without her parents' permission. Everything hinged
on Binder's coming back.

"I could go home," Tracy said hopefully. "My mom's
there. She won't let anything happen to me."

"You need to have a trained police officer with you."

"How could we explain that to my mom? Even if I told
her I was pregnant, I couldn't tell her the other stuff. I've
got to talk to my dad first. Maybe you could drive me
home, and we could tell my mom that you were at the
school giving a presentation and I got sick, so you offered
to give me a lift. Then you could pretend to get sick and
ask my mom if you could stay there for a little while until
you felt better. You could stay until my dad got home."

"Your mom isn't going to buy that, Tracy. She's bound
to know something is fishy."

"No, she won't. You don't know my mom."

Laura looked at the girl and decided she didn't have
any choice but to go along with her. She needed to be
home, where she would feel safe. In order for Laura to
leave, though, she would have to confide in the chief, and
that would be breaking her promise to Tracy. How did
she get herself into these messes? Tracy's health and
safety came first; she would have to leave quietly so Mac-
Namara wouldn't see her.

"We can give it a try," she reluctantly told Tracy. "You
wait here while I get my coat. I'll be back in a few minutes."

Laura's eyes were focused on the floor while she

walked to her office, but she was so deep in thought, she didn't see it, nor was she aware of the people around her.

"Hi, Adam," she said automatically and without glancing up.

Laura wrote a note to Binder telling him that Tracy had been in, and that she had something very important she had to discuss with him. She asked him to come home as soon as possible. She sealed the envelope, wrote urgent across the front in big red letters, and gave it to the sergeant's secretary, who promised she would give it to Binder the moment he came in. She walked as inconspicuously as possible by MacNamara's office on her way back to the detectives' office to get her coat. When she reached for her coat, her arm stopped in midair, as though she were suddenly transported to another scene only she could see.

How did I know I was passing Adam earlier? she thought. I was looking down and thinking about Tracy. I didn't see him. He didn't have his mop bucket with him, so I didn't hear that.

Goose bumps sprang across her body, chilling her to the bone. It was the sound! The sound from my dream. The sound I heard Saturday night. That's what I was missing when I tried to remember the dream. It was the sound of keys clinking together on a chain, but it wasn't the ordinary sound of keys. It was the sound I associate with Adam. Most men who wear keys from their belt have a bunch of keys. Adam has only two keys on his ring. I've always thought they sounded rather pathetic and lonely. But these murders couldn't have anything to do with our sweet janitor. Anyone could wear a couple of keys hanging from a chain, and Adam couldn't possibly know about the women at the clinic. I am going to see if anyone there is in the habit of wearing keys from a chain, though.

Laura grabbed her coat, then stopped again as she remembered Tracy's reaction to the janitor. I'm sure it's a waste of time, she thought, but it's no flimsier than some of the other leads we've checked. She closed the door to the detectives' office, which, amazingly, was empty except for her, and called headquarters and asked them to see if they had anything on Adam Smith, janitor at the Third Precinct. Then she went back to the interrogation room and got Tracy.

"How do you know there is a man working with the child?" Tracy asked as they pulled into the Binders' residential street. "How do you know it isn't the child who is committing the murders? If he is the one causing the lightning storms and the earth tremors, he could kill the women himself."

"I'm sure there is someone else involved for several reasons. The child seems to have the power to alter nature to his purposes, but several people have seen the man we suspect is the killer. Unfortunately, no one has been able to give us a description of him. Also, Saturday night when he tried to lure the woman I was guarding into his trap, I went instead. He thought I was her and tried to kill me. It was a real man who wrapped something around my neck and tried to strangle me, not a supernatural force.

"He tried to kill you?"

"Yes, but he didn't succeed, and he won't succeed with you either."

"If the man doesn't get me, the child can come after me with his lightning, like he did those people in the restaurant," Tracy said nervously.

"I don't *think* he'll do that. For some reason it seems important to him to have the man kill the women."

"Sometimes I feel like it is a game to him," Tracy said gloomily.

"I'm afraid you're right," Laura said as she pulled into the Binders' driveway. "I've noticed there are limits to his power, though. He tried to frighten me at home last week, like you said he did to you in your bedroom. I fought him by concentrating on something else until he finally gave up and went away."

"I don't think I could think of anything else. I get too scared."

"You could, and you will if you need to. You will win. We will all win against him."

"I can't tell my dad about him unless you back me up.

Unless a grown-up verifies my story, he'll think I'm crazy or lying."

"I guess neither one of us has any choice but to tell everything we know. If it's any consolation, Tracy, I'm going to be in trouble, too, for not telling the chief sooner. Have your dad call me after you talk to him. I'll back you up."

"Laura, are you pregnant too?"

"No."

"Then why is he after you? The rest of us are pregnant. Where do you fit in?"

"That's the million-dollar question. If I can figure it out, maybe I can solve the case."

Adam sat in the back of the XXX-rated movie with the darkness surrounding him like a warm cocoon. Outside it was only four-thirty P.M., but in the theater it was perpetually the witching hour. He watched a series of couples writhing and moaning in Technicolor and wiped perspiration from his forehead when the camera zoomed in for closeups. The scenes were similar to the ones he had seen on his own television during the past month, but today was different. As he sat in the dark theater, he was planning what he was going to do to Laura Bernhardt.

I thought you were pure, but Jeremy showed me I was wrong. How could I have been so blind that I didn't notice how you throw yourself at every man who comes through the door of the precinct house. You'll never be my wife now, or Jeremy's mother. You're a whore, and I'm going to treat you that way. You may fight me at first, but before I get finished, you will be begging me for more. At least you aren't as bad as the baby killers. There may be hope for you, with a good man to whip you into line.

Tracy lay huddled on her bed. Her conversation with Laura flashed in images of black and purple across her mind. Her mother had believed their story about Tracy's getting sick at school, and it hadn't been necessary for Laura to pretend she didn't feel well. Her mom had invited her in, and they had been sitting in the living room chatting for an hour.

Tracy had gone directly to her room. Her bedroom,
which she had always loved because it was warm and
cozy, now seemed overwhelmingly large. She wanted to
hide someplace safe. She went into her walk-in closet and
locked the door behind her. She sat in a corner with her
arms wrapped around her drawn-up legs and rocked
slowly. Talking to Laura hadn't solved anything. Now
she would have to tell her dad, and the child would get
her anyway. Her eyes became wide and unblinking as the
tension of the past few weeks overwhelmed her. Her subconscious spotted an escape route deep within the recesses of her mind, and she began weaving her way toward that peaceful blank area from which she would
never need to emerge. She no longer felt the floor under
her, nor was she aware of her rocking as she sank deeper
into the safe blackness of her mind. She saw a dark tunnel ahead. It was warm and secure. She could travel forever in the tunnel without worrying about anything. She
wouldn't need feet and legs; her body would cease to exist
there. Her mind would soar effortlessly through the
warm, empty mist.

She was almost at the entrance. She sank deeper into
her subconscious and the tunnel drew toward her, helping her bridge the gap. A few more feet and she could
enter and stay forever. Her despair and fear were disappearing. She felt nothing, and the nothingness was wonderful. There was no longer a need to keep up pretenses
of normality.

The closet was gone. Her body was gone. Only the
tunnel existed.

"Tracy," a melodious voice called to her from just outside the tunnel.

She smiled at the voice. It had no body, but she saw its
shadow.

"The tunnel will give you peace, Tracy. You belong in
the tunnel. You'll be happy there. No one can hurt you in
the tunnel."

She knew the voice was right.

"But they won't let you stay there, Tracy. They'll
make you come back. They'll keep you from it."

She frowned and jerked toward the entrance frantically, but it was pulling away.

"I can help you, Tracy. I know an entrance that they can't steal from you. No one can force you back if you enter the tunnel my way."

The shadow wanted to help her. She loved the shadow.

"Come with me, Tracy. I'll lead you to the tunnel."

She stood. Her eyes still did not blink. They were unfocused and unaware of her surroundings, but she could see perfectly. She was following the shadow.

"Follow me," the shadow whispered softly, like a lover.

She followed the soothing voice's instructions and walked quietly out the side door of the house and down the driveway. At the bus stop she automatically pulled out her money and followed the appropriate motions. When she was in her seat, she smiled at the friendly voice and the helpful shadow that had settled in her mind. She was not aware of the bus moving or stopping and picking up passengers. She listened only to the sweet sound of the shadow's young voice. When it directed her to stand and get off the bus, she moved in a daze.

She was walking through the city, but she wasn't aware of the people or the traffic. The only thing she saw was the benevolent shadow.

"Do as I say, Tracy, and soon you can enter the tunnel."

Tracy nodded and listened to the shadow's gentle whispers. She followed it into a building and knocked on a door.

"I'd like a room," she said when someone answered.

A hand took the money she pulled from her pocket, then held out a key.

"Welcome to the Arms Apartments, Tracy," the shadow whispered.

Laura nodded and smiled at Mrs. Binder. She was trying to pay enough attention to what the woman was saying about fudge recipes to interject an appropriate remark occasionally. Most of her attention was focused on listening for unusual sounds from Tracy's room. She had

heard nothing since Tracy said she was going to bed, and
Laura hoped she had fallen asleep. If she wasn't asleep,
she probably was in there working herself into a frantic
state, worrying about her upcoming conversation with
her father. Laura hoped that for once in his life, Greg
Binder would show a little sensitivity. She was beginning
to think the man was never going to get home when she
saw his car pull into the driveway.

"Greg's dentist appointment must have been worse
than he expected," Mrs. Binder said. "He never leaves
the office early."

"Speaking of the office, I'd better be getting back,"
Laura said as she quickly put on her coat. She wanted a
chance to talk to the sergeant alone for a minute.
"Thanks for the coffee, and I'll try that fudge recipe," she
said on her way out the door.

"What's going on, Bernhardt?" Binder asked as soon
as he saw Laura. "Is something wrong with my daughter? Has she been hurt?"

"She's fine, but she needs to talk to you right away."

"What was so urgent it couldn't wait until this evening?"

"I'd better let her tell you, Sarge. I'll be at the office,
then at home, if you want to talk to me later."

Binder looked irritated and more than a little puzzled
as he turned to go into his house. Laura got into her
Dodge, fastened her seat belt, and reached into her purse
for her keys.

Darn, where are they, she thought. The last thing I
want to do is hang around in the sergeant's driveway.

When she couldn't find them, she pulled everything
out of her purse and laid it beside her on the seat. They
weren't there. She finally thought to check her pocket.

Oh, good, she thought with relief. I was beginning to
think I left them inside, and I don't want to go back in
there.

She started the car and began to pull out of the driveway when she heard Binder calling to her.

Rats, she thought. I didn't get away fast enough. I'm
surprised he is drawing me into this. Tracy couldn't have

had time to tell him the whole story. I don't even see how she had time to tell him she was pregnant.

She rolled down her window as he walked up to her.

"I think it's time you told me what is happening here, Bernhardt. Tracy is gone. We've searched the entire house."

"That's not possible. I personally drove her home, and I've been waiting here until you got back to make sure nothing happened to her."

"What made you think something might happen to my daughter in her own home?" Binder shouted.

Mrs. Binder was standing at the front door, looking worried.

"Get in, Sarge. I'll tell you about it while we look for her. There's no time to waste." She yelled to Mrs. Binder, "She probably went out for a soda. We'll find her."

"You'd better start talking, Bernhardt," Binder said.

"If we don't find her in a few minutes, we'd better put out an all-points bulletin," Laura said. "I have reason to believe she is in serious danger." Laura reluctantly told the sergeant the story while they searched in vain for Tracy. Her service as a decoy in the botched arrest attempt Saturday had been easier, she now reflected, than having to tell this man his little girl was pregnant and possibly being stalked by a psychopathic killer.

Greg Binder seemed to age fifteen years while Laura talked. When she'd finished, he picked up her police radio and said, "All units be on the lookout for Tracy Binder, a sixteen-year-old Caucasian female, five feet five inches, one hundred fifteen pounds, red hair, blue eyes, last seen in the vicinity of Pinehurst and Elm, wearing blue jeans and a rose-colored ski jacket. She is possibly being pursued by an unidentified male who is believed to be armed and dangerous."

"Binder, is that you?" the chief's voice came over the radio when the sergeant finished his broadcast.

"Yes, sir."

"Is Bernhardt with you, by any chance?"

"Yes, sir."

Oh, boy, Laura thought, now there is going to be hell to pay, and I guess I deserve it. I was sure Tracy would be okay if I stayed with her until the sergeant came home. If anything has happened to that kid, I'll never forgive myself.

46

Jeremy's swing moved to and fro as he sang his favorite songs. He stopped singing now and then when he couldn't suppress giggling over how well his game was going. He was still mad about the Martha woman getting away, but he'd make up for it. Before long he would be strong enough to lure her back to the city. He would let her have her little victory for now, because he was tired of playing with her anyway. He was going to play with the silly-nilly Tracy girl. She was downstairs dreaming about how wonderful it would be when she died. He'd have to do something to make her frightened before the daddy person killed her. It wasn't fun unless they were afraid.

The daddy person wasn't home yet. Jeremy wasn't mad at him for not coming straight home from work, because he was thinking bad thoughts about Laura Bernhardt. That was good. He wasn't supposed to like anyone but his darling son. It was too bad she was making it so easy to turn him against her. Jeremy insisted on winning, but he didn't like his games to be too easy.

"I should have you suspended for misconduct. In fact, I should throw you off the force this very second and make sure you never work in law enforcement anyplace, ever again, Bernhardt."

Laura sank deeper in her chair as MacNamara shouted at her. She had never seen the chief so angry, and the fact that she had provoked his wrath through her own stupidity made the tongue lashing even worse.

"I've worked with you. I've listened to you. I've stuck my neck out for you on this case, and you have held back important information; you've gone off half cocked, taking things into your own hands; and now, Bernhardt, you've endangered the life of a minor. What I want to know is, why?"

"I'm not going to make excuses for myself, sir. I know I've behaved like a fool, but when Tracy came in today, she begged me not to tell you. I knew you would have to know tomorrow, but I wanted to give her a chance to talk to her parents first. I thought if I did tell you, there wasn't anything you could do besides have me keep an eye on her."

"Well, you are wrong. We could have taken her downtown and had her hypnotized like we did you. She might have remembered something from her dreams under hypnosis. We could have put a closer surveillance on her. We could have, oh, I don't know. We could have done something."

"You couldn't have had her hypnotized without her father's permission, Chief, and believe me, she wasn't up to it anyway. Emotionally she was hanging by a thread. That's why I thought I had to get her out of here and home. I didn't come and tell you I was leaving because I would have had to explain why, and that would have been violating Tracy's confidence. Once we got to her house, I don't know what happened. It doesn't make any sense. She couldn't have left the house without me seeing or hearing her."

"She did get away, though, and we'll be damned lucky if she is alive when we find her."

Laura didn't respond. She was trying not to cry. She was an officer of the law who had blown a vital responsibility. She genuinely liked Tracy, and the girl might die because of her.

The chief sighed, then said, "In all fairness, Laura, I might have done the same thing myself if I had been in your shoes, but this other situation of you holding back information is intolerable. You've even been ordering lab reports without my knowledge. What is this about a gold necklace?" he asked accusingly.

"It was Martha Gibbons's," Laura replied guiltily. "I found it on my nightstand this morning at the YWCA."

"Why didn't you tell me about it when we talked this morning?" MacNamara's voice rose angrily.

"I didn't know how to explain it."

"You mean you didn't know how to explain it without filling me in on the rest of the information you have been withholding?"

"Yes, sir," Laura said, wishing she could disappear into the floor.

"The lab personnel can't explain it, either, Bernhardt. They said they have never seen anything like it. The links of that necklace were not pulled apart. Every tiny link exploded apart. You don't look surprised, Bernhardt."

"No, sir."

"What do you think caused the necklace to explode?"

"The child, sir," Laura responded miserably.

"The child?" MacNamara asked sarcastically. "Could you perhaps be referring to the child that you have so conveniently forgotten to mention in our previous conversations?"

"Yes, sir," Laura muttered.

"And why haven't you mentioned him, Bernhardt?" the chief shouted.

The tears that Laura had been holding back through sheer willpower broke loose, and her voice changed from meek to frustrated.

"I haven't told you, Chief, for the same reason Tracy didn't tell anyone. I didn't tell you for the same reason none of the murder victims told anyone. Would you have believed me if I told you? Look at the trouble you had accepting that I might be having precognitive dreams about the murders. What would you have done if I had come to you and told you that there was one more little detail I know about the case, that the murderer is working with a supernatural ghost child who creates lightning and fog and earth tremors and makes necklaces explode?" MacNamara looked surprised and somewhat subdued by Laura's outburst.

"Do you think it has been easy for me to keep that information to myself? But if I had told you, you not only would have thrown me off the force, you would have made sure I was locked safely away where I wouldn't be a danger to myself or others. That's why I didn't talk, and that is why no one else has talked either.

"Besides, if you think about it, Chief, you'll realize I didn't hide the existence of the child from you. He was in the drawing of my dream, and you chose to ignore it. Granted, I didn't volunteer information about the shadow, but you hardly gave me the chance. You looked at the picture and told me plain and clear you thought the shadow was nothing more than a dream manifestation."

The chief sat quietly for a minute, frowning at her, then said, "God knows, Bernhardt, I'm in no mood to agree with you on anything today, but fair is fair. Your analysis of the situation is pretty close to correct. Maybe I was afraid to ask you about the shadow because I was afraid of what you would say. If I had listened to your story about the child last week, I might have been convinced you were crazy. I still expect to find out that, somehow, you, Tracy, and Martha Gibbons are suffering from mass hallucinations. Nevertheless, I do have to admit there is no evident explanation for the necklace you sent to the lab, or for several other aspects of this case. If I hadn't seen that crazy fog myself Saturday night, and felt the earth tremors, I still might not believe you. That fog was limited to the exact radius of our stakeout operation Saturday, so if you're crazy, I guess I am too; because I believe you. I'm not going to suspend you, or take you off the case. In fact, I guess I owe you an apology for yelling at you. It wasn't fair of me to take my frustration out on you, and as far as the way you handled the situation with Tracy Binder, you probably did the only thing you could do. It's not your fault."

"Thank you, sir," Laura replied with relief. "Does that mean I can go help look for her?"

"No, it does not. You and I are going to get lots of paper and sharp pencils, and you are going to tell me every little incident that has happened to you, real or imagined, since the beginning of this mess."

Laura's relief changed to dread. She should have anticipated this, but she didn't feel like going over the grue-

some details right now. "May I call my husband first and
tell him I'm going to be late?"

"Of course, Laura. How is your husband holding up
under the strain of this case?"

"Not very well, sir."

"You have my sympathy there. The pressures of this
job are hell on marriage. That's why I'm divorced. Now,
go make that telephone call so we can get this over with."

The precinct secretary waylaid Laura momentarily on
her way back to the detectives' office. "Laura," she called
from beneath a mountain of mail, "can you give me a
hand with this? We just got the evening delivery from
headquarters. Joan asked me to hand-deliver this one to
you," she said, balancing the papers precariously so she
could hand Laura the routing envelope. "She said it was
the report you asked for after lunch."

Laura looked confused for a moment, then remem-
bered having asked for a computer check on the janitor.
She couldn't understand why she had even asked for it.
The tension must be making her grasp at straws.
"Thanks, and thank Joan for me too. You two don't get
enough credit for the help you give us around here."

Laura was sincere. The secretaries and clerks had the
most overworked and underpaid positions in the department, and she felt guilty that they had gone to extra work
researching and delivering something so insignificant.
She helped the secretary carry the mail to the detectives'
office for the first drop, then started looking for a quiet
phone where she could call Darryl. She folded the routing envelope and stuffed it into her purse, immediately
forgetting it.

47

Darryl let the phone ring three times before picking it up.
If it was Laura, he didn't want her to know that he had
been waiting for her to call.

"Who is this?" he asked coldly in response to her greeting.

"Don't be that way, sweetheart. You know it's me, Laura."

"Laura? The name rings a bell," he replied caustically. "I remember now. I used to know a Laura, but she hasn't been around here in ages."

"Please, sweetheart. This isn't easy for me either."

Darryl steeled himself against the fatigue he heard in his wife's voice. She had brought it on herself, and he was determined not to feel sorry for her. "Since it is six-thirty and you aren't here yet, I assume you are calling to tell me you either are going to be late, or you aren't bothering to come home at all again tonight," he said angrily.

"It will only be a couple of hours. I want to come home, but I can't. I'll be there as soon as I can. I'm so anxious to see you, I can hardly wait."

"Sure. Tell someone who is going to be convinced," Darryl shouted. "How much longer do you expect me to put up with this, Laura? I'm supposed to be a married man, but I don't have a wife anymore."

"Bear with me a little longer, Darryl. Please. I love you, and I need your support right now."

"And what about what I need? Is my purpose in life to be your cheering section when you decide to pop in for a few minutes once a week?"

"You know that isn't true. I'll be home in a couple of hours, then we'll talk."

"Come home now, or I may not be here later."

"The chief won't let me leave. He knows about the child, and he insists I stick around and tell him everything that's happened to me in the past month. I don't want to do it, but I don't have any choice. I'll be home by nine at the latest, though. I love you, Darryl."

"If you love me, you'll come home now."

"I'll be there as soon as I can."

Darryl hoped his wife would come to her senses, right up to the moment she hung up. Then he slammed the phone down. After a month of worrying himself sick about his wife, his concern had turned to rage. He wasn't going to put up with any more nonsense about her re-

sponsibilities as a detective. She was going to have to
decide whether she wanted to be married to her job or to
him, because she couldn't have it both ways. His job was
important, too, and it brought in twice as much money,
but he hadn't let it interfere with his responsibilities to
her and to their home. Laura not only had let their marriage slide, she wasn't even showing a sensible concern
for her safety.

Darryl looked around the kitchen and noticed something on the kitchen table.

That's strange, he thought. That piece of paper wasn't
on the table a minute ago. He felt an irrational sense of
panic and a desire to flee.

There's no reason for me to overreact, he thought. It's
nothing but a folded paper. I apparently laid it there and
forgot about it.

Despite what he told himself, he did not want to look
at it. Interior warning bells seemed to ring in his head
when he forced himself to walk the few steps to the table
and pick up the paper.

As soon as he unfolded it, he dropped it and yanked
his hand back as if he were pulling away from a rotted
corpse. His stomach clenched into an involuntary knot
and his hands began to perspire as he looked in horror at
the picture of Martha Gibbons with the ghost suspended
partway inside her head.

"We burned it," he whispered. "I personally set it on
fire."

As he watched in terrified fascination, the picture began to move and change. He groaned as the shadowy
figure squirmed against the woman's head, trying to get
in. The woman covered her face and shook her head.

Darryl grasped the back of a chair to keep from falling
as the picture continued to move like a television cartoon.
The ghost was almost all the way inside the woman's
head now, and she had stopped struggling. She was
slowly moving her hands from her face.

He wanted to run from the house, but he was riveted to
the spot, unable to move his eyes from what he was seeing. The moving picture could not exist, but it was as real
and solid as the table.

The woman moved her hands from her face, and Darryl's scream bellowed through the house. It was no longer a picture of Martha Gibbons. It was Laura in the telephone booth with the ghost entering her.

He didn't hear Laura's car pull into the driveway or the front door open as she came in. He was aware only of his terror as he continued to scream.

"Darryl, what's wrong?" Laura asked frantically.

He pushed her away, sure it was a trick and that she was the woman from the picture. The room was out of focus, and so was the fake Laura. He muttered incomprehensibly and sank into a chair.

Laura dropped to her knees next to him and held him. "It's okay, darling. Whatever happened, it's over now."

He looked up at his wife as though he were seeing her there for the first time. The room was back in focus and he saw Laura looking at him with concern. "Laura?"

"Yes, it's me. What happened?"

"The picture is back. We've got to get out of here," he said frantically. "You are in it this time. It's there on the table." He held her tightly. "I thought I had lost you. I thought it had killed you too. We've got to get out of this town tonight, Laura. If we stay here, you are going to be murdered."

"There's nothing there."

"Darryl jerked his head toward the table in disbelief. "It was here," he said, crawling under the table to look.

"I believe you, darling, but it's gone now. Forget it."

"How can I forget it? Laura, you've got to quit this case. We can take that trip to Hawaii we've been talking about."

"I can't walk out, Darryl. I have to see this through."

"Why can't you understand that you are not going to get the murderer? He is going to get you. Your detective work is not going to help. You don't need police training, you need an exorcist to solve this case," he shouted as Laura followed him to the bedroom.

"We are going to solve it, and put a stop to this nightmare. We are getting close, I swear," she said.

"I've had it, Laura. I can't take any more. I can't go through every day wondering if you will be alive in the

evening. You have to decide if this case is more important
than me. I'm walking out of this house in five minutes. If
you don't come with me, we are finished."

Laura shook her head no, tears running down her
cheeks. "Don't give up on me now," she begged while he
threw clothes into a suitcase.

"Please don't go, Darryl. Give me a few more days."

He turned and walked into the cold night air.

The hint of a smile stretched across Adam's face as he
sauntered home from the movies. Soon his life would be
perfect. He and Jeremy would be together, and Laura
would realize she was in love with him. She would beg
him to let her come to his apartment. He couldn't allow
that, of course—he had to shield his son from her corrup-
tion—but eventually he would show mercy on her and
agree to meet her at a hotel near the precinct house.

Images of the triple-X-rated movies he had just
watched swam through his head, all the actresses becoming Laura Bernhardt.

He stored his dreams of Laura in the corner of his
mind reserved for her and turned his attention to his son
as he neared the apartment. He paused in front of the
showroom window of a new-car dealership and eyed an
Oldsmobile station wagon. He decided he would pick it
up Saturday so he could start finding a house for himself
and Jeremy. He had never driven a vehicle, but he was
certain it would be easy. His smile turned to a full-fledged
grin of anticipation.

When he finally began his ascent up the fire escape, he
was preparing excuses for Jeremy. His son didn't like for
him to be late, and Jeremy could make it very unpleasant
when he was angry.

The shadow on the swing was waiting when he unlocked the door.

"I've been looking for a car for us," Adam said hastily.
"I wouldn't have been late otherwise, honest, son. When
you leave the television and come to live with me, we'll
need a car. We're going to move to the suburbs, where
they have good schools. I've mentioned that before,
haven't I?" Adam spoke rapidly, defending himself be-

fore Jeremy had a chance to unleash his anger. "It won't be long now, will it, son?"

"No, Daddy, it won't be long at all," Jeremy said sweetly.

Adam flopped on the saggy bed in relief. Jeremy wasn't mad after all, but he would have to be careful from now on. If the boy got mad, he might not come and live with him, or he might punish him again.

"We'll live next to a park," Adam said excitedly as he grabbed a loaf of bread and smeared peanut butter across a piece to make a sandwich. "You and I will play ball in the park, and I'll take you swimming. How does that sound? Would you like to learn to swim?"

"We'll have lots of fun soon, Daddy," Jeremy said, the shadow on the swing soaring almost out of sight at the upper edges of the television, then descending quickly. "First, you need to punish a couple more of the baby killers. Then I can be set free."

Adam wolfed down the last of his sandwich and sat eagerly in front of the television. Punishing the baby killers was a pleasure he could enjoy now.

"Who is it this time, Jeremy?" he asked eagerly.

Jeremy's swing faded from the television, replaced by scenes of Tracy Binder in the backseat of a car with her boyfriend. Adam recognized her and laughed. The deep, vindictive sound welled up inside him and rolled out. He had recognized her immediately. It was the stuck-up daughter of the stuck-up police sergeant.

"Let's see how uppity you act when your pregnant teenager is found with her little neck snapped, and the whole city knows she was a slut," Adam hissed gleefully. "I'm going to enjoy punishing this girl. So the sergeant's little angel is another whore, a baby killer. "You thought you were too good to even say good morning to me, Binder, when all along your little girl was getting laid by every boy she could find." He laughed some more. Then his eyes squinted vengefully as he remembered Tracy coming into the precinct house.

"You looked at me like I was scum, little whore, but you're nothing better than a two-bit streetwalker. You even made Laura ignore me. You'll be sorry. So will your father."

The scenes of Tracy disappeared from the screen and Adam jumped up to grab his coat.

"Not yet, Daddy," Jeremy said firmly. "You can punish Tracy tomorrow night. Tonight I'm letting her know she has been a bad girl."

His frown of disappointment disappeared when he contemplated the terror Jeremy would inflict on his enemy.

"What about the other woman?" Adam asked hopefully. "You said there were two left to punish. I could take care of the other one for you tonight."

"No!" Jeremy shouted. "The other one has to be last. She has to see that there is no escape. She is the worst of all."

Adam squirmed excitedly. "Just tell me who she is."

"She is your worst enemy," Jeremy said coldly. "She is the devil in disguise. She is the enemy of all babies. She wants to catch you and lock you up so that all babies can be killed. She would laugh over the graves of a thousand babies. She would stand over your grave and toast your defeat."

An empty examining room at the Family Planning Clinic sprang onto the screen. Adam gasped when Laura Bernhardt walked in. His mind was in a turmoil. He knew she wasn't pure, as he'd originally thought, but there must be some mistake. She wasn't one of the baby killers. She wasn't his enemy. Laura loved babies. He had seen her comforting that baby at the precinct a few weeks before.

"She's worse than the others, Daddy," Jeremy's voice taunted through the stereo speakers. "She pretended to be pure. She pretended to be your friend when all along she was one of them. She was their leader. She has been helping all of them, Daddy. She has been trying to find out who we are so she can kill us and keep on helping the women kill their babies. She is going to kill her baby."

He sat transfixed as the door to the examining room opened and the doctor walked in. Adam was left looking at the door he closed behind him. He pounded on the television screen in frustration, but he couldn't see what was happening in the room. The agony of her betrayal increased as he imagined what was happening behind that closed door. He envisioned Laura naked on the table, a look of ecstasy on her face while the doctor reached inside her.

When the door finally opened, Laura spoke loudly. "Pregnant? I can't have a baby now. I won't have a baby. The last thing I need is a squalling kid hanging around. When can I get an abortion?"

It was true. Adam sobbed while he listened to Laura tell everyone in the clinic she wanted an abortion, that she wasn't going to let a kid interfere with her life.

Then the television flashed abruptly to Laura putting on Martha Gibbons's clothes, and Jeremy said, "You almost killed her once, Daddy. Next time you won't fail."

Adam gasped. "It was her in the fog that night? How could I have had her in my arms and not have known?"

Adam felt as though he had been stabbed in the heart. He had been willing to forgive Laura for her previous sexual transgressions, because he had been certain that from now on she would save herself for him. What Jeremy had just shown him, though, was unforgivable. In his wildest imagination he had never considered hurting Laura. Now his rage was so intense, he could not imagine a death hideous enough to repay her deceit. He thought about the excitement he had felt last weekend in the fog when Marie's scarf was tightening around her neck. He wished he had killed her then, but at least now when he did punish her, she would know it was him and why she had to die.

On top of the television Adam found a watch and a charm bracelet.

48

Laura warded off her growing depression with denial. She didn't blame Darryl for being upset, but it was inconceivable that he might have walked out for good. Until these bizarre murders began, they had been almost blissfully happy. He must realize they would feel that way again. She began fixing dinner for the two of them, both to stay busy and as an act of faith. He was bound to be home by the time she finished baking the chicken and potatoes; then, somehow, she would make him understand that she was not giving up on their marriage, and that their lives really would be back to normal soon.

She continued to stay busy with the ordinary acts of cleaning and straightening, taking comfort in the feel of her home around her. It should have been wonderful being home after having spent three days in the dingy room at the YWCA. With Darryl gone and Tracy missing, what she felt was guilt and despair.

She vacuumed and dusted while dinner cooked. When the chicken was done and Darryl still was not home, she watered the plants and cleaned the bathroom. Darryl still had not come back by the time the laundry was clean, folded, and put away, so she put their dinner in the refrigerator. She would warm it in the microwave when he came in.

She had been so wrapped up in her concerns about her fight with Darryl, as well as in her anxieties about Tracy, that she had forgotten to call Martha Gibbons. When she remembered, she dialed the number reluctantly. If Martha had not arrived safely, she didn't know if she could handle the responsibility she would feel. The phone rang several times, and Laura was beginning to fear something had happened to the woman on her way to Taylorsville when a sleepy voice answered.

"I'm sorry I woke you, Martha. I didn't realize how late it was getting. I wanted to make sure you were okay."

"It was sweet of you to call, Laura. I'm fine. I don't

think I'll ever get enough of hugging my babies, though."
Martha's voice sang with happiness.

"What about the child? Any more trouble?"

Martha lowered her voice to a whisper, and Laura
knew she still hadn't told Harold about her strange experiences. "He's gone," she said. "I'm not sure when I first
felt it, but the farther we got away from the city, the
more difference there was. It is like he has a force field,
and I broke out of it. Why don't you leave the city, too,
Laura? You'll be free."

"I'm glad you are okay, Martha. I bought you another
necklace today. They promised to mail it to you. Let me
know if there is anything else I can do for you," she said,
evading Martha's suggestion, which painfully reminded
her of her fight with Darryl. She hung up, relieved that
Martha was safe, but aching to feel the peace that the
woman radiated.

She finished putting her house in order, still hoping
that Darryl would return at any minute.

It wasn't until she was immersed in a hot bath that she
became aware of the silent emptiness of the house and
acknowledged that Darryl might not come home that
night. She pushed the thought from her head and put on
her sexiest nightgown, then crawled between the fresh
sheets she had put on their bed. He would be home, and
she would be ready for him. She was acutely aware of the
house's night talk as she lay awake in the dark bedroom.

As she lay in bed waiting, the comforting noises
seemed to change. The difference was so subtle that at
first she didn't notice, but soon the gentle hummings and
creaks seemed to turn into frantic cries of warning, and
she felt the energy around her become oppressively
dense.

Suddenly the house became deadly silent, as though
the night sounds had fled in terror. The total silence
jolted Laura more than if she had heard a loud crash.

"Darryl?" she called out hesitantly, but she knew it
wasn't her husband's presence she felt. It wasn't Darryl
who had caused her home's night symphony to retreat
into the walls and floorboards and wait for a safer time to
sing their songs.

She slid into her bathrobe and grabbed her revolver from the nightstand in one fluid motion, then stood in the bedroom listening nervously. It was the complete absence of sound that convinced her something had invaded her home. She walked quietly down the hall, all her senses alert and the safety off her gun. A rancid odor assailed her in the hall and grew steadily as she moved stealthily toward the living room. She knew the smell. It was the child. She cocked the gun and gripped it tightly, knowing her precaution was irrational because a gun would be of no use against the intruder she was going to face.

Laura froze at the living-room door. An eerie glow illuminated the walls, while in the middle of the room the shadow of a child on a swing hung suspended from the ceiling, its pendulum motion engulfing the room. Laura moaned and gooseflesh stood out on her arms. The shadow did not play against the wall and floor where shadows belong. It was in the air, self-contained and without a source. It didn't appear to be giving off the glow on the walls, rather it seemed to be sucking it in.

Laughter burst through the house like the wind from a tornado, and Laura's gun was knocked from her hand and discharged.

"I'll beat you," Laura said vehemently to the child, "or die trying."

"That will be a fun game," Jeremy responded cheerfully.

Laura was picked up by unseen hands and thrown across the room. Her head collided solidly with an edge of the piano, and she slumped, unconscious, to the floor. Blood ran from a wound on her temple onto the carpet.

49

Tuesday, February 12
"Laura called in sick about a quarter to eight, Chief," Harry said, putting his most convincing face forward. "I

know I should have told you earlier, but I got busy and forgot."

"If she is sick, why didn't she wait to talk to me?" MacNamara countered irritably.

"I'm sure she was telling the truth. I should know. She's my partner. Laura sounded terrible when she called. It was definitely a cold. No one could fake those coughs."

At ten-thirty, when Laura still had not shown up for work or called, Harry had decided to cover for her.

"Why didn't you transfer the call to me?" MacNamara asked.

"I tried, boss, but your line was busy," Harry lied. Despite the problems he and Laura might have had in the past, she was his partner, and he was determined to keep her out of trouble if he possibly could.

"Chief, Laura wanted to stay on the phone and wait for you, but I talked her out of it," Harry lied expertly. "I'm not surprised she's caught a bug. She's only taken a couple of days off work in the past month. There seems to be a virus going around. The janitor called in sick this morning too. I've never known the janitor to miss a day any more than Laura. That must be one hell of a virus to keep those two workaholics away. I'm sure glad they aren't here spreading it around. Can you imagine us trying to solve these murder cases with the whole department flat on their backs?"

"If Bernhardt is home sick, why isn't she answering her phone, Winchell?"

"She said she was going to the doctor," Harry lied.

"Are you telling me Laura Bernhardt went to the doctor's office without being dragged there in handcuffs?"

Harry winced. Maybe he had gone too far. He was going to have to do some quick talking. "I think it was pretty close to that, Chief," he said with a big smile. "She said her husband was driving her."

"Okay, Winchell, get out of here and let me get some work done, but in the future, if someone calls to talk to me, I expect you to transfer the call. Don't ever take it upon yourself again to screen my calls."

Harry ducked quickly out of the office just as Binder

walked in, looking twenty years older than he had yesterday. Harry felt a pang of sympathy for the sergeant. Everyone knew about his daughter. They still hadn't found
her, but he was too busy patting himself on the back for
the fast one he'd pulled on the chief to think about the
sergeant's problems.

Ten miles away in the suburbs, Laura was still seeing
and feeling nothing. No doctor was going to show up at
the door and discover her condition. No one from the
precinct was going to come and check on her and rush
her off for medical treatment. Harry Winchell thought
that his partner wanted to be left alone for the day, and
he had ensured she would be.

Adam ripped another sheet of baby-shower paper off
his shoe box and slammed it across the room, where it
fell with an infuriating lack of force next to the six other
sheets of paper that had preceded it. The women's posses-
sions lay in a pile at the edge of the table, waiting to be
put back in the remodeled box.

To Adam, covering the box was not a question of making it pretty. He was converting it into an altar for the
babies. After he called in sick from the corner telephone
booth, the idea of the box as a religious symbol became
an obsession. Each item in the box represented a gift to
Jeremy and the babies. When Jeremy came from the television to live with him, he would present the box to his
son, in the way the wise men had brought presents to the
Christ child. The more he struggled with the paper, however, the more miserably he failed. His hands trembled as
though they were operated by an internal vibrator as he
clumsily attached his last sheet of wrapping paper. Tiny
pink and blue teddy bears on a yellow background clung
precariously to the box when he finished.

There had been no question of his going to work that
day. With what he knew about Laura Bernhardt, he
could not possibly face her without showing his rage.

"I loved you, and you betrayed me," he said aloud. His
voice was deceptively calm. Even the shaking of his
hands could be misconstrued as mere nervousness, but

his eyes showed a seething volcano that had been building pressure for fifty years. The four murders he had committed during the past two weeks had not relieved the churning anger. They had only brought it to the surface, where a full-fledged eruption was inevitable.

The eye of the television stared with innocent blankness while Adam picked up Sister Mary Xavier's ring. He looked at the symbol of godliness that had belonged to the creature who had feigned the purest of positions among women. The confused guilt he had felt since he was sixteen years old because of his sexual longings for the nun were replaced by hot rage. He dropped the ring into the shoe box and picked up Ann Locke's earring. His molten anger bubbled freely as he remembered the nearly sexual release of tension he had felt when he squeezed Marie's scarf around Ann's pretty neck.

Whirling fury and desire clashed with his confusion as the angry rivers of his emotions forced their way upward. He rubbed the soft nap of Rhonda Hackman's gloves and remembered how she had called out for Laura just before he killed her. The proof of Laura's betrayal had been there all along, if only he had looked for it.

Heather Evans's ring fell against Sister Mary Xavier's ring when he dropped it into the altar, reminding him of the sound her neck had made when he snapped it. He longed to hear that sound again and to feel the power of his hands as he twisted Marie's scarf until the fibers threatened to break.

His hands clenched around the scarf as he anticipated his next victory, but the absence of Martha Gibbons's necklace reminded him that he must proceed with caution and follow Jeremy's instructions carefully. It also reminded him of the night in the fog when he'd had Laura in his hands, and she had slipped away. His fury threatened to erupt as he remembered how close he had come to terminating his mortal enemy. His entire body jerked and quivered in his attempt to contain his feelings, for contain them he must. Tracy Binder's charm bracelet reminded him that he still had a job to do before he could take care of Laura. He wanted to kill Tracy now, but Jeremy insisted he wait until tonight.

It had been less than four days since Heather Evans had walked obligingly into his trap, but for Adam, killing again was the only hope of relief from the raging fire within him, so he squeezed Laura's watch in his hand and waited for darkness to overtake the city.

Jeremy's smile stretched across the inside of the round television. His daddy wouldn't see him until he wanted to be seen. He was waiting to play the end of his game, and he didn't want to deal with the silly daddy person's questions. The Laura woman had kept the daddy from coming to the master as easily as he had expected. The master would win, though. Of that there was never any doubt.

Jeremy considered creating a nice lightning storm across the city. Little dramatic effects helped build the terror on which he and the master thrived.

He and the master would be well fed tonight when the daddy person killed Tracy Binder. He would wait until then to create a storm. The strength he and the master gained from the fear the lightning caused barely exceeded the energy he expended creating it. The strength he gained from the daddy's anger, however, was like being plugged directly into a power plant. The daddy had lots of anger to draw on, and after he killed Tracy, Jeremy knew he and the master would be stronger than ever.

After the daddy killed Laura Bernhardt, the master would be invincible; then the daddy would belong to the master completely, and Jeremy's job would be done.

Adam didn't hear Jeremy's laugh. If he had, it would have made him very nervous.

50

Adam had no awareness of the passing of time while his mind whirled through confused memories of his days at the orphanage and the institution. The scenes became jumbled and he saw Sister Mary Xavier at the institution and the attendants from the institution at the orphanage.

As he drifted through his fantasies, Laura's face replaced Sister Mary Xavier's in the nun's long habit as she seduced and belittled him simultaneously. The image he had held of Marie for twenty years receded and she, too, became Laura Bernhardt. She stood in his apartment, the blood that should have sustained Jeremy running between her legs.

Jeremy interupted his thoughts. The sun was setting.

"I'm sorry, Darryl, but Laura isn't here. She called in sick today."

Darryl's hopes soared at José Martínez's words. Maybe his wife had come to her senses after all. She probably had been trying to reach him all day. He cursed himself for not having called her earlier, but he was so confused, he had to have time to work out his feelings. It was one thing to tell Laura he was leaving her. It was an entirely different matter to wake up at the Holiday Inn and consider continuing his life without her.

Already Darryl was digging twenty cents out of his pocket and putting it in the coin slot to call Laura.

The continued ringing of the telephone filled him with dread and anger. Ten rings and still no answer; he hoped maybe she was in the shower and taking a while to get to the phone. Twenty rings and he slammed the receiver down, cursing his stupidity in thinking a reconciliation might be possible. He walked back to his barstool and ordered a double Scotch. Later he would go home, pack some more clothes, and check back into the motel. He gulped his drink and ordered another.

"Laura." The voice called to her firmly, but kindly, through the safe blankness of her mind. Laura resisted, struggling to stay where nothing could hurt her again.

"You must wake up, Laura."

Laura shook her head. She would not listen to the voice. The darkness where she had dwelt for the past ten hours was where she wanted to stay.

A young woman penetrated the blackness, radiating light as she walked forward. Laura tried to turn away, but wherever she turned, the woman was moving toward her, calling her name softly, with sympathy. The blue wool scarf that covered her head emphasized her simple beauty.

"You must wake up and read the report." Sadness dripped from the woman's voice like rain from a weeping willow.

"I don't know what you are talking about," Laura muttered.

"Get up and read the report," the woman insisted. Her image began to fade. In the distance Laura heard the melodious voice say, "He was a good man once."

Laura opened her eyes. She was still lying in a huddle on her living-room floor. She looked around the room, her muscles resisting the movement. Her bathrobe clung limply to her damp body; blood was caked in her hair and across her face. The room was dark and she tried to stand to turn on a light. At first her legs resisted, as if they knew more was at stake than her life. If she lost, it meant her immortal soul.

Laura was confused by her dream. Who was the woman, and what had she meant about reading a report? Then she remembered the report she had asked for on Adam Smith.

She couldn't mean that report, Laura thought. I don't know why I even asked for it.

But the woman's voice kept echoing in her head, "Read the report."

Still in a daze, she stumbled to the kitchen and pulled the report from her purse and starting reading.

The neon lights from the bar across the street had been shining in Tracy's face since it had gotten dark. She considered closing the curtains, but it was too much effort. She didn't know where she was, and she had only the vaguest notion of how she had gotten there.

She didn't care.

She was sitting on the bed, holding several bottles of pain medication. The prescriptions were made out to someone named Rhonda Hackman. The name sounded familiar to Tracy, but she didn't stop to think about it. She had done her thinking when she woke up in this

strange room. She considered her conclusions to be irre-
futable. She had no future. Her only choice was to take
the pills that Rhonda Hackman had so conveniently left
for her.

Periodically Tracy felt the child trying to reach inside
her mind, and she was aware of his anger at failing. He
was trying to frighten her, but she was beyond fright. She
was going to be okay as soon as she took the pills. She
would take them as soon as she mustered the energy to
remove the childproof lids. For now, she was content to
stare out the window at the neon lights.

Finally she sighed and removed the lids from four bottles and poured the pills onto the worn bedspread. She
smiled for the first time in days. The pills were the same
colors as the lights across the street. It was an omen she
was doing the right thing.

"Pretty little pills. Tiny candy-coated pills. You're so
little, and, oh, so very pretty."

Her left foot was tingling. Her legs were falling asleep
from sitting too long on the bed. It didn't matter. Soon
her whole body would be asleep, and at peace. She
stretched out her legs and made neat lines of pills on
either side of her, delighting in the patterns of colors.

"Yes, yes, my friends. I know you all want to sit next
to me, but I can't play favorites. That wouldn't be fair.
What's that, my friends? I know you are excited to see
me, but you must take turns talking.

" 'Take me first.'

" 'No, take me.'

"Don't worry, little friends. I'll eat you all." She began
casually popping the pills into her mouth and swallowing
as she entered the tunnel.

"It's my game, and they'll play by my rules," Jeremy
screamed. "The stupid Tracy girl can't kill herself. The
daddy has to kill her, and she has to be afraid."

The earth shook and the sky exploded with fiery light.
The child was feeling stronger now. A man had beaten
his wife to death in the city today, and Jeremy had been
able to tap into the anger to replenish his and the master's strength, but unless the anger emanated from the

daddy person, it was weak nourishment; so he had gone
searching for a more substantial meal. He had sucked up
all he could from hatred here and there across the city,
but it was like feeding a starving man a few grains of rice.

"It's Laura Bernhardt's fault," he hissed. "If she
hadn't kept the daddy from killing Martha Gibbons, we
would be plenty strong."

The television glowed red from the heat of his anger.
Not only was Tracy killing herself, the mama person had
gotten through to Laura while his attention was diverted.
It still wasn't too late, though. It might even work out
better this way. Daddy would have to kill Tracy now, and
Laura right afterward. The force of the two murders so
close together would make the master all-powerful.

The television sprang to life.

"Daddy, help me," Jeremy cried with innocent desperation. "If you don't do exactly what I say right away, the
evil Laura woman is going to destroy us both."

The daddy bolted forward, his red eyes crazed with
anticipation.

51

The wind furiously battered snow against the kitchen
window while Laura read the report on Adam Smith.
How ironic, she thought. The entire police department
has been searching for the killer, and he was right under
our noses all the time. No wonder every time I came out
of a meeting, I tripped over him. He has been keeping
close tabs on the investigation. He is so unobtrusive, if it
hadn't been for his keys and Tracy's reaction to him, I
never would have thought to check him out.

The wind continued beating snow against the house,
but Laura's shiver was from the memory of the woman in
the blue wool scarf telling her to wake up. On an emotional level Laura knew the woman was Marie. On an
intellectual level she still could not accept that a ghost
had talked to her. But on an intellectual level nothing

that had happened to her during the past month made sense.

Laura washed her hands and face and threw on the first clothes she found, a pair of blue jeans, a sweatshirt, and her snow boots. She picked up the telephone to call MacNamara, but put it back down. She remembered how useless the chief's reinforcements had been the last time, and she was certain they would be of no more use this time. She had to do this alone.

She thought about Darryl and wished she could do as he demanded and run away. She was nearly overwhelmed with grief when she realized she probably would never see her husband again, because her chances of making it through the night alive were slim.

Perhaps it's better this way, she thought. If I had to kiss Darryl good-bye, I don't think I could force myself to go; and I must go.

She wanted to write him a letter, to explain, but the words wouldn't come. Finally, she wrote simply, *I love you. Please forgive me.*

Then she bundled up and walked into the storm.

"It's the damndest thing I've ever seen," the man yelled over the jukebox to the bartender. Darryl looked up resentfully when the man brushed the quickly melting snow off his jacket and into his drink. He was about to offer to teach this intruder some manners when the man said, "It's the thunder and lightning that makes it really freaky."

Darryl jerked to attention as the man continued. "For the past month my Millie and me have been saying we don't want to see no more lightning without good old-fashioned clouds in the sky, but I'd take those other storms over this one any day."

"I saw snow and thunder once," the bartender said, handing the man a drink. "It's rare, but it's not unheard of. I've got to admit, though, I was pretty spooked. You could hear the thunder, but all you could see was a blanket of white. That was up in the mountains in the spring. You expect weird weather up there."

Darryl bolted toward the door, with the man yelling

behind him, "You'd better stay here, too, mister. No
one's going far in this freak show."

Darryl ignored him. His only thought was of Laura.
He should never have left last night. The child had set
out to scare him and had succeeded in driving him away
from his wife. If his intention had been to make sure no
one was around to help Laura, he had gotten his wish.
Darryl kicked himself for being such a fool. He hadn't
even caught on when he found out she hadn't been at
work and when she didn't answer the telephone. Now it
might be too late. If not, there wasn't a doubt in his mind
that if he didn't find her soon, she would be dead.

He halted momentarily outside the bar. The sky had
been clear when he went in a couple of hours before.
Since then four inches of snow had fallen and it was coming down as if it were determined to bury the city by
midnight. Darryl rushed to his truck and struggled to
clean the snow off the windshield. He turned the hubs to
four-wheel drive and climbed inside, praying the windshield wipers and defroster would keep up with the on-
slought. He put the truck in four-wheel low and inched
away from the curb onto the unplowed street, impatiently
maneuvering his way through the crawling traffic.

"Be home, Laura. God, let her be home," he prayed.

Soon accidents brought traffic to a standstill, and Darryl was forced to turn off the main street and grope
through the abandoned side streets until he was close to
the freeway. He steeled himself for the regular bursts of
lightning and agonized over the horrors his wife must be
suffering at the hands of the child.

At the moment he finally grew confident he was going
to make it to the freeway, he spun out of control and
plunged into a snowbank.

"Damn," he said, frantically throwing the truck in reverse and revving the engine. The tires spun deeper in the
snow and the truck skidded sideways, further entrapping
it. He jumped out of the cab into a snowbank up to his
knees. He waded to the back of the truck, pulled a shovel
from the truck bed, and started digging.

After digging, trying to move the truck, and digging
some more, he finally pulled free. The storm had reached

blizzard proportions and he could barely see the road, but he continued to inch along. He gave a sigh of relief when he saw the entrance to the freeway and turned onto the ramp. By the time he had driven five miles, he had bitten his fingernails to the quick.

He was squinting to see the edge of the road and fervently hoping he would recognize his exit when Laura passed him on the other side of the freeway, heading into the city. Darryl saw only another freak show of glowing snowflakes as the sky erupted in an attempt to blow itself apart.

It took him two hours to make the thirty-minute drive to his house. His heart sank when he pulled into the driveway and Laura's car was not there. Despite the evidence that she wasn't home, he rushed through the house calling her name. Silence answered. He paled when he saw a bullet hole in the wall in the living room and dried blood on the carpet. Thunder drowned his sobs as he trudged defeatedly to the kitchen. His fear mingled with self-loathing. He had walked out on his wife when she needed him, and now he was too late.

The glimmer of hope he felt when he saw her note turned to dread when he read it. The short message confirmed his worst fears without giving him a clue as to his wife's whereabouts. She had gone after the killer, and all he could do was wait.

He saw the routing envelope when he walked across the kitchen to start a pot of coffee. He picked it up, without much hope, and began to glance through it. After the first couple of pages he understood. He rapidly finished reading the report, then rushed to the telephone to call MacNamara.

Let Laura have told him already, he prayed as the phone rang. Don't let her have gone off to catch Adam Smith by herself.

A harried voice finally answered the phone at the precinct and put him on hold before he had a chance to say a word. It was five minutes before the voice came back and asked what he wanted. It was several more minutes before he got through to MacNamara.

* * *

Laura pulled up in front of the Arms Apartments. She had seen cars in ditches, spinning out of control, and careening into each other all the way, but she had moved steadily through the chaos unscathed, as though something had been pulling her forward. The lightning hadn't frightened her. In fact, she had expected it.

The neon lights at the bar across from the Arms Apartments gave off an eerie glow, but the snow was too heavy for her to see them clearly. The snow decreased momentarily and she gasped at the sign, which said:

WELCOME

LAURA BERNHARDT

"Stay where you are, Mr. Bernhardt," Chief MacNamara said when he finally understood what Darryl was trying to say. "All you'll accomplish by coming out in this storm is to get in an accident. You probably wouldn't make it a mile, anyway. We're only five blocks from Smith's apartment. Chances are we'll have him in custody before Laura even gets there."

"Thanks for the advice, but she is my wife, and I'm coming in."

"I'm ordering you to stay where you are, Mr. Bernhardt."

"You can't order me to do anything, MacNamara. I don't work for you, and this is a free country. I'll go where I want when I want."

"I can charge you with interfering with police business too," MacNamara threatened, but he was talking to an empty line. Darryl Bernhardt had hung up on him.

"Shit," MacNamara muttered as he hurried down the hall to the dispatcher. "I want every available unit sent to the Arms Apartments, Twenty-second and Spear," he barked. "Last known address of Adam Smith, murder suspect. He may be armed, dangerous, and holding a detective and teenage girl captive."

"I can't, Chief."

"You what?" MacNamara shouted.

"The radio just went out. It must be the storm."

"Then get on one of the hand units. Do it now!"

"The whole system is out, sir."

"That's impossible."

"I know, but it's true."

The chief spun around and started barking orders to every officer and detective he saw. "Spark, Martínez, Applebee, Phelps, Livingston, Fields, come with me on the double. We've been scouring the city for the murderer and all along it was the janitor right here at the precinct. Now Bernhardt has taken it upon herself to go out and apprehend him single-handedly."

MacNamara told them where they were going while they grabbed their coats. He was the first one to the big double doors. "What's the matter with these things?" he shouted when they refused to budge under his weight.

"They were unlocked a few minutes ago," Phelps said, mystified. "They're never locked."

"I don't supposed anyone has a key?" MacNamara asked. "I figured as much," he said in response to their blank expressions. "Okay, we'll go out the back way."

But they soon discovered that door also was jammed. Not a door in the precinct house would budge. They couldn't even go through a window. This was the Third Precinct. All the windows had bars on them. Phelps shot off the lock on the back door, but it still wouldn't open. It was as though the building were encased in steel.

"The phone is dead, too, sir," Clark said.

The men were spooked, and MacNamara didn't blame them. They were being held prisoners in their own precinct, totally without communication with the outside world. He stood looking helplessly at the raging storm outside, with its weird flashes of lightning, while the men tried in vain to unjam one of the doors. He could almost hear Laura's voice in his mind, saying, *Are you really surprised, Chief? If the child had let me have help, I would have called you in the first place.*

Good luck, Bernhardt, he thought.

* * *

Laura trudged through the deep snow toward the entrance to the Arms Apartments, then stopped. There was no need to ask which apartment was Adam's. She could feel evil and anger pouring from the dark alley. It came at her in waves that threatened to double her over. Her first inclination, to run and hide, was replaced by anger and determination. The child had haunted and terrorized her for a month. It was responsible for the death of four women, and it had ruined her marriage. She was going to stop it, and Adam.

She pulled her gun and headed cautiously through the snow in the darkness.

A man darted from a shadow and lunged at her.

"Stop, or I'll shoot," Laura yelled, automatically assuming the familiar police stance, her gun in front of her body, her finger on the trigger.

It was Adam. He backed off slightly, but even with the frozen snow partially obscuring her vision, Laura could see the wild look in his eyes. She struggled to keep from sliding in the slick snow while she kept an eye on the janitor. Her hands were numb from cold and she was shaking with fear. She could feel the force of the child around her. She knew its power too well. She had to force herself to concentrate her attention on Adam. She wanted to spin around and find the source of the evil and attack it directly. Logic told her that was impossible. Her mind and body were still suffering the shock of her supernatural journey the night before. To Laura it seemed only minutes since she had tumbled into the child's deadly world, where she had nearly lost her life.

The snow was flying into her face like tiny darts. She struggled to keep her panic under control.

Adam seemed to sense her hesitation and began moving slowly toward her. "You won't shoot," he hissed. He carried a blue wool scarf pulled taut between his hands.

Laura winced when he relaxed it, then snapped it tight. She knew the feel of that scarf around her neck. She remembered the smell of the musty fibers that had nearly been the cause of her death once before.

She reacted out of training and habit. "You are under

arrest, Adam Smith, for the murders of Joyce Jenkins, Heather Evans, Rhonda Hackman, and Ann Price." Her feet were slipping in the snow and the wind was blowing her body, making her position feel even more unstable, but she kept talking as though she were in charge of the situation. "You have the right to remain silent. You have the right to an attorney. If you can't afford an attorney, one will be appointed for you. Do you understand your rights?"

Adam laughed. "You have a right to say your prayers before you die, slut." He continued to walk casually forward.

"I don't want to shoot you, Adam," Laura said shakily. She could taste her fear as clearly as she tasted the snow that blew against her lips. This man bore no resemblance to the shy janitor she knew.

"My son won't let you shoot me, bitch. Jeremy wants me to punish you, like I did the other baby killers."

"You don't have a son, Adam. You don't have any children."

"No?" he responded in mock surprise. "I have a son, and he is all-powerful. Look at your gun, Detective Bernhardt."

Laura felt something wiggle in her hands. She looked down and screamed. Her gun had turned into a rattlesnake. Its wide head was gaped open, its fangs ready to sink into her hand. She screamed again and threw the snake from her hands. In her panic she lost her tenuous balance and found herself sprawled in the snow. The snake, which should not have been able to exist in the frigid weather, reared its head above the snow and struck at her leg. She yanked it back and pushed herself out of its way. It disappeared beneath the white blanket while she struggled to get back to her feet.

"My son doesn't like for baby killers to threaten his daddy," Adam said threateningly.

The snake has to be an illusion, Laura thought. I will not let an illusion and a sick man turn me into a cowering wimp. She stood and faced her assailant. The snow clung to her body and numbed her hands. Perhaps she was going to die, but she would do it with dignity, as a police officer.

"I'm not a baby killer, Adam. I'm your friend."

"You can't lie to me. Jeremy showed me you at the baby-killing place. You were worse than any of the others. You were bragging that you were going to kill your baby."

Laura remembered all too clearly her performance at the Family Planning Clinic, and how she had bragged that she had fooled everyone. Her idea to use herself as bait had seemed so logical at the time. Only now did she realize how she had tightened the noose around her own neck. She weighed her odds of constraining the janitor. She was unarmed, but she was well trained. The janitor, on the other hand, had the advantage of size and strength. She had no doubt she could have done it if her body were not racked with pain from her ordeal last night, and now from cold. She tried to move her fingers, but the cold had immobilized them. She had only her wits as a defense. The child's evil hovered around her like a physical presence. It, more than the cold and snow, took her breath away. She could feel the entity's glee over her impending death. She could feel his triumph, but in the back of her mind she heard Marie's voice telling her that Adam had been a good man. Laura had sensed that goodness and gentleness in him at the precinct. Her only hope was to bring his basic goodness to the surface. She had to break the child's grip on him.

"I'm not pregnant, Adam. I was only pretending. I didn't know you were involved in this. I only knew that the child has been terrorizing me for a month and that all the other victims were pregnant. I wanted to draw him into the open so I could end the nightmare I've been living—the nightmare you've been living. I never wanted to hurt you, but the child has been hurting all of us. He has been ruining my life. He's ruining your life, too. Let's stop him. We can, if we work together."

Adam loosened his grip on the scarf and looked confused, then composed himself. "No. You are lying. Women always lie. My son is the only person I have in the world. I let him down before, but I won't fail him again. You were supposed to be second tonight, though. Jeremy told me to kill Tracy Binder first. My son must have changed his mind. Good. I'm going to enjoy punishing you, Laura Bernhardt; then I'll take care of Binder's little tramp of a daughter."

"Tracy is still alive?" Laura asked, her voice showing her relief.

"Not for long."

"Where is she, Adam?"

"You are trying to fool me into telling you. I won't."

"But it won't matter, will it Adam? You are going to kill me first. Look at me. I have no gun. I'm defenseless against you."

"You're right. You are at my mercy, and after I kill you, I'll go to the apartment Rhonda Hackman stayed in and kill Binder's daughter."

So that was it. Laura felt like kicking herself for not guessing. The child had lured Tracy as it had Rhonda, and it was so obvious, the search teams hadn't even thought of it. Rhonda Hackman's apartment was the one place in the city they had not even considered checking. While Adam and she struggled, Tracy was just inside the Arms Apartments. Laura only hoped the girl would run away while she had the chance.

Adam had been slowly walking forward while they talked. He was only a couple of feet away from her now. She could feel his warm, rancid breath, but it was his eyes that frightened her. She jerked back from his crazed expression. The man was completely insane, and there is no reasoning with a crazy person. Still, she had to try.

"Tracy Binder wants to die," Adam said. "She knows she deserves to be punished. What are you going to do now, Miss Detective? You don't look so brave without your big, bad gun."

"This isn't you talking, Adam. It's the evil creature that is pretending to be your child. He is using you."

Adam stepped forward.

Laura stepped backward.

"They're all afraid of me in the end," he said. "They never ignore me when I have Marie's scarf." He laughed and snapped the scarf in front of her face.

Laura saw her chance. She quickly reached out and
tried to trip the janitor with a judo throw. Adam grabbed
her and they both tumbled into the snow, struggling in
the life-and-death contest. But Laura was too cold and
too weak and he soon overpowered her. He held her
wrists tight with one hand while he gripped the scarf in
the other.

"I never ignored you, Adam," Laura shouted while she
struggled to free herself. "I always thought we were
friends. We used to say hello to each other. Remember?"

"You just did that to trick me," he cried, lunging toward her neck with the scarf.

Laura twisted her head out of the way and said, "No,
that's not true. I liked you. I still like you. It's the child I
don't like. He wants to hurt you, like he made you hurt
those women."

"Jeremy would never hurt me. I'm his daddy." He
balled his free hand into a fist and slugged Laura in the
face. The pain made her nauseous and she felt warm
blood trickling out of her nose.

"I don't believe you really want to hurt me, Adam. I
don't think you ever wanted to hurt anyone. You didn't
want to hurt Marie either."

It was the right thing to say. At Marie's name Adam
loosened his grip. Laura pursued her advantage.

"It was an accident, wasn't it? You were upset, and she
was weak from the abortion. You loved her, didn't you?"

Adam released Laura and rocked to and fro on his
knees in the snow, sobbing. Laura cautiously inched her
way out of his reach.

"Yes, I loved her," he cried in anguish. "I loved you,
too, and you both betrayed me. You would have killed
me if Jeremy hadn't taken your gun away; and Marie
killed my baby. I loved you both, and now I hate you
both."

"You loved me?" Laura asked in surprise. "So that's
how I fit in. I didn't know, Adam. Honest I didn't." Once
again the missing link had been under her nose all along
and she hadn't seen it. She remembered Darryl's description of the warning at the restaurant. It had been Adam
he heard.

"I loved you, and you repaid me by tracking me down like an animal," Adam said. "I wanted to marry you and make you Jeremy's mother. I thought you were different from the others, but I was wrong. You were worse. The others just ignored me. You pretended to like me so you could lock me up again."

Laura and Adam both rose to their feet, watching each other carefully, like animals about to attack.

"I wasn't pretending. I did like you."

She felt the child's fury growing. His game was not going as he'd planned. She was supposed to be dead. She must be getting through to Adam, or the child would not be getting desperate. But the hatred was replenishing Adam. She saw it in his eyes, and she feared she was doomed. She used the only weapon left to her.

"Marie came to me and talked to me, Adam. She told me she loved you. She said you were a good man. I believe her."

"No," Adam screamed, and lunged at her with the scarf. He twisted it around her neck and started shaking her. "You're lying, lying. Marie never came to you. Marie is dead."

Laura's lungs felt as if they were going to explode. She had escaped before, but there wasn't a troop of cops to help her this time. She had tried, and she had lost. Even when she wrote Darryl the note, she hadn't really believed she was going to die. The world was spinning, and Laura felt herself stop struggling. In her death hallucination she thought she saw a woman walking across the air toward them. It was Marie welcoming another of Adam Smith's victims to the afterlife.

Adam released his hold on the scarf and Laura dropped to the ground.

Marie spoke: "Breathe, Laura."

Laura's lungs remained still. She had given up fighting death.

"You will breathe, Laura," Marie repeated.

Laura felt as if her mouth were being forcibly opened, though no one was touching her. Marie blew a gentle breath in her direction. It filled her lungs, and she coughed. The pain was wrenching, but Laura reacted automatically, gasping for more life-giving air.

It had not been a hallucination. Marie was floating toward her and Adam.

Laura's breaths were coming on their own, painful, difficult, but strong. She felt the snow and cold, but the discomfort was welcome, a sign that she was alive, for now.

"Marie?" Adam asked as the woman floated toward them.

"You will not kill her, Adam. Too many women have died because of me, my love."

Laura could see the snow falling through Marie's ghostly image, like teardrops that engulfed her entire body in sadness.

"You killed our baby," Adam cried, reaching out for Marie with the blue scarf. He grabbed at her translucent shape, but his hands went right through her.

"I loved you, Adam. You were my life," Marie said sadly. As she spoke, the snowflakes stopped falling through her. Her figure took form, and Adam dropped to the ground, bowing at the woman's feet and crying. Marie gently reached out and took her blue scarf and wrapped it around her head, where it belonged.

"I waited for you to come back all these years, Marie, until I remembered what you did. Why, Marie? Why did you kill our baby?"

"You never gave me a chance to explain that day, my love." She lowered herself to her knees and pulled Adam's face to hers and kissed him, while Laura backed quietly away. Marie kissed him on the forehead and cheeks while Laura looked on.

"There is no explanation. You betrayed me and our son," Adam sobbed.

"I didn't, darling. Remember how we used to be able to read one another's thoughts. We laughed about not having to finish sentences."

"We also talked about getting married and having children, but when you were going to have my baby, you killed him."

"Please hear me out this time, my love. You owe me

that much. Remember how excited we were when we discovered we could almost read each other's mind?"

"I don't understand, Marie. What does that have to do with you killing our child? Reminding me how close we were just condemns your hideous action more."

"When we were dating, my mother kept telling me to drop you, that you were no good for me. I ignored her. Then when I found out I was going to have your baby, I was the happiest woman in the world. I'd sworn I'd never speak to my mother again, but I wanted to share the news with her." Tears were running down Marie's cheeks. "When I told her, she laughed. It was a hideous laugh. She asked me if I remembered the walks we used to take when I was a child, and how we used to walk by the orphanage. At first I didn't remember, but she jogged my memory. I remembered her stopping and looking through the fence at the children, as if she were looking for someone in particular. It was you she was looking for. The reason we could read each other's minds was because we were twins. I was carrying my twin brother's child. That's why I had to have an abortion."

"No, you're lying. It's not true," Adam shouted, pulling himself out of the snow and running toward the fire escape.

"It is true, Adam. It explained so many things we didn't understand. Our mother wasn't a very nice person. She said she gave you away because she couldn't afford to keep two children, and that a girl would be less trouble than a son."

"Liar," Adam screamed, running past her and up the fire escape.

Laura heard sirens in the distance, and Marie calling to Adam, "Stop the killing. Let it end now." Then the woman faded, and Laura felt her gun in the snow. She picked it up and ran after Adam. The steps were icy and snow-covered, and Laura's injured head pounded furiously while she struggled to catch up with the janitor. She reached the landing just behind him. At the bottom of the fire escape she heard shouting and recognized MacNamara's voice and the other men from the precinct. She heard them start to climb the fire escape, then felt it

buck and jerk like a rodeo bull. Adam rushed into his
apartment, and she was jolted forward with him. Below,
her fellow officers were cursing their lack of progress as
the fire escape continued throwing them off.

The door slammed shut behind her, as though through
the will of an unseen force.

Adam stood hunched dejectedly in the middle of the
shabby room. His red, weathered hands hid his face, but
not his despair, as racks of sobs shook his body.

"Come with me, Adam," Laura said. She walked
slowly toward him, speaking gently. "It's over now."

As she reached out and took him by the arm, the TV
sprang to life. Laura's eyes were wide with horror as the
shadow child laughed and hissed, "It's not over, Daddy.
It's just beginning."

A vacuum seemed to be sucking Adam and her toward
the TV. The janitor was still too convulsed with grief to
fight, and Laura fought to pull him and herself back. She
lost her grip on his arm and screamed as he was sucked
into the TV.

She had no time to think, as she, too, was sucked
through the leering eye.

52

Her head was splitting, as if from a sudden change in
pressure. She felt as though she had been catapulted into
another dimension.

She cried for her husband, but he couldn't help her. He
had warned her to escape, and she had ignored him. Now
she must face the consequences. She felt a cold, rough
floor under her, like the slabs of rocks in a medieval cas-
tle, and wrapped her arms across her chest for warmth.
She was startled by the feel of her bare breasts. What was
left of her jeans and sweatshirt hung in tattered strands
from her shoulders, providing little warmth or cover. Despair overwhelmed her as she realized that in this latest
game, she was to be totally vulnerable.

"Where am I?" she cried. Silence. "Adam, where are you?"

No voice answered.

"I want to go home," she screamed. The child laughed in response and the glass window and the apartment disappeared. She was in total darkness. She gasped for air, certain that such complete blackness could not contain oxygen.

I've got to calm down, or I'm doomed, she thought. She concentrated on taking even breaths and sat huddled on the cold floor, willing herself to disappear from this hideous nightmare. Logic told her she must be dreaming. Her senses told her she was wide-awake.

The blackness that surrounded her was complete, but as she grew accustomed to it, she could feel eyes penetrating the darkness, staring at her hungrily.

Then she heard a voice in the distance crying out to her, "Help me, Laura. Please help me. You promised."

"Rhonda?" she whispered.

"Help me. You said it was over, but you lied."

Laura saw a faint light far away, in the direction of the sound, and struggled to her feet. It's a trick, her mind told her. Don't go. Rhonda is dead. But the anguished voice cried out to her more urgently, and she felt the eyes that she could not see closing in around her. She ran barefoot across the rough stones toward the light. Clammy, inhuman hands grabbed at her as she fled toward the light, and slime clung to her body where they touched her. The creatures were gaining on her, pulling her back as she struggled to break their grip. She was running now not to save Rhonda, but to save herself.

She was almost to the light. She gave one final jerk forward and fell into a tunnel. The creatures stayed in the darkness, muttering angrily, but apparently they were afraid of the light. Laura limped forward, sobbing. She still hadn't seen the creatures that were after her, and she was grateful for that mercy.

"Help me, Laura," came Rhonda's anguished cry in the distance. Laura did not want to go forward. Whatever lay ahead was treachery. She stood rooted to the floor, staring down the dim tunnel, then peering back at the darkness, where the creatures grunted longingly. She couldn't go forward and she couldn't go back, but it wasn't in the game for her to stay where she was. The edge of the light, which had been well behind her, was creeping forward. It was just out of reach, and she could feel the creatures' hot, rancid breath as they inched eagerly ahead, ready for the darkness to overtake her again.

At first she moved slowly through the narrow tunnel as it twisted treacherously. She seemed to be in a cave. She was surrounded by gray granite walls, which became so narrow in places that jagged rocks tore at her flesh as she pushed through. Periodically the tunnel forked, but she continued to follow Rhonda's voice.

As the darkness moved more rapidly toward her, she increased her pace until she was running toward Rhonda's voice. In places the tunnel was so low, she had to crawl on her hands and knees, but she was forced relentlessly in the direction of Rhonda's tortured voice. Despite the creatures' even pace in the darkness directly behind her, she feared she was not running for her life, but rushing to her death.

Rhonda's voice was much nearer now, and its urgency was growing.

Laura stopped and leaned against the wall, gasping for air and struggling to regain her courage. She did not want to go forward. She was certain that whatever lay ahead, it was far worse than anything she had suffered so far.

"I won't go," she cried to the unseen child. "If you are going to kill me, you will have to do it here, because I won't play your game any longer."

The child's laughter echoed through the tunnel, and the wall Laura had been leaning against began to suck her inward, like a vertical wall of quicksand. She twisted and screamed as her hips and back sank farther into the quagmire. The ceiling and the opposite wall breathed excitedly while she fought the hold that threatened to completely immobilize her. Laura's panic gave her a strength she hadn't known she possessed, and she pulled forward at her shoulders with all her might. She broke loose and fell to the floor, but her feet fell back against the wall and were sucked in. The wall was patiently claiming her as a victim while she struggled. She tried to dig into the floor, but her fingers slid off the hard stones. Behind her the darkness was growing closer and she could smell the vile creatures it brought with it.

She managed to turn enough to get into a half-crouching, half-sitting position. It brought her entire body closer to the wall, but it was her only chance. A cramp rocketed through her back, nearly paralyzing her. She cried out in pain as she reached for one of her legs and yanked it free. She could feel the wall begin to harden, and she knew she had to hurry before it once again became stone, trapping her forever. She grabbed her other leg, tore it loose, and rolled to the middle of the floor. The walls screamed in rage, and she could see veins in what she now knew was not stone. The ceiling and walls were breathing deeply, chanting her name, while she pulled herself to her feet and ran toward the waiting horror as though it were her salvation. When she reached a door at the end of the tunnel, she threw it open and lunged blindly forward . . . where the shadow child loomed huge over Adam. Laura stood rooted to the spot, unable to control her terror.

"You wanted to see me as I really am," the shadow said to Adam. "Now you are. The master created me just to fulfill your wish for a child. You can never hold me like a child. You can't hug a shadow."

"But the babies," Adam sobbed. "You cared about the babies."

"Don't be a fool. I care only about the master. I used the babies to bring you back to the master, where you belong."

Laura turned to escape, but the door had disappeared. There was no way out. There was nothing she could do to help Adam or herself. She watched and listened, without understanding what the shadow was talking about. She assumed the babies were the children growing in the wombs of the women planning to have abortions, but she didn't know what the shadow child meant by the master.

"You remember the master, don't you, Daddy? He remembers you. You are his, and he sent me to claim you.

You have been his since you slept with the nun. She belonged to him too. That's why the others discovered you. When you joined with the nun, you joined with the master too. He showed himself through the nun, and you screamed and screamed until the other nuns came and found you naked in Sister Mary Xavier's room."

Laura was horrified by what she was hearing, but the janitor's resigned sobs told her it was true.

Adam turned to run, but met the resistance of thick glass. On the other side Laura could see the apartment and dared to hope there was a way out of this living nightmare. Adam pounded against the glass and screamed in agony.

On the other side of the glass MacNamara and the other officers finally had made it up the fire escape and stormed into Adam's apartment. They saw a man in a round television, apparently beating against an invisible wall. The scene was too foggy for them to make out his features. They searched the apartment while the eerie TV character screamed, but Laura and the janitor were not there. Chaos reigned.

"Quiet!" MacNamara ordered. He thought he had heard Laura's voice. The fog had cleared from the TV and the officers stared in amazed fascination at a picture of Laura and the janitor in what appeared to be a dungeon. A shadow loomed above them, changing shapes, laughing, taunting its captives.

Laura looked at the glass hopefully, recognizing the distorted apartment on the other side. There had to be a way back to her own safe world. But as she watched, the glass zoomed backward, away from Adam. In front of him a pit seemed to grow from nothing. Laura couldn't see the bottom of it. It appeared to descend to the very bowels of hell. She could see the apartment through the glass on the other side of the pit, but it was much too far to jump, and if the glass didn't yield, she would fall to her death.

"It's time to meet your master," Jeremy screeched. "Since you didn't follow my instructions and kill this

Laura woman, the master is angry. He will take care of her himself."

Behind Adam and Laura the wall crept forward, pushing them closer to the pit. Soon the floor was a mere ledge, with Adam and Laura standing side by side, awaiting their fate.

From within the pit they heard hissing and a million muted rattles. Laura didn't want to look down, but she couldn't stop herself. She screamed at what she saw.

Ascending from the pit was a multiheaded demon. The snakelike heads gaped open, shooting balls of fire in their direction. The necks swayed as though under the spell of a snake charmer, then connected to a massive dragonlike body. Hundreds of tails vibrated rapidly, making the rattling sound of the combined fury of a huge den of snakes.

"You can't have Miss Laura too," Adam shouted. Before she knew what he planned to do, the janitor had grabbed her and flung her across the pit.

Laura screamed as her body flew over the demon and toward the glass. She was certain she would fall into the dripping fangs and prayed to God to save her immortal soul.

She just heard Adam's anguished scream as she plunged once again through the spinning void. She felt as if her body would be torn apart by the pressure, when she lost consciousness.

The next thing she saw was MacNamara leaning over her, surrounded by detectives. The chief wrapped a blanket securely around her. He, and the others, looked nearly as bad as Laura.

"We saw it all through the TV," MacNamara said. "I don't understand it, but I hope to God I never see anything like it again."

"Adam?" Laura whispered hoarsely, trying to turn her stiff neck to look at the apartment.

"He fell to that thing," MacNamara said with a shudder. "Then you flew back through the TV, like there was no glass on it."

They looked suspiciously at the round TV, which appeared ominously similar to one of the eyes of the demon. It flashed electronic snow across the screen, replaced by a

shrinking red retina that seemed to wink at the assem-
blage of shocked police officers.

Then it vanished.

Laura wanted to sink into unconsciousness again, but
something kept nagging at the edges of her mind.

"Tracy!" she exclaimed. "You have to get her. Adam
said she was killing herself. She's in Rhonda Hackman's
apartment downstairs."

Greg Binder, who was standing out of the way in a
corner, cried out and rushed out of the apartment to find
his daughter.

Laura let the peaceful fog veil her mind. Through the
haze she heard Darryl's voice.

"I don't give a damn about police regulations. She's
my wife."

"Let him in," MacNamara said.

Laura felt her husband's arms wrap around her. "I
love you," she said.

Epilogue

The warm sun enveloped Laura's body, filling her with a
sense of security and well-being. She felt the crisscross of
the plastic lawn chair beneath her and Darryl's hand in
hers. The sound of the ocean lapping against the shore
made her smile and she inhaled a deep breath of clean
salt air.

It had been a month since Laura had been drawn into
the depths of hell and had escaped. She spent the first two
weeks in the hospital. For the first few days she remembered nothing, then she remembered Tracy Binder visiting her and kissing her on the forehead. Later the doctors
told her it had been touch-and-go for both her and Tracy.
They said that five more minutes, and the pills would
have done too much damage to bring the girl back. A
serious concussion and what the doctors called the worst
state of shock they had ever seen had left Laura precariously balanced between life and death. The doctors said

they believed her strong will, and her husband's constant presence at her side, had brought her through.

In the background Laura heard the strains of Hawaiian music and was amazed that she and Darryl were finally on their dream trip.

"Let's take a quick dip," Darryl said, squeezing her hand. They walked slowly to the shore, Darryl providing support. Laura still had to take it easy. The waves languished gently across Laura's body, and she felt as though they were washing away the pain and horror. After a while they returned to their chairs and let the sun warm and dry their tanned bodies.

"I think I can talk about it now, Darryl, here in the sunlight, far from the city."

"There's no rush, sweetheart."

"I want to talk about it."

She shivered and wrapped a beach towel around herself while she told Darryl about what had happened to her and Adam Smith. At first she spoke hesitantly, then her words poured out in a torrent. He listened in amazement and horror at her bizarre story. When she finished, he reached out and pulled her gently to him and held her close. Finally he released her and said, "There are still some things I don't understand. This Jeremy, the shadow child, was he Adam's aborted son?"

"No, he was an extension of the demon, a creature the demon created to lure Adam back to him. He only pretended to be Adam and Marie's aborted child so he could get Adam to commit the murders. That way he and the demon could feed off the anger and fear."

"But where did the demon come from?"

"I had Harry Winchell do some checking for me while I was in the hospital. One of the old nuns at the orphanage remembered Sister Mary Xavier and Adam well. She said Sister Mary Xavier was sent to the orphanage after she had helped with an exorcism. The church officials knew the young nun was under stress and thought working with the children would be good for her. They had no idea she had become the host for the demon after the exorcism. In seducing Adam she literally sacrificed him to the demon within her. After she and Adam were discovered, she committed suicide."

"Why did the demon wait so long to come back?"

"The old nun said it needed Adam's invitation to claim him, and he had to ask for the demon's help. Adam had blocked out the experiences at the orphanage, so he didn't know he was inviting the demon in when he asked for a son."

"How did that let the demon loose?"

"Because only he could grant Adam's request. The janitor's wish unchained him."

"And you were involved because Adam was in love with you?"

"Yes, and the shadow child was able to use that love to build Adam's hatred and sense of betrayal."

"I can understand that, but how did Marie come back from the grave?"

"I think Adam willed her back. We hear about people calling forth the spirit of loved ones through séances. Maybe that was similar to what Adam did—or maybe Marie was sent by a good force to intervene. If there is intelligent, thinking evil in the world such as I experienced, there must also be intelligent, thinking forces of good."

"That gives me hope. And the doors locking at the precinct and the fire escape bucking were the child's way of stopping anyone from interfering?"

"Yes. It gave the child a chance to suck Adam and me into the demon's trap."

"Do you think there's any hope for Adam?"

Laura hesitated, then said, "Maybe. Adam was basically a good person who was used. He brought that goodness to the demon's dwelling place. There was another force in there at the end. When Adam flung me across the pit and back into this world, he had a strength that he couldn't possibly have possessed on his own. Maybe that same force will save him."

"Do you mean you think he might get catapulted back into this world? That scares the living daylights out of me," Darryl said with a shudder.

"No," Laura replied sadly. "Adam Smith is dead. I felt

his death when the TV disappeared. His body is lost, but maybe someday his soul will be saved."

"You'd like that, wouldn't you, sweetheart?" Darryl said, squeezing her hand again.

"The Adam who wasn't under the demon's spell was a kind, loving man. He saved my life at the moment when his own personal nightmare became a reality. How could I not be grateful and pray for his soul?"

They sat quietly for a while, both lost in their own thoughts. Then Darryl said, "Just one more question. What happened to the TV?"

Apparently the demon created the TV, just as it created the shadow child, to gain control of Adam. When the demon had Adam, there was no more reason for the TV to exist."

Darryl shook his head and reached over and embraced his wife.

Laura put the thoughts of Adam and the child and the demon out of her mind. Soon the sun lulled her into a comfortable sleep. Instead of the nightmares that had plagued her since January, she dreamt of planting strong young plants in the greenhouse Darryl promised to start building as soon as they returned home.